# COWBOYS OF THE SKY

# COWBOYS OF THE SKY

CARL MICHAELSEN

Boxhead Books

# AUTHOR'S NOTE

When I finished writing *The Last of A Dying Breed,* the wheels were already turning for a sequel. I wanted this series to be an anthology and follow different sets of characters, so creating a new cast that was unique was imperative. During my senior year English elective course, I wrote a short story about an Ironworker turned bank robber named Boyd McTiernan. It was a good starting point and *Cowboys Of The Sky* soon followed.

At the end of *The Last of A Dying Breed,* I also made the decision to introduce John Shannon from the Phantom Soldier series into this world. Bringing him into this book and getting to write that character again was super, super awesome for me as a writer. John is one of my favorite characters that I've created, so having him in more work was definitely an easy decision. I think this time around, we get to learn so much more about him, and I really tried to flesh him out more as a character.

The feedback I got from everyone who read *The Last of A Dying Breed* was greatly appreciated. I am super proud of that book and am excited to keep the series going with this new book. Noah Riordan is another character who I love writing. There is going to be much more of him and I hope to keep creating interesting and exciting adventures for him to navigate!

I'd like to thank my mom, Kathy, for yet again helping me proofread and edit this book. Her willingness to have serious conversations about the plot and character helped make this possible. I would not be the writer I am today without her help. A lot of the subject matter I write about is not something she would normally indulge in. Yet, she has never once judged me for it and has always been willing to offer honest feedback, which is an invaluable quality in a good editor/proofreader.

Tyler at Boxhead Books has been an incredible publisher and friend. He's let me do whatever I want without any stipulations and creatively, it works. I appreciate that he continues to trust me with turning out quality work and is always willing to provide feedback on an idea. This Anthology is something I plan to continue and I am glad that Tyler is equally enthusiastic about it as I am.

I have to give a shoutout to my cover artist and one of my best friends in the world, Taylor Piggott. She has designed all of my covers and knocked it out of the park with this one. The Chicago skyline and the character silhouettes all lend to an awesome and attention-grabbing cover. Without her, none of these books would've gotten off the ground. Through thick and thin, highs and lows, Taylor has consistently been there for me, and that is something I truly appreciate. Whether it's to talk about an idea for a book, a new cover, or just to vent, thanks for always having my back!

I can't write a book about Ironworkers and not give a shout out to my dudes with the Chicago Ironworkers. Erik and Matt have been great friends over the last few years and even though we don't see each other often, it's always a good time when we get together to knock back a few cold ones. Ironworkers are a rare kind; fearless and a little crazy, but it's an absolutely necessary job. Their culture and community is something I really admire, dating all the way back to the original Ironworkers who built the first skyscrapers.

I hope everyone enjoys this book and enjoys getting to know the Chicago crew!

A Novel by Carl Michaelsen

Cover Designs by Taylor Piggott

Proofread by Kathy Michaelsen

Published by Boxhead Books

# Prologue

The night was eerily quiet, still and unassuming. Even in the dense forest preserve, no animals, not even an insect, dared to move. It was almost as if the entire forest knew what was happening and understood to keep still. The only source of light came from the two lights on the small excavator next to the large pile of dirt. The hole next to it was dug as deep as the machine could dig; exactly twelve feet.

He was on his knees and shivering, but not from the cold. His hands were bound behind his back with a strip of duct tape; another strip of tape was across his mouth. His graying hair was completely disheveled, his shirt was ripped. He was easily 75 pounds overweight and was missing a few teeth. The man was severely beaten, blood leaking from a fresh wound on the left side of his face. Low and guttural sobs escaped from him, that being the only sound in the entire forest. His left eye was swollen shut, but he could still see well enough out of his right eye. The three men stood around him in a semi-circle, looks of disgust across each of their faces.

The man in the middle had a Chicago Police Badge on his belt, right next to a holstered pistol; there was also a radio and a pair of handcuffs attached to his belt. His massive arms were folded loosely across his chest as he watched the bound and gagged man begin to cry.

"Detective Kavanaugh, come in over," the radio squawked. "Klint, do you copy?"

Detective Klint Kavanaugh turned the dial off and the radio went silent. Whatever dispatch needed could wait, there were more pressing matters to attend to at the moment. Klint turned to the man on his right and studied his stoic expression, looking for any kind of hesitation. He saw none of the usual giveaways that his younger brother had when he was trying to act tough.

Kade Kavanaugh, the youngest of the Kavanaugh brothers, didn't have to act tough anymore. He'd just finished his career with the Army, ending as a Major in the Army's elite Delta Force special operations unit. No, Kade didn't have to prove he was tough to his older brothers anymore. They knew, which is why they were all standing out in the middle of the Thatcher Woods. The two Kavanaugh brothers - Kade and Klint - looked very similar to one another. Tall, brown hair, and strong facial features. Each man was darkly handsome and in top physical condition; although Kade was definitely in better shape than his older brother.

"Who is he?" Kade Kavanaugh inquired.
"Malcolm Welsch," Klint answered immediately.
"What did he do?" Kade asked, staring at the whimpering man on his knees. His nose was leaking a grotesque mixture of snot and blood.
"Does it matter?" John Shannon muttered in his signature deep voice, also not taking his eyes off the man before them.

John Shannon was a former Navy SEAL Master Chief, but had been run out of the military following a conflict with a high ranking CIA Agent. Since then, John had found a career working in various cities all around the United States, protecting America from the shadows. John was well-known around Chicago, especially with the Police, due to his efforts to stop Gray Saxon - the ex-soldier who had attacked *Lollapalooza* a few years ago in an attempt to start a war. Like Klint, John had a pistol tucked against his hip - minus the holster. Kade was the only brother who was unarmed. In his right hand, John held a small 10-pound sledgehammer - it was dripping with blood.

"I don't mind the killing, I've done plenty of that," Kade said quietly. "I've just never killed someone who was helpless. I've never executed someone before,"

"You want to talk about helplessness?" John asked, taking a step toward Malcolm, who instinctively tried to fall away from him. John grabbed Malcolm by the throat and hauled him back to his knees, Malcolm wailing in terror.

"That's enough, John," Klint said, calm as ever. John spat on Malcolm before reassuming his position next to the Kavanaugh brothers.

"I gotta know..." Kade whispered, his eyes still completely focused on Malcolm. Klint put his hand on Kade's shoulder.

"He raped and killed an 11 year old girl, Kade," Klint said. "Her parents are going through a nasty divorce. Mom got drunk and passed out, Dad left in a fit of rage, leaving the poor girl to fend for herself. Unbeknownst to her, the next door neighbor was a spawn of Satan, and took advantage of the situation. Strangled her to death and dumped the body in a ditch off the side of the road,"

Kade felt his blood boil. Of all the despicable crimes humans could commit, Kade couldn't think of something worse. Malcolm looked down in shame, earning him a vicious punch to the face courtesy of John.

"You keep your eyes up here, you piece of shit," John snarled. He put the sledgehammer on Malcolm's shoulder and left it there, warning what was to come if Malcolm didn't comply.

"Why don't you want him?" Kade asked Klint. "They love pedo's, he wouldn't make it a week in GenPop,"

"His lawyers will most likely get him into protective custody so he can stand trial. After that, no one will be able to touch him," Klint said, matter of factly. "The girl's dad was an associate of ours a few years ago. Nothing of this nature, he did some forensic accounting for us. He's the one who called me, begging me to get justice for his daughter. *Real* justice. You see, that's the problem, Kade. There is no justice, no law and order, out there. There is just us. And our version of justice. Hammurabi's Code - an eye for an eye. Or in Mr. Welsch's case, a life for a life,"

Malcolm shook his head frantically, his right eye bugging out in terror. He was mumbling words beneath the duct tape, but nothing coherent for the brothers. Slowly, Klint reached behind his back and pulled out a second pistol - a Glock 30. He racked the slide back and spun the weapon in his hand, holding it out toward Kade. Kade grabbed the gun by the grip, the polymer feeling oddly comforting to him.

"Take the tape off," Kade muttered, looking at John. Walking up to Malcolm, John gripped the piece of duct tape across his mouth, and ripped it off in one fluid motion. Malcolm coughed violently and doubled over, sucking in as much air as his lungs would allow him to. Picking up the sledgehammer, John walked away as Kade stepped up to Malcolm. He crouched down so he was eye level with Malcolm.

"I'm sorry," Malcolm whispered, blood spewing from his mouth as he spoke. Kade shook his head and stood back up.

"Do you believe in God?" Kade asked. Malcolm nodded slowly. "Then I suggest you use whatever time you've got left and pray for forgiveness,"

Malcolm hung his head and began crying softly. Kade pressed the barrel of the gun to Malcolm's forehead.

"Pray!" Kade screamed.

Malcolm instantly began mumbling to himself, breathing shallowly as he tried to stop himself from hyperventilating. Kade lowered the weapon and walked back up to Klint, keeping his back to Malcolm.

"He's getting off easy," Klint said, his hard stare unwavering. "You and I both know that,"

"I know, I know," Kade agreed. "I've just never killed a man who couldn't defend himself. It feels different,"

"And it is different," Klint stated. "But only for a minute or two,"

Klint put his arm around Kade's neck and moved him away so John couldn't hear.

"If you want in, little brother, this is what you have to do to earn my trust back. I've been doing this for years, you left. You got out while you still could. If you're not ready, I'm not going to hold it against you. But I just want you to think for one second... What would you do if someone did that to Hailey?"

Kade stopped dead in his tracks. Hailey was his daughter, only a few years younger than the victim. This entire time, he'd been trying desperately not to think of her, knowing it would cloud his judgment. But the second the name left Klint's lips, Kade knew what he had to do. Gripping the gun, Kade spun on his heels and marched back toward Malcolm, his eyes burning with rage.

"No!" Malcolm screamed, as Kade raised the gun.

A single gunshot rang out, snapping Malcolm's head toward the side as the bullet bore a hole through his temple. His lifeless body fell into the hole unceremoniously. Kade stood over the hole and blasted off the remaining nine rounds into Malcolm's face and chest.

John Shannon lowered his head and shot Klint a nod of approval before he walked over to the excavator and climbed into the cab. The machine roared to life and John began filling in the hole before the body even had time to cool. Putting his hand on Kade's shoulder, Klint took the pistol back and stuffed it in his waistband. Kade turned and nodded at his brother.

"You guys can trust me," Kade said quietly, his heart still beating a million miles an hour.
"I know we can," Klint responded. "I just had to make sure,"

Klint turned to watch John backfill the hole and stuck his hand out to Kade.

"Welcome home, little brother,"

# PART 1

# The Bandit, The Model, and The Man Called 'Shannon'

*"The only defense against evil, violent people is good people who are more skilled at violence" - Rory Miller; Author*

# CHAPTER 1

# Klint

The feeling of nervousness or anxiousness had vanished long ago. Most people would feel something along those lines if they were summoned to the Mayor's office, but not Klinton 'Klint' Kavanaugh. Sure, his first few trips to visit the Mayor alone, he'd been nervous, but now it was more tedious than anything else.

Klint Kavanaugh was a hotshot, and he knew it. A Detective with the Chicago Police Department, Klint had risen through the ranks about as fast as anyone possible could. At 36 years old, Klint still felt like he was in the prime of his crime fighting career. Although, contrary to general perception, Klint wasn't a crime fighter in the traditional sense. He carried a gun and a badge and collected a paycheck from the City of Chicago, but his duties were far more than those of an average Detective. Anyone who was anyone in Chicago knew who Klint Kavanaugh was and understood the power that was associated with the name.

"Detective Kavanaugh?" a young woman in a pantsuit said into the small waiting room. She was carrying a clipboard and her brown hair was tied back in a ponytail.

"Yep," Klint said with a nod.

"Mayor Hart is ready for you," the woman informed. Klint stood up, buttoning up his jacket before following the woman into Mayor Hart's spacious office in City Hall.

Mayor Kelly Hart stood behind her large mahogany desk, looking out onto LaSalle Street. She wore a black jacket over a light blue blouse and a black skirt. The Mayor, unlike previous Chicago Mayor's, was young, attractive, and as stubborn as they came. It had been pretty shocking, at least in Klint's opinion, that the 35-year old politician had won - especially since she was running on a much more libertarian platform than her predecessors. Klint wasn't overly political, he couldn't be in his position. Politics did nothing but complicate his job and that wasn't something Klint put up with. His job, while on paper was pretty standard, was much more complex and complicated than that. Meetings with Mayor Hart had become a regular occurrence. It was something that she had initiated, knowing Klint was the best candidate for the job.

Turning around, Mayor Hart smiled to see Klint standing before her desk. She sat back down behind her desk, gesturing to one of the large leather chairs in front of her. Nodding respectfully, Klint sat down and propped his foot up on his knee.

"Can I get you anything else, Mayor Hart?" the young woman asked from the doorway.

"No, I think we're good, Molly. Thank you so much," Mayor Hart said pleasantly. Molly closed the door behind her. "She's very thorough,"

"I bet," Klint shrugged.

"Do you want something to drink?" Mayor Hart asked, reaching into her desk and pulling out two small rocks glasses and a bottle of Johnnie Walker Blue Label. Knowing he didn't really have a choice, Klint nodded and accepted one of the glasses after the Mayor poured a few fingers of whiskey into each glass.

"Cheers," Klint muttered, holding up his glass. He took a sip and set the drink back down on the Mayor's desk.

"So, how's the recruiting going?" the Mayor asked, pulling a black binder. She opened it and began scanning several different files.

"John's on board, one hundred percent," Klint informed her. "Kade is good to go too. He's green and is going to need to get acclimated to how we do things, but he's ready. I still need your permission to bring in the last two,"

"Yes, that's why I wanted to talk with you," Mayor Hart said, closing the binder. "I have no problem with the girl, she's a real badass. Acknowledgements in marksmanship, physical fitness, and leadership. Retired from the Army honorably as a Staff Sergeant. I like her. Hell, I want to be her, she's got it all. But this other guy. Noah Riordan..."

"He's just a construction worker, Kelly," Klint countered. Mayor Hart looked at Klint and rolled her eyes.

"Come on, Klint," she groaned. "Don't give me that. Just tell me why you need a bank robber on the team..."

"Many reasons. None of which I care to bore you with, but he's valuable to what we're doing here. He's got the eye for the job and he knows how to fly under the radar. Clearly," Klint defended. Mayor Hart sighed and took another sip of whiskey.

"Fine, you can have the bandit too," Mayor Hart relented. "But, let's make sure we're clear. This is your responsibility. I'll sign the checks, but you're in charge of keeping them all in line. Don't forget, Klint, we're alone in this. The cops don't see it the same way you and I do,"

"Oh, trust me," Klint said quietly. "I'm well aware,"

"Did you take care of that problem?" the Mayor inquired. Klint nodded ominously.

"It's been dealt with. Do you want the body found or not?"

"Not necessary, just as long as he doesn't do that to anyone ever again," Mayor Hart shuddered.

"He won't," Klint whispered.

"I'll let you know if I get any more customers this week," the Mayor said knowingly. Klint nodded and stood to leave, downing the rest of his drink.

"Thanks for the drink," he said, handing the glass back to the Mayor.

"Of course," she said with a sincere smile. "Maybe sometime we can finally do this outside of the confines of my office,"

"Yeah," Klint lied. "Maybe,"

"Say hi to Kara for me," the Mayor winked.

Klint smiled, though less sincere than the Mayor, and left City Hall a few minutes later. His black supercharged Dodge Charger sat along the street, waiting patiently for him to return. Slipping behind the wheel, Klint turned the engine over and listened to it roar to life, growling in anticipation to be released into the wild once more. The car was outfitted with discreet blue and red strobes under the grill - the only thing that gave it away as a police vehicle. Once it was clear, Klint threw the car into gear and sped off, loving the roar of the engine as he shifted through the gears.

\*\*\*\*

The building was located on the corner of State Street and Ida B. Wells Drive. Included was a private gym, sun deck, and a business center that Klint had never even stepped foot in. He was proud of his condo, he'd done quite a bit of work to it when he bought the place. The granite countertops, stained hardwood floors, and matching cabinets had all been done by Klint. It wasn't particularly large, just under 1,400 square feet, but it was all that he and Kara needed.

"Hey, I'm home," Klint called out as soon as he entered the condo. He threw the deadbolt and kicked off his shoes toward the mountain of footwear by the door. The small puppy came running over to Klint, sliding on the hardwood floor. She'd still been unable to figure out how to gain traction on the new floors. She was a yellow lab, a clumsy, but lovable yellow lab. Scooping the small pup in his arms, Klint held her close to him and walked into the kitchen. "How are you, little Koda?"

"Hey dad," Kara grumbled, not looking up from her computer, notebooks, and textbooks. Kara looked tired and agitated, not a good combination. "Sorry, I'll be done soon. Fucking chemistry is not my thing,"

"*Fucking* chemistry wasn't my thing either," Klint said, grabbing a bottle of Gatorade from the fridge. Kara looked up at her father, horrified.

"I'm sorry," she said, her cheeks getting red. "It flew out..."

"Dude, I don't care," Klint laughed. "You're eighteen, you can swear if you want,"

"Sorry, dad," Kara cracked a smile and went back to her homework.

Deciding to let his daughter work in peace, Klint took Koda and his gatorade into his bedroom. He set the puppy on his bed and changed out of his work clothes into a much more comfortable shorts and T-shirt combo. His nightstand had a large 8x10 picture of Kara, her senior graduation picture. She was now a freshman in college, her first semester at DePaul, and Klint could hardly believe it. He still vividly remembered the day she'd been born as if it was earlier that day.

They were exactly eighteen years apart. She'd been born just a few months after Klint graduated high school, while he was in the Police Academy. It was a total surprise to Klint and his girlfriend at the time. They both had agreed they wanted to go through with it, but once Kara was born, his girlfriend had a change of heart. She took off without warning, leaving the brand new baby with Klint, Klint's parents, and Klint's younger brother, Kade. Since then, neither Klint nor Kara had heard a word from her. Klint had virtually raised her by himself, both of his parents had long passed away. He was forever grateful for how close they were, knowing how different things could've been. At the end of the day, everything that Klint did or didn't do was for the betterment of his daughter's life. So far, he liked to think he'd done a good job of giving her a solid life.

Little Koda sat on the bed, wagging her tail enthusiastically as Klint dropped down next to her. He scratched her head and accepted a few gracious licks on the cheek. Unintentionally, Klint rested his head on his pillow and ended up drifting off to sleep, exhausted from the previous night's activities. It wasn't the first time in recent weeks that Klint and John Shannon had disposed of an exceptionally disgusting individual. And, Klint doubted it would be the last.

Klint and John had met years earlier through a mutual friend, FBI Agent Riley Hanna. At the time, Klint had been fresh out of the police academy and working a case in Los Angeles, where he met Riley Hanna - the FBI Agent in Charge. It was hard to tell exactly, but Klint had assumed that John had been a boyfriend or something. Klint and Riley had kept in touch somewhat frequently since then; Klint had actually been one of the first Detectives on the scene of the *Lollapalooza* massacre. News of Riley's death had deeply hurt Klint. He'd attended the funeral and seen John Shannon there, confined to a wheelchair. When Mayor Kelly Hart had recruited Klint for the task of cleaning up Chicago's crime problem, he knew John was going to be an invaluable asset.

And since they had started working together, John had proved his worth a hundredfold. The former Navy SEAL was an expert in urban warfare and was a brilliant strategist; his expertise combined with Klint's detective skills had made them very popular with the Mayor's office. In less than six months of working in Chicago, John and Klint had managed to cross off several high value criminals, either by turning them over to the police or killing them. Fortunately for Klint and John, Mayor Hart wasn't particularly picky.

Klint was awoken by the banging and crashing of pots and pans in the kitchen. He rolled over and checked his phone, groaning when he realized he had been sleeping for almost two hours. Koda jumped up and started licking his face, wagging her tail as fast as she could.

"I'm up, I'm up," Klint groaned, getting out of bed. He walked out of his room and into the kitchen. Kara was making an absolute mess in an attempt to cook spaghetti, red sauce, and meatballs. She was cursing under her breath while vigorously stirring the pot of boiling water and pasta.

"Are you doing good?" Klint asked, trying hard not to laugh. Kara whirled around, her eyes fiery.

"Why is this so hard?" she complained. "I figured it'd be easy,"

"It is easy," Klint said, taking over the stirring responsibilities. "You just don't have any patience,"

"Uh huh, yeah, that's it for sure," Kara rolled her eyes. Klint smirked and took over cooking dinner. As was her nightly duty, Kara took Koda outside and fed her. Once Koda was done eating, Klint and Kara sat down at their small kitchen table and dug into their food.

It was a rule that Klint had instilled when Kara was still very young. If Klint wasn't working, the two of them had dinner together. Sometimes they went out, but most of the time they cooked something together. No matter what kind of a day they'd had, dinner was always peaceful and nice. Klint loved that they could bond over dinner and it was more meaningful now that she was becoming an adult.

"So, did you ask out the Mayor yet?" Kara asked, almost as soon as they sat down. Klint smirked and shook his head.

"No, I did not," he said. Kara rolled her eyes dramatically. While she didn't know the specifics of Klint's job, she knew that he worked closely with the Mayor and had met her on a few different occasions. The Mayor was a pretty woman and very clearly was interested in Klint.

"What are you waiting for? She's practically throwing herself at you,"

"I don't mix work and pleasure," Klint shrugged, taking a sip of water. He couldn't pretend the thought hadn't crossed his mind, but he'd never allowed himself to entertain the thought for too long. "Besides, we have a rule. I don't date, you don't date,"

"I have a boyfriend, Dad," Kara shook her head. Klint laughed and rolled his eyes as dramatically as Kara did.

"I know," he grumbled. "And I'm so very happy about that,"

"You're sarcasm is not appreciated,"

"Noted,"

The rest of the meal went by without any mention of the Mayor or of Kara's boyfriend. Klint had still yet to meet the man, but he'd heard nothing but good things from Kara. The jury was still out, as far as Klint was concerned. Afterwards, Kara handled the dishes while Klint took the garbage to the big chute at the end of the hall. When he got back to his condo, Kara tossed his phone at him.

"John's calling," she informed, returning to the dishes. Klint thanked her and went out onto the deck to call John back, not wanting Kara to overhear his conversation. She already probably knew too much about what he did.

"Yo," John answered in his signature deep voice.

"What's up?" Klint asked.

"That Santos guy you wanted me to tail, he's having a meeting right now at the brother's place. Looks like a few shot callers, maybe some enforcers. What's the call?"

"You got Kade's number?"

"Yep,"

"You know the drill," Klint said ominously. "No witnesses, understood?"

"Copy," John answered.

"Be careful and be smart. I've got the new recruits approved, we're meeting at the end of the week. I need you in one piece for that,"

"Trust me, this is gonna be a walk in the park,"

# CHAPTER 2

# John

The house was the typical tall and skinny home that one would find in a large city like Chicago, on a street with other ones identical to it. On the narrow city block, the homes were in various states of disarray, years of poverty had taken a toll. Beat up old cars lined the road, except for the home on the corner. Black Cadillacs were parked on the street and in the alley beside the house. It was like shooting a beam into the sky, broadcasting their position to the entire city. The men who drove those cars were flashy and arrogant. Of course they were. For years, the cops in the city hadn't dared to cross the men and women associated with the Sinaloa Cartel, for fear of retaliation against them and their families. Fortunately, John Shannon was not a cop, he had no family, and he certainly wasn't afraid.

John drove his own vehicle, a 2001 Ford Excursion XLT with a Super Duty Front End that he'd installed himself. Additionally, John had added several other features to turn the truck into a virtual battle tank; bulletproof windows, run flat tires, and a reinforced chassis. The backseat and trunk were filled with enough weapons and equipment to fight a small war. John liked being prepared for anything and everything.

He did another pass around the block, confirming that all four black Cadillacs were still there. John pulled over on the next block, parking his truck along the sidewalk. After a few minutes, John saw a familiar looking Dodge Ram pickup park behind him. Kade Kavanaugh climbed down from the truck, walked around the side of John's truck, and into the passenger seat.

"It's a beautiful night for a gunfight, my friend," Kade said, bumping his fist against John's.

"Isn't that every night?" John grumbled.

"I've been itching for some action," Kade admitted. "I love my daughter and all of that, but this stay at home dad needs some excitement,"

"Going through a dry spell?" John asked with a sneer. "I know a guy who sells Viagra down by the United Center. $25 a pop. Those gas station pills give me the shits, I wouldn't recommend them,"

"You are a real asshole, you know that?" Kade snickered. "No, I don't need any of that shit. Jenna's just been working a lot, barely seen her these last few weeks,"

"The perks of being married," John grumbled.

"Aren't you married?" Kade asked, pointing to the gold band on John's finger. Instantly, John moved his hand so Kade couldn't see the ring anymore.

"Sure," John shook his head. Kade didn't ask anything else, seeing that the comment obviously bothered John. Clearly, there was a lot that Kade did not know about John Shannon. "Alright, I confirmed that Miguel Santos is in the house along with at least two other shot callers for the cartels. Far as I'm concerned, everyone in the house is considered hostile,"

"Cops know to steer clear?"

"I'm gonna assume Klint took care of that," John said, shutting his vehicle off. "Come on, let's gear up,"

John and Kade got out of the truck, John moving around to the rear of the truck. Using Kade's truck as cover, John quickly went to work putting a tactical vest over his gray Carhartt hoodie. The vest was filled with spare rifle and pistol magazines, half a dozen 'flashbang' grenades, and a spool of zipties. John strapped a thigh holster to his leg, snapping it around his belt so it was secure to his body. He grabbed two large gun cases from the trunk and popped them both open, revealing his primary and secondary weapons. The rifle was John's preferred variant, a Heckler and Koch HK416; he'd fit the weapon with a holographic optic, vertical foregrip, and a suppressor. It was one of the standard rifles in the SEAL community and John had carried it through most of his career as a Navy SEAL. For his sidearm, John carried a Heckler and Koch USP45 also fitted with a suppressor.

Kade grabbed his own tactical vest, filled with similar items to John's. He was quick with his weapons selection, opting for a simple M4A1 rifle and a Glock 17 handgun. After a quick weapons check, Kade nodded that he was ready to go.

"Alright, let's do this," John whispered, reaching into the back pocket of his jeans. He pulled out a black ski mask and pulled it over his head, adjusting it so he could see through the eye holes. Kade pulled on his own mask. Keeping their identities a secret was imperative in their newfound line of work.

John locked his truck and with Kade on his heels, they took off across the street and down a narrow alley, moving as quietly as they could. For the most part, the street was quiet, minus a few houses that were blasting music. One of which being the house they were moving towards.

"What's the play?" Kade asked. "Smash the door in, shoot first, questions later?"

"That's my favorite," John admitted.

"Mine too,"

"Then that's the play,"

Sticking to the shadows, John and Kade exited the alley and turned left, moving toward the house with the Cadillacs parked out front. This was not the first time that John and Kade had been on a raid like this, but it was the first time that Klint hadn't been with them. Since Kade had joined the crew, they had hit a dozen houses like this. Some of them were low level drug dealers, some were sex traffickers, and some were highly affiliated gang members. It didn't matter, if you were a scumbag in the city of Chicago, chances were sooner or later you'd get a visit from a team of highly armed masked men.

Being back in the fight, having a mission, had saved John's life. The monotony of construction work had been slowly killing him. Although that was still his official cover while in Chicago, going on these night raids and working closely with Klint made him feel whole again. John Shannon was a man who needed a mission, needed action. Without it, he didn't know who he was. There was still an offer from the Director of the Central Intelligence Agency, but John wasn't ready for that kind of work. Not yet, anyway. For now, playing vigilante was all that John wanted to do.

"Stack up on the door," John whispered as they approached the house. Moving quickly so the wood stairs wouldn't creak, John and Kade climbed onto the porch, taking up positions on either side of the front door. Slowly, John tested the handle. Surprisingly, it was unlocked. These guys clearly weren't expecting any trouble. If only they had any idea who was outside on their porch.

"You want the honors?" Kade asked. John grinned underneath the ski mask and gently unhooked a flashbang from his vest; he pulled the pin. Taking a step forward, John threw his foot back against the door as hard as he could. The rickety door nearly snapped it two, collapsing into the house with splinters of wood spiraling into the air. John chucked the flashbang inside and turned away, covering his ears. Kade did the same, not wanting to catch any residual effects from the flashbang. The grenade went off with a blinding flash of light and emitted the incredibly disorientating high pitched ringing.

John Shannon was first through the door, bringing his rifle up to bear as he crossed the threshold of the home. The first thing he saw were the AK-47 rifles all over the front room, leaning against the wall. A young Hispanic man was stumbling toward them, clearly still disorientated from the flashbang. Flicking the safety off his rifle, John pulled the trigger once, blasting the man in the side of the head; he dropped dead.

Kade moved in behind John, sweeping left into the family room. A trio of heavily tattooed cartel enforcers were scrambling to get their guns, one even managed to raise his pistol and fire off a shot in the general direction of Kade. Rushing to Kade's side, John yanked the trigger and blasted off a three-round burst, gunning down the first enforcer. Kade unloaded on the last two, popping two bullets into each of them. John backed up and crept toward the kitchen, hearing a few people hissing and whisperering in Spanish.

"Miguel Santos!" John called out, adding a Mexican accent to his voice. "The Tijuana Cartel sends their regards, motherfucker," "Fuck you, *cabron!*" a voice yelled back from the kitchen. John snickered to himself and brazenly stepped into the kitchen, rifle raised.

Miguel Santos was feeding a magazine into his flashy, silver plated AK-47. His black hair was gelled back and his arms were covered in tattoos. The two cronies on either side of him were drawing their pistols. Miguel's eyes went wide when he saw John standing there, assuming it was a rival from the Tijuana Cartel.

"Adiós, Miguel," John sneered, squeezing the trigger. He mowed them down, emptying the rest of his magazine into the three gangsters, his bullets shredded their chests and faces, spraying blood all over the rotting appliances and filthy kitchen table.

"Kitchen clear," John called out.
"First floor clear," Kade echoed. "Moving upstairs,"
"Be right there,"

Now with Kade leading the way, they climbed the staircase to the second floor, spreading out as soon as they hit the landing. There were three rooms and the doors were all closed. John cocked his head toward the first door. He and Kade slid over to the door; John put his foot through the door, knocking it off the hinges. Kade rushed inside, sweeping the room like he'd done so many times before. There was a bed and a few dressers, nothing else of any real value.

"Clear!" Kade called out. He reentered the hall and moved across to the second door. This time, he booted the door open and John moved inside. Once he determined there was no one inside the room, John lowered his rifle and knelt down next to a massive stash of weapons and drugs. Bundles of rifles, pistols, and shotguns were neatly laid out on the floor, along with two suitcases full of small baggies of cocaine. This was more than just a safehouse for the cartel, it was a storage facility too. No doubt these guns were on their way to the streets of Chicago to arm the local gangs. This was exactly the type of thing John had been brought on to prevent.

"Jackpot," John said to Kade.
"Whatchu got?"
"Drugs and guns,"
"Two of the main food groups," Kade muttered. "What's the move?"
"Take the guns, dump the drugs," John said. "Same as always,"
"Sounds good to me,"
"Hit that last room," John gestured toward the end of the hall. "I'm gonna give your brother a call and I'll start getting these guns ready to go,"
"Copy that,"

Kade raised his rifle and marched toward the final door at the end of the hall. He didn't pause or take a moment before kicking the door in. It was reckless, for sure, but Kade got the feeling that no one else was in the house. He'd been on plenty of raids like this in places like Afghanistan, Libya, and Iraq. Over the years, he'd developed a sort of sixth sense when clearing homes. And his internal radar wasn't going off at all, he felt confident that John and him and cleared out the remaining enemy combatants.

The room was dark and the smell attacked his senses instantly. Kade let go of his rifle, letting it hang from his harness. He drew his pistol, along with a flashlight, illuminating the room in front of him.

"Holy shit," Kade breathed as soon as he angled the light onto the bed. He holstered his pistol. "Hey, John!"

"What?"

"Get in here, man!" Kade yelled back. Kade heard John mutter *'motherfucker'*. But a few moments later, John stepped into the room

"What's up, man?" John asked, his face contorting as he smelled the room. Kade shined the light on the bed. John took a step back. "Well, fuck,"

\*\*\*\*

Keeping his hand on the grip of his pistol holstered on his hip, Klint Kavanaugh hurried up the front steps, through the busted front door, and up to the second floor of the small home. He ignored the smells of death, blood, and gunfire emanating from the first floor; the bodies strewn about like ragdolls. It never failed to impress Klint just how efficient John Shannon was. But that was to be expected, he guessed. After all, John had spent the better half of his adult life being forged into a living, breathing weapon.

John and Kade stood outside the bedroom at the far end of the hall, leaning against the wall, their backs to the room. John had called Klint a little less than a half hour ago. He'd been pretty cryptic, imploring Klint to get to the house as soon as he could. Klint had been relieved that his daughter was already asleep when he'd gotten the call. He hated having to go back into work after he'd been home for the night. And judging by John's tone, Klint was figuring he was in for another late night.

"What's wrong?" Klint asked, seeing the looks on John and Kade's faces. Kade shook his head and handed Klint his flashlight; he looked pale. John, however, looked like he was boiling at the seams with rage. Klint hadn't seen that look in his eye before and it made him extremely uneasy.

Taking the flashlight, Klint turned it on, and slowly walked toward the bedroom. The stench hit his nostrils and Klint felt his stomach turn. He pulled his shirt up and over his nose in a futile attempt to save his nose from inhaling anymore of the horrid smell. Klint scanned the room with the flashlight, picking out the giant oil drum right next to the bed.

On the bed was the body of a young boy, probably thirteen or fourteen years old. Klint hung his head and walked out of the room. He didn't need to investigate any further.

"Here," Klint muttered, tossing Kade his flashlight back.
"What do you want us to do?" John asked. Klint was already pulling out his cellphone and rubbing his forehead.
"Get out of here," Klint shook his head. "I gotta call this in. Come back in like twenty minutes after everyone gets here. Ditch the gear and shit, as far as everyone else is concerned, this was a rival hit,"
"You got it," John nodded. He and Kade hurried out of the house as Klint called in his location to the 9-1-1 dispatcher, giving her his name and information.

\*\*\*\*

It wasn't the first time Klint had seen something like what was in the back bedroom of the house. The cartels loved to use middle school and high school aged boys to help traffic the drugs. They were easy to manipulate, with promises of huge paydays for simply carrying a bag from one location to another. The first couple times, the kids usually got some money. Some. Always promised more. That's why they kept coming back. But it all ended the same way. The kids were a dime a dozen and when one was no longer needed, they'd be shot and dumped in a vat of acid, ceasing to exist.

No one really questioned Klint's version of the events. He'd been driving by the area when he heard gunshots. After going to investigate, Klint made the discovery. He assumed it was a retaliation hit against the cartel from a rival cartel. The other detectives he spoke to seemed to agree with his theory.

The uniformed officers taped off the entire street, drawing a crowd of spectators and news reporters in mere minutes. Kade and John were allowed under the yellow tape, the patrolmen recognizing both men. They had changed out of their tactical gear; only carrying compact pistols in their waistbands. Klint came and got them as soon as they entered the crime scene.

"Alright, they bought it," Klint whispered, pulling the two men aside. "We're good. They're gonna bag up the bodies and drugs. I didn't mention anything about the weapons,"

"I got 'em. I'll unload them all at the safehouse tonight," John said.

"Kade, give him a hand," Klint turned to his brother. Kade nodded. "We're gonna need to see what happens with this. If Sinaloa thinks they got hit by a rival, we may be looking at something a little bit more serious. Cartel retaliations are not something this city needs,"

"Don't really see a better alternative. We stirred the hornet's nest here, now's the time to put our boots over their throats, not let off the gas," John shrugged.

"John's got a point," Kade agreed. "Whether we want to admit it or not, we're fighting a war. And a dirty war at that,"

"I know," Klint muttered. He shook his head, trying to clear his thoughts. "Listen, just handle the weapons tonight. I need both of you at the safehouse Friday. Meeting the rest of the crew,"

"Looking forward to it," John said. He and Kade turned around, ducked under the yellow tape, and walked back to their vehicles.

Klint headed back into the house to finish up with the other detectives inside. The CSU Technicians had finished their examinations of the house and bodies, clearing the way for the Medical Examiner to begin bagging up the bodies for transportation to the morgue. The two detectives stood in the kitchen, hovering over the body of Miguel Santos.

"Everything ok?" Klint asked, leaning against the wall. He didn't make eye contact with the detectives as he fired off a text to his daughter, just letting her know he'd be home soon.

"Fine, fine," the older detective, Richard Brown, said. He was holding something in his right latex glove covered hand. "But we found this. Not sure exactly who to pass it off to,"

"Let me see," Klint said quietly, pulling on his own pair of gloves. Rich handed him a notebook, small enough to fit in your back pocket. The brown cover was stained with blood. Klint was especially careful as he opened it and flipped through the pages. The book was filled with addresses all over the greater Chicagoland area;

Klint saw locations in Naperville, Burr Ridge, Elk Grove Village, and Markham.

"What're you thinking?" Rich asked, seeing Klint's eyes narrow as he skimmed the book.

"I think... we might've just stumbled onto a gold mine," Klint muttered. "Turn that into evidence. But not before you make a copy of every single page in this book and give it to me. Me. No one else,"

"You got it," Rich nodded. He, as well as the other detective on scene, knew Klint's power and influence around the city of Chicago. "I'll have it to you tomorrow,"

"Good," Klint handed the book back to Rich. "You guys finish up here, we'll be in contact,"

# CHAPTER 3

# Klint

The safehouse wasn't anything more than a small warehouse on the corner of two relatively low traffic streets in the Bridgeport neighborhood of Chicago. It was the perfect place to keep a low profile, right in the middle of a majority working-class residential neighborhood. John and Klint were the first ones to arrive, they'd both parked their vehicles inside the warehouse.

Klint had been up late again the night before, diving into the packet of addresses that he'd gotten from the notebook. Richard had done what Klint had told him to and turned the book in as evidence, but not before ensuring that Klint had a copy of every page. With the book sitting in evidence, Klint doubted anyone would be looking through it anytime soon, giving him ample time to investigate the lead. Fortunately, Klint knew a few people who might be able to help.

"Kade's almost here," Klint said, tucking his phone away in his pocket.

"So, who's the other one?" John asked, dropping the liftgate on his Excursion and hoisting himself up; he let his legs hang off the side and he cracked open a bottle of Gatorade. He offered an unopened bottle to Klint, who accepted.

"You'll see soon enough," Klint said with a knowing smile. "But no matter what, I want you to trust me. Please,"

"I don't trust anybody," John said, dryly. "But I know we have the same goal here. I know you and Kade both have the stomach for it. Who's to know if these rookies do?"

"I think you'll be surprised," Klint countered.

The rumble of Kade's truck shook the rickety garage door of the warehouse. A minute later, Kade pulled the garage door up and entered the warehouse, pulling it down behind him.

"Speak of the fuckin' devil," John muttered, bumping his fist against Kade's.

"A lot of pomp and circumstance for the newcomers, huh?" Kade commented.

"I don't think you two would disagree with me when I say we could use some extra hands. The three of us can't be in seventeen places at once and we've all got our own lives outside of this. Kade and I are still fathers. We need some help,"

"I'm not arguing," Kade said, throwing his hands up. John shrugged. Klint's phone buzzed. He pulled it out to read a text.

"Be right back," Klint muttered. He hurried out through the front door of the warehouse.

"This should be good," Kade said aloud.

"Oh yeah," John smirked.

The front door opened again and they heard Klint and another man talking quietly to each other. John jumped down from his liftgate, leaning against it with Kade. The two men appeared in the warehouse, Klint stepped aside so John and Kade could get a look at the second man. John recognized him; he and Klint had met the man on his wedding day, almost a year ago.

The man was tall and slim, but obviously in good shape. He'd very clearly just come from work as he was still wearing dirt-caked boots and jeans and a Hi-Vis Carhartt jacket. A pair of Mechanix gloves stuck out of his back pocket. His brown hair was spiked up in the front, cut short and neat all around. He wore a thick gold chain, a cross hung from the gaudy piece of jewelry. There was a black wedding band on his ring finger.

"Kade, John," Klint said formally. "I'd like to introduce Mr. Noah Riordan,"

"How's it going?" Noah asked with a nod. John stepped forward and stuck his hand out.

"Good to see you again," John nodded. Noah shook John's hand firmly and returned the nod.

"Hey, man," Kade said, following suit with a handshake. "I'm Kade,"

"Noah. Pleasure,"

"We're just waiting on one more and then we can begin," Klint announced.

John held up a bottle of Gatorade and looked at Noah, offering it to him. Noah nodded.

"Thanks man," Noah said with a smile. John tossed the bottle and Noah cracked it open, taking a massive sip. "Long day,"

"Where are you working?" John asked.

"Highway up by O'Hare," Noah said.

"Yeah? I've been there for a while too,"

Klint's phone rang once again and he answered with a pleasant 'Hello'. After a few 'uh-huhs', Klint strode back outside of the warehouse. Noah walked over to a chair and sat down, chugging the rest of the Gatorade. He leaned back in the chair, groaning loudly.

"You got any idea who else is coming?" Kade asked.

"No, not a clue," Noah admitted. "I'm still pretty unsure what exactly I'm doing here,"

"So are we," Kade muttered. "Klint's been pretty tight-lipped about all this,"

John was about to say something fairly sarcastic, but before he could, the door to the warehouse opened. Again, Klint's friendly voice filled the silence. He was talking excitedly. The voice talking back to him was a woman, young and full of life. John and Kade looked at each other, raising their eyebrows with suspicion. The footfalls and Klint's animated voice got closer and closer, coming around the corner to the actual warehouse portion of the building. Klint came around the corner first and gave the three men a quick glance.

The woman stepped out into view, stopping next to Klint. She was carrying a large camo duffle bag in one hand and a massive weapon case in the other. Her hair was lightly curled and long, falling to the middle of her back. Although more brunette towards the roots, her hair was a dark blonde that complemented her tan skin very well. She had sparkly diamond earrings in both ears and a thick steel bracelet on her right wrist. She wore no makeup, not that she needed any. Unlike the men, she dressed more practical for the uncharacteristically hot day in Chicago, a pair of white Nike gym shoes, a pair of denim short-shorts, and a low cut black crop top that exposed a bit of her toned stomach.

John and Kade looked at each other with surprise. Noah cocked his head toward Klint, spinning his wedding ring around his finger. This woman was not at all who they'd been expecting. Not by a long shot. Klint could see the surprise on their faces and bit his lip, enjoying their immediate discomfort with the gorgeous woman in their presence. He'd expected them to be surprised, but John's look of sheer disbelief was very amusing.

"Gentlemen," Klint said loudly. "This is Kayley. Kayley, this is the rest of the team,"

"Hi," Kayley said with a small, yet serious, smile. She set her bag and gun case down next to her.

"That's my brother, Kade, John Shannon, and Noah Riordan," Klint said, pointing to each man as he listed them off.

"Uh, yeah," Kade grumbled. He waved at her. "Nice to meet you,"

"Nice to meet you guys," Kayley said, still smiling with her perfectly white teeth.

"She just flew in from LAX, so I'll try and make this quick," Klint said. He turned to Kayley. "I'm sure the last place you want to be is in a dirty old warehouse,"

"I've been in worse places," Kayley shrugged. "Kandahar makes this look like the Four Seasons,"

"Kandahar?" John asked, not bothering to hide his astonishment. Kandahar was a city in Afghanistan that the US Military had a heavy presence in. John had been stationed there during one of his tours with the SEALs. "You're military?"

"Army," Kayley said proudly. "40th Infantry Division,"

"No shit," Kade muttered. He looked impressed, but also very surprised. Kayley looked more like a model than a soldier. "I was Delta Force, just retired a few months ago,"

"My dad was Delta Force," Kayley nodded. She turned to John. "What about you?"

"SEALs," John answered curtly; he barely paid her any attention, instead glaring at Klint. His shortness with her caught her somewhat off guard, but she was used to it. Most men, especially military men, had not taken her seriously. There was nothing she could say to change their opinions, only her work would reflect her level of commitment.

"And you?" Kayley asked, looking at Noah. She shook off John's harsh attitude like a pro. "Are you military, too?"

"Nope," Noah shook his head with a wry smile. He was loving the very obvious tension between John and Klint. "I'm just the kleptomaniac,"

"O-kay," Kayley said, not exactly sure how to respond to that. Noah laughed.

"We all have our special skills, right?" Noah shrugged. "Mine are probably less legal than yours,"

"Sounds exciting," Kayley raised her eyebrows. Noah touched his wedding ring again. He knew exactly who she was, but wasn't about to say anything in front of the rest of the guys.

"Now, that we're all affiliated with one another..." Klint said, crossing his arms. He shot John a rough look before straightening up. "I want to talk a little bit about why I've gathered you all here. Again, I'll try and keep it brief. We've all had long days and I want us to enjoy the weekend,"

Klint reached into a backpack and pulled out the packet of addresses he'd gotten off the notebook. He tossed them onto a table off to his right, more for dramatic effect than anything else.

"You all have been picked by me because of your unique skill sets. It doesn't matter if everyone else sees it right now, or not. I see it. I brought you all here because I've been tasked with cleaning up this city. As I'm sure you're all aware, Chicago is routinely one of the more dangerous places in the country. Our weekend shooting rates are astounding and the Mayor is sick of it. The five of us have been granted immunity from any legal repercussions, assuming we actually start making progress," Klint paused, letting everyone grasp what he was explaining.

"John and Kade have been hitting targets for the last few weeks," Klint continued, nodding to his brother and John. "It's hard to tell, but I firmly believe we are causing some damage, especially to the Sinaloa Cartel. They've got a huge footprint in Chicago and contribute to a lot of the violence with other gangs. That packet is a list of addresses we pulled off one of the cartel shot callers. I've been researching the locations, it's a mix of commercial and residential properties. Some occupied, some aren't. The investigation is ongoing,"

"Probably safehouses," John offered. "The cartels have plenty of local contacts who aren't exactly affiliated but still love the money,"

"Fair point," Klint agreed. "Like I said, I'm investigating on my end. Once I have something actionable, I'll let you all know,"

"For our safety, we all need to maintain some semblance of normalcy. The last thing any of us needs is our identities getting out there. Safe to say, anonymity is our friend," Klint explained. "As far as anyone is concerned, I'm just a simple detective waiting for retirement. John and Noah are working construction. Kade's a stay at home dad. And Kayley's here opening her new office for the talent agency,"

"I knew I recognized you," Kade suddenly blurted. The comment got him a hard backhand on the arm from John. Kade looked at John and shook his head. "Hey! The fuck was that?"

"Keep it in your pants," John muttered, still glaring down at Klint.

"Part of my arrangement with the Mayor..." Klint matched John's glare. "Is making sure that you all have adequate accommodations. This doesn't apply to Kade or John, but Noah, Kayley, you two have two standing rooms at the Ritz Carlton. Suites,"

Klint pulled out two room keys from his wallet. He handed one to Kayley and the other to Noah.

"Room numbers are written on the back," Klint said with a smile.

"Wow," Noah muttered. "Thanks, dude,"

"Yeah, thank you," Kayley echoed.

"That's all I have for you guys as of right now," Klint finished up. "You all have my cell, I'm available if you have any questions or concerns. We'll plan to meet up again on Monday and get to work. Have a good weekend,"

After a few more pleasantries, Noah and Kayley left the warehouse. Kade followed them out, firing up his Dodge Ram, and driving away as Kayley hopped into an Uber. John remained motionless, still staring at Klint with narrowed eyes. Klint stood his ground, trying his best to act unafraid. As confident as Klint was, he knew precisely just how dangerous John Shannon was. He was not a man you wanted to make angry.

"Something to say, John?" Klint asked, stuffing his hands in his pockets.

"What the hell?" John spat. "I really didn't have an issue with the bank robber. That actually makes sense to me and the guy can clearly handle his own in a gunfight. But, come on, man. You brought on Kayley fucking McKenna?"

"She's a highly decorated soldier, John," Klint defended, his voice and attitude as calm as could be. As usual, Klint remained cool and collected.

"Give me a break, man. She's a goddamn pornstar, Klinton," John groaned. "I mean, seriously? I don't care if she's a soldier or not, she sticks out like a sore thumb. She's actually famous, Klint. Famous. Noah recognized her, for Christ's sakes,"

"Exactly," Klint smiled. "That's exactly why she's perfect. She's combat ready, deceptively beautiful, and recognizable. No one is going to look at her and think she's anything more than a pretty face. These gangbangers aren't PHD candidates. You throw a woman like that in front of them and they'll melt. We have leverage. And leverage that we can trust with our lives should things go bad,"

John crossed his arms and fell silent. After almost a minute, he pulled out his sunglasses and slipped them over his eyes. Walking over to the large garage door, John firmly gripped the handle, and yanked the door open. Returning to his truck, he flipped the liftgate on his truck up and walked around to the driver's side door, throwing it open. Looking back, John pushed the sunglasses up onto his forehead so Klint could see his eyes.

"You better know what you're doing, Klint," John said cryptically. "I've seen what happens when guys get complacent,"

And with that, John climbed into his truck, fired up the engine, and pulled out of the warehouse. His truck roared down the street as he drove away, kicking up a cloud of dust and exhaust.

Sighing, Klint proceeded to lock up the rest of the warehouse before getting into his Charger and driving out of the warehouse, back onto the main road. Hurrying back over to the building, Klint pulled the garage door down and threw the lock on it.

****

Klint stepped out of his shower and felt lightyears better than he did before. The day had kicked his butt, in more ways than one. He was positive he'd assembled a solid crew to achieve his goals, but John's words kept echoing in his ears.

*You better know what you're doing, Klint. I've seen what happens when you get complacent.*

Was he complacent? Had he made a mistake bringing in someone like Kayley? Klint shook his head free of those thoughts. No, he hadn't. He had gone over different possible candidates for weeks. Kayley McKenna gave them a distinct advantage. And, she was a combat veteran, a decorated marksman. She was the right woman for the job. None of the other guys Klint had recruited could play both parts. Kayley could. It was that simple.

After getting dressed, Klint slid into bed and sighed loudly. He was relieved that the day was finally done, Kara was safe and sound in her room; he could finally try and relax. Relaxation didn't come easily or naturally to Klint. While he always conveyed a calm, collected, and level persona, it was growing increasingly difficult to maintain that even keeled personality. The weekend would be a good break from the week's events. He and Kara had planned on going to Lincoln Park Zoo for the day. She was admittedly way too old for the zoo, but they both had gone so many times when she'd been growing up that it was more nostalgic than anything.

The coming week was going to be challenging. Klint would finally get to see if the team he'd put together would actually be able to achieve what he'd hoped. But first, Klint had to find out more about the addresses. Fortunately, he had plenty of friends from all walks of life.

****

The Pilsen neighborhood in the Lower West Side of Chicago was predominately Hispanic, making up more than 80% of the demographic of the small community. Some of the best and most authentic Mexican cuisine could be found in the Lower West Side. Because of the ethnic ties to Mexico, many immigrants gravitated to Pilsen. And because of that, there was a strong cartel presence. Not obvious, not even very intimidating, but they were there just the same. The men and women of the Sinaloa Cartel lurked around every corner, watching and waiting. Miguel Santos had been shot and killed, presumably by a rival cartel. That was not something to be taken lightly. In fact, that was the type of thing that could start a cartel war.

Klint Kavanaugh was tempted to stop and get some food, but decided against it. He was in a bit of a rush and stopping for food would only delay his rendezvous at the warehouse with the rest of the team. John stared out the window from the passenger seat, his tinted sunglasses hiding his ferocious eyes from passersby on the street. They barely talked during the drive, which didn't bother Klint. At the end of the day, Klint had to stick to his gut. The Mayor had chosen him to clean up the city, not John Shannon. As much as John may have disagreed with Klint's logic, Klint knew he was right.

"You still pissed at me?" Klint asked as they came to a stop before an intersection. It was an occupational hazard, but Klint scanned the street in front of him, waiting for something horrible to happen. John rolled his neck around and Klint heard it crack a few times.

"I just don't get it," John grumbled, his voice especially gravelly today. You want me to trust you and buy into this, but this just doesn't make any sense to me. It's like you're asking for more attention,"

"You're missing the point, John," Klint said as the light turned green.

"No, I get it. Leverage," John responded.

"What?"

"Well, Klint," John pushed his sunglasses up on his head. He reached into his back pocket and pulled out a half empty pack of Marlboro Golds and a beat up Bic lighter. John flipped the pack open and thumbed a cigarette into his mouth, though he didn't light it yet. "The last time I was working closely with a woman, she got shot in the head. I'd rather not deal with that again,"

Klint looked over at John, studying the man carefully. John didn't speak much about his past life prior to moving to Chicago, but Klint knew enough. John Shannon still wore his wedding ring, even though his wife had passed away years prior. Klint knew that

John had been close with Riley Hanna and her death clearly had had a profound effect on John. It was only just occurring to Klint that John blamed himself for Riley. And that made much more sense. Klint was going to say something else about it, but John rolled down the window before he lit his cigarette and shook his head.

"Are we almost there?" John asked, blowing a cloud of smoke out the window.

"Few minutes," Klint muttered, turning left down a narrow street. Small homes and four-story flats lined either side of the road. "It's the house on the right,"

Klint parallel parked into an open space in front of the rundown white home. There were two men sitting on the porch, one of them was shirtless and sporting an entire body full of tattoos. He was very clearly carrying a pistol in his waistband.

"Best behavior, ok? The last thing I need is for these guys to have an issue with me. Javier isn't someone I can replace. Building this relationship has taken a lot of work, don't shoot your mouth off," Klint said seriously, glaring at John. John scoffed and pinched his smoke with two of his fingers.

"Yes, mom," John rolled his eyes under his shades and hopped out of the car, popping the cigarette back into his mouth. He puffed on it while he waited for Klint to get out and walk around the front of his car.

"Let's do this," Klint whispered, adjusting his t-shirt to cover his own pistol he had tucked in the small of his back. John, always prepared, also had a gun in his waistband and a compact pistol around an ankle holster beneath his jeans; both guns were locked, loaded, and ready for action.

The shirtless man on the porch smiled when he saw Klint. He got up and opened the front door to the house.

"¡Yo, Javier!" he called into the house. *"Policía está aquí,"*

"Que pasa, Carlos?" Klint asked, bounding up the stairs. Klint and Carlos 'bro-hugged' like they'd known each other their whole lives. Turning to the shirted man, Klint greeted him the same way.

"It's been a while, *jefe,*" Carlos said with a grill of gold teeth smile. "You good?"

"Good as one can be," Klint shrugged. "Hey, I wanna introduce you to John,"

"How's it going?" John asked, slowly climbing up the stairs behind Klint. He put his cigarette out of the bottom of his boot and flicked the butt into the bushes.

"Any friend of Klint's is a friend of mine," Carlos said, offering John his tattooed fist. John bumped knuckles with Carlos. Carlos pointed to the second man on the porch. "This is Tomás,"

John nodded respectfully. Tomás returned the nod. John felt a little more at ease, but still wasn't fully comfortable. Even if these guys were cool with Klint, they were still cartel affiliated. He recognized the ink on Carlos as a dead giveaway.

"Javi should be out in a minute," Carlos said. "Want a beer?"

"No thanks," Klint shook his head. "When I'm not working, I'll take you up on it though,"

"Imma hold you to that, homes," Carlos grinned.

The front door opened and Javier 'Javi' Rodriguez stepped onto the porch. He wore sunglasses, a flannel shirt, and a pair of expensive jeans. Wallet chains hung from his right side and he had rings on most of his fingers. His hands and neck were covered in tattoos.

"Klint, so good to see you, my friend," Javi said with a bright smile. He and Klint hugged.

"Good to see you too. Sorry it's been a while, just been busy,"

"How's Kara doing?" Javi asked, leaning against the house.

"She's good, started her first year at DePaul," Klint said proudly.

"I hope you got the graduation gift I sent," Javi smiled. Klint nodded.

"Of course. That was very nice and completely unnecessary of you,"

"You let me know if she needs anything, alright?" Javi insisted. "We take care of our own,"

"I appreciate it, Javi,"

Aside from Javi and Klint, no one else on the porch was aware of the level of respect that Javi had for Klint. Many years ago, when Javi was first rising through the ranks of the Tijuana Cartel, Klint had helped him out of a very dangerous situation. Javi had been married at the time and they'd had a young daughter when he'd crossed a pair of *sicarios* from the Sinaloa Cartel. If it hadn't been for Klint, Javi and his family would have surely been killed. It was something that Javi had never forgotten and even though he ended up getting divorced and losing custody of his daughter a short while later, he always appreciated the risks Klint took to keep his family safe. Klint was a brother, as far as Javi was concerned, and he looked out for him as best he could.

"So, what can I do for you?" Javi asked. Klint reached into his jacket and pulled out the packet of addresses.

"I pulled these off of Miguel Santos," Klint said, handing the packet to Javi.

"I heard Santos was gunned down," Javi grinned. "That your handy work?"

"I can't take credit for it," Klint nodded his head toward John. Javi looked at John, and smiled.

"All in a day's work," John muttered.

"I like this guy," Javi laughed. He opened the packet and began skimming through it.

"They're all in the greater Chicago area. But I have no way of knowing what they are. I was hoping maybe you'd have some idea,"

"Well..." Javi sighed, his eyes narrowing as he read. "What I know and what I suspect are two very different things. I know that Tijuana has many local contacts around here. My guess is they've got safehouses all over the place. I suspect this is a log of sorts, but I have no way of knowing that. It's worth looking into for sure. My only question would be why did Santos have this? Clearly it's important if he had it on his person,"

"That's what I was thinking too," Klint muttered. "Ok, I know it's a lot to ask, but anyway you can have your people do some snooping around at some of these? I don't have the time or resources to look into all of these, but John and I can split some of them up between our team,"

"For sure," Javi nodded. He turned to Carlos and said something in Spanish. Carlos rushed inside and came back a few minutes later with a burner cell phone; he handed it to Klint. "Mine and Carlos's numbers are programmed in there. Text us the addresses you want us to take a look at and we'll handle it,"

"Awesome," Klint said, slipping the phone into his pocket. Javi handed him the packet back and they shook hands. "I'll reach out later today,"

"Don't be a stranger," Javi smiled. He turned to John and offered his hand. "Nice to meet you,"

"Likewise," John said, minus the smile.

Klint said goodbye to Carlos and Tomás before heading back to his Charger with John right beside him. They jumped in the car and Klint sped off, heading back toward the warehouse in Bridgeport.

"You really trust these guys?" John asked after a few minutes of silence.

"With my life, John," Klint nodded. "With my life,"

\*\*\*\*

"Thank you all for coming, once again," Klint said to his team. This time, they were all seated on rolling chairs around a large folding table. Klint had several things laid out on the table, mostly newspaper articles and things of that nature. "Again, I'll try and make this quick, but I want us to all be clear on the goals for this week. Just so everyone is aware, I meet with Mayor Hart every two weeks to discuss our progress. When we've made progress, those meetings are quite pleasant. When we haven't, less so. We're not going to fix a city like Chicago in a week. It's going to take a lot of time. But, we still need to be making strides towards that goal, even if it's just little victories. Taking down Miguel Santos was a huge victory for us, so thank you to John and Kade,"

John Shannon and Kade Kavanaugh were seated next to each other. After hearing their names called, Kade stuck out his fist to bump with John. John stared at Kade for a moment before turning back to Klint, ignoring the fist. Kade slowly put his fist back down on his knee. Noah Riordan sat next to John and Kayley McKenna was next to Kade. Each of them had a different drink from Starbucks in front of them, all in various degrees of consumption.

"This week, we're going to be working in teams," Klint continued. He reached into the bag by his feet and pulled out two manilla folders. "John and Kayley, you two will check out a handful of addresses and report back your findings. Kade and Noah, you guys have a different set of addresses. Same thing, check 'em out and see what's up. I've got a few meetings with the Department this week, but I'll be around should anything come up,"

"What exactly should we be looking for?" Kayley asked. She reached over the table and picked up the manilla folder with her and John's name written on it. John looked extremely displeased about the pairing, but that was to be expected. Klint had purposefully assigned them to work together. John needed to get over his issues with Kayley and Klint knew the best way for that to happen was to have them work together.

"Anything you deem suspicious," Klint said simply. "I don't expect you all to do full on stake outs, but check them out, and see what's up. That's all I want you to do this week. Just surveillance. I've got some other contacts looking into the rest of the addresses. I want all of these locations checked out by the end of the week,"

"Sounds doable," Kade grabbed the second manilla folder and handed it to Noah.

"I'm hoping it's fairly easy," Klint said, focusing on the only person who Klint figured would have an issue. John didn't look any more miserable than usual, which Klint mistakenly took as a good sign. "Any questions?"

Seeing none, Klint stood up and smiled at his newly formed team. They got up and headed out to their respective vehicles without any more friendly banter. He had nothing to worry about from Kade and Noah. John climbed into his Excursion and fired it up, not bothering to get the door for Kayley. Klint almost felt kind of bad for Kayley, knowing what she'd have to deal with this week. He kept reminding himself that this was the best way to get John more comfortable with the idea. Klint needed John on his A-Game. Hopefully, this would do the trick.

# CHAPTER 4

# John

The first address on their list of ten was located in Burr Ridge, Illinois; a little more than a half hour outside of Chicago. It was known for the sprawling mansions and homes. Burr Ridge was as wealthy an area as they came. Neither John nor Kayley could relate to that. John had been mostly quiet throughout the drive from Bridgeport, only asking for directions once when traffic got so bad he took the next possible exit off the highway. Kayley was friendly, but not exactly a conversationalist. However, the constant silence was getting to her.

"So, you were in the Navy right?" she asked, looking over at John.

"Yep," John grunted, not taking his eyes off the road. His dark sunglasses were covering his eyes, making it hard for Kayley to tell if his eyes were even open.

"What made you choose the Navy?" she asked another question. "You see, I went into the Army because both my parents were in the Army. My mom was more on the Administrative side, but my dad... he did some interesting stuff. He retired from Delta Force,"

Delta Force was the Army equivalent of the Navy SEAL Teams. The very best of the very best.

"Delta, huh?" John repeated, trying to not be rude. He didn't have anything against Kayley as a person. She was pretty, friendly, and chatty. But he absolutely resented Klint for bringing her into this and that wasn't easy for him to hide. "Yeah, I knew a few Delta boys in my day,"

"I'm not trying to pry," Kayley said.

"But why'd I go to the Navy?" John finished the rest of her sentence for her. She nodded. "Honestly, I don't know. But as soon as I was in, I knew I was going to be a SEAL. Nothing else was going to satisfy me,"

"I understand that," Kayley nodded. "That's how I felt when I first joined the Army. I did two tours in Afghanistan and I don't know, guess I changed my mind after that,"

"Things go sideways?" John asked, hearing the same tone in her voice that he used when he talked about his time overseas. Not many civilians picked up on it, but vets could sniff it out in a heartbeat. The reluctance to talk, but also the yearning to relieve yourself of carrying the burden of what you did or saw alone.

"Something like that," Kayley shook her head and stared out of the window.

He looked over and could see it in Kayley's eyes. The same haunted look that he saw every time he looked in the mirror. His heart hurt for her. She was a young girl still, probably only 25 or 26 at the most, with a full life ahead of her. But that youthful innocence, that was gone. This poor girl had bought into whatever bullshit her parents had fed her about glory and country. John shook his head in disgust. It never failed to amaze him how ass backwards his country was. But, then again, John owed his entire life to his country. Without the military, who knows what he would've ended up doing.

"So, can I ask you something?" John asked, changing the subject rapidly.

"Sure," Kayley said, still looking out of her window.

"How's a combat vet get into... your current line of work?" John asked. "Just seems like a bit of a leap,"

"I was waiting for someone to bring it up," Kayley said, smirking at John. "When Klint pitched me this whole thing, I was wondering why the hell he'd want me, but he was pretty adamant,"

"That sounds about right," John didn't know what else to say.

"I kind of got into it by accident. A lot of things just fell into my lap, but I ran with it. It's worked out pretty well, I can't complain," Kayley admitted, not really knowing how to explain everything about her new career to a man she barely knew.

Quite simply, Kayley McKenna was an adult film star, going by the stage name 'Kaye Lee'. Not the most original name, but it worked for her purposes. She was only 26 years old, but had become a superstar in the industry; not only as a performer, but also as a director and talent agent. Despite her successes and rise to fame, the job from Klint had been welcome, as she'd started to miss the thrill and excitement of the armed forces. Under the cover of trying to open a Chicago branch of the talent agency she owned, Kayley knew her cover was rock solid. Although John clearly didn't see eye to eye with Klint, Kayley understood and respected Klint's plan for her. She wasn't naive at all, she knew her value to the team was more than just her ability to shoot.

"Hey, I'm not judging," John said, feeling the need to make sure she knew that. "I was just asking,"

"I get it's a little unconventional," Kayley shrugged. John nodded, but didn't say anything else.

Suddenly, John pointed toward a massive white house on the right side of the street.

"Right there. Big white house with the gate," John muttered, slowing down just a little bit so he could get a good look at the property. It was a sprawling home with a beautifully manicured front lawn. He noticed there were four black SUVs parked on the long driveway that lead up to a four car garage.

"Security?" Kayley asked, eyeing the cars as well.

"Could be," John muttered. He pushed his sunglasses up on his eyes and kept driving, trying to be as incognito as possible. "We'll do a few passes and see what's up. Klint just wanted us to see if we saw anything worth noting,"

"Sounds good to me," Kayley nodded in agreement.

John turned down the next block and made another loop around the subdivision, once again driving slowly past the big white house. This time, A group of men were walking out of the house toward the SUVs. Kayley pulled her iPhone out and zoomed in on the camera as close as she could, snapping picture after picture.

"Got 'em?" John asked.

"Yeah, I got 'em," Kayley nodded, scrolling through the photos. "I don't recognize any of them,"

"Let me see," John stuck his hand out for the phone. He pulled over in front of another house down the street and began scrolling through the photos. He stopped on one particularly clear image of the group and zoomed in on one of the man's faces. "Well, shit,"

"What?" Kayley asked, leaning over to see what he found. John turned the phone so she could see.

"That's one of the Lieutenants for the Chinese Triad in Chicago," John muttered. He looked in his rearview mirror. The SUVs hadn't left the property yet. "You got your gear in the back, right?"

"Uh, yeah," Kayley said. "Why? Didn't Klint say just observe?"

"Klint's not here right now," John sped off down the road, turning right to make another lap around. "Get your gun and gear ready, we're going loud,"

"Are you sure about this?" Kayley asked, tying her hair back in a ponytail.

"Yes," John grunted. "I am,"

\*\*\*\*

John reached behind his seat and shrugged into his tactical vest, adjusting it over his hoodie. He handed Kayley one of his spare vests, it was going to be too big on her, but it would still do the job; he made a mental note to make sure he got a vest that would better fit her. Kayley pulled the vest over her black Under Armour shirt and tightened the straps as much as she could.

"Have they left yet?" John asked. He was grabbing his rifle and pistol, making sure they were loaded, and that his vest was properly equipped with spare magazines and flashbang grenades.

"Doesn't look like it," Kayley reported.

"Here," John groaned, heaving a kitted out M4A1 rifle toward Kayley. Accepting the rifle, Kayley spun it around so the barrel was pointed at the floor, and racked the charging handle - priming the weapon. John handed her half a dozen extra rifle magazines, which she promptly fit into the pouches on her vest. "You want a sidearm?"

"Nah," Kayley shook her head. "I'm good,"

"Alright then," John said, grabbing his USP45 and sliding it into his waistband. Last but not least, John reached into the center console and pulled out the ski masks. He tossed one over to Kayley and pulled the second one over his face; Kayley followed suit. Her blonde hair still fell below the mask, but her identity was at least concealed.

John Shannon didn't really get nervous in situations like this. Times like this were when he felt most comfortable, most capable. The only thing that made him uncertain was Kayley. Yes, she was military. But being in the military and being a Navy SEAL were two very different things. And even so, John still had no idea what exactly she'd done in the Army. Looking back, maybe he should've tried to talk to her more on their drive out here. None of that mattered now. They had a mission to execute.

"Let's go," John whispered, stepping out of the truck. He took the lead, immediately moving onto the sidewalk, and raising his rifle. Kayley filed into position behind him, keeping her rifle pointed downward, but still ready to engage. John knelt before a large brick pillar that connected to the gate in front of the house. Slowly, he peered around the pillar. Sure enough, the men were still talking in front of the SUVs.

There were two options, John decided. The first of which was to storm the property and kill anyone who moved. The second involved a more tactical approach and getting the men back inside the house, overpowering them, and then asking them some very pointed questions. Knowing he was already going to be on Klint's shitlist for this, John figured it'd be better to at least bring him back some intelligence he could use.

"Alright, I got a plan," John whispered to Kayley. "We gotta pick off the bodyguards quick and fast, force the rest of them back inside the house. Then we storm the house and have a nice friendly chat with whoever feels like talking. Sound good?"

"Got it," Kayley nodded. She brought the stock of her rifle into her shoulder to check the optics.

"Follow my lead, don't get shot," John said.

And with that, John Shannon stood up and stepped forward, leveling his rifle. He peered through the optic, steadied his aim on one of the bodyguards, and pulled the trigger. The rifle barked and kicked back, but the guard went down instantly, a hole where his face used to be. The group of men whipped around in panic, looking for the shooter. In their confusion, John was able to drop two more guards. Without the suppressor on the end of the 416, the rifle sounded like a cannon. Kayley laid on the ground next to John's feet and slowly selected her targets. She took a deep breath and squeezed the trigger, shooting one of the Triad enforcers through the chest. He spun in a circle and Kayley shot him a second time through the back; he fell in a mess of his own blood.

"Front gate!" John heard someone yell.

"Here we go," John muttered. He dropped to one knee and fired off six more rounds, injuring another enforcer and killing a second. After a few seconds, John and Kayley began taking return fire; granted it wasn't any real threat. The gangsters accuracy wasn't anything to write home about. John spotted a handful of Triads heading for one of the SUVs, no doubt in an attempt to escape.

"Shoot the cars!" John yelled over the gunfire to Kayley. Calmly adjusting her aim, Kayley put a round through each of the engine blocks and then shot out the tires, ensuring that no one was going anywhere. Rolling onto her back, Kayley leapt to her feet, and blasted off the rest of her magazine before taking cover behind the brick pillar across the driveway; she reloaded like a true soldier. John could tell in the first few seconds of shooting alongside her that she meant business. He almost felt bad for judging her so quickly. Almost.

As expected, once the gangsters deemed the cars were useless, they began darting back inside, spraying wildly at the front of the property. While they managed to shoot off a ton of bullets, their rounds didn't come close to causing actual harm to John or Kayley.

"They're heading inside!" Kayley called out. John nodded and ran over to her just as the last of the gangsters were running back inside.

"Ok, we don't have long," John said. "Someone will surely call the cops and those guys are probably calling whatever backup they've got. Our advantage is that they have no idea how many of us are out here. Let's get in and get out, alright?"

"You take the front, I'll take the back," Kayley suggested. John didn't like the idea of splitting up, but tactically, it made the most sense. He grabbed two flashbangs from his kit and passed them off to Kayley, who attached them to her vest.

"Be careful," John said, staring at her intently.

"You too," Kayley answered with a wink.

John watched for only a moment as Kayley ducked and took off toward the rear of the house, sticking to the property line, and using the trees and bushes to cover her movements. Gripping his rifle, John moved quickly toward the front of the house. He was slightly surprised a cocky triggerman didn't bust a window and start shooting at him, but he wasn't complaining. Instead of going to the front door, John tried his luck with a side door attached to the garage. Miraculously, it was unlocked. Never failed to amaze him how lazy bad guys could be. He moved inside the garage and crept past four parked cars toward the door that lead to the house. Keeping one hand on the trigger of his rifle, John grabbed a flashbang from his vest and used his thumb to pop the pin out. Letting his rifle hang for a moment, John yanked the door open and launched the flashbang inside.

He heard the panicked screams and shouts before the grenade went off, silencing whoever was in the general area. The effects of the flashbang were incredibly disorientating, even lethal depending on how close you were when it detonated. Kicking the door open, John moved inside, knowing he'd have to be careful to not kill everyone. He still needed some information. The first man he saw was in a blue suit, probably a *mafioso*. John spoke in heavily accented Spanish, ordering the man to keep his hands where he could see them. He had no way of knowing if the man could hear him. But, the man stretched his hands out and John zip tied his wrists and ankles. At least he had one.

Standing up, John heard a second flashbang detonate, followed by a concussive exchange of gunfire. He heard a pistol, submachine gun, and an M4. Luckily, the M4 was the final gun he heard. Moving around into the kitchen, John shot a cartel enforcer dead as he was trying to reach for a compact shotgun. Two Triads, including the Lieutenant that John had recognized, were still trying to orientate themselves from the flashbang.

"Hands above your heads," John snarled, kicking the Lieutenant in the gut. The man ground and mumbled something in a language that John didn't understand. John jammed his rifle into the man's back. "Roll over and keep your hands up!"

Reluctantly, both men complied, blinking their eyes to try and get their eyesight back. John knelt down and zip-tied them both as fast as he could. He grabbed his rifle and moved quickly through the rest of the first floor. Kayley spun around the corner and fell into position next to him.

"We're running out of time," John muttered as they cleared a back room.

"I didn't see anyone else," Kayley whispered back. It was a huge risk to not clear the rest of the house. "It's your call,"

"Screw it," John grumbled. "Watch the front for cops. I'll get what I can out of these guys,"

"Ok," Kayley nodded. She ran toward the front door and took up an overwatch position in front of the large window looking out at the front of the property.

Reentering the kitchen, John dragged his three prisoners in front of the fridge. They all stared up at him with hate in their eyes. He began throwing open drawers and cabinets in the kitchen, looking for anything he could use against them. He struck gold when he opened a junk drawer and found a pair of large shears. Picking up the tool, John crouched down in front of the three men.

"I don't give a shit how tough you three think you are," John growled. "You can either talk to me or I'm gonna hurt you until you do. Is that clear?"

As expected, none of them said anything. The man in the blue suit even spit on the floor in front of him. John narrowed his eyes on the man.

"Looks like you're up first," John snarled, grabbing the man's bound wrists. He fought back, but once John drew his pistol and stuck it in the man's mouth, he stopped. John opened the shears and grabbed the man's pointer finger, applying just enough pressure for the man to know John wasn't messing around. The two Triads looked over in horror.

"Now," John looked into the man's terrified eyes. "You're going to tell me your name. You're going to tell me who these two are sitting next to you. And, you're going to tell me what the hell the cartel and the Triad is doing all the way out here. Understood?"

The man didn't say anything, but he was shaking. His eyes were narrowed and filled with a blinding rage.

"Last chance," John said, squeezing the finger hard enough to draw blood. The man shrieked in pain, but didn't offer up the information that John wanted. "Your choice,"

The shears did most of the work, John only had to apply enough pressure to snap the bone like a stick. Blood squirted out from the newly formed stump on the man's hand. He screamed in pain, his body shaking uncontrollably. John set the discarded digit in the man's lap and moved his attention to the two Triads. This had always been his intention; show your not messing around and they'll always break. Wiping the shears on the man's suit coat, John opened and closed them a few times for effect.

"Do you two feel like sharing anything with me?" John asked.

****

The sounds coming from the kitchen sent a chill down Kayley's spine. After hearing the bone chilling screams, Kayley was relieved that John had assigned her to watch the front of the house. Whatever he was doing in there, Kayley wanted no part of it. She wasn't naive, not by any stretch of the imagination. Kayley had seen the ugly side of war quite a few times; she'd taken a few lives and done some pretty horrible things in the name of her country. But when it came to torture - 'enhanced interrogation' - Kayley just didn't have the stomach for it. There was something evil about inflicting that much pain on someone who wasn't actively fighting back, someone who wasn't innocent, but was completely helpless in that moment.

She could hear John's low voice, sounding much less frightening than it had been. Someone was talking back, which she was relieved about. Whatever John had done, he'd gotten his point across. Kayley was feeling herself relax a little bit when three impossibly loud gunshots rang out from the kitchen; she covered her mouth to avoid yelping in surprise but she jumped from the startle.

"Let's go," John called, walking out of the kitchen. He had his ski mask rolled up on his forehead, exposing his face. Kayley was glad she still had hers on so he couldn't see the expression on her face. "The cops will be here any second,"

As if on cue, John saw a duo of squad cars come to a screeching halt at the front of the property. Their lights were flashing, but the sirens were off. One by one, more police cars started showing up.

"Damnit," John muttered. "Alright, let's move. We're going out the back,"

"I'm right behind you," Kayley said, showing no hesitation. She followed John back through the kitchen, past the corpses against the fridge, and toward the back door. The men that Kayley had taken out upon her intrusion to the home were sprawled on the ground.

"Cut through the lawns and double back to the truck," John explained. "Don't worry, they won't come after us. Not for a while, anyway,"

"How do you know?"

John didn't answer but he picked up a discarded AKMSU from one of the gangsters. Releasing the magazine, John made sure there was sufficient ammo before slamming it back into the rifle and cocking the gun.

"Go," John encouraged, nodding toward the door. "I'll catch up,"

"John..." Kayley whispered, having a bad feeling about what he was going to do. John grabbed her shoulder and looked at her seriously.

"Go!" he urged. Kayley sprinted from the house into the back-yard, crossing over into a neighbor's yard once she was far enough away.

Jogging back toward the front door, John sidestepped into the living room and raised the AKMSU, barely aiming as he pulled the trigger. He sprayed rounds all over the front yard, purposefully missing any of the actual emergency personnel. All he was doing was forcing them to take cover, regroup, and reevaluate. Now that someone was shooting at them, they would most certainly wait for SWAT. And in that window, John and Kayley would be in the clear.

Once the gun ran dry, John dropped the rifle, and sprinted out the back door after Kayley. He followed the same route she'd taken, hoping he'd catch up to her soon. The sirens were now ever present as John tore through a neighbors yard; moving quickly to avoid scrutiny. Trying to hide his rifle under his hoodie, John hurried onto the sidewalk and down the street. Kayley was nowhere in sight and that was extremely alarming to him. He was desperately wishing he and Kayley had radios.

All of a sudden, John saw his Excursion come flying down the road. The truck came to a screeching halt and Kayley leapt out of the driver's seat. John did a double take, knowing the keys were still in his pocket.

"How the-?"

"Just get in!" Kayley hissed, interrupting him. "Come on!"

John shook his head and climbed into the truck while Kayley jumped in next to him. Ripping off his ski mask and rifle, John tossed them both in his backseat before slamming on the gas. He took a left turn and sped out of the subdivision, away from the cops amassing in front of the white home. Once John pulled onto Interstate 55, he and Kayley both audibly sighed in relief. He looked over at her and smiled nervously. Kayley chuckled, relieved that they had both made it out unscathed. Her blood was still flowing as she was coming down from the adrenaline high.

"So, did you get anything from them?" Kayley had to ask. John nodded slowly.

"They always talk, Kayley," John muttered. "That's the worst part of the job, but they always talk…"

She looked over at him and knew at that moment that he had done that before. Many times. John Shannon was a total enigma to her. He had this protective, fatherly instinct to him that made her feel safe. But at the same time, she'd seen his capacity for violence, and the ease with which he inflicted it upon others. Strangely, he reminded her of her own dad.

"Yeah…" John nodded somberly. That same vacant, almost haunted look came across his stubbled face. "Like I said, worst part of the job,"

"I can't imagine," Kayley shook her head. She wondered whether or not her dad had ever had to interrogate someone like that.

"Yeah, well," John grunted. He looked like he was about to say something else, but was interrupted when his phone started vibrating in the cupholder. John picked up the phone to see who was calling.

"Well, that lasted long," John muttered, showing Kayley that Klint was in fact the one calling. John answered and put the phone on speaker. "Hey, Klint,"

"Where are you?" Klint asked, annoyed.

"Driving back to the city," John answered.

"Warehouse. Now. Bring Kayley," Klint hung up.

"We're in trouble," Kayley commented.

John scoffed, but had a small smile on his face.

# CHAPTER 5

# Klint

Klint couldn't seem to comprehend what he was watching on the laptop open on the folding table in the middle of the warehouse. ABC Chicago was live reporting from outside an extravagant home in Burr Ridge, detailing a brutal shootout that had occurred between local gangs. So far, there wasn't an official number, but more than a dozen people had been shot and killed.

John and Kayley were quiet, staring straight ahead like the pair of soldiers they were. Klint knew he wasn't going to get a straight answer out of either of them; he could tell. Whatever they'd gotten up to, there was a newfound bond between them.

"I asked you two to survey the locations and report back," Klint muttered, crossing his arms and leaning against the table. "I remember specifically saying that was all I wanted you to do. I put you two together because I figured the two of you understood the value of actionable intelligence. I also figured you two were intelligent enough to understand the values of being incognito. Clearly I was wrong,"

"It was a gang shooting, Klint," John gestured to the laptop. He lied with such conviction, Klint was almost impressed. A guy like that could withstand a police interrogation and a polygraph without breaking a sweat. "Had nothing to do with us,"

"Don't give me that shit, John," Klint spat back. "I was born at night, but it wasn't last night. What happened? You're gonna have to tell me something, the Mayor is gonna be calling my ass soon ready to ream me out. I have to let her know before I have my guys kick down doors and drop bodies, otherwise this could get out of hand real fast,"

"Theoretically speaking..." John began, maintaining an absolutely unbreakable poker face. "If a pair of highly trained military operatives happened to drive by a meeting between two different organizations and then those operatives decided the best move was to take action, rather than let those men leave and continue to cause havoc, you would consider that the right move, correct?"

"Depends," Klint said through gritted teeth.

"And, if upon further questioning, one of those operatives was made aware of some highly sensitive information regarding the gangs in Chicago, you would be pleased that those operatives were able to gather such information," John continued, still straight faced.

"Yes," Klint nodded. Although he didn't show it, Klint was impressed. John was cunning and Klint hadn't expected that from him. He'd figured, based on everything he knew about him, that John was more of a blunt instrument. "I would be,"

"Well, then," John finally smiled. "I think you're going to want to hear some things,"

"Go on,"

"It was a meeting between the Triad and Sinaloa," John explained. "Low level guys in the grand scheme of things, but it's still an interesting turn of events. Anyway, I spoke to two Triads who were eager to chat about the meeting. Sinaloa is convinced that the Tijuana boys are the ones who've been hitting them, which is good for us. Unfortunately, they're planning retaliation and the Triad is helping them. Territory is on the line here, the Triad stands to gain a lot from helping the Sinaloa guys. There's a lot at stake for both parties. I guess the house was a mutual staging ground. They were meeting to discuss when and where they'd strike first,"

Klint let this marinate in his head before he said anything. While it wasn't exactly groundbreaking information, having it confirmed that the Sinaloa Cartel and the Triad were in bed together was a big deal. It foreshadowed what was to come. But on the other hand, at least they were convinced it was their rivals, the Tijuana Cartel, who was hitting them, and not a group of police officers and former soldiers. The gang-on-gang violence wasn't anything new to Chicago and with any luck, they'd kill each other off. Still, Klint would have to try and contain the fallout. The Mayor would be understanding, at least Klint hoped she would be.

"Alright, John," Klint finally sighed and looked at the ground. "Is that all you have to tell me?"

"That's it," John replied. Klint turned to Kayley.

"Anything to add?"

"No, sir," Kayley answered with rigid military conduct. Klint scoffed.

"Uh-huh," Klint rolled his eyes slightly. "Well, ok. I'm not going to thank you for doing the opposite of what I asked you to do, but I appreciate the information,"

"Of course," John nodded politely. He waited a beat before asking, "Can we go now?"

"Yeah, yeah," Klint waved them off. "Tomorrow I want you two to tackle the rest of the addresses I gave you. Please try not to get into anymore shootouts,"

"Can't make any promises," John shrugged. Kayley stifled a laugh.

Klint was in the process of coming up with a sarcastic retort when his phone started ringing. He pulled out his phone and raised an eyebrow. The Mayor was calling him. From her personal cell phone number.

"Hey, hang on a second," Klint said to John and Kayley, holding his hand up to stop them from leaving. John and Kayley looked at each other, picking up on a distinct shift in Klint's mood and demeanor. He slid his finger across his phone to answer the call and put the phone up to his ear. "This is Klint,"

Klint could hear someone breathing heavily on the other line, but they didn't say anything. Finally, the woman was able to speak.

"Klint?" Mayor Hart whispered, her voice was breaking. Klint could hear in her voice that she'd been crying.

"Kelly?" Klint was automatically concerned. "Kelly, what's wrong? Are you ok?"

Klint marched outside to take the rest of the phone call in privacy.

"What was that?" John muttered, giving Kayley a strange look.

"Who's Kelly?" Kayley wondered aloud.

The door to the warehouse burst open a few moments later and Klint rushed inside. He ran over to the table and grabbed his car keys.

"Come on!" he cried. "Follow me!"

"What's going on?" John asked, rushing out to his truck after Klint. Kayley was right behind them. Klint didn't answer. He jumped into his Charger and turned the car on, instantly putting on his flashing lights and sirens. Rolling down his window, Klint pulled up alongside John's truck just as John and Kayley were getting in.

"Kade and Noah are gonna meet us!" Klint said. "Follow me and try to keep up!"

****

Klint was already yards ahead of John and Kayley, weaving in and around news personnel, bystanders, and police officers. The entire road was locked down, traffic being forced to detour from both directions. Chicago Police cruisers lined the streets, the flashing blue and red lights bouncing off of the tall buildings on either side of the street. Four uniformed officers were stationed on each side of the road, blocking the news crews from getting any closer to the crime scene. Yellow tape was blocking the road and sidewalks, discouraging anyone from getting through the virtual blockade. Upon seeing Klint rushing towards them, one of the officers lifted the tape up, letting Klint duck under.

John and Kayley chose to keep their distance from Klint. They could tell something was up and he needed the space. Before Klint took off, he'd given both of them credentials that could be worn around their neck. It was a formality, but it allowed John and Kayley access to duck underneath the yellow tape to see what the situation was. Once under the tape, John adjusted his shirt, showing the world that he had a pistol holstered to his hip. Kayley had also insisted on carrying a weapon on her hip, just in case. They looked like undercover cops; no one bothered them as they explored the crime scene.

It was two vehicles, the massive armored cash truck was overturned on its left side and still smoldering. Firefighters were dousing the inside with water, being especially careful. The SUV was a white, unmarked, police Interceptor. The driver's side door was wide open, the windshield and windows were completely shredded from probably a hundred bullet holes. Shell casings littered the ground; John saw that at least three different calibers had been used. As they got closer to the Interceptor, John and Kayley both saw the pool of blood around the car, as well as the blood stains on the white paint job.

Something bad had happened. Really bad.

Running over to fellow detective Richard Brown, Klint grabbed him by the shoulder and pulled him away from a duo of Crime Scene techs he'd been talking to.

"Where is she?" Klint asked, the worry obvious in his voice.

"Right over there," Richard nodded to the curb where a pair of uniformed cops were standing above Mayor Kelly Hart. She was seated on the curb, wearing a hat and a hoodie, trying to be as incognito as possible. The last thing anyone wanted was the bloodthirsty media seeing the Mayor sobbing at a crime scene.

"Is he...?"

"Dead," Rich nodded, folding his arms in a grim way. "Dead before we got here. Nothing anyone could've done. M.E. already moved the bodies,"

"Bodies?"

"The guards too," Rich explained. "Absolutely riddled,"

"What happened?" Klint asked, mouth open as Rich informed him of the casualties. Rich pointed to two buildings, one on either side of the street. Klint noticed that there were two cables hanging from each of the buildings.

"Four attackers. According to a few witnesses, they were decked out in black and wore gas-mask, motorcycle type helmets. Apparently, they rappelled out of those windows, tossed smoke on the truck, and then swarmed it. Our boy was just down the street and saw the whole thing happening. Lit up the sirens and lights, and drove over. Barely had time to get out before they shot him, probably thirty times if I had to guess,"

"Automatic weapons?" Klint asked.

"Yeah," Rich nodded. "Witnesses confirmed,"

"Jesus," Klint shook his head. "You figure out what the haul was?"

"Just got off the phone with the carrier company before I got here. It was on route to the depot. $5.7 million and some change," Rich explained. Klint shook his head in disbelief.

"That's a lot of fucking money," he muttered. Rich nodded in agreement.

"Waiting on the Feds right, we'll see who takes point on this," Rich shrugged.

"Keep me updated," Klint clapped Rich on the shoulder. "I gotta go talk to her,"

"Good luck, brother," Rich said.

Walking over toward the Mayor, Klint made eye contact with the two cops protecting her, and cocked his head. They both nodded and walked away, leaving the Mayor and Klint to themselves.

Her eyes were on the ground and her hands were trembling. She was breathing shallowly in between painfully quiet sobs. The sight broke Klint's heart. He sat down on the curb next to her and put his arms around her. She buried her face in his shoulder and continued sobbing. Klint held her against him, gently rubbing her shoulder and back.

"I'm so sorry, Kelly," Klint choked out. "I'm so, so sorry,"

Mayor Kelly Hart sniffed, wiped her eyes, and looked up at Klint; her make-up was streaked down her cheeks. She looked pale, like she could throw up at any given moment. Klint didn't blame her at all, she had every right to be distraught.

The cop that had been killed trying to stop the heist had been Danny Hart, Kelly's younger brother. Her only brother.

"I don't know what to do," Kelly spoke in a voice that was barely audible. Her voice was hoarse from crying and she was still breathing heavily, trying to compose herself again.

"There's nothing you can do now," Klint said, knowing it sounded harsh. But he needed to be firm with her. She was still the Mayor of the city. "It's not your fault, Kelly,"

"I have to tell my parents now," Kelly whispered, tears starting to fall once again. Klint didn't know exactly what to say; he couldn't imagine having to deliver that kind of news. As much as he wanted to stay there and comfort her, Kelly needed to leave the crime scene immediately.

"Kelly, we have to get you away from here," Klint said back to her gently. "This is still an active crime scene and the last thing you or your family needs is the media running video of you crying here. Your family cannot find out from the media,"

"I know," Kelly hung her head again. "God, Klint, how could I have let things get this bad?"

"It's not your fault, Kelly,"

"But it is," Kelly shook her head. "I waited too long to start doing anything significant about crime. You know, I asked Danny first. I asked him to handle this stuff, before I asked you. He refused, saying he wouldn't do anything to dishonor the badge. That's the kind of guy he was Klint, he was a good and pure man,"

"I know, Kelly," Klint comforted. "He was a good man,"

Kelly was quiet. She stared at the shredded Interceptor, the pool of blood on the ground next to it, and the shell casings that littered the road. The cables that the thieves had used to rappel onto the road swayed gently in the wind.

"I don't care what you have to do, Klinton," Kelly said, her voice unwaveringly intense. "I do not care what you're in the middle of. I want you to find whoever did this. I want you to find them. My family will not be put through trials and appeals. You will find whoever did this. And you will kill them,"

\*\*\*\*

Discreetly escorted by four police officers, Mayor Kelly Hart was able to sneakily get away from the prying eyes of the media. The officers stuffed her into the back of an unmarked SUV and drove off. As she left the crime scene, Kade and Noah were just arriving. They both wore credentials around their neck and Klint waved them through past the officers on guard. John and Kayley were standing off to one side, talking quietly to each other. Klint marched right up to Noah. Fate seemed to be at play, as it would seem.

"Alright," Klint said in a low voice. "Take a look around, let me know what you think,"
"Got it," Noah nodded, gulping a little bit. "Four guys, right?"
"Yeah," Klint confirmed. "Four guys,"
"Ok, ok," Noah whispered. "Give me a few minutes,"

At his own pace, Noah walked around the crime scene. He didn't touch anything, but he did crouch down to inspect the shell casings and other pieces of debris. Klint watched him carefully. Noah was muttering to himself as he continued his walkthrough, coming to a stop in the middle of the road. The cables. Rappelling out of windows to hit the truck. That wasn't something that would've ever occurred to Noah. It just didn't make sense when you could just as easily hit the truck already being on the ground. Klint could see the wheels turning in Noah's brain.

"Hey," Noah asked Klint. "How'd these guys escape?"
"I didn't ask," Klint admitted. "But I'm assuming a car. Why? What are you thinking?"

Noah put his hands on his hips and looked at Klint.

"A lot," Noah said, taking a deep breath. "Find out how they escaped. These guys were professionals. Even more so than me. Hitting the truck out in the open like this means they knew the route. So, either there's an inside man or they've been doing some pretty serious stalking. Automatic weapons means they've got some pretty good gun dealers, especially for the Chicago area. My guess is the ammo is either homemade or bought on the black market. Yeah, man, these guys are pros. But..."

"What?"

"Rappelling onto the ground, though... That doesn't make much sense to me. I mean, why increase the risk? Why take more chances than necessary? You're going to have to have a car ready to move the money you steal anyway, so why not just drive up behind the truck and swarm it that way? That's just adding more complication to an already impossible feat,"

Klint nodded, taking it what Noah was saying. He had a point. Rappelling onto a busy road to conduct a truck heist didn't make much sense. There had to be something they were missing, some extra piece to the puzzle.

"Unless..." Noah kept thinking aloud. "Unless that's part of it for them,"

"What do you mean?"

"Well, think about it," Noah said. "Most guys rob banks and trucks out of desperation. A few rob them because they have seen too many movies and think it's easy. And then, there's a very select group that'll steal things for the high, for the rush. Maybe that's part of it. Deliberately making it complicated so that high, that rush, is there,"

As strange as it sounded to Klint, everything that Noah was saying made sense. Clearly, they were dealing with a different kind of crew here. One that wasn't afraid of dropping bodies or spilling blood.

"You think we're dealing with pros who are also adrenaline junkies?" Klint clarified.

"Possibly," Noah nodded.

"So where should we start then?" Klint asked. Noah cocked his head.

"I'd start with the cables," Noah shrugged. "That's the unique thing about this one. Start with that, see where it leads. I'd also see if there are any unsolved heists involving some type of signature like this. My guess, this probably isn't the first time these guys have hit something. Let's see if we can find something to compare it to,"

\*\*\*\*

Noah and Klint each sat behind computers at the Chicago Police Precinct, scrolling through case files of unsolved heists from all over the country. So far, they'd noted half a dozen possible heists that could be connected to this recent one. Similarities were noted in their swarming techniques, use of automatic weapons, similar disguises, and the extracurricular activities that made this most recent heist unique. For example, there was a heist in Indianapolis eleven months earlier in which the bandits had rappelled down a building after hitting a bank vault. There had been another heist in Milwaukee where the bandits escaped by BASE jumping off a building and deploying wingsuits.

The media had branded this crew "The Marauders of the Midwest" and the articles on them walked a very thin line between news reporting and elaborate fan fiction. Vivid details of their brazen heists read more like a James Patterson thriller than actual reporting. The more and more Klint read about them though, the more intrigued he became. These 'Marauders' were a different type of criminal. Sophisticated, daring, but absolutely reckless.

Upon Noah's suggestion, Klint sent the cables that had been recovered at the scene of the crime off for further analysis. That would take a few days to bring forth any results, so until then, there wasn't much that Klint could do except try to find a connection to another heist. There had been a few truck robberies in Chicago over the last few years, but most of the big ones had already been solved. The list of open cases was interesting but none of them had an obvious connection to their crime.

"What do you think?" Klint asked, after close to two hours of looking through files. Noah sighed and rubbed his eyes.

"I'm thinking I'm tired," he grumbled. "I'm thinking I'd like to go home to my wife,"

"I meant about the case,"

"I know," Noah scoffed. "Yeah, I mean there's no way to if any of these are connected,"

"Alright," Klint muttered, somewhat defeated by the day. "Go home and get some rest. I'll give you a call when I get the analysis on those cables back,"

"Please do," Noah said, standing up. "I'm curious,"

"Have a good night," Klint waved as Noah left.

Klint waited only a few more minutes before deciding to call it a night as well. Kara would be home from class by now and he wanted to spend the rest of his night with her. Maybe he'd take her out for dinner, anything to forget about the day.

He left the Precinct and walked to his car, eager to get home. It wasn't until he was closer to his Charger that he noticed John's Excursion parked right next to his vehicle. John Shannon leaned against the truck, smoking a cigarette.

"Hey," John said, blowing a cloud of smoke in front of him. "Going home?"

"Yeah," Klint nodded. "Gonna take my daughter for some dinner,"

"Good, good," John muttered, inhaling from the smoke.

"If you've got something to say, John, please just say it," Klint sighed. "I've had a long day and I just want to get home,"

"What are we going to do about the Cartels and the Triad?" John asked. Klint shrugged.

"I've been told by the Mayor to focus on nothing else other than finding whoever killed her brother," Klint admitted. "So, as far as I'm concerned, we're not doing anything,"

John took this in, nodding slowly. He put the smoke up to his lips and took another drag, flicking the rest of the cigarette onto the ground.

"You know that isn't smart, right?" John looked at Klint seriously. "We've been hitting them hard. Taking our foot off the gas right now is not a good idea. I know you know that,"

"What am I supposed to do, John?" Klint threw his arms up, getting tired of the constant questioning from John. "I can't fix the entire city by myself,"

"You don't have to," John said, surprisingly much calmer than Klint. "Give me Kayley and we'll handle it. Focus on the investigation and when I need backup, I'll take Kade,"

"John, no offense, but the last thing anyone needs is you starting a gang war in Chicago," Klint responded.

"I'm not starting anything," John said with an actual smile. "I'm finishing it before it starts,"

Klint didn't want to admit it right then and there, but John was right. Ignoring the current issue wasn't a solution. John could handle this, Klint was sure. And if he wanted Kayley's help, clearly she had proven her worth already.

"Alright, John," Klint nodded. "Do what you have to do. I'll send you a list of targets. You do what you see fit, ok?"

"Copy that," John Shannon said with a grin.

# CHAPTER 6

# John

Kayley had her phone hooked up to the AUX in John's truck and was playing music from her 'Favorites' playlist. None of it was anything John would normally listen to, but he didn't really mind. The music Kayley was playing was exactly the type of thing his wife Anna would've listened to. In fact, he really didn't mind Kayley's company either. She was pretty easy to be around, all things considered. That was all he allowed himself to feel towards her. Ever since Riley Hanna had died, John hadn't let a single woman into his life. He just would not. And that was fine with him. At least, he tried to convince himself it was.

It was close to midnight and they were parked outside a stretch of Southside projects, watching the beat up red Mustang that belonged to a triggerman on Klint's list of targets. John felt right in his element, stalking his targets before the actual hunt began. He'd lost track of the amount of times he'd been on missions like this overseas. Being back in the action was doing wonders for his mood. He needed a mission, a higher purpose.

"What do you want to listen to?" Kayley suddenly asked, adjusting in her seat. She wore a faded Army hoodie and a pair of leggings.

"I really don't care," John sighed, chuckling a little bit.

"Oh my gosh, was that a laugh? I didn't think Navy SEALs were allowed to laugh,"

"We are, but only once a week," John said. "Nah, my wife used to ask me that same question every single time we went anywhere. I never cared, but she always liked that hip-hop, rap shit you got playing,"

"Sounds like a smart woman," Kayley said, lowering the volume. He'd never mentioned his wife. However, she'd noticed the gold band on his finger almost as soon as she'd met him. "How long have you been married?"

"I'm not married anymore," John said softly, looking out the window. "She passed away a few years ago,"

"John, I'm sorry," Kayley said, genuinely. "I had no idea,"

"It's ok," John shrugged, still not looking at her. He paused for a second. "There's only been one other woman in my life. She was also kinda like you. FBI Agent. Real hotshot, cocky, and confidence I wish I had. We were together before my wife and I got married and then after she passed away,"

"Yeah?"

"Yeah," John nodded, again with a sad smile. "I don't know if you remember the name Gray Saxon, he was big in the news a few years back. But she and I were tracking him down and he... Well, he shot her. Killed her right in front of me,"

It suddenly occurred to John that he had no idea why he was confiding so much into a virtual stranger. He didn't talk this much to anyone, let alone someone he didn't really know that well. Maybe it was just the fact that she was a vet and understood some of what he'd been through. Or maybe it was that ever since Riley and Anna died, John hadn't had a truly meaningful conversation with a single person. He had never been a huge talker, but not being able to really talk to someone bothered him, more than he cared to admit.

"Jesus, John," Kayley whispered, touching his hand. She had no idea about any of what John was telling her. "I'm so sorry. I don't know what else to say. I'm so sorry,"

"That's why I was kind of a dick to you, though," John admitted, finally looking at her. "Call me sexist if you want, I really don't give a shit. But the last time I worked with a woman, she got killed. Can't have any more innocent deaths on my conscious, I got enough of that as it is,"

Studying his hardened face, Kayley felt guilty for having judged him almost as soon as she laid eyes on him. He didn't have to say anything, Kayley knew he was former military just by the way he carried himself. It was her unfortunate reality that many of the male military officers she'd encountered had been quick to make assumptions about her just because of the way she looked. Her father had prepared her though, she knew she'd have to work twice as hard to prove her worth in a male dominated career. Throughout her first few years living on military bases, she'd put up with more than enough bullshit; constant sexual comments towards her, getting her panties and bras stolen from the laundry on a regular basis, and the unwanted ass-grab every once in a while.

But that wasn't John Shannon, not even close. She could see the hurt, the pain in his eyes. He was in mourning, actively grieving. And he was still risking his life on a regular basis. He was capable of such violence, she'd seen that up close and personally. But, in little moments, she'd seen that there was kindness to him that he clearly never let to the surface. John cared about people, he cared about keeping people safe. She saw her father in him and that made her heart ache.

"I told you my father was Delta Force, right?" Kayley asked. John nodded. "Well, he was constantly redeploying throughout my childhood. He was never home and every single time he came home, he left a piece of himself over there. I saw it. He changed. The constant war, the fighting, it changed him. When he came back, he just wasn't the same. The last time he redeployed, when we were saying goodbye... It was right before I left for bootcamp. He promised he'd see me at my graduation, told me he was proud of me, all that father stuff,"

John was listening intently, fearing the outcome of the story Kayley was telling him.

"A few months before I graduated, he was killed," Kayley wiped her eyes, speaking in a small, nearly inaudible voice. "Killed in a gunfight with Afghani Police... It still doesn't make any sense to me,"

Leaning across the center console, John put his hand on her shoulder. They remained like that for almost a minute, not caring one bit about the stakeout they were on. The catharsis of the moment was much needed. For both of them.

"Thank you," Kayley whispered, squeezing John's hand. "I needed that,"

"I needed that, too," John said, squeezing her hand back. "For what it's worth, I know your dad would've been proud of what you accomplished,"

"I know," she nodded. Kayley looked at John and smiled softly. "Your wife was a lucky woman. You're a good man, John,"

"No, Kayley," John shook his head. He chuckled softly and looked at her with a sad smile. "That I am not. Anna knew it too, but she loved me regardless. She was an angel,"

Kayley didn't know how to respond to that, but she didn't have to. Three African American men in dark hoodies approached the red Mustang, she could see one of them was openly carrying a pistol. They climbed into the Mustang and a few seconds later, the car roared to life.

"What do you want to do?" Kayley asked quietly. The Mustang slowly pulled away from the curb and began driving. Without a word, John Shannon fired up his Excursion and began following, keeping enough distance to not draw suspicion.

\*\*\*\*

Almost a full twenty minutes later, the Mustang pulled into a parking garage that connected to a building with luxury apartments and condos. John drove past the garage and parked on the street, putting his hazards on. He opened his glove box and grabbed the packet of addresses that Klint had gotten from the notebook. Sure enough, one of the Chicago addresses matched up with an apartment in the building.

"Could be meeting an employer," John muttered, stuffing the packet back into his glove box. "What do you think?"

"Something's up, for sure," Kayley said. "They were armed,"

"Alright," John nodded. "You take the truck and go around the block. Get into that building across the street and set up somewhere..."

"Not a chance," Kayley interrupted. "You're not sticking me on overwatch. If you're kicking down doors, I'm right there next to you,"

John didn't let her see it, but he almost smiled. She was a lot like him, not at all willing to be sidelined from the action. He respected that and it made him like her even more.

"Ok, then gear up,"

They went to work donning tactical vests, holsters, and ammo pouches, as well as newly acquired radios which they both clipped to the shoulder straps of their vests. John handed Kayley her rifle and pistol before grabbing his own weapons. Kayley reached into a pouch on her vest and produced a shemagh, a military scarf-head wrap that she'd always worn while on deployments. Expertly, Kayley wrapped the scarf around her head and face, only leaving her eyes exposed. To conceal his identity, John threw on a dark Carhartt baseball hat and pulled a neck gaiter above his nose.

"Let's go," John nodded, throwing open the door to his truck.

Hurrying over to the building, John and Kayley moved into the lobby. The doorman instantly stood up, but John stuck his hand out firmly, flashing the credentials from Klint.

"Federal Agents!" John hissed at the doorman, keeping his rifle low so as not to frighten the man. "Make sure no one leaves this building until we come back downstairs, understand?"

"Uh, yeah," the man nodded, scared. "No one leaves 'till you come back. Should I call the police or anything,"

"No," John shook his head. "Just let us handle this,"

"Ok, ok,"

"Good man," John nodded. He hit the button to call the elevator and waited a few painful seconds before the doors creaked open. John and Kayley rushed inside and John tapped the button for the 23rd floor.

They ascended in silence, no words needed to be said. John Shannon and Kayley McKenna were trained professionals. As soon as the doors opened, John and Kayley rushed into the hallway, barely making a sound as they took up positions on either side of the hallway. Hugging the wall, they moved down the corridor toward the apartment. John looked over to Kayley and held up two fingers, followed by four fingers. Unit 24.

Kayley spotted the corresponding door and held her fist up, the universal motion to stop. John swung around on to the other side of the door as Kayley approached from the opposite side. Pressing his ear to the door, John listened intently. He could hear a muffled conversation taking place inside the apartment. Nodding at Kayley, John took a step back and knocked on the door four times.

"Who is it?" an aggressive sounding man asked. John didn't answer and put a finger up, silently telling Kayley not to say a word. He knocked once again, rapping his fist on the door three times. After a brief pause, the door was unlocked from the inside and very slowly, the door began opening and one of the men from the

Mustang peered his head through the gap. His eyes went wide as soon as he saw John and Kayley in the hallway.

John lunged toward the door, putting his shoulder through it as hard as he could. The door flew inward and the man opening the door was knocked on his back, a gun clattered on the floor, away from his grasp. He rolled over onto his back and threw his hands up.

"Federal Agents!" John announced, stepping over the man on the ground; he kicked the gun down a small hallway. Kayley ripped a pair of zip-ties from her vest and cuffed the man's hands together before following John deeper into the apartment.

They came to a living room and saw three men in there, the other two from the Mustang, and one man they hadn't seen before. The two men from the Mustang were on their feet, brandishing weapons in their hands. But the third man was still seated, a foot propped up on the table in front of him. There was a substantial amount of cash on the table.

The man sitting down was darkly handsome and wore a pair of black pants, black collared shirt, and a black long coat. His red-brown hair was neatly combed over and his facial hair was meticulously clean and trim, not a single stray hair on his head. John thought he bore a striking resemblance to Leo Messi, the star soccer player. But as the man sat there, watching two armed assailants enter the apartment, the faintest hint of a smile crept on his face.

"Hands in the air, weapons on the ground," John growled, training his rifle on the two armed men. Kayley swung into the room and moved a few steps over so they had the entire room covered.

Neither of the men moved. They hadn't raised their guns at John yet, but they were holding pistols at their side. They looked at each other, as if each one was trying to figure out what the best option was.

"I'm not gonna ask again," John barked, taking a step toward them. He glanced at the man in the chair. "Don't you fucking move,"

"Of course, sir," the man said with a smile, completely sarcastic. He put both his feet on the ground and raised his hands slightly, indicating to John and Kayley that he wasn't armed.

"Last chance," John said to the two men. "Or you get put down,"

"Fuck you!" one of the men yelled, raising his pistol.

John wrapped his finger around the trigger, but before he could pull it, Kayley shot the man dead, blasting three bullets into his chest. Blood exploding onto the table and couch, the man fell back, his chest riddled. The second man took the opportunity to try and raise his own gun, but John shot him through the face, and the man collapsed, dead before he hit the ground.

"Clear!" John barked.
"Clear," Kayley echoed.

Turning to the man on the couch, John raised his rifle at him. The man put his hands up a little higher, but that smile didn't go away. He wasn't afraid or annoyed. No, he was amused. Amused by all of this. Something felt incredibly off about him to John. The way he looked at the bodies without as much as breaking a sweat told John that this was a guy who'd seen some stuff in his day, possibly even done some stuff. He could've been a former soldier, he appeared to have the physique for it.

"Who are you? Who were those guys? What's going on?" John rattled off. The man remained utterly calm.

"Those were three members of the local chapter of the Crips," the man said. "The man who just shot was a hitman for hire, so to speak,"

"So, you in the market for a hitman?" John asked, gesturing the money on the table.

"Not at all," the man continued. "The money was for other things,"

"Care to be more specific?"

"Not really,"

"Alright then," John nodded. "Hands up, you'll be coming with us,"

"No, I don't think I will be," the man said. John blinked a few times. "You and your partner over there aren't 'Federal Agents', that's for sure. You're certainly not cops, so I'm wondering what type of authority you have to take me into custody for simply being in the wrong place and the wrong time,"

Before John could answer, four gunshots rang out in the apartment. John instantly dove to the ground while Kayley took cover behind the fridge. The first man they'd encountered stormed into the living room, shooting wildly. His hands were still zip-tied, making it hard for him to properly handle the weapon, but he was shooting nonetheless. John cursed himself for being so complacent. He crawled toward Kayley, taking cover in the kitchen.

Kayley steadied her aim and returned fire, shooting half a dozen rounds in the direction of the shooter. He ducked down that small hallway, avoiding being shot.

"Imma kill you fuckin' pigs!" the man screamed, blasting off another series of rounds.

The man in the chair flipped over behind the chair and couch in one fluid motion. One of the stray bullets hit the sliding glass door that led onto the balcony. When the man reappeared from behind the couch, John saw him draw a gun from within his coat. The man raised a pistol and aimed it right at Kayley.

"Watch out!" John screamed, leaping to his feet as the man pulled the trigger. John realized instantaneously that the gun was a machine pistol, capable of firing extremely rapidly. Kayley wheeled around and her eyes went wide as John Shannon tackled her to the ground, just as the first salvo of bullets crashed all around them. Drawing her pistol, Kayley fired around John's body, desperately trying to buy her and John some time to get to cover.

"Move to me, Trev!" the man yelled, emptying the rest of his machine pistol. He swung his coat to the side, revealing a belt around his waist that had several spare magazines for the weapon.

The first shooter hurried into the living room and as soon as he exposed himself Kayley shot him in the side. He fell to the ground and Kayley shot him again.

John rolled onto his back and unloaded at the second man, firing his rifle as fast as he could. Diving behind the couch again, the man popped up a second later, and squeezed the trigger, sending a hellish barrage of bullets toward Kayley and John. Ducking down, the man ran toward the balcony, and fired a quick burst toward the door before putting his shoulder down, smashing through the glass. Groaning, John got to his feet and hurried after him.

The man produced a coiled up cable from inside his coat and already had it anchored to the building. John stepped outside just in time to see the man leap from the balcony. The cable went taut and the man swung back toward the building, smashing through a glass window nearly eight floors below. John stood at the edge of the balcony and stared at the cable, which was now fluttering in the wind. Kayley stepped outside, pulling her shemagh down.

"What the hell was that?" she breathed, wiping sweat from her forehead.

"I have no fucking idea," John shook his head. He winced slightly, realizing he was in a lot of pain. John looked down and saw blood. "Oh shit,"

"Oh shit what?" Kayley asked. She looked at John and her eyes went wide. He'd been shot in the arm, back, and stomach. "Oh my god, John!"

"Can you believe that?" John said, almost laughing. He took a swipe at his stomach and his fingers were covered in blood. "That asshole shot me,"

He turned and tried to walk back inside. The adrenaline wearing off rapidly, John stumbled back and felt his legs give out. Kayley caught him and dragged him back inside the shot up apartment.

"John, hang on!" Kayley cried, laying him down. She yanked out her cell phone and dialed 9-1-1 as fast as she could.

# CHAPTER 7

# Klint

Kayley was being nothing short of methodical as she relayed what had happened to Klint. The paramedics had come and rushed off with John; she had followed in John's truck. She described the shootout, the men they'd killed, and the man who'd escaped; not that any of it made much sense to Klint, he was still half asleep trying to understand what had happened.

He jumped out of bed and got dressed as fast as he could, clumsily knocking over a picture on his nightstand. Luckily for Klint, Kara was spending the night with some college friends, so he didn't have to worry about waking her up as he darted out of his apartment. Koda hadn't been the least bit bothered by Klint's sudden departure; she remained sleeping soundly on the edge of Klint's bed.

"I don't know what I'm supposed to do, Klint," Kayley was saying. "This guy literally jumped off the building, what the hell is that? And John, Jesus, Klint, he was bleeding from everywhere!"

"Ok, calm down," Klint said as he ran down the stairs toward the parking garage. "Where are you?"

"I'm at Rush with him," Kayley said. She sounded very upset. "They rushed him into surgery as soon as we got here. I haven't seen him since,"

"How bad was it?"

"Bad, Klint," Kayley stressed. "He was shot at least three times. There was so much blood when they put him in the ambulance, I don't know if the bullets hit an artery or something,"

"Jesus Christ," Klint groaned. "I knew letting him go off on his own was a bad idea. Ok, send me the address of the building you were at. I'm gonna go to the scene, assuming PD has the building locked down. Stay by your phone and do not leave that damn hospital until I tell you. Is that clear?"

"Copy that," Kayley said. "Just sent you the address. I'll keep an eye on things here. The cops were already on the scene when I left,"

"Ok, I'll handle that. Are you still armed?"

"Is that a real question?"

"Fair enough," Klint smirked, climbing into his Charger. "I'll be in contact,"

Speeding out of the garage, Klint flipped a switch in his car, igniting the lights and sirens on his Charger. Clearing traffic ahead of him, Klint accelerated. Keeping his eyes on the road as best he could, Klint dialed his brother's number.

"Yeah?" Kade answered rather quickly.

"We got a situation developing," Klint muttered. "John's at Rush, couple holes in him,"

"Are you serious?" Kade groaned. "What happened?"

"I'll explain when you get here. I'm texting you an address right now, meet me there ASAP,"

"I'm on it," Kade said.

"Hailey alright?"

"She's fine. Jenna's asleep with her in our room so they're fine for a while," Kade reassured his older brother. "Do you want me to grab Noah?"

"Might as well," Klint muttered.

"Copy, I'll see you soon,"

\*\*\*\*

Klint waited until Kade and Noah arrived before entering the building, figuring it would be better for them to walk the crime scene together. While he waited, a couple of patrolmen filled him in on everything. The more he heard, the less it made sense to him. Three dead gangbangers in a luxury Chicago high-rise, a mysterious fourth man who can swing off buildings like he's Spider-Man, a boatload of money left on the table, and a hospitalized Navy SEAL.

The entrance to the building was tied off with yellow tape and per procedure, a pair of patrolmen were on guard, making sure only police personnel crossed the threshold. Once they saw Klint, Kade, and Noah approaching, the officers held the yellow tape up so the three men could duck under. The trio ascended the elevator together in relative silence, Noah groaned loudly and stretched. Klint looked at him and smirked slightly.

"Late night?" Klint asked.

"Eh," Noah shrugged. "Just not used to waking up in the middle of the night anymore,"

"No kids, then?"

"Hell no,"

"Smart man," Kade chimed in. "Don't have kids. Unless your wife is demanding, then you gotta do what she says,"

"Is that what happened with Jenna?" Klint asked his younger brother.

"One-hundred percent," Kade nodded.

The doors to the elevator opened and the three men exited, following the commotion toward unit 24. A few restless residents had their doors open and were gabbing amongst themselves. Some were genuinely interested in what was going on, a few were terrified that a shooting had just taken place in their building, but most were annoyed that the noise had woken them up.

Klint ducked under the yellow tape blocking the doorway into the condo and held it up for Kade and Noah to slip under. A handful of techs moved around the condo, snapping pictures of the bodies. They saw Klint and nodded, showing their respect.

"Jesus," Kade muttered, looking at the sheer volume of shell casings that were on the ground. The drywall in the kitchen had been shredded from the bullets. "It's a miracle anyone walked away from this..."

"John's still in surgery," Klint muttered. "That was the last I heard from Kayley,"

"Is she ok?" Kade asked. Klint just shrugged. He looked over to Noah, who was standing close to the shattered glass door, staring out onto the balcony.

"Hey, what's up?" Klint asked, walking over to Noah. "You see something?"

"You got any pictures of the cables used in that heist?" Noah asked, stepping onto the balcony. He knelt down, examining the cable that was attached to the railing.

"Hold on," Klint pulled out his phone. He scrolled through his photos, hoping he had something. There was one crime scene photo of one of the cables that had been hanging from the building. Klint handed his phone to Noah. "Yeah, here,"

"Son of a bitch," Noah shook his head after merely glancing at the phone. "I can't believe I didn't notice it before,"

"Notice what?" Klint asked, taking his phone back from Noah. Kade leaned against the doorframe, arms folded across his chest. Pulling out a pair of blue rubber gloves from his back pocket, Noah yanked them on, and grabbed the cable.

"This is a crane cable," Noah said, almost with a smile. "Sometimes called a hoist rope. Every type of crane in existence has cables so the operator can lower and raise the hook, extend the boom, that kind of stuff. This is a spare crane cable. The ones from the other day were also crane cables. Super strong, made of steel wire. Not ideal if you're trying to rappel down them, but with the right equipment and gloves, you could definitely do it,"

"So you're saying whoever robbed that truck and killed the Mayor's brother was here tonight too?" Kade asked. Noah stood up and yanked the gloves off.

"That would be my guess," Noah nodded. "This is too specific of a material for it to be a coincidence. I think you're looking for guys like me. Operators or steel workers or ironworkers. Someone who clearly understands how to use this kind of thing and has access to it,"

"Holy shit, Noah," Klint commented with a nod of approval. "That's excellent work. So, where should we start looking?"

"Well, if you can figure out what type of crane these cables go to, you'll narrow down your search. But if it were me, I'd start with local crane companies," Noah explained. "Check steel and iron working companies too. Where there's steel going up, there's always a crane,"

Klint was writing all of this down on a small notepad he always had with him, just in case. He couldn't have been more impressed with Noah's extensive knowledge and he was glad he'd taken a risk on the bandit from California. No one could understand crime better than a former criminal, regardless of whether or not it was his choice. But, he was also incredibly relieved to have his first real lead for the Mayor. She'd be thrilled to know and Klint would make it a point to tell her as soon as he could.

"Ok, I'll get to work on this immediately," Klint said, tucking the notepad away. "Great work, Noah,"

"Thanks," Noah shrugged. "If that's all you need from me tonight, I'm gonna head back to the hotel,"

"I'll give you a ride," Kade offered.

"I'm right behind you guys," Klint said. "I'll meet you downstairs,"

After giving the cops and techs at the scene some final instructions, Klint hurried back down to the ground floor. Kade and Noah were waiting by Kade's truck. Klint hopped in his Charger and turned the car on before getting back out to talk to them.

"I'm gonna start tracking down this lead as best I can," Klint said. "If something comes up, I'll let you both know. Until then, low key as usual,"

"What about John and Kayley?" Kade asked.

"We'll cross that bridge when we get there," Klint said. "Kayley's not going anywhere until John does, so who knows when that'll be. As much as I'd like you two to help me with this, you aren't cops. I'll take it from here,"

"Let us know if you need anything," Kade muttered. He and Noah climbed into Kade's truck and drove away.

Klint didn't even have time to wonder what his brother's sudden pissy attitude was about. He jumped back into his car and sped off, knowing there was one person he needed to talk to immediately.

****

Although you couldn't see them from the street, the small home on the North Side of Chicago was protected by a heavily armed squad of retired police officers. They tried to be as inconspicuous as possible, but everyone on the block knew that Mayor Kelly Hart resided there.

Klint parked a few doors down from her house and walked the rest of the way, not wanting to draw more attention to himself than was necessary. He hurried up to the front door and knocked three times, pulling his badge and ID out while he waited. The door opened a crack and a middle-aged man peered through the gap. He saw the badge and ID and relaxed a little.

"Detective Klinton Kavanaugh," Klint introduced. "I need to speak to the Mayor as soon as possible,"

"Is it an emergency?" the man asked. "She's sleeping, I don't really wanna bug her. Been a tough week for her as it is,"

"She'll want to hear what I have to say, trust me," Klint reassured the guard.

"Alright," the guard sighed. "Come on in, you can wait in the living room. I'll go get her,"

"Thanks," Klint said, stepping inside the home.

The other guards looked at Klint skeptically, but showed him into the living room. It clearly had been furnished by Kelly. The room, as well as the entire house, was completely immaculate and was decorated like a museum. Kelly was a history fanatic; her favorite time period being the Revolutionary War era. Sitting down on the long leather couch, Klint pulled his phone out and sent Kayley a quick text, asking for an update on John. He hadn't even had time yet to properly worry about John Shannon. Klint absolutely needed him to be ok. Without John, Klint would lose a distinct advantage over the criminal elements in Chicago. Not to mention, he considered John a friend.

After a few minutes, Klint heard some muffled voices just outside of the living room. Mayor Kelly Hart entered the room wearing a comfy looking robe and a pair of slippers. Her hair was in a messy ponytail and she looked like she hadn't slept in a week. Upon seeing her, Klint felt bad for having woken her up. The poor woman had been through enough. But at the end of the day, Klint knew she'd want the update in person. Even though Klint figured what her answer would be, he still wanted to hear her give him permission to track down this lead in whatever way he saw fit. There was always the potential for things to get ugly and Klint wanted to keep her in the loop as best he could.

"Sorry to wake you, ma'am," Klint said, standing up. He stuck out his hand formally. Mayor Hart stopped in her tracks, glaring at Klint.

"You are not going to wake me up at this ungodly hour and then give me the whole 'ma'am' bullshit, Klint. Is that clear?"

"Of course," Klint nodded without missing a beat. "My apologies, Mayor Hart,"

"Kelly! My name is Kelly, so just call me Kelly,"

"Ok, ok," Klint relented, throwing his hands up in the air. "I'm sorry for waking you up, Kelly,"

"Please don't apologize, Klint," Kelly sat down on the couch next to him. She rubbed her eyes softly. "What can I do for you?"

"There's been a breakthrough in that thing you wanted me to focus on," Klint said, deliberately trying to be vague in case the guards could still hear him. The less people knew what he was up to, the better.

"A breakthrough?" Kelly adjusted on the couch, crossing her legs. "What kind?"

"John and Kayley were following up on a lead tonight," Klint began. "There was a shootout and one of the shooters managed to escape. John is at the hospital right now, he was shot a few times,"

"Oh my god! Is he ok?"

"Not sure at the moment," Klint shrugged. "Time will tell. Kayley's with him right now and I haven't heard anything, so I'm assuming he's fine until I hear otherwise,"

"I hope he's ok," Kelly said softly.

"That's not what I came to tell you," Klint continued. "The shooter who escaped, he used a specific type of cable to scale down to a different floor. Noah inspected the cable and identified it as a crane cable, something used on construction equipment,"

"Ok?"

"It was the same type of cable that was used during the truck heist," Klint revealed. Kelly cocked her head and raised her eyebrow. There was a moment of silence between them.

"What're you saying?"

"I'm saying, it's very likely that whoever robbed the truck was at the apartment tonight. I have no idea why, but Noah has given us a few leads, and I'm going to start pursuing them. I just wanted you to know and I wanted your permission,"

"You have it, Klint," Kelly said immediately. "Pursue any lead you need to,"

"Alright," Klint nodded. "Thank you. I'm sorry I woke you,"

"I already told you it's fine," Kelly said, sounding somewhat annoyed. Klint wasn't sure what to make of her tone and felt uncomfortable. Other than her, the only woman he dealt with on a regular basis was his daughter, and he knew how to navigate her different tones like the back of his hand. He stood up awkwardly and sighed.

"I'll get out of here," Klint muttered. "I'll keep you updated on the case as it progresses,"

Kelly stood up and stared at him, folding her arms across her chest. She gave him a look, a mix of annoyance and impatience. He couldn't understand what she was trying to tell him, as much as he was trying to. After staring into his soul for what felt like forever, Kelly finally lowered her gaze and mumbled something incoherent under her breath.

"Ok, Klint," she stepped aside so he could leave the living room. "I'll talk to you soon,"

Klint left the property less than a minute later and hurried back into his car. He got inside, fired it up, and started driving home. Once he felt comfortable enough, Klint began letting his mind wander. As long as he'd known Kelly Hart, he'd felt strange whenever he was around her. He wasn't intimidated or scared by her position, not by a long shot. No, it was something else. Klint had never denied the fact that he found her attractive, but that was a high school emotion, not something that Klint spent much time pining over. Kelly had made a few comments over the course of their meetings about getting a drink sometime, but Klint never thought that was more than friendly banter. Was that the problem? Was she looking for more from him? Aside from the fact that it would complicate their working relationship, Klint couldn't be that bold, especially with his superior. He wasn't ever one to take the lead in a relationship, not that he had much experience with it. Since the birth of his daughter, he'd only had one serious girlfriend, and that ended seven years ago.

As he continued driving slowly through the city, his image of Mayor Hart was slowly changing into just Kelly Hart. He began to realize that maybe there had been more behind him going to her house in the middle of the night. He'd wanted to see her, to check on her, to talk to her.

"Shit," Klint muttered to himself, shaking his head. "This is bad idea,"

Slamming on the brakes, Klint spun the wheel and drove his Charger into a perfectly executed U-Turn. He took his foot off the brake and punched the accelerator, speeding back the way he'd come. The engine roared loudly, blocking out the sound of Klint's heart pounding in his chest.

\*\*\*\*

When Klint knocked on the door again, he was shocked to see that Kelly Hart answered it herself, almost immediately. She was still wearing that same robe and slippers. Seeing Klint standing there, Kelly's face broke into a shy smile.

"I'm sorry..." Klint muttered, not really knowing what to say. "I just..."

"Shut up, Klint," Kelly said, grabbing him by the collar and pulling him inside her house.

# CHAPTER 8

# John

The explosion of the sniper rifle echoed in John's ears. He saw Riley Hanna, running in slow motion toward him. Before he could shout a warning, Riley's head vanished in a nanosecond, ripped apart by the bullet. There was nothing he could do. No matter what he did, it always ended the same way, with Riley's body dropping right in front of him. An image he'd never be able to get out of his head.

He shot up in the hospital bed, still half thinking he was back in Los Angeles. It always took a minute to remind himself that he had just been dreaming. His vision was blurry and he could feel his heart beating a million miles an hour.

"Hey, hey, hey," a female voice whispered. John Shannon felt someone touch his arm. She gently forced him back down in the hospital bed. "You're ok, you're ok, John,"

"What... What happened?" John grunted, reluctantly laying back down on the pillow. He looked around the room and saw he was in a hospital room; hooked up to a bunch of different machines, including an IV which had been pumping pain medicine into his system.

"You were shot," the woman said softly. "Three times. But, you're going to be fine. You're ok, John,"

His vision finally coming back to him, John saw Kayley standing next to him, holding his hand gently in hers. She had a sympathetic smile on her face.

"Kayley..." John muttered. "Are you ok? You weren't hurt?"

"No, I'm fine," Kayley assured John. "I promise, I'm ok,"

"Where am I?" John asked.

"Rush," Kayley answered. "You've been asleep for a while. They rushed you into surgery as soon as you got here. You lost a lot of blood, but the bullets missed all of your major organs. There's going to be a lot of pain as they heal, but the doctors all think you're going to be just fine,"

"Good," John groaned, slamming his eyes shut.

"I don't mean to pry," Kayley pulled up a chair next to the hospital bed. "But I saw your back and chest. You've got more scars than anyone I've ever seen in real life..."

"Yeah," John grunted. "Long career, it's part of the job,"

"You've been shot before,"

"Yeah,"

"Stabbed too, by the looks of it,"

"Are you writing a book?"

"Sorry," Kayley looked a little embarrassed. "I'll let you get some rest,"

"Kayley," John said as she got up to leave the room. "I'm sorry, didn't mean to snap at you. Thank you,"

"What was I supposed to do? Let you bleed out?" Kayley said back.

"Thank you," John said in a quiet voice, as sincerely as he could.

Kayley smiled at him and sat back down in her chair. She pulled out her phone and texted Klint, letting him know that John was alive, awake, and going to be ok. By the time she put her phone away, John was already asleep again.

\*\*\*\*

When John awoke a second time, it was clearly early in the morning. Sunlight bled through the curtains, giving the room a strange lighting. There was a nurse to his right, checking his heart rate. Kayley was on the left side of the hospital bed, talking quietly to Klint Kavanaugh. When John moved in the bed slightly, Kayley and Klint both turned to look at him.

"Hey, you're awake," Klint said with a smile. John was doped up on pain meds, but he still could tell that something had changed with Klint. His eyes looked a little less serious, some of the tension was gone from his face. "How're you feeling?"

"Fine," John grunted, trying to sit up. The nurse looked over and shook her head.

"Try not to move, don't want you to rip the stitching," she warned, placing a strong hand on John's shoulder. "Good news is all your vitals are good. You should be able to eat regular food tonight or tomorrow morning. Until then, we'll keep you on the IV and you can have some water and jello,"

"Wonderful," John rolled his eyes. He hated being confined to a bed, especially when he was in the middle of a mission. "Klint, as soon as I'm out of here, I'll be good to go. We need to find the asshole-"

"Don't you worry about that," Klint said before John could finish his sentence. "Just get better, dude. We've got this for now,"

"Klint, come on," John groaned. "Don't sideline me. I'm gonna be fine, I'll be ready to go as soon as I get out of here,"

"One step at a time," Klint tried to be firm.

"Fuck you, Klint," John rolled his eyes. Klint sighed and shrugged.

"Alright, John. Do what you want, you're a grown ass man. Just be smart, ok?" Klint turned to Kayley. "Let's talk outside, I don't need Captain America's comments right now,"

"Hey Klint?"

"Yeah?"

"Go fuck yourself,"

Klint smirked and stepped out into the hall with Kayley while the nurse went to work doing a full check-up on John's wounds. Kayley looked like she could use a full day of rest, but Klint appreciated that she'd stayed with John. Despite their rocky start, he was also pleased that her and John appeared to have formed some type of bond.

"What's up?" Kayley asked, leaning against the wall. She yawned dramatically and tossed her hair over one shoulder.

"We've got a lead," Klint said, lowering his voice. Kayley cocked her head to the side. "On the robbery and the guy who shot John. We think they might be one in the same,"

"Really?"

"The cable he used to escape out the condo was the same type the bandits used to rappel onto the road," Klint admitted. "Noah gave us a lead and I'm gonna shake that tree pretty hard, see what falls out,"

COWBOYS OF THE SKY  -  111

"Ok," Kayley nodded. "What do you need from me?"

"I need a description of the guy who shot at you," Klint said, pulling out a pen and his notepad.

"Yeah, ok. He was tall, slim, and had reddish-brown hair. Beard too. He smiled a lot, for some reason. Like he thought it was funny we were there or something,"

"Any tattoos, scars, anything like that?" Klint asked.

"Not that I could see," Kayley shook her head. "He was wearing a long coat,"

"Ok," Klint said, tucking the notepad away. He was slightly disappointed that Kayley didn't have a better description, but it would have to do for now. "I'll keep you updated,"

"Please do," Kayley nodded. "He should be good to go in a few days. I'm hoping, anyway,"

"Talk to him, ok? Maybe you'll have more luck than I will,"

"How much do you know about him?" Kayley suddenly asked.

"Know about John?"

"Yeah,"

"I know enough," Klint muttered.

"Do you know if he's ever had a psych eval?" Kayley asked softly. She angled her head back toward the hospital room.

"I'm not his mother," Klint snapped. He didn't mean for it to sound so harsh, but he didn't like Kayley's accusatory tone. Kayley shot him a disgusted look and put her hands on her hips. Klint softened his tone. "Look, the best thing for a guy like John is to give him a mission. The less downtime he has, the better,"

"So why do you want to sideline him?"

"I don't want to sideline him," Klint groaned. "But if he dies, then I lose my tactical advantage. I need him, he's more valuable to us than he realizes. There's not another John Shannon I can just scoop up. Ok?"

"Ok, I get it," Kayley said quietly. Klint reached out and touched her shoulder.

"Stay by the phone. Keep him here as long as you can. I'll be in touch soon enough,"

# CHAPTER 9

# Klint

Klint and Noah walked out of the Ironworkers Local 1 Union Hall with their heads hanging low after yet another unsuccessful visit. It was just starting to get dark out and they'd spent the entire day visiting steel companies, crane companies, and local labor unions. No one had any useful information or seemed willing to share much. The Labor Unions were especially tight-lipped, but according to Noah, that was normal.

"I don't know about you, but I need a drink," Klint muttered as they climbed into his Charger. "You want to stop and get some dinner?"

"I appreciate the offer, but I've got plans with my wife tonight," Noah said. "Sorry to disappoint,"

"Eh, don't worry. I'll hit up Kade, see what he's doing,"

"What about your daughter?" Noah asked as they started driving. Klint laughed out loud.

"She's with friends again," Klint said. "We're close, but I'm still her dad, you know?"

"Sure," Noah mumbled. He looked at the list he'd made of potential companies to investigate. "Hey, we're pretty close to one of these companies. You got one more in you?"

"Might as well," Klint shrugged. "Where's it at?"

"Stickney, it's like 30 minutes from here,"

"That's not close," Klint retorted.

"Come on, I'm in full detective mode," Noah argued. "What's the worst that could happen? We're gonna get stuck in traffic if we head back into the city right now anyway,"

"Fair enough," Klint relented. He really didn't feel like driving out of his way, but he had nothing else going on tonight, and would rather keep himself busy than worry about his daughter.

Noah pulled up the directions on his phone and turned the volume up so Klint could hear. Klint wasn't feeling too optimistic after the day they had just had, but Noah still seemed to be in good spirits. He had a naivete to him that Klint found kind of funny, especially considering that Noah was no stranger to this sort of life. They drove in silence for a few minutes until Klint's curiosity got the best of him.

"So, you weren't the one who robbed the truck, right?" Klint asked. "I hope you're not just wasting my time,"

"Ha!" Noah laughed. "Good one,"

"Can you blame me for wondering?"

"Not really," Noah smiled. "I was kind of waiting for you to ask,"

"Yeah?"

"Makes sense. I know you know what I did,"

"You didn't seem surprised either," Klint admitted. Noah merely shrugged.

"One thing that I learned doing that kind of stuff, people always know more than you,"

"Do you ever regret it?" Klint asked. Noah paused for a moment, looking out the window at the passing street.

"No," he said. "No, I don't. It wasn't right, I know that. But I was forced into it. I did it to protect people I care about and love. For that reason alone, I'll never regret it,"

"Fair enough," Klint nodded.

He had to respect Noah's blunt honesty about the entire thing. It's not like Noah was trying to pretend he didn't do bad things, just the opposite, in fact. Noah owned it and carried it with a sense of pride that Klint had only seen in the criminals he almost wished he hadn't caught. Those were few and far between, but Noah fell into that category. He was a good man, Klint could see that. Noah had morals, principles, and a code; most men didn't have any of those, let alone all three. But, there was always a small part of Klint that still looked at Noah as a criminal, which he was. It was a tough line to walk, but Noah had earned Klint's trust, and until he proved otherwise, Klint would continue to trust him.

****

Turning the wheel, Klint spun the Charger into the parking lot of McTiernan Steel Construction. The building itself was in an older part of town and it looked like it. Atop the front of the building was the company logo, which was fading. There were only a few other cars in the parking lot, mostly pickup trucks.

"Alright, let's do this," Klint said, shutting off his car. He and Noah stepped out and headed toward the door. "What do you know about these guys?"

"Not much," Noah admitted. "Their website was pretty vague, but they do steel construction. Bridges, buildings, warehouses, that sort of stuff. I think it's a family-owned company, but they pretty much all are at this point,"

"Well, let's hope this is at least a little bit productive,"

Noah held the front door open for Klint, letting him lead the way inside the small lobby. Klint immediately took everything in. There was an American flag hanging on the wall and a small plaque that contained a picture of a young man who was obviously in the military; there was also a Silver Star and a Bronze Star in the plaque - prestigious awards given out by the US Armed Forces.

"Damn," Klint muttered, looking at the wall. "They don't hand those out easily,"

"What is it?" Noah asked, peering over Klint's shoulder.

"Silver Star and a Bronze Star," Klint said, pointing to the different medals.

But before he could explain any further, a door opened and a small, petite woman stepped into the lobby. She wore glasses and had a disarming, friendly smile.

"How can I help you gentlemen?" she asked. Klint stepped up toward her, flashing a smile of his own.

"Pleasure to meet you ma'am," Klint stuck his hand out. "My name is Detective Klinton Kavanaugh with the Chicago Police Department. This is my associate, Noah. We were hoping to talk to the owner here, we have some questions,"

"Mr. McTiernan isn't in right now," the woman said, still friendly as ever. She didn't appear to be phased at all by the presence of the police. "But, our Principal Foreman is in his office. I can let him know you're here,"

"Thank you, ma'am," Klint said. The woman returned through the same door she'd come. Noah sat down in one of the chairs and propped his foot up, yawning loudly. They sat in silence while they waited, neither man having much to say.

A little more than five minutes later, the door opened again and a man wearing jeans, black work boots, and a collared shirt appeared. Klint noticed the company logo on the front of the shirt. He looked the man up and down, sizing him up as best he could. The man was older, probably in his fifties. Graying brown hair, stubble, and sunken eyes. Klint could smell the cigarettes as soon as the man stepped into the lobby. He was slightly overweight, but his height made it less obvious.

"Craig Trasker," the man introduced himself. He didn't stick his hand out, which Klint found odd. "What can I do for you guys?"

"I was hoping we could talk to you for a few minutes," Klint said, pulling his coat aside to flash the badge on his belt. "I promise to be quick,"

"Sure thing," Craig said. "Follow me, we can talk in my office,"

Holding the door open for Klint and Noah, Craig led them through the front office. There were a handful of people at desks, including the woman who had greeted them. Klint noticed four doors that had name plates on them, indicating different offices for different higher-up employees. Craig's office was at the end of the hall, the door was open, and soft rock music was playing from his iPhone. Shutting off the music, Craig closed the door to his office as soon as Klint and Noah were inside, giving them some privacy. He took a seat behind his desk and leaned back in his chair.

Klint could tell he was uneasy.

"So, how can I help?" Craig asked. Klint opened up his notepad.

"Just have a few questions for you about this company and such. We're investigating a particular case and I'm hoping you could provide some insight for us,"

"Depends on the questions, I guess," Craig shrugged. He didn't look Klint in the eye for too long.

"Can you just give me a brief overview of what it is you guys do here?" Klint began with something easy to hopefully relieve the tension in the room. Craig adjusted in his seat and cleared his throat.

"Of course. Um, well, the company was started in the 80's by my father-in-law, my brother-in-law took over until he passed away a few years ago, and now his kid is running the show. We're basically a one-stop shop for all things steel construction. Bridges, skyscrapers, warehouses, that kind of stuff. It's our bread and butter,"

"Sounds like an interesting operation," Klint commented, jotting a few notes down. "And the current owner, his name is...?"

"Boyd," Craig confirmed. "Boyd McTiernan,"

"Perfect," Klint nodded, writing that down. "Now, how familiar are you with crane cables?"

"Very," Craig said. "We've got several cranes in our fleet,"

"Tell me about the cables, specifically,"

"Well, what do you want to know?"

"Anything you think I should know,"

"That's kind of an open-ended question," Craig shrugged.

Klint narrowed his eyes. He'd interrogated and questioned many people over his career. Every person had a tell that let him know they were either lying or not sharing all of the information they had. And right now, Craig was giving off such a dishonest vibe that Klint was actually kind of impressed. The man was lying right through his teeth with such confidence and ease, like he thought he was truly pulling one over on the authorities. Deciding it was useless to pursue an ambiguous approach, Klint switched on his true detective self.

"There was an armored truck that was robbed last week," Klint said, watching for any shift in Craig's expression. He surprisingly saw nothing, but he continued nonetheless. "The crew used cables to rappel onto the road and hit the truck. Those cables have been identified as ones that are used in cranes,"

"Interesting," Craig said. He seemed genuinely surprised to hear that. He seemed to relax a little bit. "I mean, it's definitely possible, with the right equipment. Those cables are made out of steel, so whoever used them had to know they'd need a specific type of gloves. Otherwise, you're gonna shred your hands trying to rappel down that,"

"Anything else you think I should know?" Klint asked.

"Is there a reason you're asking me all of this?" Craig suddenly asked.

"We've been talking to every company in the area that uses these types of cables. Still have plenty to visit, we're just gathering information at this point,"

"Smart," Craig commented. He put his hands behind his head and sighed. "Those cables are expensive. Anyone who's leaving them behind, using them for anything other than their working purpose, clearly isn't too concerned with money. Either that, or they knew they were going to get a hefty payday soon,"

Klint and Craig locked eyes. Silence fell over the room. Nodding, Klint got to his feet. He'd heard all he needed to. Sticking out his hand, Klint smiled.

"Pleasure to meet you, Mr. Trasker," Klint said. "Thank you for meeting with us,"

"Always a pleasure to help Chicago's finest," Craig shook Klint's hand, sarcasm oozing from the comment. Klint scoffed and shook his head, impressed by the guts Craig was displaying. The man thought he was untouchable and he acted like it. Fortunately, Klint had made a career of dealing with men like Craig.

"I'm sure we'll be seeing each other again soon," Klint said, giving Craig a knowing wink.

Hurrying out of the office, Klint pulled out his phone and sent a text to Kade. Noah was right on his heels, keeping up with him.

"We found our guys," Klint muttered as they reached the lobby. "That man was lying through his teeth,"

"Are you sure about that?" Noah asked. "He didn't say anything too different from the other guys we talked to,"

"Trust me, Noah," Klint said. "He's lying. Our guys are here,"

As they stepped outside the building, Klint saw a man jump out of an expensive looking Ford pickup truck. He wore work boots, dirty jeans, and a Hi-Vis long sleeved shirt. Klint saw spiky reddish-brown hair poking out from a backwards baseball hat. Making eye contact with him, the man smiled brightly at Klint and Noah.

"How are you doing, gentlemen?" the man asked, walking past them into the building. He kept that smile on his face until Klint and Noah were behind him. Klint stopped and watched the man disappear into the building.

"What?" Noah asked.

"Yeah," Klint muttered, remembering Kayley's description of the man who'd shot John. "These are our guys,"

# PART 2

# The Marauders Of
# The Midwest

*"Sinful and forbidden pleasures are like poisoned bread; they may satisfy for a the moment, but there is death in them at the end"* - Tryon Edwards; Theologian

# CHAPTER 10

# Boyd

From the front office of McTiernan Steel Construction, Boyd McTiernan watched the two men get into the Dodge Charger, and slowly pull out of the parking lot. He lowered his head and sighed heavily. Running his hand through his hair, Boyd stepped over to the woman who had greeted the two men. Leaning down, he lowered his voice so he wasn't broadcasting for the entire front office to hear.

"Did you have them sign in?" he asked. She shook her head, slowly.

"No, I'm sorry. Completely forgot,"

"Who did they meet with?"

"Your uncle," the woman answered. "They were looking for you. I told Craig that, but he said he could handle it,"

"Wonderful," Boyd rolled his eyes. "Carole, please let Craig know I want to see him. In my office,"

"You got it,"

Walking back toward his office, Boyd bumped fists with one of the ironworkers who was in the front office, making copies. His office was located in the back corner of the front office; he kept it locked at all times when he wasn't actually in the building. Not because he didn't trust people, but he just didn't like the idea of anyone being in his office when he wasn't there. He was particular and liked things the way he liked them.

Unlocking his door, Boyd flipped the lights on and turned the small AC unit on. His office wasn't especially large or grand, but still a nice place to work, complete with his own bathroom, shower, and small kitchenette. He had a large wooden L-shaped desk, and two swivel chairs in front of it. The office had once belonged to his father.

One of the most prominent items in his office was the print on his wall. The image was titled 'Lunch Atop A Skyscraper' and depicted 11 grisly ironworkers sitting across an iron girder and eating lunch during the construction of the RCA Building in Manhattan, New York. Photographed by Charles C. Ebbets, the image had become synonymous with ironworkers and ironworker culture. Everytime Boyd saw that picture, he felt proud to be carrying on the legacy of those men. Fearless, brave, hardworking. They represented everything Boyd wanted to be.

Sitting down behind his desk, Boyd flipped open his laptop and began checking his email. He had a meeting the following day with a potential client who was interested in hiring McTiernan Steel to construct a new warehouse in the Lisle area. Boyd was slated to meet with the developer and the General Contractor. Even though he still spent a fair amount of time on actual job sites, Boyd certainly enjoyed the business end of working at the company. Meeting with clients, attending forums, and trying to grow his father's company was something he took great pride in.

"Knock, knock," Craig said, stepping into Boyd's office. "You wanted to see me?"

"Yeah, shut the door," Boyd said, closing his laptop. Craig gently closed the door and took a seat in front of Boyd's desk.

"What's up?"

"Why don't you tell me? Who were those guys?"

"Police," Craig admitted.

Boyd sat back in his chair, watching Craig like a hawk. He set his folded hands on the desk.

"Relax," Craig said, adjusting in the chair. "I didn't tell them anything,"

"You don't always have to say anything," Boyd answered. He shook his head. "Names?"

"The one said his name was Klint. Klint Kavanaugh. I don't think the other one said his name, actually,"

"Klint Kavanaugh," Boyd repeated, writing the name down on a piece of scratch paper. He looked up at Craig, trying to hide his annoyance with Craig's knack for getting them in trouble. "Look, get the guys together after work today. I want to meet and talk,"

"Where?"

"Anywhere," Boyd snapped. "Just pick a place and figure it out. I have to make sure you didn't just screw us over,"

"Real nice, Boyd," Craig grumbled, standing up and stuffing his hands in his pockets.

"Why you felt it necessary to handle that is beyond me," Boyd said, raising his voice a little. "If they were looking for me, you tell them to come back when I'm here. You don't *handle* it for me. We've had this same conversation before,"

"You weren't here!" Craig tried to defend his action. "What was I supposed to do? It's still my family's name on the door!"

Boyd reached over the desk and grabbed Craig by the collar of his shirt, narrowing his eyes on his uncle. Craig tried to fight back, but he was no match for Boyd, who was much stronger.

"It's not your name. And you don't own a goddamn thing in this building. You'd be wise to remember that," Boyd snarled.

Keeping a grip on Craig's shirt, Boyd walked around and opened his door before throwing his uncle out of his office. He slammed the door shut and took a deep breath, trying to calm himself. No one on the planet could piss him off the way Craig Trasker could. Boyd had to respect his father for being able to put up with him for as long as he did.

Craig had married Boyd's aunt - his mom's sister. He'd been a decent guy, or so Boyd had been told. In a time of temporary desperation, Boyd's father had hired his brother-in-law as a Foreman. Craig had worked in construction, had experience, and was family. What could possibly go wrong? It didn't take long for Boyd's dad to realize his own mistake. Craig was woefully inept and exuded a disgusting sense of superiority amongst the crews he ran. Within the first six months, Boyd's father fielded over a dozen complaints about Craig. But, the deed had already been done. People found a way to put up with Craig or they left for a different job. Boyd's father hated it, but that was the reality of the situation. Since the passing of both of Boyd's parents and his aunt, Craig had become slightly less of an asshole, but that wasn't saying a whole lot. Boyd still dealt with a number of complaints regarding his behavior, but he knew that Craig was better kept happy. An angry Craig was unpredictable and Boyd couldn't have that, especially given their side job.

\*\*\*\*

They met in the back lot of McTiernan Steel, where the heavy equipment and fleet of work trucks were parked. All of the other employees had gone home for the night, there were only three personal vehicles in the back lot remaining. As he walked toward the three trucks, Boyd popped a Newport into his mouth and lit it. He took a long drag as he approached the three men standing in the back lot. Per usual, Craig was the loudest, talking obnoxiously to the two other men who knew better than to show their annoyance with him. They looked somewhat relieved to see Boyd approaching and once Craig saw him, he wisely closed his mouth.

"How's it going, boss?" Patrick asked, nodding respectfully to his boss. Patrick Cross was another foreman at McTiernan Steel and an Ironworker by trade. He'd been working for Boyd for almost a decade and was one of the hardest working employees at McTiernan.

"Oh, it's going," Boyd answered. He bumped fists with Patrick and then with the second man, Juan Alarcón, the Lead Mechanic. "Are you guys good?"

"All good," Juan shrugged. "Got the cranes ready to go for tomorrow,"

"Good, good," Boyd nodded, blowing out another cloud of smoke. "Listen, I'll make this fast, don't want you guys hanging around here any longer than you have to,"

"Eh, don't worry," Patrick shook his head. "Leah's got the kids this week, I've got nothing going on,"

"Be that as it may, I wanna get home," Boyd said, getting a chuckle from Patrick and Juan. Craig was still pouting from their earlier encounter, which Boyd guessed would last another day or two.

"Here's the deal, there were some cops that came by the shop today," Boyd began. "They spoke to Craig and were asking questions about the heist,"

"They said they were talking to several companies, but they identified the cables we used," Craig huffed.

"You're kidding me?" Patrick asked, his mouth slightly open. "What does that mean?"

"Well..." Craig started to answer.

"It doesn't mean anything," Boyd interrupted, pinching his cigarette between his thumb and pointer finger. He shot Craig a look that made it perfectly clear that he didn't want Craig saying anything else. "We are and always have been one step ahead of the cops. They got nothing on us so far. We hit pause for a little bit. I still have to give the haul to the fence, but once I've got this most recent total, we'll know how many more jobs we have to pull,"

"You haven't gone to the fence yet?" Craig blurted out. Boyd ignored him. "Punk ass, I asked you a question? Why in the hell have you not done that?"

And that's when Boyd turned on him.

"You're the reason we're having this conversation," Boyd snapped. "If you hadn't wasted the guards and that cop, it would've been just a heist, and I could've gotten us our cash already. But no, now we're wanted killers, no thanks to you,"

"It's not like you've never killed cops," Craig muttered.

"Fuck you, Craig," Boyd snapped. Craig lowered his gaze. Patrick fidgeted with his jacket. Juan stared at his boots.

"I'm not concerned about this, at least not yet," Boyd continued, composing himself once again. "We go about our business as usual and I'll let you all know what the next move is. I'll have your cuts by next week, so until then, just keep a low profile. I'll make sure we link up and get everything figured out. Just trust me, ok?"

"Hey, I trust you," Juan said. "I just don't want to get cornered. Cops know me, ya feel?"

Juan didn't need to spell out what he meant. He was a two-time felon who'd served time for drug trafficking and was the only man on the team who'd done hard time. His perspective inside the criminal world had been invaluable to Boyd when he was first developing his plan.

"No one's getting cornered," Boyd reassured him. "We are fine. You guys go home, have a good weekend, and we'll talk next week,"

"Have a good one, boss," Patrick said, walking back to his truck and climbing inside. Juan followed suit and Boyd watched them drive away while he finished the cigarette.

"You really believe that shit?" Craig asked, lighting up his own cigarette. Boyd looked at him and shrugged a little, flicking ash away from his smoke.

"Yeah, I do," Boyd finally said, taking one final puff from the cigarette. He threw it on the ground and stomped it out with his boot. "I'll see ya around,"

Boyd started walking back the way he'd come, but Craig reached out and grabbed his arm. Not hard, but firm enough to annoy Boyd.

"Hey," Craig said, seriously. "Don't get complacent,"

"It's not gonna happen," Boyd responded, not even making eye contact with his uncle. He jerked his arm away and marched back around the building.

****

The Starbucks was located on the corner of Jefferson and Main, right in the center of Downtown Naperville, about an hour west of Chicago. Naperville was routinely listed as one of the nation's wealthiest areas, in addition to being one of the safests towns in the United States. Both of those facts were the main reasons why Boyd had chosen to make his home right in the bustling Downtown area. The irony of that alone was amusing to him, a man wanted by over a dozen agencies for countless heists, sleeping in the safest town in America. Hollywood couldn't write something that ironic.

He sat alone in the rather large Starbucks branch, sipping on an overpriced coffee that he could barely pronounce. His laptop was open and he scrolled through a few different articles about the recent 'Marauders of the Midwest' heist. If he was being honest, he wasn't crazy about the name the media had given him. He would've preferred something a little more theatrical, but it wasn't bad. After all, not many crews could pull off enough impressive heists to earn themselves a nickname. That in and of itself made him appreciate the name just a little bit more.

A pair of burly Naperville Police Officers stepped into the coffee shop, each of them looking like they had just come right off the set of a cheesy cop TV show. A few pounds overweight, balding, mustaches, it was almost enough to make Boyd chuckle. The officers looked at him and nodded, he of course nodded right back, raising his coffee toward them in a polite gesture. They had no idea who he really was, no idea who was sitting mere feet away from them. No idea that by not arresting him, they were missing out on an insane amount of publicity, the talk show circuit, and maybe even a book tour. Ironic.

Boyd closed his laptop and slipped it inside the backpack resting by his feet. He kept his phone face-up on the table, awaiting a text that would be coming through any second. Checking his watch and then the time on his phone, he sighed and took another sip of coffee. It was a few minutes before 8 o'clock and the morning rush was just about to pick up. He knew the daily schedules of the coffee shop by heart and was expecting today to be a rather busy morning. Sure enough, people started filing in and suddenly the shop was filled with a line of thirsty patrons.

*Buzz.*

The phone lit up and he saw a text notification with a single word.

*Here.*

Tossing the backpack over his shoulder and grabbing both his phone and coffee, Boyd slipped past the bustling line and stepped out of the shop. He slipped on an expensive pair of Oakley sunglasses and began walking toward the Naperville Riverwalk, probably the most popular attraction in Naperville. The Riverwalk was a stretch of the Dupage River with beautiful wooden bridges, walking paths, and a few little parks along the way. Every night, street musicians would gather at the various fountains and play music. Couples would walk hand in hand, stopping to take selfies or have a stranger snap a cute photo. Older couples would usually have a dog with them and would sit by the fountains, enjoying the live music. It was a rather unique thing to witness, but it was cozy and remarkably romantic for a rather boring suburb.

This Saturday morning, however, there were no musicians or couples or dogs, just a few 20-somethings jogging or walking. Boyd smiled or nodded at pretty much everyone he passed, no use in being rude or walking around angry at the world. He liked to consider himself a generally nice person, he tipped well, made conversations with the cashiers, stuff like that. Being miserable or angry hadn't gotten him anywhere in his earlier days.

He spotted Rob sitting alone at one of the picnic benches under a large pergola, overlooking the Riverwalk. Blue jeans, plaid shirt, glasses, short black hair under a tan Carhartt baseball hat. As simple as a disguise could get. To any passersby, Rob looked like a regular suburban dad, no one would've guessed his real job or who he kept as friends.

"Good to see you, bro," Boyd said, sliding onto the picnic bench across from his friend. The man smiled and nodded.

"Glad to see you're still breathing," Rob muttered. He rubbed his forehead and pulled out a pack of Marlboro Reds. "You want a dart?"

"Sure," Boyd chuckled, grabbing a smoke from the pack. He couldn't remember the last time he smoked Marlboros. Lighting the cigarette, Boyd sighed loudly in relief as the nicotine flooded his system. Boyd held the cigarette between his thumb and pointer finger, making a mental note to buy a fresh pack of Newports on his way back to his apartment. Rob followed suit, lighting his own cigarette and taking a long drag.

"Dare I ask how it went?" Rob asked, flicking some ash away with his middle finger. "Or does the new coverage do it justice?"

"The score was good, the plan worked to perfection," Boyd shrugged. "Fireworks weren't my doing, obviously, but it definitely complicates things. Every cop in the city is gonna want a piece of us,"

"Sounds like it was a close one," Rob said, blowing out a cloud of thick smoke. "How did it go with guys I recommended?"

"Not well," Boyd shook his head. "Two special forces-lookin' assholes kicked the fucking door down and started shooting. The hitters bit the dust, I barely escaped with my life. Took one of them out in the process, though,"

"Jesus Christ, Boyd," Rob breathed, shaking his head. "You really need to start taking it easy, they could've busted you. Plus, if you guys are dropping bodies regularly now, that's going to create more complications. You drop a few gangbangers, no one bats an eye. But you drop some cops, that's gonna bring a lot of unwanted attention,"

"Cops came to the shop yesterday," Boyd muttered, changing the subject. He took another drag of the cigarette. "They talked to Craig,"

"Shit," Rob swore, spitting on the ground. "That is not good, Boyd,"

"We're fine, ok?" Boyd said. "I'm not worried about it at all. They don't know anything, just following up on a lead,"

"That's what I'm afraid of," Rob shook his head. "I understand you're in a tough situation and all, but you're gonna get yourself killed if you don't start taking this more seriously,"

"I'm not in the mood for a lecture, buddy," Boyd said, his tone a very clear warning that Rob was dangerously walking the line along a forbidden topic.

Boyd couldn't blame him, they had been like brothers for nearly a decade. Through the ups and downs, Rob had been a pillar of consistency and dependability in the life of a man who had none of that. Rob had every right to be concerned, even if Boyd didn't want to admit it. He knew they'd screwed up the heist. Craig's actions had brought dire consequences and an unprecedented level of attention.

"I'm not trying to lecture you, but no one else is going to tell you these things," Rob said. "I just don't want to have to bury you. I've buried enough of my friends over the years,"

"Hey, stop that. You're not gonna have to bury me," Boyd waved the idea away and popped the cigarette back into his mouth.

"Then look at me and be honest," Rob challenged. "Tell me the rush you get has nothing to do with why you keep doing these jobs? You are addicted. So, just admit it. When you quit drinking, what did you do?"

"I bought the bike..."

"Yeah, you bought the bike," Rob interrupted. "And you still drive that thing like you have a death wish. You need a vice, for whatever reason. I'm glad it's not the booze and pills anymore, but I don't know if this is much better. You're walking a fine line and you know it. I do not want to bury you, but you seem to be fine with rolling the dice every single time,"

Boyd didn't answer. Rob could feel the weight of his gaze through the sunglasses. He put his cigarette out on the ground and sighed heavily. There were certain things that he knew he couldn't bring up around his friend, but sometimes it was hard to keep his mouth shut. He had to ask, despite knowing it was going to set his friend off.

"When was the last time you saw her?" Rob asked in a whisper. Boyd didn't move for a few seconds, the cigarette burning down to the filter. He tossed the butt on the ground and squashed it under his boot. Rob knew he was crossing one of the forbidden lines, but he had to ask. He had every right to know what was going through his friend's head.

"She has nothing to do with any of this," Boyd answered coolly. "Call me whatever you want, but we got the job done. How I did is of no concern to you,"

"Bullshit," Rob fired back. "Of course it concerns me,"

"No, it doesn't," Boyd growled. Rob threw his hands up and relented, shaking his head.

"Alright, it doesn't," Rob grunted. "Where is it?"

"Back seat of my truck," Boyd cocked his head back toward the Downtown area. "Black Nike duffle bag,"

"Ok," Rob nodded. "I'll grab it on my way out. You'll see the changes in your account by the end of the week. I'll cut a check for the others and bring them to you myself,"

Rob stood up and was about to start walking away when Boyd set his phone on the table and pushed it toward Rob. Slowly, Rob sat back down and picked up the phone, studying the picture on the phone. He took a deep breath.

"You're insane, you know that, right?" Rob looked at his friend and handed the phone back to him.

"We can do it," Boyd said. "It's gonna be relatively simple compared to the job we just pulled,"

"I have no doubt in your ability to pull it off," Rob agreed. "But I can't trust you to not make a stupid decision that would risk your life,"

"What do you want me to say, Rob?" Boyd asked, raising his voice. "Yeah, I love the rush, ok? I need it, it keeps me sane. I'm not turning back to the bottle or the pills, so this is all I got. If it kills me, so be it. It's my choice how and when I risk my life,"

"Ok, ok, ok," Rob put his hands up, feeling bad for riling him up so badly. "Calm down,"

Both men fell quiet. Boyd instantly felt guilty for snapping at his friend. Rob didn't mean any harm, he was trying to do the same big-brother routine as always. He was a good friend and the closest thing that Boyd had ever had to a brother. In fact, Rob was the only man Boyd considered to be his family. There was a bond between them that wasn't going to be broken, especially by an argument. Just like real brothers, they argued all of the time, but they still were there for each other, and that was what counted.

"I'm sorry," Boyd grunted, suddenly very focused on a group of people walking along the Riverwalk. "But I'm not gonna stop. I can't. I don't have a choice in it anymore. The banks are gonna take the company, the house, everything. I can't let that happen. I owe it to him to at least do this. I hope you can understand that,"

"I understand, trust me," Rob stood up and clapped Boyd on the shoulder. "And I'll look into that, ok?" he said, gesturing to the phone. "But, you need to seriously ask yourself if this is worth it. An empty house that you don't live in and a business you never really wanted. I understand where you're coming from, but you need to think about this, Boyd. Otherwise, you're going to waste your entire life. And for what?"

Hanging his head, Boyd fought the sudden and powerful urge to get emotional. He typically was good at keeping a poker face, but the more and more he repressed the pain he felt, the more his facade threatened to crack.

"Call me if you need anything, ok?" Rob said quietly.

Boyd turned to watch Rob depart, walking confidently back toward the parking lot where Boyd had left his truck, along with a spare key in the gas tank. That was the procedure. Rob would take the haul from the last heist and in a few days, Boyd would be several million dollars richer.

He waited a full ten minutes before he made the fifteen or so minute walk back to his apartment building. His truck would be back in his designated parking space later that day. Crossing into the back parking lot, Boyd fished out a set of keys from the pocket of his leather biker jacket. He grinned as he approached his pride and joy, a black Suzuki GSX-R1000 motorcycle. The bike had been a celebratory purchase after his first heist, which coincided with when he finally got sober. It was a reminder of both of those accomplishments and also just an awesome toy to have.

Revving the engine, Boyd shifted into gear, and expertly piloted the bike out of the parking lot. The wind whipped through his hair as he shifted into second gear and tore down the road, the bike's engine roaring to life. The GSX-R had a zero-to-sixty time of just under 2.5 seconds, making it one of the fastest street bikes on the planet. Even so, there were certain times when Boyd wished it could've gone faster. Maybe Rob was right, maybe he did have an addiction. The rush he used to get on his bike was becoming less and less significant, it took maxing out the bike or doing a wheelie on the highway to really get the adrenaline flowing. Even skydiving

COWBOYS OF THE SKY - 139

had become a bit of a bore for him. The most reliable and intense rush came from the heists. Nothing compared to it anymore.

The route was ingrained in his subconscious, he didn't even have to think as he swerved in and out of traffic. He'd made the drive from his apartment to that office so many times that it was pure muscle memory, knowing when to turn and where to go. He came to a stop at a red light, first in the line of awaiting cars. The office was just off the road, in a plaza with a movie theater and a large shopping mall. As soon as the light turned green, Boyd cranked the throttle and shot off toward the office, braking and leaning into the turn for the parking lot.

Rolling to a stop, Boyd planted his feet on the ground, but kept the bike idling. He checked his watch again. The office wouldn't officially be open for another few hours, but the staff would start arriving right now to start getting ready. Boyd was parked in an adjacent parking lot, far enough away from the office to not attract much attention from anyone heading in there, which was the point. The last thing he needed was for her to see him. When Rob asked about her, he didn't have the heart to admit that he'd been doing this a few times a month. It was pathetic, but he didn't have anything else, or anyone else, for that matter. Boyd was as alone as one man could be.

The grey SUV came to a stop in front of the office and she stepped out, her long brown hair blowing in the wind. She smiled at the driver and leaned in to kiss him before walking away toward the front door. Boyd watched her closely, memorizing every step she took with the focus of a man who'd lost everything. And just like that, she disappeared into the building, ready to start a new day.

Boyd always thought about going in and trying to talk to her. He had rehearsed the speech so many times, he knew it by heart. But he stopped himself, every single time. There was nothing to talk about, he knew that. Anything he'd possibly say would just make things worse than they already were. Plus, it was better for him to be alone. It made his job a lot easier knowing there was no one worrying about him to come home safely. That second part he told himself to make himself feel better, knowing it was a complete load of crap.

"Bye, baby," Boyd whispered to himself. He twisted the throttle and spun the bike around, flying back onto the road, and toward the highway

# CHAPTER 11

# Kayley

Kayley was very much surprised at how relieved she was to see John Shannon walking under his own power. He was moving slowly, but definitely feeling much better. John was able to sign himself out of the hospital and finally able to leave. Since Klint had virtually assigned her as John's personal bodyguard, Kayley felt an incredible responsibility to make sure John was taken care of. Maybe it was the guilt she felt from her military days or something deeper than that, but she felt the need to make sure John was ok.

John climbed into the passenger seat of his Ford Excursion after finally surrendering the keys to Kayley. His arm was wrapped in a sling and the wounds had all been stitched, stapled, and glued up. Despite being on a heavy amount of painkillers, John felt much more like himself. This certainly wasn't the first time he'd been injured. But, comparatively, this had been one of the worst stays of his career. Being sidelined, especially with so much going on, was a horribly vulnerable feeling for someone like John. Kayley was all too familiar with those feelings. She'd seen her dad go down that same path.

"So, what have I missed?" John asked, closing his eyes so he didn't have to witness someone else driving his truck.

"Well, Klint thinks he found a lead on the guys who robbed that truck. Maybe the one who shot you too," Kayley said, driving back toward the city.

"Good," John grumbled, balling his fist. "Has he got a location yet?"

"Relax, John," Kayley said, looking over at him. "This is going to require a little bit more precision than just kicking doors down. I'm just giving you a warning, but Klint is still pretty heated at both of us for that apartment thing,"

"Let him be heated, I could care less," John finally opened his eyes and looked at Kayley. "Thanks for taking care of me, I do appreciate it,"

"Of course, John. I wasn't about to leave you hanging there," Kayley smiled.

"When does Klint want to meet up again?" John asked. Kayley shrugged.

"No clue, I haven't heard much from him. He's been following up on this lead pretty hard. Something about what the Mayor said to him is weighing on him, you can just tell,"

"Interesting," John grunted. For a few weeks now, John had had his suspicions about Klint's true relationship with Mayor Hart. He had no real evidence to support his theory, but John nonetheless didn't believe for one second that their relationship was strictly platonic. "Are you ok? I mean, with everything that happened..."

"I'm good, trust me," Kayley said before John could finish his thought. "I've been in worse situations than that,"

"Just checking..." John mumbled.

"You know, John..." Kayley once again looked over at him as they came to a stop at a redlight. "It's ok to care about people,"

"I do care about people," John stared out the window. "I just care about them from a distance. It's better that way, for everyone involved,"

"Do you seriously think that?" Kayley asked.

"One hundred percent," John answered almost immediately.

The light turned green and Kayley drove through the intersection, turning her attention back to the road. She felt incredibly sympathetic towards John. The constant pain he felt was written all over his face, Kayley could just see his internal struggle playing out in real time. No one deserved to be alone, especially someone who clearly cared about people as much as John did. The reality of the situation was that John Shannon reminded her too much of her father for her to truly want to get closer to him. That look in John's eyes was the same look that Kayley had started to see in her father. It was incredibly confusing and uncomfortable for her.

Kayley wanted to tell him all of that and more, but just couldn't find the words. As much as she wanted to comfort him, Kayley always felt like there would be a barrier between her and anyone she tried to date. Not that she was trying to date John, but there had always been problems with men that she tried to let into her life on a personal level. When it was purely professional, never an issue. But the second actual emotions were involved, Kayley turned tail and usually ran or put up walls. Relationships were just virtually impossible for her. It had been that way ever since her dad had passed away. All of the unanswered questions about his death constantly ate away at her. Not having answers made it extremely difficult for her to feel any kind of closure or peace.

After making the final stretch of the journey in silence, Kayley pulled over in front of the hotel they'd both been staying at. Noah Riordan and his wife also had a room there. All three of them were on separate floors and the rooms were being paid for by the Mayor's office. As soon as Kayley threw the truck in park, the valets ran over, and opened the door for her and John. Kayley expected John to wait for her, but as soon as the door was opened for him, he hurried into the hotel, and disappeared.

She stood there, on the sidewalk, watching John Shannon limp onto an elevator. Looking up at the cloudy Chicago sky, Kayley felt tears coming on. All she ever wanted was to see her father, talk to him. Right now, those feelings were amplified tenfold.

****

Walking into the warehouse for the first time in almost two weeks, Kayley felt a little nervous. She didn't really know what Klint had been up to on his own time with Noah and Kade. And she certainly hadn't been expecting the sudden phone call from Klint, imploring her to get to the safehouse as soon as possible. She saw John's truck parked outside, which made her feel a little relieved. At least he was included; she knew she would've felt worse had he been excluded.

"...But I'm still glad to see you up and about," Klint was saying, almost certainly to John.
"Yeah, me too. I'm all good, ready to go," John answered.

John was sitting on a swivel chair, an unlit cigarette hanging from his mouth, and a pair of sunglasses resting on his forehead. As usual, Klint stood in the center, around that white folding table that was getting more and more crowded with files, pictures, and various other reports. Noah and Kade stood off to one side, each of them looking a little more tired and rundown than the last time Kayley had seen them. Klint, Kade, and Noah had clearly been burning the candle at both ends, trying to compensate for the fact that John and Kayley had been sidelined for the last two weeks. Kayley pulled up another swivel chair and sat next to John, touching his arm discreetly.

"How're you feeling?" she asked in a low voice.

"Fine," John grunted. He stood up and walked over to the table to stand by Klint. "Alright, we're all here,"

"Kayley," Klint smiled, looking toward her. "You are needed over here,"

"What's up?" Kayley asked. She walked over to the table. Klint opened up a manila folder and pulled out a picture of a man. It had been taken from a website. The man was smiling. Kayley, and John, both recognized him in an instant.

"Is this the man who shot at you guys?"

"That's him," John nodded, narrowing his eyes. Klint turned slightly, angling the picture so Kayley could clearly see it.

"Yeah, that's definitely him," Kayley confirmed.

"You're both sure about this?" Klint clarified.

"Without a shadow of a doubt," Kayley nodded. "That's him,"

"Who is he?" John asked; a natural and practical follow-up question.

"Everyone, meet James Boyd McTiernan II," Klint said, setting the image down on the table. Noah and Kade stepped over and filled in the gaps around the table. Noah picked up the picture of Boyd and showed it to Kade.

"Damn good lookin' dude," Kade muttered. "Why is it that the big-time criminals are always so good looking?"

"I'm going to choose to ignore that comment," Klint said. "But, Kade, if you ever want to come out to the group, feel free to. We're all very supportive,"

"Ha, ha," Kade rolled his eyes.

"Who is he?" John repeated, folding his arms across his broad chest. The cigarette was still hanging from the corner of his mouth, just begging to be lit.

"Well, he's a lot of things," Klint said ominously. "Born in Chicago, raised in Naperville. Mother, Jennifer Smith. Father, James Boyd McTiernan I. Mom died in a car accident when he was 13. Enlisted in the Army right after high school graduation. Did five tours, including two with a special ops combat team. Silver Star and Bronze Star accommodations, honorable discharge. By all intents and purposes, a perfect soldier. Once he got back stateside, got into the family business. Once the father died from liver failure, Mr. McTiernan took over the construction company. Been running it for about six years now,"

"He's a soldier?" John asked, his mouth slightly open. Klint nodded.

"And a damn good one. From what I understand, they don't just go passing out Silver and Bronze stars like it's nothing,"

"No," John shook his head. "They don't,"

"You should see the lobby of that place," Noah commented. "Like a fuckin' shrine to him,"

"The other guy we met..." Klint continued, pulling out a picture of Craig Trasker. "Is this man, Craig Trasker. He's got a rap sheet, DUI, DWI, felony assault and battery, disorderly conduct, stuff of that nature. Nothing to the caliber that we're talking about right now. He was married to Mr. McTiernan's aunt before she died in that same car accident with the mom. Mr. Trasker also works at

McTiernan Steel Construction. Makes over six figures, plus pension, benefits, and bonuses. I pulled some financial records and last year it looks like Mr. McTiernan made just over a mil. So, neither of these men have any reason to need to rob a bank. At least, it appears that way,"

"Well, there's got to be a reason," Kade commented.

"Always is," Klint agreed. "Right now, we have means and we have people. What we don't have is a motive for these guys. We have John and Kayley's testimony, but that won't be enough. If you two are the only evidence or witnesses I have, they'll call you to testify. And that will expose a lot of icky shit the Mayor doesn't have the stomach for. So we work the case, the old fashioned way,"

"Meaning what, exactly?" Noah asked. Klint smiled at him.

"I'm glad you asked," Klint reached into his backpack and pulled out a stack of different colored folders, each with a name on it. He passed the folders out based on the assignments. "Noah, as of next week, you're starting at McTiernan Steel Construction. I made a few phone calls and got you in as an operator. Get in with the guys, keep your ears to the ground, and see what you learn. You'll fit right in, just be incognito. Pay attention to what the guys say. If anything stands out to you, I want to know about it,"

"Got it," Noah said with an enthusiastic nod.

"Kade, I want you on Craig Trasker outside of work. Follow him, but be invisible. Do *not* make any direct contact with him whatsoever. There's a good chance he's not apart of anything, but he's still worth looking into,"

"Sounds good," Kade answered, opening his folder to see an entire file on Craig Trasker.

"And Kayley..." Klint said, turning toward her. He could feel John Shannon's eyes on him. "You get Mr. McTiernan,"

"What do you mean I get him?" Kayley asked.

"I need you to get close to him. I want to be clear, I'm not asking you to do anything you're not comfortable with. I ain't asking you to sleep with him or anything like that. Just get close to him, work him a little bit. You have one thing that the rest of us do not have, use that to your advantage,"

"And what is that, exactly?" Kayley said, folding her arms. She knew damn well what *it* was, but she wanted to hear the words come out of Klint's mouth. A little ego boost never hurt anyone.

"Your feminine appeal, Ms. McKenna," Klint answered. Kayley shook her head and chuckled.

"That's about as politically correct as you could be, huh?"

"I try," Klint gave her a sarcastic smile.

"What about me?" John suddenly asked, glaring at Klint.

"John, you're with me," Klint said, locking eyes with John. He nodded slowly, indicating to John that they would talk later - in private. Klint turned his attention back to the group. "Alright, if there are no questions, you guys are free to go about your day as planned. Keep in contact, stay by the phones, we'll link up again in a few weeks,"

One by one, the group dispersed until only Klint, John, and Kayley remained. She had known all along that she might be asked to do this type of thing. But now that that moment was upon her, she felt oddly uncomfortable by the idea. Kayley wasn't a prude, not by any stretch of the imagination. And she had zero problem having casual intimate relationships with people. Sex and intimacy were things that Kayley had made a career, a name for herself, out of. The line between work and her personal life rarely blurred, if ever. She was able to separate the two, as were most other actresses or actors in her profession. But this... this was not that. This felt more crude, more dishonest. Kayley had certainly flirted with guys that she had zero intention of doing anything with, who hadn't?

For whatever reason, there was just something that made her feel slightly anxious about the entire thing; maybe it was because she'd seen Boyd's capacity for violence. Maybe it was because he was an Army vet, like her. Just another person suddenly in her life who was a constant reminder of her father.

"Are you ok with this?" John Shannon's voice interrupted Kayley's internal dialogue. She shook her head clear of any intrusive thoughts.

"With what?"

"Nevermind," John grunted. He rolled his eyes and stomped out of the warehouse toward his truck.

"Is he ok?" Kayley asked Klint as soon as John was out of earshot.

"John is a damaged man, unfortunately," Klint said sadly. "Until he decides to admit that to himself, he's just going to be the same lovable asshole,"

Klint reached into his pocket and checked his phone, clearly satisfied with what he saw.

"Alright, you and I are all set," he said. Tucking his phone away. "Mr. McTiernan has a dinner reservation at Perry's in Oak Brook tonight. You and I have reservation thirty minutes after them,"

"Well, alright then," Kayley muttered. "Looks like I don't have to order room service again tonight,"

****

The hostess walked Klint and Kayley to their table in the dining room, right in front of the extravagant wine rack. Klint pulled out Kayley's chair for her and slid it in for her as she sat down.

"Here's the wine menu," the hostess said with a bright smile, handing the menu to Kayley. "Your server will be over in just a few moments,"

"Perfect, thank you," Kayley returned the smile.

Once the hostess left, Kayley set the wine menu down and adjusted in her seat. She was wearing a form-fitting and strapless black dress and a pair of matching black heels. Before going out for the night, Kayley had curled her hair and done her makeup the way she would before a photoshoot. Being that done up definitely made her feel confident, but it only increased her rising discomfort with the scenario. Kayley pushed those feelings down and forced herself to smile, putting on the facade that she was happy to be on a date. Surprisingly, she saw Klint looking equally as uncomfortable as she felt. He was wearing jeans and a dress shirt, but threw on a sport coat over it. Everything else aside, Kayley did think he looked handsome, but Klint was not at all the type of guy she'd ever be interested in dating.

"Are you ok?" Kayley asked, picking up on Klint's discomfort. He shifted in his chair awkwardly. "You could at least look like you're happy to be on a pretend, fake date with me,"

"Yeah, I'm fine," he muttered. "This just feels kinda weird,"

"How so?"

"I just can't tell you the last time I took a woman to dinner," Klint half-heartedly laughed. "The amount of dates I've been on in the last twenty years I could count on one hand,"

"Come on!" Kayley shook her head. "There's no way,"

"I'm serious, I don't date,"

"Why?"

"Ever since I had my daughter, nothing else really mattered. Stuff like dating and relationships just took a backseat. Between my job and being there for her, didn't really have time to be worrying about a woman,"

"How old's your daughter?" Kayley asked, resting her arms on the table. Klint smiled and sat back in his seat.

"18, now," he said proudly. "Her name's Kara. She's a freshman at Depaul,"

"That's crazy, you definitely don't look old enough to have a kid in college," Kayley commented.

"I'm not," Klint said with a smirk. "Had her when I was 18. Her mother took off, haven't heard from her since Kara was born. As long as I can remember it's just been me and my girl, ya know?"

"That's nice for her, though," Kayley said, doing her best to hide her sadness. "Having a dad that's so devoted to you,"

"I'm sure it's a gift and a curse," Klint shrugged. He looked at Kayley and chose to risk making an awkward situation even more awkward. "You and your dad get along or...?"

"He passed away, unfortunately," Kayley admitted. "We had an... interesting relationship to say the least,"

"I'm sorry for your loss," Klint said simply. He could tell Kayley didn't want to open that door any further and Klint respected that. Changing the subject, Klint looked around the expensive steakhouse and nodded approvingly. "Yeah, this is a good place to take a date,"

"You got someone in mind?"

"Maybe," Klint gave Kayley a wink.

Their waiter came over, took their drink order, explained the specials for the evening, and headed back into the kitchen. Once their drinks arrived, Klint finally turned on the Detective inside of him. Scanning the dining room discreetly, Klint tried to locate Boyd McTiernan. It only took him a few scans to zero in on the man he was looking for. Boyd was seated at a table close to the kitchen, but away from the central crowd of people. Klint recognized Craig

Trasker sitting across from him, but the other two men were new. They were all dressed to the nines, and were drinking an expensive bottle of whiskey, like they were celebrating something. Craig was making a toast, which appeared to be getting a humorous reaction from the two other men. Boyd, on the other hand, looked more embarrassed than anything else.

"I see our friends," Klint muttered to Kayley in a low voice. "Behind you, over your right shoulder. Close to the kitchen,"

"Ok," Kayley nodded. "What now?"

"Now we enjoy dinner and we wait and see," Klint said. Using his menu as cover, Klint opened the camera on his phone and snapped a few pictures of Boyd's table.

A while later, Kayley and Klint placed their order and thoroughly enjoyed the food. For the most part, their conversation was relatively superficial, Klint kept most of his focus on the table of suspected bandits. Only twice, did Kayley glance over toward her mark. He looked oddly out of place. The fancy setting, the expensive food, it just didn't seem like he cared too much for it. Kayley found this interesting, especially since Boyd clearly had *money*.

"Perfect," Klint suddenly said to himself, taking a bite of the monstrous pork chop he'd ordered.

"What?"

"He noticed you," Klint said, keeping his gaze on his food. He stole a quick look toward Boyd while taking a bite. "Yeah, we are a go. Do your thing, Ms. McKenna,"

"Here goes nothing," Kayley sighed.

With the grace of an ice dancer, Kayley stood up, pushed her chair in, and started walking to the bathroom. As casually as she could, Kayley looked over toward Boyd. She caught his gaze and gave him a wry smile, followed by a wink. Knowing he was probably checking her out now, Kayley added a little extra shake to her walk. Looking over her shoulder, she gave Klint one last seductive look, biting her lip for ample effect.

When she left the bathroom a few minutes later, Kayley expected Boyd to be staring in that direction, waiting for her to come back out so he could get another look. But much to her surprise, she saw Boyd getting to his feet, shaking hands with the three men he'd had dinner with, and hurrying out of the restaurant. He didn't even so much as glance in Kayley's direction. She sat back down across from Klint and saw the same confused look on his face that she must've had on her own.

"Something happened," Klint informed her. "He got up to take a call and when he came back, he was definitely different,"

"I wonder what's going on. He was in a big hurry to get out of here,"

"Well, there's one way to find out," Klint shrugged, slipping his credit card out of his wallet.

# CHAPTER 12

# Boyd

Boyd rolled his bike into the parking lot of York Tavern and spotted the familiar blue Infiniti sedan instantly. He parked as closely as he could to the car and shut the bike off, leaning it on the stand. Leaving his helmet on the handlebars, Boyd headed into the bar, smoothing out his jacket and jeans. His hands were covered in a film of sweat and his heart beat a little faster as he entered the busy bar, looking around for her. The phone call had come as a surprise and he'd been panicking ever since he'd hung up, wondering what she wanted.

Brittany Phillips was sitting at a high-top table at the far end of the bar. Her brown hair was wavy and long, coming all the way down to her hips. She wore a pair of black jeans, a teal tank top, and a pair white Nikes. As Boyd had expected, she was still the most beautiful woman he'd ever had the privilege of seeing. He smiled to himself, relieved that she was actually there.

"Hey," Boyd said, sliding into the seat across from Brittany. She looked up from her phone and smiled, although her eyes were less inviting. Her annoyance was evident from the way she sat on the barstool and the way she was carrying herself.

"Hello," she said, taking a sip from the martini she was drinking. "It's nice to see you,"

"It's nice to see you too," Boyd smiled. He reached over and held her hand. "I'm really glad you called. I've been dying to talk to you. About everything,"

"Boyd..." Brittany began, shaking her head slowly. He stopped speaking and looked at her, realizing that this was not the type of conversation they were going to have. "That's not really why I called you here tonight,"

"Oh?" Boyd said, cocking his head slightly. "I just figured, I mean..."

"I know what you were probably thinking," she said. "But this isn't that,"

"What is it then?" Boyd asked, finding it hard to mask his disappointment.

"The office has security cameras," Brittany said, narrowing her eyes. "And I know what your bike looks and sounds like. I don't know why you've been coming around the office, but that has to stop, ok?"

"I never..." Boyd started to lie.

"Don't," Brittany snapped. "Don't lie to me right now, that's the last thing I want to hear out of your mouth,"

"Ok, ok," Boyd shook his head. "Just calm down, I didn't know why the hell you called me. This isn't what I was expecting,"

"Well, what were you expecting, Boyd?" Brittany asked. "I have moved on, I figured you were trying to do the same,"

"You... You moved on?" Boyd hated how pathetic he sounded. Brittany lowered her eyes, not wanting to see how much it was clearly hurting him to hear those words.

"I love you, Boyd," Brittany said quietly. " I never stopped loving you,"

"I love you too," Boyd replied, touching Brittany's knee. "I never stopped loving you, either. I told you I'd wait for you, I meant it,"

"I never asked you to do that. I told you right from the start, I didn't have a crystal ball. We broke up for a reason,"

"Because you said you needed time, you needed space..." Boyd argued back. "You said all these things making me think that it was a temporary break or something,"

"That was a year ago, Boyd," Brittany defended herself. "A year. You could've reached out if that's how you felt, but you never did. I honestly figured you had moved on,"

"You told me not to contact you!" Boyd yelled. "You said you needed space, I gave you space! You can't say one thing and want another, I'm not a mind reader, Brittany,"

"Boyd, I called to tell you I'm moving," Brittany said flatly. "I met a man and he and I are moving to Florida in a few weeks,"

Boyd felt like he'd been stabbed right in the heart. All this time, he'd been waiting, praying, yearning for the day that he and Brittany would get back together. They could finally do everything they had talked about when they were together. The trips to Europe, the perfect wedding, the home in the suburbs, the dog, maybe even the kids. The future that Boyd had envisioned for himself had been with Brittany, not without her. He couldn't even begin to process what she was saying. It didn't make sense, it wasn't fair. Brittany had been perfect for him, their issues as a couple hadn't been from anything that either of them had done, just Brittany's own emotional baggage that she'd carried with her.

They had met at a grocery store shortly before Boyd went away for his first deployment. Brittany had been short a few dollars for a purchase - a Starbucks Iced coffee and a bag of pretzels - and Boyd has covered the extra three dollars. Afterwards, they'd gotten to talking, and exchanged phone numbers. While nothing romantic happened for almost a year, they kept in contact while he was away. Boyd wrote to her every month from Afghanistan and she wrote back. He had enjoyed the correspondence and when he got home, Boyd finally asked her on a date. They started dating and it got fairly serious. But, they broke up when Boyd redeployed. The long distance proved to be too hard.

When Boyd's father had died, Brittany had come to the funeral, which sparked them trying to work things out until tragedy struck. Her father, Bill, had been murdered during an attempted carjacking. It was shocking, horrific, and devastating for Brittany. The murder had been a mistake as Boyd had been the target due to a mob debt from Boyd's father. Boyd had tracked down the men responsible and killed them for it, but the damage had been done. It didn't take long before Brittany ended things with him, stating that she could no longer prioritize a relationship. A few times since then, they'd exchanged texts, but nothing more than that. And all this time, Boyd had been holding out hope that Brittany would come around again. Now, that was seeming to have been a complete and utter waste of his time.

"Twice, Brittany," Boyd muttered. "We've been through this twice before and after everything this is how you want to end it? Who was there for you through everything? Who stayed up 'till two in the morning with you when you couldn't fall asleep? Who held your hair back when you cried so hard you'd throw up? Who was by your side through thick and through thin? I was, Brittany. I was always there for you, whenever you needed me, I was there,"

"And I love you for it, Boyd," Brittany answered, her eyes welling up. "My family and I appreciate everything you've done for me. I'll never be able to thank you the way you deserve. I know you might find it hard to believe, but I am sorry. Truly, I am sorry,"

"So that's it?" Boyd asked. "I mean, after all of that, this is it for us?"

"I guess it is," Brittany whispered, wiping her eyes.

Boyd felt his heart breaking all over again and instantly wished he hadn't gone to see her in the first place. For months, Boyd had imagined what it'd be like to see, to talk to Brittany again. But not once did he imagine this scenario playing out. He fought back the urge to start crying. The last thing he wanted was to cause a scene. Instead, he shook his head and remained quiet. Brittany gathered herself and stood up, looking at Boyd one last time.

"Goodbye, Boyd," she whispered before walking out of the bar.

Boyd stood straight ahead, gripping the bar top. His mind was racing and his stomach was turning. He felt like he wanted to throw up.

"Big fight?" a woman asked. Boyd turned to his left and saw the woman leaning on the bar top to his left. She turned and looked at Boyd.

"Yeah, uh, something like that, I guess," Boyd exhaled.

The woman was tall and slender, but very muscular. She wore a black dress and a matching pair of black high heels. Her hair was wavy and a dark blonde shade. Her eyes were dark and striking, but gave away a sense of sadness that Boyd picked up on. She was very beautiful, Boyd couldn't deny that. It took him a second glance, but he recognized her from the restaurant earlier that night.

"I've seen you before," Boyd said, pointing at her. "Tonight. At Perry's,"

"Yeah," she nodded, flashing a small smile. "Yeah, I was there,"

"With a man, if I remember correctly,"

"Don't worry about him," the woman rolled her eyes. "Nothing serious,"

"Are you following me or something?" Boyd asked, raising an eyebrow.

"I'm guilty of a lot of things, but stalking isn't one," the woman gave Boyd a knowing wink. "Must be a coincidence,"

"I don't believe in coincidences," Boyd muttered. He ordered a stiff drink from the bartender. The woman slid over to the seat that Brittany had previously been occupying.

"Put it on my tab," she said to the bartender,"

"Look, whatever it is you're looking for, I'm not interested," Boyd said firmly. "Now is not a good time,"

"Was she your wife or girlfriend?"

"Why would I tell you that?" he asked. The bartender set a drink down in front of Boyd and he downed the entire glass in one sip.

"Get him another," the woman said to the bartender.

"Are you trying to ply me with alcohol?" Boyd looked at her. "You're gonna be here all night, I come from a long history of alcoholics,"

"Just trying to be friendly," the woman said. "Looks like you could use one,"

"Girlfriend," Boyd relented. "Ex-girlfriend now, actually"

"Sorry about that," the woman said somberly. "Her loss,"

"Sure," Boyd muttered. He took the full glass from the bartender and sipped it.

The woman watched him carefully, almost like she was sizing him up in her head. Boyd noticed from her posture that she was probably military or law enforcement. No one else sat like that. After Boyd finished his drink, the woman slapped a few bills on the bar. She pushed off from the bar top and stood in front of Boyd. Stopping on a dime, the woman angled her head back over her shoulder. "I'm going for a walk. Care to join me?" she offered.

"No, I'm fine," Boyd shook his head. "Like I said, not really in the mood for someone to be friendly with,"

"I'm not expecting you to be friendly," the woman shrugged. "But I am good at listening,"

She started walking away, not looking back towards him again. Boyd wasn't the type of person to ever make conversation with strangers, outside of his job of course. He was still reeling from the conversation with Brittany and not really willing to dish all of those feelings onto someone whose name he didn't even know. But, for reasons that Boyd couldn't understand at that moment, he caught up to her. He stuck his hands in his pockets and they started walking out of the bar after her. Boyd saw two guys smoking cigarettes outside the bar and jogged over to them.

"Can I have one?" he asked, gesturing to the pack of Newports. The guy nodded and held the pack out to Boyd.

"Need a light?" he asked. Boyd nodded, popping the cigarette into his mouth. The guy tossed him his lighter and Boyd torched the smoke, inhaling the nicotine. He sighed in relief and handed the lighter back.

"Thanks,"

"No worries brother," the man said, turning back to his conversation with the other smoker.

Puffing on the cigarette, Boyd slowly walked toward the woman, cursing quietly under his breath. This wasn't like him. This was stupid. This was impulsive. Why was he doing it?

"What was the fight about, if you don't mind me asking," the woman looked up at Boyd and smiled more warmly than before. She looked pleased that he'd had a change of heart.

"Well," Boyd muttered, debating whether or not he wanted to unload everything on a total stranger. "We've known each other for a long time. We dated for a while and then it got serious. She lost her dad rather tragically and I don't know, just kind of changed her. Nothing either of us did, just grew apart, I suppose,"

"I feel that," the woman nodded in agreement. "I lost my dad too. That's a tough loss, even when you're an adult. I still don't think I'm really over it,"

"Same," Boyd scoffed, shaking his head. "My dads been gone about seven years now,"

"Wow, look at that," the woman said, clearly being sarcastic. "Looks like we got something in common,"

"You're military, aren't you?" Boyd asked, suddenly. The woman nodded, but was clearly caught off guard.

"How'd you know?"

"Just the way you carry yourself," Boyd shrugged. "You've got the rigid soldier posture, ya know?"

"Army?"

"Yes, ma'am," Boyd nodded, proudly. "You?"

"Army," she said with an equal amount of pride.

"Looks like we got more than one thing in common then," Boyd muttered. "Are you retired or just on leave?"

"Retired," she admitted. "I'm new to the area, I guess you could say. I've been working out in L.A. since I got out,"

"Long way from home," Boyd commented.

"Sometimes you just need a change of scenery," the woman shrugged. Her hand grazed Boyd's hand and felt himself flinch instinctively. He felt bad almost instantly, but it just felt weird, knowing that it wasn't Brittany's hand touching his.

"I think about leaving here all the time," Boyd admitted. He didn't know why he was opening that can of worms with her, but there were definite similarities between them. "Honestly, I just thought my life would've turned out a little bit different, ya know?"

"How do you mean?"

"When my dad died, I kind of got handed his company. I was never really sure I wanted to work there, which is why I went into the Army. But, I don't know, I guess I just felt like I owed him. Like I was responsible for it, if that makes sense,"

"It makes a lot of sense. But that sounds like a lot of pressure for you. What kind of company is it?"

"Steel construction," Boyd said. "We do buildings, warehouses, that sort of thing,"

"Sounds like a good job, though," the woman offered.

"It is, I can't complain. It was good to my family and it's been good to me so far," Boyd shrugged. He looked at the woman and gave her a small smile. "So, what do you do? If you don't mind me asking,"

"I don't mind you asking," she said, lowering her eyes a little bit. "Just as long as you don't mind me not answering,"

"I don't," Boyd chuckled. "But now I'm just gonna assume the worst,"

"Most guys, when I tell them what I do for a living, they have two reactions. Neither of them are good or make me feel good about myself. So..."

"Most guys, in all honesty, suck," Boyd responded, getting a laugh out of the woman.

They came to a stop on the bridge overlooking a narrow river. The woman bent over and leaned her arms on the railing, resting her head atop her arms. Boyd settled in next to her, standing close to her, but still apart enough so he didn't feel too uncomfortable about it. He was honestly surprised to be enjoying talking to her as much as he was.

"My dad was Delta Force," she admitted. "When I was growing up, we were always moving around. And after he died, my mom couldn't handle being in a house where she was constantly reminded of him, so we moved again. I never really felt like I had a home, you know?"

"I've lived in this state my whole life," Boyd offered. "And most of the time, it still doesn't feel like home. Too many painful memories here,"

"Yeah, except almost everywhere is like that for me," the woman said in a quiet, sad voice. "L.A. at least isn't tainted by that sort of thing. Everyone in that city is so fake you can kind of just be someone else,"

"Sounds nice," Boyd admitted. "Can't tell you how many times a day I think about leaving here, but I just can't,"

"You feel trapped?"

"In a way, I guess I do," Boyd shrugged. "I don't have any family left. There's nothing, aside from my job, that's holding me back,"

That was a lie. But Boyd didn't think a stranger would want to know about his secret double life. That wasn't good conversation etiquette and it was a great way to end up in jail. Most of the time, it was just easier for Boyd to pretend that the man who robbed trucks and banks was a different entity altogether.

"I'm sorry, I don't mean to complain," the woman suddenly said. "It's just exhausting sometimes, trying to smile when you really don't feel like smiling,"

"Trust me, I know," Boyd smiled. He wrapped his arm around the woman and gave her a small hug. It felt like the right thing to do at that moment.

"Two of a kind," she chuckled, leaning into him. "That's what we are,"

"Yeah, I guess we are," Boyd said.

"I'm Kayley, by the way," she said, looking up at him with her striking eyes.

"Boyd," Boyd introduced himself, smiling warmly at her. "Boyd McTiernan,"

Kayley leaned up and wrapped her arms around Boyd's neck, pulling him in closely and sealing her lips over his. She kissed him passionately, moaning into his mouth. Boyd hesitated at first, but fell into the kiss, throwing his arms around Kayley's waist. He kissed her back before pulling away.

"Woah," Boyd breathed dumbly.

"What?" Kayley smirked. Boyd shrugged, stuttering over his words.

"Nothing. Just a little quick, that's all," Boyd muttered, feigning embarrassment. Kayley smirked and giggled.

"With me it's always been now or never," she admitted, holding tightly onto Boyd's arms.

"Ever consider later?"

"Depends. How much later?"

"Tomorrow night? Same spot, on the bridge," Boyd offered. Kayley leaned up and kissed him on the cheek.

"I'll be there,"

\*\*\*\*

Wiping the sweat away from his brow, Boyd retied the green bandana around his forehead before putting his white hard hat back on. The hardhat was filthy from years of work, but was covered in a plethora of ironworker and union stickers; most journeymen adorned their hard hats with stickers of the company and trade that they worked in.

"Boyd, unhook that girder for me, would you?" the crane operator, Andy, said over the radio. Andy, who worked at McTiernan Steel Construction, was almost 40 feet below Boyd, in a Liebherr LTM 1055-3.2 mobile crane. To date, the crane had been one of Boyd's most expensive equipment purchases, but it was well worth it.

"Yeah, copy that," Boyd said back into the radio strapped to his shoulder. He unclasped his hook from the railing of the boom lift he was on, attaching it back to his safety harness. Per regulations, anyone working on site had to wear a safety harness and fall protection harness when going up in a boom lift or man lift. Given the nature of his work, Boyd was used to this.

He'd walked across many girders in his day. The first couple of times he'd been jittery, but now it was as easy to him as walking down the street. Expertly climbing over the railing of the lift and onto the girder, Boyd swung his cable around the beam and attached the cable to his harness, securing himself to the beam. Standing to his full height, Boyd walked toward the center of the girder where two straps were connected to the crane's hook. Instead of bending down, Boyd used his foot to dislodge the straps before unhooking them from the crane, unwrapping them from around the girder, and then hooking them back up.

"Alright, you're good," Boyd said into the radio.
"Coming down," Andy warned, slowly turning the crane's boom and hook away from Boyd.

For the last week, Boyd and one of his crews had been working in Bolingbrook, Illinois. A new warehouse was being constructed and McTiernan Steel had been hired to handle all of the ironwork involved. Typically, Boyd wasn't up in the air hanging girders on a day to day basis, but with a few guys out this week either on vacation or sick, he was filling in where needed. He didn't mind in the slightest, there was something extremely freeing and liberating about this job that he missed nowadays. Most of his days now consisted of responding to emails, meeting with potential customers, and checking on a few sites a week. Actually working a jobsite was something that he missed and was happy to do once again.

"Hey Boyd, you got a copy?" Patrick's voice came over the radio. Groaning more out of habit than actually annoyance, Boyd clicked on his radio.
"Yeah, go ahead," he said, slowly walking back toward his boom lift. "You got great timing, Patty,"
"I know, I see you tight-rope walking up there," Patrick answered.
"And you thought now was a good time to radio me?"
"Sorry, boss. I got the G.C. down here yelling and screaming, figured you're more equipped to handle it than I am,"

"What is he all bent out of shape about?" Boyd asked, unhooking from the girder and climbing back onto the platform of the lift.

"Trucks are here to start hauling away some of the extra dirt, but there's no operator. Some miscommunication with the excavating subs,"

"Tell him I'll be right there," Boyd groaned, now fully annoyed.

Not bothering to hook back into the lift, Boyd worked the controls and began lowering the boom back toward the ground. He could see Patrick standing by their trucks, getting an earful from a pair of men in jeans, matching collared shirts, and spotless white hard hats. Although Boyd couldn't see from that far away, he was willing to bet money that they had 'Project Manager' stickers on their hard hats. Once on the ground, Boyd stepped out of the lift, and hurried over toward Patrick, who looked to be simply ignoring the two men.

"What's up, Patty?" Boyd asked, walking up to his employee. Patrick looked over to the two men and gestured his hand toward Boyd.

"Here you go," Patrick grunted. He threw his hard hat on. "I'll fill in for ya,"

"Thanks," Boyd said, clapping Patrick on the shoulder. Jogging back over to the boom lift, Patrick got in the lift and began ascending up to where Boyd had been working. Boyd turned his attention to the two men.

"You're the superintendent?" the younger of the two asked. Boyd shook his head.

"Boyd McTiernan," he introduced. "I own McTiernan Steel. What can I do for you guys?"

"Do you know anything about why the excavators aren't here?" he asked, clearly not at all impressed by Boyd's claim of ownership.

"No, sir," Boyd shook his head. "I don't have anything to do with them. We're just here to do the iron work, that's it,"

"I can't believe this," he threw his hands in the air. "We're already a month behind schedule,"

"All due respect, that's not our fault," Boyd defended himself. "And chewing out my foreman is not going to make someone magically appear,"

"We've got at least six trucks waiting to get loaded up!" he yelled, gesturing to the trucks waiting outside the lot.

"Hold on," Boyd rolled his eyes.

Boyd looked around the jobsite and spotted an excavator parked next to a mountain of dirt that had been dug out for the foundation of the warehouse. He ran over to the excavator, a massive Link-Belt 490 X4, and climbed up to the cab. Thankfully, the door to the machine was unlocked. Looking around the cab, Boyd found the keys in the cupholder. Most contractors locked up their machines after each shift, but clearly someone had forgotten. Jumping down from the cab, Boyd jogged back over to the two Project Managers.

"Look, the keys are inside," Boyd said. "I'll load up the trucks, ok? Just start sending them in,"

"Can you do that?" the same guy asked. Boyd didn't necessarily think he was trying to be condescending, but Boyd still didn't appreciate the tone.

"You need to see my fucking operator card?" Boyd asked.

After getting no response from either man, Boyd spun on his heels and walked back toward the piece of equipment. Climbing back into the cab, Boyd fed the key into the ignition, and turned. The excavator roared to life. He slammed the door shut and got comfortable in the operator's seat. Turning the throttle up, Boyd released the parking brake, grabbed hold of the two joysticks, and swung the machine toward the pile of dirt. Opening up the bucket, Boyd drove the stick and boom down while curling the bucket, cutting through the dirt like butter.

The first dump truck pulled up alongside the excavator and Boyd immediately went to work loading it with material. It had been probably a full year since the last time Boyd operated an excavator, but it was just like riding a bike; once you knew how to, you pretty much always knew how to. He was definitely a little rusty, but after half a dozen scoops, Boyd felt much more comfortable. He loaded up the entire truck in about three minutes, evening out the material as best he could with the teeth of the bucket. Once he felt satisfied, Boyd honked the horn on his machine, signaling to the driver that he was good to go. As soon as the dump truck left, another filled its place, and Boyd repeated the process.

After the last truck pulled off the site, Boyd lowered the bucket and gently rested it on the ground before turning the throttle down and climbing out of the cab. With the excavator idling, Boyd sat down on the treads and ripped off his sunglasses, wiping the steam from the lenses on his shirt. Looking up, he saw the two project managers approaching him. This time, they looked much less agitated than before.

"Hey," the younger one said. "Sorry for being a jerk earlier. First project we're managing on our own, just don't want any major screw-ups, you know?"

"No hard feelings," Boyd shrugged. "I get it, trust me. If that ever happens again though, just let me know,"

"Thanks again, I appreciate it,"

"Don't mention it,"

Boyd checked his watch and decided it was close enough to quitting time for him. He climbed back into the excavator and shut the machine off, leaving the keys exactly where he'd found them. Walking back to his truck, Boyd began thinking about Kayley. Until now, he hadn't really given much thought to going back tonight to meet her. She probably hadn't been serious anyway. They hadn't even exchanged numbers or settled on a specific time. Although, it wasn't that far from his home in Naperville. Maybe it was worth a shot? At this point, anything to numb the pain over Brittany was worth a shot to him. Even though he hadn't actively been thinking about her during the day, there was a nagging pain in his heart, just a constant reminder that the woman he'd wanted to spend his entire life with, was gone.

"Any plans tonight, boss?" Patrick asked, throwing open the passenger door to his work rig. All McTiernan Steel work trucks were F-450 utility rigs or the much bigger International utility trucks, which required a CDL to drive; Patrick's was an F-450 and Boyd drove an International.

"Nah, nothing exciting," Boyd said. "How about you?"

"Dinner with the kids," Patrick smiled. "Looking forward to it,"

"Enjoy yourself, buddy," Boyd clapped him on the shoulder. Parked a few trucks away were another duo of McTiernan Steel Construction work trucks. One belonged to Andy and the other was being driven by the new guy, Noah Riordan. Boyd hadn't officially introduced himself to Noah and didn't feel like doing it right now. He made a mental note to officially meet the man tomorrow morning.

"How's the new guy?" Boyd asked Patrick, throwing his hard hat inside his rig.

"Solid," Patrick nodded with approval. "He's got an operator card too so I figured he'll be pretty versatile,"

"Good," Boyd was pleased to hear that. He climbed up into his truck and turned it on, rolling the windows down as soon as he could. "See you tomorrow,"

"You too, boss," Patrick waved. "Have a good night,"

Turning the radio on, Boyd slowly drove off the site and headed toward Interstate 355 to head home. He relaxed in his seat and just focused on driving. After a particularly long day, the calmness of driving home was extremely cathartic. Boyd tried to keep his mind clear, but no matter how hard he tried, thoughts of Kayley were never too far away. During the drive back to his house, Boyd made up his mind that he had nothing to lose. It was worth a shot.

****

Rumbling into the parking lot, Boyd piloted his motorcycle into a parking space as far away from the bar as he could. Dismounting the bike, Boyd slipped his helmet over the handle bar and followed the sidewalk, walking toward the center of the bridge. He smiled to himself when he saw Kayley, sitting alone on a park bench. Upon seeing him, she stood up and walked over to him.

"You came," she grinned. "I have to admit, I'm kind of surprise,"

"Me too," Boyd shrugged.

"I wasn't sure if I had scared you off,"

"Take a lot more than a kiss to scare me off," Boyd squeezed her hand as they set off walking the length of the bridge. "It's good to see you, I was wondering whether or not you'd actually be here,"

"I was wondering the same thing," Kayley admitted. "I was looking forward to this all day,"

"You know what? Me too," Boyd said, squeezing Kayley's hand.

All of this was new territory for Boyd. He and Brittany had been together for so long, he'd only ever been with one other woman in his life aside from her. The thought of not having a future with Brittany was painful, heartbreaking, and nauseating. But Boyd could not deny that things had gotten bad with Brittany. They had grown further and further apart from each other. He didn't really know why he had come to meet Kayley again, but something told him he would regret it if he didn't. And as they walked, hand in hand, Boyd genuinely felt happy. He felt content, just walking with her, talking with her. There was a feeling of comfort with her that he'd stopped feeling with Brittany.

"...And that was kind of the last straw for me. After that, I knew I needed a change of scenery," Kayley was saying. Boyd felt guilty for having zoned out and chuckled, trying to hide his embarrassment.

"I'm sorry," Boyd said. "I totally missed the first part of that. You've got my undivided attention now, sorry about that,"

"Don't worry," Kayley brushed it off. "I was just telling you about my last boyfriend and why I moved out to Chicago,"

"Oh, do tell," Boyd sneered. Kayley laughed and started her story over.

"Once I got out of the Army officially, I had settled in San Francisco for almost a year. It was the longest I'd ever really been in one place and I just loved it. I mean, it gets a bad reputation for obvious reasons, but I really liked living there," Kayley explained. "Anyway, this guy started buying me drinks one night while I was out at this bar. We started seeing each other casually, but it got kind of serious,"

"Serious?" Boyd raised an eyebrow.

"Yeah," Kayley nodded, a hint of pain in her eyes. "But he ended up cheating on me with his ex. So, that was the last straw for me and after that I was excited to leave San Fran. I headed down south to L.A. for a little bit and then came out here,"

"Well, that's his loss," Boyd said, stopping and spinning Kayley into him.

He ran his hand through her blonde locks and pulled her in for a tender kiss, rubbing her back as they came together for another intense kiss. Kayley pulled away and giggled, blushing hard as she looked up into Boyd's dark eyes.

"I haven't been kissed like that in a while," she admitted, throwing her arms around Boyd's neck.

"I'm hoping that can be a regular thing," Boyd smiled. Kayley giggled again and pulled out her phone.

"Give me your number, maybe we can grab a drink or dinner soon?" She handed her phone to Boyd. He quickly tapped his number into Kayley's phone and handed the device back.

"I'd love that," Boyd grinned. "Maybe you can finally tell me what it is you do for a living?"

"We'll see, won't we?" Kayley winked.

Boyd leaned in and pressed his lips against Kayley's, falling into another deep kiss.

# CHAPTER 13

# John

Lighting another cigarette, John hung his hand out the window of Klint's Dodge Charger, blowing a cloud of smoke as they drove through Chicago's Englewood neighborhood. A Glock 17 rested on John's leg, locked and loaded. Despite Klint's insistence that nothing would happen to them, John was less convinced. He'd heard the horror stories and seen the news reports about Englewood. No way he would take a drive through that neighborhood without a gun. Klint was as relaxed as John had ever seen him, which made no sense in and of itself.

"You sure you know where we're going?" John asked, touching the Glock on his leg.

"Yep," Klint nodded. "Just a little bit further, we're almost there,"

"This isn't something we do in broad daylight," John muttered, taking another pull from the cigarette. "We come back at night and..."

"Let me guess, kick the door in?" Klint finished John's thought. "Not everything requires your level of action, my friend. We're just going to have a friendly conversation with Mr. Jamal Williams. His brother, Trevon, was one of the guys who you shot in the apartment. Figure he might be able to give us some insight as to why McTiernan was meeting with them,"

"What makes you think this guy will know anything?" John asked.

"I don't know, but it's worth asking, don't you think?"

"Seems like a waste of time to me," John grunted, tossing his cigarette.

"Let's just see, ok?" Klint said, pulling over in front of a run down looking house.

Two men were sitting on the front porch, both of them were wearing red bandanas. Although Klint couldn't tell, he was positive they were both packing firearms. John sighed and tucked his Glock into his waistband, adjusting his shirt so it covered the grip of the weapon. Klint double checked his service pistol before slamming it back into the holster on his hip.

"Let's do this," Klint muttered, stepping out of his car. John followed suit, letting Klint lead the way up to the front porch. The two men were glaring at them as they approached, looking incredibly mean. "How're you doing, gentlemen?"

"Fine," the one spat. "Whatchu want?"

"Looking for a guy named Jamal Williams," Klint said, putting his hands in his pockets. "I have some questions to ask him about his brother,"

"We don't know any Jamal," the second man said instantly. Klint played along, for the time being.

"Well, maybe it's my mistake. This is the address I have on file for him," Klint said. "No one's in trouble here or anything, I just want to ask about his brother. He was killed recently,"

"Yeah, well, like we said," the first man said, glaring up at Klint and John. "That name don't ring a bell,"

Before Klint could try to come up with a clever response, he and John both heard a door slam from around the back of the house. Klint and John exchanged looks. The two men's eyes went wide and they jumped up, drawing their pistols. John whipped out his Glock and shot them both through the chest before they could even produce their weapons.

"Runner out back!" John said, moving up and over the bodies and kicking in the front door. "I'm in pursuit, go around and cut him off!"

"On it," Klint called back, running back toward his Charger. By now, a few nosy neighbors were peeking out of their front doors, not alarmed in the slightest, but just curious about the gunshots.

Bursting through the house into the backyard, John turned left, and saw a man hopping over a chain link fence. Without a second's hesitation, John took off after him, climbing up and over the fence as fast as he could. As soon as his feet hit the ground on the opposite side of the fence, John regretted being the one chasing after Jamal. His injuries, while better, still prevented him from being able to run and maneuver as well as he could. Jamal whirled his head around and saw John in pursuit. He reached into his waistband and drew a handgun, shooting wildly at John.

"Holy fuck!" John yelled, throwing himself on the ground as a bullet flew over his head. He rolled onto his back and got back up, squeezing off two rounds at Jamal before continuing to chase him. John felt his phone buzzing in his back pocket; he grabbed it with his free hand and saw Klint was calling him. Rolling his eyes, John slid his finger across the phone to answer.

"Yeah, what?" he barked, breathing heavily.
"What's with all the shooting?" Klint yelled. "I told you, I want to talk to this guy,"
"I ain't the one shooting!" John screamed back, hanging up. Stuffing his phone back in his pocket, John kept running after Jamal as fast as he could, bounding over another fence. Jamal darted around a house and headed left, back toward the road. He came to a stop and gripped his handgun with both hands, shooting a ten round barrage at John. Ducking for cover, John returned fire, narrowly missing hitting Jamal in the leg. He didn't want to kill the man if it could be avoided, but if Jamal didn't stop shooting at him soon, John wasn't going to hesitate to put him down. Permanently.

When his gun ran dry, Jamal turned and sprinted toward the street. Leaping up to his feet, John gave chase once again. He was gaining on Jamal, who was running out of steam. Even though John was injured and smoked like a chimney, his stamina was still better than the average person. Looking over his shoulder, Jamal was clearly surprised to see John so close behind him.

"Fuck you!" Jamal said, willing himself to go faster.

Suddenly, John stopped dead in his tracks. Jamal grinned for half a second, only to realize he'd ran right into the middle of the road. Klint's Dodge Charger screamed on the brakes, but still hit Jamal right in the side, sending the man flying down the road. Throwing the car in park, Klint jumped out of the vehicle, gun drawn. Jogging over to Jamal, John kept his gun trained on the man.

"Don't you move," John growled, sucking in air. "I got him, cuff him,"

"Cuffing," Klint muttered, holstering his weapon as he knelt over Jamal. He slipped Jamal's wrists into a pair of handcuffs. Klint took one look at Jamal's leg and knew it was broken. Once the adrenaline wore off, Jamal would be in a world of pain. "Listen to me, Jamal. Your leg is shattered. You need a hospital. I can get you to one immediately or I can wait until the pain becomes so mind-numbing you'll try and knock yourself out just to get some peace,"

"Fuck you," Jamal spat. "I ain't no snitch,"

"As you wish," Klint shook his head. "Grab him and let's move,"

Putting his gun away, John Shannon grabbed hold of Jamal's collar. The instant he started yanking Jamal to his feet, the man started screaming in pain. John delivered one strike to the side of Jamal's head, knocking him out cold. He dragged him back to Klint's Charger and stuffed him in the trunk.

\*\*\*\*

John threw a vicious right hook, connecting his fist with the side of Jamal's face. The hit snapped Jamal's head the one direction, but he came to a few moments later, spitting out a wad of blood on the ground in front of him. His hands were suspended above his head, hanging from a hook that was attached to the rafters. The building, now abandoned, had once been a meat packing facility. It was scheduled to be demolished in a few short months.

"I've been friendly, Jamal," Klint said, stepping in front of Jamal. "I've given you every opportunity to tell me what you know,"

"I keep telling you! I don't know nothin!" Jamal cried. "I don't know!"

"I find that incredibly hard to believe," Klint shook his head. "You and your brother were close, you worked together. Odds are he would've said something to you about who he was meeting or why he was meeting them,"

John Shannon stepped up behind Klint; his knuckles were dripping with blood, but he didn't even seem to notice. He made eye contact with Jamal and the man shuddered under the gaze of John. John cracked his knuckles menacingly, more for the effect than intent. He'd dished out enough of a beating on Jamal, John knew he was close to breaking.

"I'm going to ask you one last time, Jamal," Klint said. "Why was your brother at that apartment?"

"I don't fucking know!" Jamal yelled, spitting at Klint. Slowly, Klint wiped his face and lowered his gaze to Jamal's leg.

"John... Do it," Klint growled, staring Jamal right in his eyes. John grabbed a metal pipe from off the floor and swung it as hard as he could, hitting Jamal right above where his leg was broken. Jamal screamed in agony, thrashing around like a crazy man. He swore at the two men profusely, tears freefalling from his eyes.

John took a step back and tossed the pipe aside. Jamal was done. As soon as he calmed down, he'd talk; John could see it in his eyes. It took a few minutes, but Jamal finally got his breathing under control and stopped fighting his restraints so badly.

"Tre got hired to take someone out," Jamal wheezed, panting heavily. "Some white guy, he came here and offered a ton of money to take out some foreman at a construction company. Tasker... Tracker... Trasker! Yeah, Trasker. Craig Trasker. This guy wanted him dead. Badly,"

"Did you see the man who hired your brother?" Klint asked calmly. Jamal nodded feverishly.

"Yes, yeah, I saw him," Jamal said. Klint pulled out his cellphone and found the same picture of Boyd McTiernan from the McTiernan Steel Construction website. He flipped the phone around, letting Jamal see the picture.

"Is that him?"

"Yeah, yeah that's him," Jamal nodded. "That's definitely him. He smiled a lot, I thought that was weird,"

"Yo," John grabbed Klint by the shoulder and pulled him away from Jamal. Once they were far enough away, John spoke in a low voice. "He ain't lying. I've interrogated plenty of guys. He isn't lying,"

"I know," Klint agreed. "This doesn't make any sense,"

"Tell me about it," John grunted.

\*\*\*\*

After dropping Jamal off at the hospital, Klint and John doubled back to their safehouse. Neither of them wanted to include the others until they had a chance to talk over what they had just found out. They sat in two chairs, in the front office of the safehouse. Klint had Boyd's file opened on the table, next to a file on Craig Trasker.

"Ok, hear me out," Klint said, standing up. He began pacing back and forth as he continued talking through his theory. "If I'm capable of robbing banks and trucks and getting away with it, then I'd definitely think I'm capable of killing someone and making it disappear, right? I mean, I definitely wouldn't be afraid to do it myself, right? And then there's the fact that he hired them to kill Craig. Sure, Craig's not blood related, but that's still the man's family. It doesn't make sense,"

"We're clearly missing something, some piece to the puzzle," John offered. "I agree, it doesn't make any sense,"

"But then again, we don't know for sure that this is even the crew who hit the truck," Klint countered. All we know right now is that Boyd was definitely at that apartment, he definitely shot me, and he hired gangbangers to try and kill his uncle. But really, all we have is a testimony from an unreliable witness, at best,"

"We should talk to the others, see if they've come up with anything," John suggested.

"I'm not sure that's the best move," Klint responded. "Until we really know what's going on, we should act like these are still our guys. Now, we just have to find some solid connection between the truck job and our guys,"

"You're the detective," John shrugged, not in the mood to argue with Klint.

Klint began skimming through his files and reports again, looking for something that he might have overlooked the first time around. John was less patient and decided it was best if he did something to at least feel productive. Grabbing his car keys from the front office, John headed out of the warehouse and got into his Excursion. Once he was away, John dialed Kayley's number and connected his phone to his truck's BlueTooth system.

"Hello," Kayley answered, speaking in a quiet voice. It sounded like she was at a restaurant or something.

"Hey, it's me," John said. "I wanna meet and talk. Where are you?"

"I'm just walking into the Starbucks right off Michigan Avenue, right across from the Art Institute," Kayley said. John checked his watch to gauge how bad the traffic would be heading into the city.

"Ok, I'll be there as soon as I can," John said, making a quick right turn. "If you have to leave or something, just let me know. I can meet you wherever,"

"Ok, I'll let you know," Kayley said.

"See you soon," John hung up and drove toward the highway, knowing it would be the fastest route into the city.

****

Parking his truck on the street, John jumped out and pushed his sunglasses up on his forehead. He locked his truck and walked toward the Starbucks, not bothering to pay the parking meter. Since being in the city, he'd gotten several tickets for parking violations. Every time he just handed the ticket to Klint, who passed it onto the Mayor, and it disappeared. There were definite benefits to being in the line of work John was in. He spotted Kayley from the street; she was sitting at a table up against the window. John didn't bother with ordering anything, he sat down across from her and set his sunglasses on the table.

"You ok?" he asked.

"I am," Kayley nodded.

"How's the mark going?"

"Good," Kayley said quickly. "Made contact,"

"Ok, good," John nodded, giving Kayely a curious look. She looked reserved, like she was being careful or cautious not to say the wrong thing. "Listen, I just wanted to fill you in on a few things.

Klint doesn't want to tell everyone yet for some reason, but you're the one who's getting close to this guy. You should know,"

"Ok, what's up?"

"That meeting we interrupted, Boyd had hired those to kill Craig Trasker. He put a hit out on his uncle," John explained. "Klint and I had a conversation with one of the dead guy's brothers. He was pretty positive about that, I guess Boyd had gone to them in person,"

"Really?" Kayley asked, surprised to hear that. "But... But that doesn't really make sense. Aren't Boyd and Craig supposed to be partners or something?"

"Well, yeah," John shrugged. "But we can't prove that they had anything to do with the truck job yet. Klint's looking for some kind of a connection between the two, but all we have so far is that Boyd put a hit on his uncle,"

"Why are you telling me this?" Kayley asked. "Especially if Klint didn't want us to know yet,"

"Because, if you're getting close to this guy, you need to have all the information," John said. "You need to be careful,"

"John, I can handle myself," Kayley said. John did a double take, her tone throwing him off.

"Hey, I wasn't trying to insinuate anything," he responded. "I was just letting you know,"

"I appreciate that, John," Kayley said, although John couldn't tell if that was genuine or sarcastic.

"What's your problem?" John snapped. Kayley glared at him.

"Nothing," she said, grabbing her coffee and standing up. "See you later,"

Kayley walked out of the coffee shop, put her sunglasses over her eyes, and crossed the street toward the Art Institute. John watched her disappear into the gardens around the museum, utterly confused about what the hell had just happened. Something was up with Kayley and that wasn't a good sign. Maybe he shouldn't have told her, but he wanted her to be careful. As much as he didn't want to, John cared about her; at least enough to be concerned about her getting close to a man who'd put a hit on his own family. It didn't matter if Klint didn't agree with him, John was more concerned with keeping people safe than abiding by Klint's rules. But something was bothering Kayley. And that made John nervous. If she was already having doubts about deceiving Boyd or anything of that nature, she was putting herself in serious danger.

# CHAPTER 14

# Klint

Klint was startled awake and shot up in bed, reaching for a gun on the nightstand that wasn't there. He was sweating and his heart was beating fast, sounding like a drum in his chest. It took a few moments for Klint to realize he was in bed and not in the middle of whatever scenario he'd been dreaming of. Swinging his legs around, he planted his feet on the ground and rested his head in his hands.

"Jesus," Klint breathed to himself, finally getting his heart rate back to normal. This was the fifth time in about two weeks that Klint had woken up like that; heart racing and sweating, like he'd been in a fight. Every once in a while, Klint had had issues with sleeping, but he attributed that more to worrying about his daughter than anything else. He still worried about her, what parent didn't worry about their kid? Over the years, Klint had seen veteran cops go through rough periods of insomnia, so he wasn't overly worried about it. It was just part of the job.

Klint felt a hand touch his shoulder and he smiled. He reached up and gently touched her hand. Kelly Hart wrapped her arms around his chest, resting her head on his shoulder. She kissed his neck a few times before going back to resting on him.

"Are you ok?" she whispered in a sleepy voice. Klint squeezed one of her hands.

"I'm ok. Sorry to wake you," he said. "I'm gonna go get some water, I'll be right back,"

"Hurry back," Kelly said, laying back down in bed.

Using his phone for light to navigate through the house, Klint grabbed a cup from Kelly's cabinet, filled it with water, and took a seat at the kitchen island. Sipping his water, Klint opened his phone and sent a quick text to his daughter, asking her to get dinner later tonight. It was 3:18 in the morning, he doubted she'd be up for at least another seven or eight hours, but he still felt better having texted her. With her class schedule being so busy now, Klint hadn't really talked to her in a few days. Whatever was bothering him subconsciously, Klint hoped a dinner with his daughter would make him feel better.

Not wanting to open up his email or anything work related, Klint grabbed his water and went back to the bedroom. Setting his phone and water on the nightstand, Klint slid back into bed next to Kelly. She rolled over and snuggled in next to him.

"Better?" she asked, opening her eyes a little bit. Klint nodded and kissed her forehead.

"Yeah, I'm ok," Klint whispered. "Sorry I woke you, didn't mean to,"

"Don't worry about it, Klint," Kelly shook her head. "I don't really sleep that well anymore, anyway,"

"Since Danny?" Klint asked.

"Yeah," Kelly mumbled. "I just keep having these weird dreams about him. I don't know, maybe that sounds crazy,"

"Not crazy at all," Klint said, wrapping his arms around Kelly. "That's a pretty common sign of trauma and grief, trust me,"

"You and I have never really talked about that sort of thing, you know? I mean, does it ever bother you? All the stuff you've seen?"

"There's only one instance that sticks with me, if I'm being honest," Klint said, closing his eyes and taking a deep breath. He'd been asked that question before by friends, acquaintances, and even a CPD psychiatrist. Usually, he just lied. But Kelly wasn't someone he could ever lie to, nor would he want to. She was the first person he'd really felt something for since his daughter's mother, lying to her right off the bat wasn't a good idea, and he knew that. Their personal relationship was already going to be complicated enough given their professional relationship.

"You don't have to tell me, I'm not prying," Kelly said after Klint didn't say anything else. "I was just kind of wondering,"

"When I first became a detective, my partner was this guy who just looked like he was right out of an action movie. Bald head, muscles, tattoos, the whole nine yards. He was a freakin' genius detective and taught me basically everything I know about solving cases. We got pretty close, I got to know his wife and his three sons to the point where they called me 'Uncle Klint'. My daughter and the two younger boys were in school together, so they were just, like, who we hung out with, right?"

"Ok," Kelly said, nodding along. She fought back the urge to yawn, not because she was bored by the conversation, but even she didn't get up before four in the morning if she could help it.

"One night, we get called to a homicide. We're walking up to this alley and I see the looks on some of the other first responder's faces and I can just tell it's something awful. And it was... it's this poor girl, maybe 15 or 16. It's bad... really bad. My partner gets all quiet and doesn't say much and a few hours later or whenever we got back into the car, he just broke down. Started crying like he'd lost his own child. I don't know, just hit him different than some of the other cases we worked,"

"Anyway, a month later to the date, there's another girl. Same age frame, same basic crime, body dumped in an alley. The similarities were there, so we decide we've got a serial killer," Klint paused, taking a deep breath before continuing. "Three months and three victims later, we finally found the sick sonofabitch. After we arrested him, my partner was looking over the case file and spotted some piece of evidence or something... to this day, I don't know what it was that set him off. But, I guess he overlooked something with the first victim. Or just didn't see it..."

"My god," Kelly muttered.

"Couple days later, he took his pistol and shot himself in his squad car. And I was one of the first guys on the scene," Klint spoke in a voice that was barely audible.

Kelly sat up in bed and looked at Klint, her eyes damp. She held his hand and hugged him, not having the right words at that moment, not that there were any words that would make Klint feel better.

"But yeah..." Klint said sadly. "That one sticks with me. Never took another partner after that, either,"

"I'm so sorry, Klint," Kelly shook her head. "I can't even imagine,"

"You know, I've never really told anyone about that," Klint said, looking at Kelly and smiling at her. "What're you doing, having me confess my deep, dark secrets to you?"

"Well, you've got to confess them to someone," Kelly said, smiling back at him.

"Can I ask you something?" Klint asked, looking at her seriously.

"Of course," Kelly nodded.

"Would you like to have dinner with me and my daughter tonight? Assuming she's available..."

"Klint, are you serious?" Kelly asked, flattered by the invite.

"Well, yeah," Klint said, feeling a little embarrassed now. "I want you to meet her,"

"I would love to," Kelly said. She pressed her lips against his, kissing him passionately. Klint grabbed the back of Kelly's neck and kissed her back, pulling her into him.

"You want to go back to bed?" Kelly asked, breaking away from the kiss. She gave Klint a knowing look.

"No chance I'll go back to sleep now," he said, winking at her.

"Good," Kelly grinned, kissing him once again. Klint wrapped his arm around her body and flipped her onto her back, immediately going for her neck. She breathed heavily and dug her nails into his back.

\*\*\*\*

With the Mayor of Chicago on his arm, Klint Kavanuagh followed the hostess to their table at Eddie V's, a premier seafood and steak restaurant located right on Michigan Avenue. It was a bit more extravagant than Klint had intended, Kelly had insisted that Klint and his daughter deserved a nice meal. They had gotten there a few minutes before their scheduled reservation, wanting to be there before Kara.

As they sat down at their table, Klint and Kelly received a few knowing looks from the patrons. Obviously, Kelly was known by the people of the city, and seeing her in public like that was a bit strange for them. As was procedure, there were a squad of bodyguards outside the restaurant in various vehicles, ready to intervene if needed. Normally, she'd be escorted by her security team, but given that Klint was a cop, they allowed her the freedom to have a more private dinner.

"I hope this is ok," Kelly said, touching Klint's hand.

"It's perfect," Klint smiled. "I'm excited for you to meet her. Definitely a little nervous, but more excited,"

"Why are you nervous?" Kelly asked, laughing.

"She's never met anyone I've been dating! I'm nervous!"

"Oh, so we're dating?" Kelly asked, cocking her head at Klint. "Is that what we're calling it?"

"We can call it whatever you want," Klint answered, giving her hand a small squeeze. "I'm just glad that whatever this is, is finally happening,"

"Me too," Kelly blushed a little. "And yes, I think we're dating,"

"Dating it is then," Klint nodded, smiling ear to ear.

They were about to lean in for a kiss, but Klint spotted Kara walking toward them, being escorted by the hostess. He stood up and grinned as Kara approached, delighted to see her. Following suit, Kelly stood up too, straightening out her jacket.

"Hi Dad!" Kara said excitedly, giving Klint a big hug. "Sorry I'm late, class ran long, and then I had trouble getting an Uber back home, and then Koda was being crazy. But here I am!"

"Oh, wow, ok," Klint said, laughing. "That's a lot,"

"Sorry, sorry," Kara rolled her eyes. "My bad,"

"It's good to see you," Klint smiled. He turned and gestured to Kelly. "Kara, this is Kelly. Kelly, this is my daughter, Kara,"

"It's so nice to finally meet you," Kelly said with a warm smile, offering Kara her hand. "Your dad has told me so much about you,"

"Very nice to meet you too," Kara said, respectfully shaking Kelly's hand. The three of them sat down around the table. "I'm glad this is finally happening,"

"What do you mean?" Kelly asked, sipping her glass of water. Kara gave her dad a cheeky smile.

"Well, I've been poking my dad for a while to ask you out," Kara admitted. Klint cleared his throat, looking very interested in the menu all of a sudden. "I'm glad he finally did,"

"Really?" Kelly asked, flattered by Kara's comments. Kara nodded.

"I couldn't vote when you ran for Mayor, but I totally would have," Kara said.

"Thank you," Kelly smiled, laughing a little. "That's very sweet of you,"

"I didn't tell her to say any of that," Klint commented, getting a laugh out of Kara and Kelly.

They ordered drinks and dinner, chatting while they waited. For the most part, the conversation was between Kara and Kelly, which Klint was happy to see. He could tell when Kara was putting on a smile for his sake versus when she was genuinely enjoying herself and the company. Fortunately and much to his pleasure, Kara appeared to be having a good time. He'd definitely been nervous to introduce her to Kelly. If he was going to seriously consider a long term relationship with someone, it was imperative that Kara liked the woman, and vice-versa.

Kara and Kelly talked about DePaul, Kara's classes, dogs, and the latest celebrity gossip that Klint was totally out of the loop on. It was kind of funny for Klint to see an entirely new side of Kelly that he'd never been privy to before tonight. She wasn't Mayor Kelly Hart at dinner, she was just Kelly. She made a few inappropriate jokes, gave Kara dating advice for her and her boyfriend, which Kara actually seemed to appreciate.

Klint often tried not to think about it, but he knew that Kara had missed out by not having her mother around. He was a good dad and he knew that, but a young girl still needed her mother. It wasn't fair that Kara had been dealt an unlucky hand, she'd done nothing to deserve it. Actually, Klint didn't really blame Kara's mother either. They were kids when she'd been born, she didn't know any better. Since then, Klint had never tried to find her or reach out to her. Maybe he should've, but he'd raised Kara all by himself without her help. It also wasn't fair for her to come into Kara's life at such a crucial stage in her life. If Kara ever wanted to meet her mother, Klint would encourage her to do so. But until Kara brought it up, Klint would leave it alone.

"So, are we getting dessert?" Kelly asked, finishing off her last bit of Norwegian Salmon.

"Oh, I like her," Kara said, nudging her dad's arm. Kara looked back at Kelly. "I certainly hope we're getting dessert,"

"It's the best part of any meal, in my opinion," Kelly shrugged. "What sounds good?"

Kara and Kelly began discussing the handful of dessert options, debating the pros and cons of each. Sitting back in his chair, Klint chuckled to himself, watching them get so excited about dessert.

The waiter came back and they ordered, anxiously awaiting their sweets. Before dessert came, Kelly excused herself, and headed to the bathroom; leaving Klint and Kara alone for a few minutes. As soon as Kelly was out of earshot, Kara moved her chair closer to her dad.

"I like her, Dad," Kara said seriously. "She has my approval. I like her a lot,"

"Kara…" Klint smiled at his daughter. "I can't tell you how happy I am to hear that,"

"You're the best dad I could've ever asked for," Kara continued. "And I mean that. I want you to be happy, you deserve to be happy,"

"I am happy," Klint responded. Kara gave him a sad look.

"I mean *happy*, dad. You can be selfish for once in your life. She really likes you, I can tell," Kara said. "Don't miss out on something like that. You deserve to have someone. I'm not always going to be around and I hate the thought of you being alone. I don't want you to be alone forever, ok?"

"Understood," Klint said quietly, his daughter's words echoing in his ears.

\*\*\*\*

Tossing his shirt on the chair in the corner of Kelly's room, Klint slid into bed next to her and threw the blankets over them. Kelly sighed happily and moved over toward Klint, resting her head on his chest. She looked up at him and kissed his cheek.

"Kara is great," she said. "Thank you for letting me meet her. That really means a lot to me,"

"Thank you for being so great tonight," Klint said. "She really liked you,"

"I'm glad," Kelly grinned. "We'll have to do that again some-time,"

"I think that'd be great,"

"Get some rest, Klint," Kelly whispered, closing her eyes. "Good-night, babe,"

"Goodnight, Kell,"

# CHAPTER 15

# Boyd

The establishment was the definition of a dive bar; a hole in the wall that drew in a loyal customer base, but wasn't a destination for anyone. Blink and you miss it. It was the kind of place that didn't attract any attention, which is why Rob and Boyd always met there. They were both fairly certain that the bartender, Big Richie, knew what they were up to, but he'd never talk. Big Richie had been around the block more than enough times; he'd never say a word. Plus, Rob and Boyd were loyal customers and they always tipped well.

They sat in the corner of the dimly lit bar, a pair of Modelos on the small bar table in between them. Boyd had just come from work, still wearing his dirty work boots, pants, and Hi-Vis jacket. Rob had his iPad out on the table, showing Boyd a route through Chicago that was marked in a blue line.

"It's a relatively simple job," Rob explained. He pointed to two different locations on the route. "Best bet would be to hit them here or here. It won't require much in terms of equipment and gear. Just pull up alongside them, jump out, and do your thing,"

"What's the expected haul?" Boyd asked, taking a sip of his Modelo. Rob pushed his glasses up on his nose.

"$1.7 or $1.8 million. Maybe $2 million at the most," Rob said grimly. Boyd exhaled and lowered his head, shaking it a few times in clear disappointment.

"That's not enough, man," Boyd muttered. "Ain't worth it for two mil. By the time I cut in the guys, I'll walk away with barely a million,"

"I know, I know,"

"I need at least 4.5 or 5 for it to be worth it," Boyd took another sip of beer. "Anything less than that isn't enough to make a dent and it ain't worth the risk,"

"Trust me, I'm aware," Rob responded. He put his iPad back in his backpack. "Trucks don't normally carry anything more than two, though. It was a one-off last time, a truck having that much cash on it. Ever since those boys in Los Angeles jacked a truck for a few hundred million, regulations stopped letting the truck companies move anything close to that. Truth is, they never should've been moving that much in the first place,"

"So, what now? Boyd asked. "I mean, do we just risk it and do a bank?"

"Banks are tricky," Rob scratched his chin. "So many variables and there's just no guarantee you'll walk away with a significant enough payout. With everything being so digitized nowadays, the amount of physical cash a bank will have on site is going to be a lot less than we want. I would not recommend a bank,"

"Any other ideas?"

"Well, there are plenty of other ways to get money. Cash isn't the only currency out there," Rob said ominously.

"Like what?" Boyd asked, a little intrigued.

"We're in Chicago, man," Rob gestured around them with his hand. "Jewelry stores, galleries, concert halls, stadiums. All of those places have something you can take,"

Boyd narrowed his eyes on Rob, a wry smile cracking through his usual look of melancholy. Rob was dropping subtle, but noticeable hints. He had something for Boyd, but was testing the waters on whether or not Boyd would take the job. Professionally, Rob managed money for professional athletes, actors, singers, and other celebrities; he currently had about two dozen current clients and a small office staff. But on the side, Rob had put together jobs for certain people when they needed money. He never got involved with actually executing the heists, but he had a knack for knowing when and where to hit. Every single job that Boyd and his crew had pulled off had been planned thoroughly by Rob, with some help from Boyd. Aside from Boyd, there was only one other crew that Rob planned jobs for anymore and they were based out in New York.

"You got something in the works?" Boyd asked.

"I might," Rob flashed a smile. "I'm still looking into that thing you showed me, that's going to take more time. But, for the time being, I have an option,"

"Let's hear it,"

"Marshall Pierce & Co," Rob said. "High end jewelry store on the Magnificent Mile,"

"Jewelry, huh?" Boyd commented. Rob nodded.

"If you can clean the place out..." Rob began. "Looking at upwards of five million. Easily. I'd say closer to six or seven, by my estimates,"

"Holy cow," Boyd breathed, leaning back on the barstool. "That would make a dent,"

"We're still going to need at least one or two more to clear every-thing you owe those motherfuckers, but this is a good way to get ahead," Rob said.

"Alright, walk me through it,"

"A store of this caliber is going to have its own security. Most likely armed with at least mace and a taser, but probably a gun. Expect one or two guards, nothing more than that. The display cases are going to be where the real showpieces are at and they should be relatively easy to smash through. You smash the cases and take the loot. I'd check some of the cabinets too, but those might be locked. You'll need a staff member to open them," Rob explained to Boyd, keeping his voice extremely low.

"That doesn't sound too hard," Boyd responded, keeping his tone even and his facial expressions neutral.

"It won't be for you and your crew," Rob continued. "The problem is the escape route. Magnificent Mile is a tough location and your best chance at escaping clean is either disappearing into the city somewhere or getting to the highway as fast as possible. The response time will be only a few minutes, stores like that will have silent alarms. With how congested the city can be, you're not going to want to use a truck or car as a getaway. I recommend motor-cycles, something that's fast, durable, and maneuverable. The slant bikes like the one you have might be a good bet, but I'd take a look at an off-road or motocross bike,"

"Shit, you're serious about this," Boyd muttered. Rob smiled and shrugged.

"As serious as I'll ever be," he gulped down the rest of his beer and thumbed out a few bills, slapping them on the table. "This round is on me. Let me know what you're thinking in a few days. If you want the job, it's yours,"

"Talk to you soon, bro," Boyd said.

Rob left and a few minutes later, Boyd left as well, but not before dropping a twenty in Big Richie's tip jar on the bar. The big man gave him a nod as Boyd walked out. He didn't need a few days to think about it, his mind was already made up. The debt hanging over his head was like constantly carrying around a 200-pound bag; burdening, exhausting, and utterly annoying. It had been years since his father had passed away, but Boyd was still cleaning up the messes he left behind, the debt being the largest. Rob was thorough and detail-oriented. If he said this was a good score, it was a good score. But Boyd wanted to get eyes on the place himself, visualize everything first, before he talked to Rob and his crew. Luckily for him, he had a good excuse to go and spend some time in the city.

\*\*\*\*

He sat at a small table at Cafe on Oak, which was a part of The Drake Hotel on the corner of Michigan and Walton. Instead of his normal workwear, Boyd wore a pair of clean jeans, dress shoes, and a white button down. Cafe on Oak was bustling with people this morning, the majority of which were staying customers at The Drake. Typically, Boyd didn't venture this far into the city. The snooty, arrogant attitude of most people around the Magnificent Mile bothered him immensely. They were the kind of people who'd turn their nose up at him if they saw him in his work gear, but wearing the right attire, no one batted an eye. To anyone else, Boyd looked like a regular old schmuck who belonged there.

No, Cafe on Oak was not his ideal spot for a breakfast date, especially on a Saturday morning. The drive from his home into the city hadn't been too bad, but just long enough for him to need a second cup of coffee while he waited. But, the little cafe admittedly offered a good spread of food, and was close for Kayley to get to. There was the added benefit that it was directly across the street from the jewelry store. For those reasons, the drive on one of his two precious days off was worth it.

While sitting at the table waiting for Kayley, Boyd tried not to think about the fact that this was his first 'first date' in a very long time. He wasn't nervous about it, just feeling out of practice. This whole thing with Kayley had come out of nowhere, but it had also come a great time. Not that it was the only reason he was interested in her, but keeping his mind off from his ex was a big bonus. Kayley was cool, she was beautiful, she was smart, and she seemed to be genuine with him. They'd been texting for a few weeks now and he had already started to get those excited butterflies whenever he saw his phone light up with a notification from her. It was a nice feeling to have again. Boyd had always been somewhat of a hopeless romantic, wanting nothing more than to fall in love, and live out his days with his person.

Looking around the restaurant, Boyd grinned when he saw Kayley approaching the table. He looked her up and down as she walked toward him, a beautiful smile on her face. Kayley wore a pair of white high-tops, a plaid mini-skirt, and a black blouse. Boyd stood up, setting his napkin on the table.

"Good morning," Boyd said, still smiling at her. Kayley returned the smile and gave Boyd a hug, kissing his cheek as well.

"Good morning to you, too," Kayley said. Boyd tried to hide the fact that he was blushing by scratching the side of his face. He and Kayley sat down at their table.

"You look beautiful," Boyd complimented. "I hope that's ok to say,"

"Of course that's ok to say," Kayley laughed. "Thank you, that's very sweet of you. You look very handsome as well,"

"Every once in a while I can clean up," Boyd shrugged. "Just don't get used to it,"

"Noted," Kayley smiled, taking a look at the menu. "So, what do you get from here?"

"No clue," Boyd said. "It's my first time here,"

"Really?" Kayley asked. "I've only been in town a month and I've been here three times already. I love it,"

"You'll have to order for me then,"

"I can definitely do that," Kayley nodded. She set her menu down and looked at Boyd, smiling in a way that Boyd couldn't quite pick up on. "I'm glad we're doing this," she said in a quiet voice, looking down at her lap.

It was almost like she was ashamed or embarrassed that she was happy to be there, but Boyd couldn't really tell. She was as un-readable as someone could be. As far as poker faces went, hers was the best he'd ever seen. Kayley was smiling and looked happy. But he kept noticing her eyes. There was a look in her eyes. He couldn't decipher if it was guilt, sadness, or hesitation. Maybe a combination of the three?

"Me too," Boyd said, reaching across the table with an open hand. Kayley put her hand in Boyd's, blushing as he squeezed it. "I like hanging out with you,"

"Yeah?"

"Oh yeah," Boyd winked. He paused for a second and then continued. "I don't know, maybe that's corny to say, but I do. I enjoy talking to you,"

"You know, Boyd," Kayley said. "I enjoy talking to you too,"

They had a relatively uneventful breakfast, but that wasn't a bad thing at all. Boyd loved just how natural and easy it was for them to talk to each other. Kayley and him swapped military stories from their early years living in the barracks and traded a few stories about particular missions they were a part of. For someone who was as naturally attractive as Kayley, she was quite the badass, and Boyd found that that made her a million times more attractive in his mind. Her self-confidence and self-sufficiency were extremely desirable qualities. She asked him technical questions about his job and he answered in a way that was easy to understand for someone who wasn't familiar with steel erecting.

"Ok, I have to ask," Boyd said. "You certainly don't have to answer if you don't want to, but what do you do for a living? You were very cryptic about it last time,"

Kayley sighed audibly and wiped the corner of her mouth with her napkin. Boyd had no trouble reading the expression on her face now. Hesitation. She clearly didn't want to tell him, but Boyd couldn't imagine why not.

"You don't have to tell me," Boyd quickly added. "I don't care, it's not gonna change my opinion of you,"

"You can't say that," Kayley muttered. She closed her eyes for a moment, opening them back up, and locking her gaze on Boyd. "After I got out of the Army, I had trouble finding a job. I did a few jobs like waitressing and bartending, but it was barely enough to pay the bills. I had a friend who'd gotten into the adult entertainment industry and she gave me a referral to a photographer and an agent. I did a few photoshoots for them and then moved into doing some videos. In less than a year, I became a partner at that same talent agency. I handle bookings, dealing with the models, and setting up locations for shoots,"

Boyd looked at her for a second with an admittedly dumb look on his face. He was slightly confused why she'd been so hesitant to tell him that, but he was also surprised. When she'd been cagey about telling him what she did for a living, he hadn't even thought of 'adult film star' as a possibility. For a second, Boyd debated whether or not that was a deal breaker for him. This was only their first date, there was absolutely nothing that said Boyd had any obligation to Kayley, or to a relationship with her. He didn't exactly love that that was what she did for a living.

He was formulating a response in his head when it hit him. Kayley was being honest. She was being vulnerable. And she was letting him in on a part of her life that she'd been nervous to share with him. Boyd was hiding a lot from her. She didn't know he was a criminal, a thief, a marauder. It would be a cold day in hell before he confessed to her what he really was. That made him reconsider, though. Who was he to judge someone for what they did to earn money? He certainly didn't have any moral high ground to stand on.

"Ok, I'm sorry, you gotta say something," Kayley finally said, uncomfortable with the silence at the table. "If it's an issue, just say it, and we can part ways like nothing ever happened,"

"No, no, no," Boyd shook his head. "I'm sorry, I was just trying to think of what to say. No, it's not an issue. I'm just a little surprised is all. The way you made it sound, I would've thought you were a drug dealer or something *real* bad like that,"

"No drugs over here," Kayley said. "Sorry to disappoint,"

"Hey," Boyd lowered his voice and leaned across the table. He took Kayley's hands with his own. "It's not an issue, I promise. I don't care. I like talking to you and, you know, I want to see you again,"

"Are you sure?"

"Of course I am," Boyd smiled. Kayley blushed before standing up a little in order to lean over the table and kiss Boyd on the lips.

"Good, I'm glad," Kayley kissed him one more time. "I want to see you again, too,"

"How about one night this week, we have dinner?" Boyd suggested.

"That sounds good to me," Kayley agreed. "Listen, I have a call later on today, but care to walk around for a while? I understand if you don't want to, but I could definitely do some window shopping..."

"Kayley, that sounds wonderful," Boyd agreed.

****

Kayley insisted she didn't need a ride back to her place, instead opting to walk back. Boyd offered to walk back with her, but secretly hoped she wouldn't accept; not for any other reason than his truck was parked at The Drake and he truly didn't want to have to walk all the way back.

"I promise I'm fine," Kayley said with a soft smile. "Don't worry about me, I'll be fine,"

"Well, just let me know when you're back safely?"

"I can do that," Kayley nodded. "I appreciate the concern,"

"Sorry, force of habit," Boyd shrugged. "Thanks again for today, I had a great time,"

"Me too," Kayley said, spinning around in front of Boyd. He leaned down and kissed her, holding onto her waist as he did.

"Have a good rest of your day, Ms. Kayley," Boyd grinned.

"You too," Kayley couldn't stop smiling. "I'll text you,"

Boyd watched her go and waited until she disappeared around the next block before doubling back toward the jewelry store. He subtly gazed through the window, seeing a few customers and plenty of staff. Confidently, Boyd strode inside the jewelry store, immediately taking in the entrance and surroundings. There was a guard on his left side wearing an earpiece. Although it wasn't being openly holstered, Boyd assumed he had a weapon of some sort on his person. He nodded respectfully at the guard and began browsing the exquisite selection of jewelry. Within minutes, a saleswoman was strutting toward him, her heels clicking off the marble floors.

"Hi! Welcome to Marshall and Pierce, what can I help you find today?" she asked, beaming at Boyd. He read her name tag.

"Hello, Dani," Boyd said, as pleasantly as he could. He came up with an easy and quick lie. "I'm looking for something for my woman, but have absolutely no idea what to buy,"

"Well, you've come to the right place," Dani said. "Come on, let's take a look around,"

Regrettably, Boyd spent the next half hour looking at jewelry pieces that were way too expensive for him to even be in the same vicinity. He managed to smooth talk his way out of putting a down payment on anything, promising to return later that week, and actually buy something; Dani gave him her business card. As soon as Boyd was outside, he pulled out his phone and dialed a number.

"Yeah?" Rob answered immediately.

"Send me the plans," Boyd said. "I want the job,"
"That's what I like to hear,"

# CHAPTER 16

# Kayley

Kayley McKenna tossed and turned in bed, getting more and more annoyed with each passing second that she was unable to find sleep. She checked her phone, refreshed her Instagram feed, and tried to fall back asleep. Fifteen minutes later, she repeated the process. Finally, she gave up trying to get any more sleep and went into the living room of her hotel room. Dropping down on the couch, she turned on the TV, lowered the volume, and was pleased to find one of the James Bond movies on. She'd grown up loving the movies, having fond memories of watching them with her entire family.

Since she'd been in Chicago, Kayley had been staying in a Luxury Suite at The Wit Chicago. The room was being comped by the Mayor's office, per the arrangement she'd made with Klint when he'd first pitched the idea to her about joining the team. She had known there would be a certain aspect of the job that involved using her looks in order to manipulate men, but Kayley never expected it to get as complicated as it currently was. Emotions and feelings were a tricky thing. As much as humans tried to be in control of those two things, logic was not something that played a role in one's own emotions and feelings. Often, they were the complete opposite; illogical, irrational, and sometimes just totally and completely absurd.

They were also undeniable and until Kayley could truly admit what she was feeling, these sleepless nights would continue to plague her. She wasn't entirely surprised with what she was feeling, ever since she discovered boys, she'd been attracted to the stereotypical 'bad boys'. Kayley was beating herself up internally. She was supposed to just be playing a part, getting close to him in order to get information. He was a criminal, after all.

But, he wasn't. When she was with him, he wasn't a criminal. He was kind, soft-spoken, even gentle; not at all capable of shooting John Shannon or being a serial bank robber. She just couldn't understand how the Boyd she'd encountered in the condo could be the same Boyd who could kiss her so tenderly, hold her hand so gently, and make her stomach twist up into nervous knots. It was against everything she'd been brought in to do for Klint. Worse, it was incredibly stupid. She couldn't develop feelings for someone that she was actively trying to put behind bars. But that reality, that taboo, that forbidden love sort of thing, made her want to see and talk to Boyd even more.

"God, I have issues," Kayley muttered to herself, rubbing her temple with the palms of her hands. She checked the time on her phone and did some quick math. It was just after 2AM in Chicago, which meant it was close to 10PM in Hawaii. Getting under a blanket, Kayley unlocked her phone and went to her contacts, clicking on a name that said 'Will'. Putting the phone to her ear, Kayley listened to the dial tone, praying he'd answer.

"Hello?" Will answered flatly.

"Hey," Kayley said, smiling to hear his voice. "I was hoping it wasn't too late to call. How are you?"

"Good, good," he answered. "Nothing exciting going on right now. What about you, how's Chicago?"

"It's a lot different than I expected, if I'm being honest," Kayley admitted. "But it's good,"

"Ah, the Midwesters are too much for you?" Will teased. He paused for a second. "It's been a while since you've called me, is everything ok?"

"I just needed some big-brother advice," Kayley confessed. "I'm having kind of a hard time with some things,"

"What's going on?" Will asked in his now compassionate, big-brother voice. "Something wrong with work?"

"No, no, work is fine," Kayley lied. Her family knew that she was a talent agent and nothing more. "It's just..."

"Hey, you don't have to worry about being embarrassed or anything," Will said, just in case his little sister was feeling self-conscious.

"There's this guy..." Kayley finally admitted. Will laughed over the phone.

"There it is!" he exclaimed.

"Are you done?"

"Alright, sorry, tell me everything,"

"From the outside, he's 100% my type, you know what I mean?"

"Oh god," Will groaned. "I thought you stopped going for anyone that could be described as your type? You need to get with a librarian or a teacher or a lawyer or something,"

"A librarian, a teacher, or a lawyer, huh?" Kayley responded.

"Something regular, something normal," Will clarified.

"Will you just listen to me?"

"Sorry,"

"As I was saying, yeah, from the outside, he looks like my type," Kayley continued. "However, I've been talking to him for almost a month, we've gone out on three dates so far, and it's been really, really great. He's super kind and sweet and just a really chill person. Like I love every second that I'm with him and we text all the time and stuff,"

"So... what's the problem?" Will asked, not wanting to get into it until he had all of the information.

"Well..." Kayley began, unsure of how to tell Will the truth without telling him the truth. "He's got a sort of reputation, I guess. I've heard some things about him that make me question whether or not he's really this nice, kind guy, if that makes sense,"

"It does," Will confirmed.

"So, yeah, I don't really know what to do about it..."

"I have a few questions,"

"Ok,"

"Who made the first move?"

"Me,"

"Why?"

She paused. How in the world was Kayley supposed to answer that? Because the super secret cop I'm working for right now wanted me to seduce him in order to get close to him to see if he really robs banks in his free time?

"I just thought he seemed interesting," she lied.

"Does he have a job?"

"Yeah, he's in construction," Kayley answered. "Steel construction. He builds like warehouses and bridges and stuff,"

"Ok, so he's not a bum," Will sounded impressed with her answer. "Last one, what are your intentions here? I mean, is he the real deal or just some fling or what?"

"He's not a fling," was all Kayley had to say for Will to understand how she felt about him. Will sighed heavily.

"Well, look, here's my opinion. If you like this guy enough to overlook those rumors or whatever, go for it. It sounds like he's an alright guy, but you have to take care of yourself. That's the only focus. You. You have to know that there might be some things about him that you don't know right now or that you might not like. You have to prepare yourself for that. That being said, talk to him. Have a conversation with the man. Three dates isn't much. Really talk to him, see if you can get a look at who he really is. That's my best advice to you,"

As always, Will was the rational and thoughtful of the two. Ever since she'd been in high school, Kayley had gone to Will for dating advice. He was a psychologist by profession and was very good at his job. He knew people better than anyone Kayley had ever seen.

"Thanks Will," Kayley said, now smiling. "I guess you're right,"

"You guess?" Will asked. "Kayley, I'm always right,"

"Alright, alright, you are always right," Kayley laughed. "Are you doing ok? How's the family?

"We're good, dude," Will said. "Meg's back to work and the twins are doing well. They miss their Aunt Kayley, that's for sure,"

"I miss them too," Kayley admitted. "Please tell them I said hi,"

"Of course. You take care of yourself, alright? Let me know if you need anything,"

"I will, I will," Kayley said. "I love you,"

"Love you too,"

\*\*\*\*

When she wasn't doing her job for Klint or seeing Boyd, Kayley worked for the talent agency out of an office in Gold Coast. In Chicago, there wasn't a huge abundance of talent looking to get into adult entertainment, but there was a plethora of men and women looking to get into modeling. Most of her time was spent either looking through headshots, setting up interviews with potential models, or overseeing photoshoots. While it wasn't the most exciting work, comparatively to the other jobs she'd had, Kayley did enjoy it for the most part. Meeting people and getting to help guide younger men and women through the industry was definitely rewarding in its own way. When she first got into modeling, one of her friends had acted as a mentor for her. Being able to return the favor was a big perk of her current job.

Kayley had her own office, which was another perk of being a partner at the agency. She sat behind her desk, looking through a potential models portfolio, when there was a knock on her door. Looking up from the portfolio, Kayley saw her assistant walking in with a steaming cup of coffee in his right hand.

"Good morning, Ms. McKenna," he said with a smile. He set the coffee down in front of her. "Your usual,"

"Ugh, thank you so much, Billy" Kayley was grateful. Morning coffee was an absolute essential for her.

"You've got a 1PM meeting with Jerry and Melissa, a 2:30 with two new signees, and an interview in about thirty minutes," Billy listed off. "I'll be at my desk if you need anything,"

"Thank you," Kayley smiled. Billy left and closed the door behind him. Kayley took her first sip of coffee when her cell phone started ringing. Without looking at who was calling, Kayley answered the phone.

"West Coast Modeling, this is Kayley," she said in her professional, work voice.

"Well, hello Kayley at West Coast Modeling. This is Boyd Mc-Tiernan at McTiernan Steel Construction,"

"And how may I direct your call, Mr. McTiernan?" Kayley asked, grinning to hear Boyd's voice.

"Just calling to see how you're doing," Boyd said, dropping the act. "I'm kinda bored at work right now, just wanted to say hi,"

"Hi," Kayley said. "I'm doing good, looking at a few portfolios right now. What're you doing?"

"Eh, nothing to exciting, just eating lunch,"

"Aw, he's calling me on his lunch break now," Kayley teased, but smiled inwardly. She felt flattered.

"Get used to it," Boyd responded, chewing his lunch. He gulped down whatever he was eating. "I hope these little lunch time chats become a regular thing,"

"I hope so too," Kayley said. And she meant that. She'd been having a pretty good day already, but hearing from Boyd just made her feel so much better.

"Listen, I'm gonna be working in the city tomorrow. I have to check the address, but it shouldn't be too far from your office. Gotta do some welding on a new building. Care to come down to the site and have lunch with me? It'll be quick, but I'd like to see you. Might be kind of cool for you to see the site and stuff. If not, maybe we could do a movie or something?"

"Text me the address, I'll bring you lunch tomorrow," Kayley responded. She stood up and walked over to the windows of her office, looking out into the city.

"You don't have to bring me lunch!" Boyd exclaimed.

"Well, I'm going to. Let me know what you want,"

"You're the best, you know that?"

"Yeah, I know.  I hear that a lot,"

"I'm sure.  Hey, I gotta roll," Boyd suddenly said.  "I'll text you after work.  Have a good rest of your day, hope work goes well,"

"You too," Kayley answered.  "Talk to you later,"

# CHAPTER 17

# Boyd

Shutting his phone off and throwing it back in the glovebox of his truck, Boyd walked into a small, rundown building on the outskirts of Chicago. The building was two stories and only a few rooms, all of which were beginning to show their age. It hadn't been well maintained at all and Boyd had been able to purchase it for close to nothing. To avoid any prying eyes, Boyd purchased the building through a duo of shell companies that Rob owned for the purpose of moving money around. The surrounding neighborhood was overrun with crime and drugs, which meant a lot of police activity. But that was what made it a perfect safehouse. So far, it had been working just fine for Boyd and his crew.

He wasn't anywhere close to the construction site, in fact, he'd taken a vacation day, not that he really had to. Boyd was dressed in all black; black boots, black cargo pants, and a black long sleeve shirt. He wore a mic around his throat, a heavy tactical vest, and a thigh holster, which held his pistol. The vest was filled with spare magazines for his rifle and pistol, along with two concussion grenades.

Juan, Patrick, and Craig sat on folding chairs in the back room of the building, dressed similarly to Boyd in all black. They weren't talking to each other, just sitting there getting into the right head-space. Craig looked up and made eye contact with Boyd, giving him a subtle nod.

"Alright, boys," Boyd muttered. "Just gonna go over the plan one more time. We're gonna drive in two separate vehicles to the target. Ditch them both and use them to create a diversion. The bikes are already in place, Patty and I took care of that yesterday. You all have your keys right?"

Three nods.

"Perfect. Look, this isn't a bank or a truck. These are just normal people not expecting us to come and shit on their day. There will be an armed guard to our left. We take him out as soon as we enter the place. Aside from the guard, no one is to be harmed, I say again, we are not to touch a single person. Apply pressure, but the key here is speed. Craig, you're on crowd control while the rest of us hit the display cases. We clean them out in under two minutes and we're golden. Use the bikes to escape and we'll rendezvous here. I'll take the score to the fence and we'll have the money in our accounts by next week. Everyone good with that?"

Again, three nods.

"Alright," Boyd exhaled. "Juan, you're rolling with me. Craig and Pat, you guys follow,"

"Let's do it," Juan muttered, standing up.

On their way out, the four men each grabbed an AR-15 from the metal crate in the room. Tucking the rifles under their arms, they left the building and walked to the two vehicles that Juan had stolen the week before; an old Jeep Patriot and a Chevy Malibu. Not exactly built for a high-octane escape, but they blended in with everyday traffic. Remaining inconspicuous was half the battle in these types of situations. This was a first for Boyd and his crew. Banks and trucks were their bread and butter, but this was a different type of heist. There were variables they couldn't plan for. But, Boyd had no doubt in his crew's ability to pull it off.

Boyd hopped into the passenger seat of the Malibu, letting Juan get behind the wheel. They pulled away from the building and began the drive toward the Magnificent Mile, soft R&B music playing on the radio. He pushed any and all thoughts of Kayley out of his mind as they drove; he was lasered in on the task at hand. Any distractions or lapses in judgment would most certainly result in failure. It was something that had been ingrained in him when he'd been in the military. Even the slightest mistake or lack of attention could destroy an entire operation.

"We got this," Juan grunted, looking over at Boyd confidently. "You ain't never steered us wrong yet, boss,"

"I try," Boyd muttered in response. He wasn't one for small talk before a job like this. "I got a good feeling about this one, though,"

"Good," Juan nodded. "That's all I need to hear,"

They continued on in silence. Boyd didn't get nervous anymore before a heist. The first time, he'd been throwing up for days before the job, his stomach a mess of nervous knots. He'd gotten over those feelings a long time ago, to the point where driving to a heist didn't feel any different from driving to work. There was nothing to worry about. Boyd had done the planning, scouting and prepping necessary to make sure that this heist went off without a hitch. And if they were successful, the payout was going to be well worth the risk.

\*\*\*\*

Juan parked the Malibu in an alley behind Marshall Pierce, leaving the engine idling. Boyd jumped out and threw the duffle bag over his shoulder, Juan did the same. Throwing open the bag, Boyd grabbed a small can of gasoline and doused the inside of the car while Juan stood guard. Once the can was empty, Boyd threw it on the floor of the car, and gave Juan a nod. Flicking open a Zippo lighter, Juan threw it inside the car before hurrying away. Seconds later, the interior of the car ignited. As they hurried out of the alley, Boyd and Juan pulled on black ski masks over their faces. Boyd touched the button for his mic.

"We are a go, I repeat, we are a go,"
"Copy, moving toward the front door," Patrick answered.
"Pick it up, let's move," Boyd said to Juan. He looked at the watch on his wrist, making note of the time.

Hustling toward the front of the jewelry store, Boyd saw Patrick and Craig moving toward the door steadily, ignoring a few confused passersby. Their rifles were smartly hidden in the duffle bags until it was absolutely necessary to start brandishing weapons. Linking up in front of the door, Boyd reached in the bag once again and grabbed his rifle. It was a standard AR-15 platform, a weapon Boyd was very familiar with from his time in the military. He drew the rifle, held it with his right hand, and pushed the front door of Marshall and Pierce open, walking in like he owned the place. Patrick, Craig, and Juan followed in after him, taking up positions on either side of Boyd.

The security guard to the left of the door gasped when he saw the four armed intruders, getting the attention of one of the saleswomen behind the counter. He went to draw his weapon, but Boyd swung his rifle, hitting the man in the side of the head. Collapsing to the ground, Craig was on the guard in a nanosecond, ripping away his pistol and taser.

"Good afternoon, ladies and gentlemen!" Boyd yelled, hopping on top of one of the display cases. He lazily aimed his rifle at the staff and customers, relieved to see less than ten people in the entire store. "I am going to politely ask that you all get the fuck on the ground right now and stay there. Heads down, hands up. No sudden movements, no one tries to run, I would certainly hate to make a mess of such a fine store,"

Slowly, the customers and staff did what they were told, laying on the ground with their hands in the air. Boyd jumped down from the display case, his boots slightly echoing as he hit the ground.

"Clean house," he muttered, walking up to the same display case. Flipping his rifle around, Boyd smashed the stock through the glass, shattering it on impact. Shoving the broken glass away, Boyd stuck a gloved hand inside and began ripping out the jewelry, stuffing it in his duffle bag as he moved through the entire case. Juan and Patrick each broke through different cases, moving methodically through the entire store as fast as they could.

There were a few startled yelps everytime one of the crew smashed through a case, but for the most part, the people remained quiet. Craig kept his gun trained on them, slowly scanning back and forth, more for show than anything else. Looking at the watch on his wrist again, Boyd smiled underneath the mask, smashing through another case and plundering the jewelry.

"Sixty seconds!" he called out, feeling the adrenaline start to course through his veins. "Hustle, hustle, don't leave anything behind!"

The shattered glass crunching beneath his boots, Boyd ran over to another case containing a display of topaz and diamond necklaces. As he swung down on the case and smashed through, Boyd saw the price tag on the display, marking the four necklaces at $30,000 a piece. With four items, he'd cleared over $100,000. Rob had certainly not disappointed with this one, Boyd couldn't even begin to imagine what the total haul would be. He'd have to shave off a percentage for Rob and the majority of it would be used to clear his debt, but Boyd would still walk away with a pretty payday. Maybe a weekend vacation with Kayley was in order.

"Oh fuck!" Craig yelled suddenly. Boyd whipped his head around.

"What?"

"We got company!" Craig pointed to the window. Boyd peered outside the store and saw two Chicago Police Interceptors parked on the street, bumper to bumper. The officers were still sitting in their cars, not indicating any aggressive move toward the jewelry store. More likely than not, they were responding to the car on fire in the alley, and not the heist itself.

"What's the plan?" Patrick asked as he cleaned out another case.

"Keep going," Boyd said, keeping his gaze solely focused on the cops. "They haven't made us yet,"

"What about escape?" Craig asked.

"We'll cross that bridge when we get there," Boyd muttered. He checked his watch again. "Twenty seconds, wrap it up boys,"

"Clear over here," Juan called, zipping up his duffle bag full of stolen loot.

"Clear here, too," Patrick echoed. Boyd turned and hurried back to the case he'd been cleaning out. He grabbed the remaining handful of diamond rings, stuffed them in his bag, and zipped it shut.

"I'd like to thank you all for participating in today's robbery," Boyd said to the people lying on the ground. "You've all been wonderful customers and we look forward to serving your robbing needs again real soon,"

"They're still out there," Craig warned.

"Where are the bikes?" Juan asked.

"Shut up and follow my lead," Boyd grunted, tucking his rifle under his arm and hurrying toward the front door. Lowering his head, Boyd pushed open the door and immediately turned right, walking toward their getaway bikes.

It had been a tough choice, but Boyd had decided on using Honda XR650L Dual Sport bikes. They were quick, maneuverable, and could be taken off road at a moments notice; perfect for a quick escape. The bigger 600-cubic centimeter engine gave the bike more speed and torque, allowing the rider to reach top speeds in mere seconds. All four bikes were identical. The license plates were missing and the VIN numbers had been removed. The four bikes were parked together in an alley opposite the Magnificent Mile, underneath a tarp. If they could get to them without attracting unwanted attention, they were in the wind. No police car could keep up with them or maneuver the way they could on a dual-sport.

Boyd didn't dare look over towards the cops as he hurried through a small group of window shoppers, bumping a woman unintentionally. She gave him a dirty look, which immediately transformed into surprise when she saw what he was wearing.

"Run!" Boyd yelled, ditching any notion of trying to blend in. The four bandits took off running as fast as they could down the alley; Juan openly brandished his rifle to wave people out of the way. Risking a look over his shoulder, Boyd saw the woman he'd bumped into running over toward the two police cruisers. He didn't need to keep watching, the sirens started blaring a few beats later.

Making a sharp right turn down a narrow alley, Boyd vaulted over a dumpster and landed next to the four bikes under the tarp. He grabbed one end of the tarp and ripped it away, revealing the vehicles. Securing the bag of stolen jewelry across his back, Boyd mounted the motorcycle, fed the key into the ignition, and flipped the bike on. The engine roared to life and Boyd twisted the throttle a few times. Still wearing the ski mask, Boyd slipped a pair of sunglasses over his eyes so nothing would get into his eyes and affect his driving.

"Split up and meet back at the safehouse!" Boyd screamed. The rest of his crew nodded and they soared out of the alley; Boyd and Juan went left while Patrick and Craig went right. At the first possible intersection, Boyd and Juan split up. Boyd could still hear the sirens, but didn't see any flashing lights in his sideview mirrors. He drove quickly down the streets, blowing through a redlight, and receiving a barrage of honks from angry city drivers. Steering the bike, Boyd shifted into high gear, and sped down Michigan Avenue, heading toward the Chicago River. He was feeling confident that splitting up had disoriented the cops enough to buy them some more time. Again, another great suggestion by Rob. While he never took part in the heists, Rob was a vital component to each and every one of Boyd's heists.

Looking behind him quickly, Boyd breathed a sigh of relief to see no one in direct pursuit of him. Still hitting the throttle hard, Boyd reached up and activated his mic.

"I think I'm clear!" he yelled.

"I'm good, circling back to the safehouse," Craig answered. Boyd couldn't make out what Patrick or Juan said. His heart sank when he saw a duo of CPD Interceptors flying towards him from the opposite lane, lights and sirens blaring.

"Nevermind," Boyd grunted into the radio.

Leaning into the bike, Boyd shifted up into a higher gear and accelerated, popping the front wheel of his bike up. Setting the front wheel back down gently, Boyd flew past the cops. They came to a screeching halt, executed U-turns, and began chasing after him.

"Boyd! Boyd, where are you?" Craig called into the radio.

"Southbound on Michigan!" Boyd screamed over the bike's engine. "I picked up a few friends, gotta ditch 'em, and then I'll meet up with you guys,"

Weaving in and out of traffic, Boyd managed to put a decent amount of distance between himself and the police officers in pursuit. Seeing the traffic get thicker, Boyd angled the bike to the right and hopped onto the median, splitting through the four lanes of traffic. He didn't dare look behind him and see how close the cops were. Judging by the sounds of their sirens, there were more coming. The bike engine was screaming as Boyd jumped back onto the street, whipping around a slow moving SUV. He felt like the sirens were all around him, coming from every single direction. It might've been incredibly disorienting for someone not used to this kind of stress and action. Fortunately for Boyd, he'd done far crazier things in the military. Sometimes, it baffled him how well his extensive military training had prepared him for a life of crime. Being able to remain calm and focused under ridiculous pressure was something that kept proving itself valuable. Even now, with the cops attempting to close in on Boyd, he felt as calm as could be. Maybe he was just cocky or overconfident, but he knew his abilities and he had a plan. There was no doubt in his mind that he'd be having dinner with Kayley in a few short hours.

As he neared the bridge over the Chicago River, Boyd saw a second group of cruisers turn off of East Wacker, and come to a stop on the bridge, blocking him from crossing. Squeezing the brakes as hard as he could, Boyd came to a screeching stop, the back wheel of his bike popping up to execute a perfect *stoppie* - a stunt done on either a bicycle or a motorcycle by abruptly applying the front brake in order to lift the back wheel and coast on the front wheel.

Boyd had a rule when it came to heists. Aside from the actual robbery portion, he never engaged in any violence unless someone engaged him first. In the military, this was usually standard rules of engagement; you can't fire a shot until someone has shot at you first. During the previous robbery, Craig had fired on the cop, and killed him. It was not the first time that Boyd and his crew had been forced to resort to violence in order to get away. And now, Boyd was being forced once again to do something he did not want to do.

The second the back wheel of the motorcycle hit the ground, Boyd planted his feet on either side of the bike, and drew his rifle, bringing the stock into his shoulder. Boyd flipped the fire selector switch to full-auto before squeezing the trigger, sending a salvo of bullets toward the two cruisers. In an instant, the world around Boyd turned to chaos; cars screamed on their brakes, some slamming into each other as they tried to stop, and pedestrians walking on the sidewalks screamed in terror, looking for anything that could be used as cover.

Blasting off the entire magazine, Boyd ejected it, and immediately smashed a fresh one into the breach. He popped off about a dozen rounds at the cops on the bridge before shifting his aim behind him, as another group of cops were heading toward him from the opposite direction, trying to surround him. Steadying his aim, Boyd fired at the cops flying toward him; his rounds shredded through the windshields of both cruisers. The cop car on the left veered to the right suddenly, hitting a parked car, and flipping over onto its side, catching fire as soon as it hit the ground. The second cop car turned abruptly to cover the crashed cruiser; both officers jumped out with their guns drawn, returning fire at Boyd.

Boyd felt a twinge of panic shoot through his system, his fight or flight system going into overdrive. Reloading his rifle once again, Boyd fired off another burst at the cops pursuing him. Slinging the rifle across his back, Boyd spun the bike around and flew down East Illinois Street, leaving a trail of destruction in his wake. He jumped the bike through the roundabout at the end of the street, cutting off a gray sedan, and receiving angry honks from another driver. Turning right, Boyd drove down Cityfront Plaza before cutting through another roundabout, and speeding down East North Water Street. The bridge crossing on North Columbus Drive was completely open.

Once he was across the bridge, Boyd looked over his shoulder and didn't see any cruisers on his tail. That being said, he didn't let off the throttle at all. Going well over the speed limit, Boyd rocketed toward Lake Shore Drive, deciding based on the time of day that taking that road to the highway would be his best chance at a clean escape. Lake Shore was busy, but it was the most direct route. The benefit of having the bike was that Boyd wouldn't get caught up in any traffic, he could cut straight through to the highway.

"Boys, I think I'm in the clear," Boyd said into his radio. "I'll meet up with y'all at the safehouse,"

"Good," Craig answered after a few seconds of silence. "Be safe,"

****

Almost an hour later, Boyd rolled his bike into the safehouse; Juan and Patrick yanked the garage door down by a rope that was attached to the handle. Boyd kicked the stand out, leaned the bike onto it, and dismounted. Without saying a word to his crew, Boyd tossed his rifle on a table and set the duffle bag of loot next to the others on a rather rickety folding table.

"You good?" Juan asked, dressed now in a blue V-neck, tan shorts, and a pair of flip flops. His bulky arms were covered in tattoos. Boyd nodded and began stripping off his tactical gear and clothing.

"Where's Craig?" Boyd asked. Juan and Patrick looked at each other, hesitant to answer. Boyd rolled his eyes, not in the mood for whatever silent code they were talking. "Guys, it's been a long day, cut the shit. Where's Craig?"

"He took off," Patrick said. "Don't know where he was going, but he seemed to be in a hurry,"

Boyd paused and took a deep breath. It was always tough coming down from an adrenaline high as intense as the one Boyd experienced during a heist. Craig's sudden disappearance didn't help either.

"Good work today, guys," Boyd said to Patrick and Juan. "Go home, get some rest, and I'll see you at work tomorrow,"

"You gonna be ok?" Juan asked. Boyd nodded, holding out his fist. Juan bumped knuckles with Boyd.

"Yeah, I'm good," Boyd appreciated his concern. "You guys have done enough for today, I'll handle Craig and the fence. Check your accounts, money should be in them quickly,"

"Sounds good," Patrick said.

"Let's grab a drink soon," Boyd suggested. "After all, it is tradition,"

After every successful job, the crew would always go out for a celebratory drink at a different bar - never the same bar twice.

"I'm in," Juan grinned. He patted Patrick on the shoulder as he headed out. "See you around, dudes,"

After Juan and Patrick left in their own vehicles, Boyd gathered up all four duffle bags of loot, and stuffed them in the backseat of his truck. Tomorrow after work, he'd transfer the bags to Rob, and await payment. Holding onto the bags overnight wasn't as big of a risk as one would assume. He triple checked that the safehouse and all of their gear were locked and secured. With the amount of homeless people in the area, there was always the risk that one would try to get into an abandoned building. Satisfied that the building was secure, Boyd climbed into his truck, threw on a hat, and started driving back home. This time, the traffic on the highway didn't bother him at all. He thought about calling Kayley, but he didn't want to bug her. A little while to himself to gather his thoughts was not a bad thing. He tried not to wonder about what Craig was doing or why he'd left in such a hurry, but knowing his uncle, he assumed it wasn't good.

A lot of Boyd's current situation could be blamed on Craig Trasker, but Boyd knew the blame was pretty evenly split between Craig and his father. It was an unfortunate reality, but Boyd's father had not been a stand up guy by any stretch of the imagination. As Boyd grew into a young man, it was one of the hardest things to realize, that his dad was not the perfect man every boy envisioned in their head. But that being said, Boyd understood why he did what he did. Boyd had never wanted anything more than to get the opportunity to work with his dad. He'd grown up idolizing him and counting down the days until they could work together. Not having his dad around anymore was hard, even if they hadn't been the closest.

James Boyd McTiernan I, who went by James rather than Boyd, had been thrust into owning a company that he wasn't sure he'd ever had any real interest in. According to Boyd's mom, James had always wanted bigger and greater things than the steel construction business, not that he was ever ashamed of what he did. When money started to get tight, fear of not being able to provide for his young family and employees drove James to make some truly poor decisions. He borrowed money from people that he had no business borrowing money from. And then he got greedy, always wanting more. He took out so many loans from so many bad people that he lost track of who was owed what. Especially in a city like Chicago, there is no shortage of rich people with hired muscle. When James tragically died, Boyd inherited an absolute mess of a company.

McTiernan Steel Construction made a decent amount of money, but wasn't necessarily profitable. They nearly broke even every month once salaries were paid, but the company was still in massive debt. Compounded with the amount of debt that Boyd had taken on from his father, he suddenly felt that he was drowning. At the time, he'd only seen one viable option to repay all of the debts and get some cash back into his family business. And he'd made a crucial mistake by involving his uncle, but at the time, he thought he could trust Craig since he was family. But Craig was not a man that could be trusted and Boyd had come to that realization too late. Craig was far too dangerous when he was angry or spiteful. It was more risky to not include him than to include him. At least, that's what Boyd kept telling himself.

# CHAPTER 18

# Klint

Angry wasn't quite strong enough a word to describe Klint Kavanaugh's emotions as he walked through Marshall and Pierce, carefully stepping around the shards of shattered glass on the floor. He kept his facial expressions as neutral as possible, hiding the fact that he was seething with frustration. Crime Scene Technicians were sweeping the entire store, trying to find any piece of evidence. He was only in the store for about two minutes before going to check out the smoldering ruins of the old Chevy Malibu.

"Quite an elaborate plan, huh?" Richard Brown commented.
"If you say so," Klint muttered. "Perimeter still in place?"
"Yeah," Rich nodded. "I got patrolmen at every block,"

Following the robbery, ensuing shootout, and escape, the Chicago Police Department had enforced a hardened perimeter around the jewelry store, which at this moment in time did little other than annoy the local population.

"Lift it," Klint shook his head. "It's not gonna help us in any way,"

"Whatever you say, boss," Rich nodded. He grabbed his radio from his belt. "Alright, bring everyone in. I repeat, close down the perimeter,"

"Copy that," a cop answered.

"CSU find anything?" Klint asked, cocking his head toward the Malibu. Rich sighed and shook his head.

"Nothing useful," he admitted. "Store was clean too. Shell casings were the same way, nothing we could use to trace them,"

"Goddamnit," Klint shook his head. He looked at Rich. "The Mayor is breathing down my neck to bring these guys in,"

"They're good, I don't know what you want me to say, Klint," Rich shrugged, getting a little defensive.

"Yeah, Rich, I know they're fucking good," Klint was fed up with everything involving this crew. "And we have no idea where they went?"

"No," Rich shook his head, hating to be the one to keep delivering bad news to Klint. "They knew the right routes to take to avoid cameras, we lost the one guy after he got on the highway. Cruisers can't keep up with guys on bikes and these guys were driving like they were the offspring of Valentino Rossi,"

"So I've heard," Klint muttered. "Keep me updated, Rich,"

"Will do, sir,"


Klint walked back to his Charger, clenching his fists. He was unable to comprehend how this crew had been able to pull off a heist in broad daylight and escape with apparent ease. It was especially confusing since John, Kade, Noah, and Kayley were supposed to be surveilling the suspected crew. Klint had been pretty positive that the guys at McTiernan Steel were the ones they were looking for. But now, there were shrouds of doubt. Maybe Klint had been wrong. Maybe they'd been wasting their time. Either way, it was time for everyone to meet again. Whatever they'd been doing so far, hadn't been enough. And two more cops were now in the Intensive Care Unit with gunshot wounds. Regardless of how Mayor Kelly Hart felt about Klint, she was not going to stand for incompetence. Right now, Klint and his team were looking extremely incompetent.

****

Last to arrive at the safehouse, Klint marched inside without greeting anyone. They noticed right away that this wasn't going to be a light hearted meeting; Klint was visibly upset. Walking right up to the folding table they'd used for briefings, Klint grabbed the table, and threw it across the warehouse. It crashed to the ground with an echoing boom. Kade and Noah exchanged concerned looks. John watched him carefully and Kayley took it all in. Continuing to display his anger, Klint picked the table up again and smashed it, breaking one of the legs in half. He picked up the discarded table leg and launched it back across the warehouse.

"Correct me if I'm wrong..." Klint said in such a dangerously calm voice. "But I thought I made it perfectly clear that I wanted this crew under surveillance so that this type of thing doesn't happen. I thought we were all in agreement as to what everyone's responsibilities were. And supposedly, you're all doing your jobs, so how did this happen?"

The room was dead silent. John looked up from his boots and glanced over at Kayley. She made eye contact with him, she was biting her lip. Klint's rant was bothering her and John's defensive instincts started coming to the surface. He knew Kayley didn't

COWBOYS OF THE SKY - 233

need protecting, but he still had those protective qualities that often showed themselves in the worst moments.

Klint narrowed his eyes on Kayley, picking her out as the unfortunate weakest link of the group. He walked across the warehouse until he was right in front of her, looking her up and down. She stiffened up, her posture rigid from her military years.

"You've been keeping an eye on Boyd, huh?"

"That's what you asked me to do," Kayley answered, her eyes unwavering.

"That's not what I asked," Klint shot back. "Has he said anything to you? You know, everyone has reported in at least once about their findings. Except you,"

"He hasn't said anything," Kayley ignored the accusation. She couldn't let on what she was really feeling. "I'm still working on him,"

"Oh, I'm sure you are," Klint let the insinuation of his words speak for themselves.

"Lay off her, Klint," John suddenly spoke up. Klint didn't even appear to hear John, his attention was solely on Kayley.

"If you are not cut out for this type of work, there's the door," Klint said to Kayley.

"Klint! Lay off her. It isn't her fault," John yelled.

"You don't seem to understand what is at stake here," Klint continued pressing her. "So go. If you can't do what you were brought on to do, then you're of no use to me,"

John crossed the warehouse in a nanosecond and grabbed Klint by the shoulder, spinning him around violently, and dropping him with a right hook. Blood shot out of Klint's mouth as he dropped to his knees, feeling like he'd been bit by a bus. Steadying himself,

Klint launched himself upwards, reeling his right hand back. He swung with massive force, but John was too quick, dodging the punch and tossing another devastating blow, this time hitting Klint square in the face. Klint's head snapped back and he once again fell to the ground.

Kade yelled John's name and went to intervene but Noah grabbed him by the arm and calmly shook his head.

"No," he muttered. "They need this,"

John hadn't even broken a sweat, standing over Klint who was bleeding badly and panting heavily. He looked over at Kayley to check on her, but she was totally stunned. Coughing, Klint slowly rolled over onto this side and spat onto the ground; his head was throbbing in pain.

"It's not her fault, Klint," John said again, keeping his voice neutral. "You want to start shit with someone, you start it with me. Leave her out of it,"

"Oh, when did you get all soft," Klint spat, sitting up. He was bleeding from his mouth and nose. "You are a tool, John. A weapon that someone points in any direction and sends you on your way,"

"You're goddamn right I am," John snapped back. He gestured to Kayley. "She went through the same training as me, she's the same thing that I am. You'd never talk to me like that, so don't you dare talk to her like that when she's got the hardest job of us all. We don't even know for certain if these are the guys who robbed the truck or the store, for crying out loud. All we know is that Boyd wants his uncle dead. You might have read this whole situation wrong, Klint. So, before you start throwing accusations around, take a good hard look in the motherfucking mirror,"

Klint couldn't defend his actions, at least not in that moment. He'd let his emotions get the best of him and he knew it. John was right, although Klint would rather die than admit it. Kayley did have a much harder job, the moral gray-area of it alone was probably enough to bother her immensely. Slowly, Klint got to his feet, wiping his face with the front of his shirt. John balled his fists, ready to go another round if he and Klint needed it. Kayley shook her head, bothered by what had transpired on her behalf.

"Relax, I'm not gonna fight you, John," Klint groaned. He looked at Kayley and gave her a half-hearted smile. "I'm sorry... Rough day,"

"I understand," Kayley spoke quietly. She didn't need to say anything more.

"We should talk about some things when we've all cooled down a little," John said, having retained the alpha male status for the time being. He fished the keys to his truck out of his pocket. "Tomorrow night, we'll meet back here and discuss everything. Until then, just go about your normal life. You can take a day off from whatever it is Magnum P.I. has you doing,"

Noah bit his lip to avoid laughing at the admittedly stupid joke. John gave him a discreet wink and walked out of the warehouse, followed by Noah. Kayley was hesitant, but after a few moments, decided if it was best to leave without saying anything else to Klint or to Kade. Once they were gone, Kade walked over to his brother, handing him a towel.

"Brother, never piss off a Navy SEAL," Kade muttered. "I know you're a tough guy and all, but John could break you in half with his hands tied behind his back. Not the kind of guy you want to egg on like that,"

"Duly noted," Klint muttered, dabbing at his busted lip with the towel.

"You ok?"

"Fine," Klint grunted. "I just don't understand what we're doing wrong. How can these guys leave no evidence behind?"

"Because they are professionals," Kade said. "Their livelihoods are on the line, same as us. We can't assume they're going to screw up, we have to find another way,"

"I was just sure it was the guys from McTiernan," Klint muttered. "There was just something about that Craig guy... He was lying to me when I asked him about the heists, I could see it in his eyes. He was lying,"

"Your gut feeling..." Kade leaned against one of the support pillars. "Is it them?"

"Yes," Klint nodded without hesitation. Kade nodded.

"If you say it's them, then it's them," Kade agreed. "Then we gotta press 'em. Get them in a room and start breaking them down. One by one. Shake their tree a little bit,"

"How?"

"Klint, come on," Kade rolled his eyes. "You know damn well how. In my opinion, let John off the leash a little bit. You said it yourself, he's a tool. Use him properly. We need to make sure these are our guys, so let John take care of that. Once we know for sure, we need to find a way to split them up..."

"Dissent among the ranks," Klint commented.

"Exactly," Kade nodded. "Break them up a little... Like we are right now,"

"We can do that," Klint muttered. "The Mayor wants these guys caught... Yesterday,"

"Right and I'm sure your anger has nothing to do with the fact that you two have been seeing each other," Kade crossed his arms. Klint gave him a strange look, wondering how he knew about that. Kade rolled his eyes. "Dude, Kara has a phone. She likes to talk,"

"That she does," Klint smirked. "Go home, Kade. Say hi to Jenna and Hailey from me,"

"You got it," Kade smiled. "Take care of yourself, Klint,"

# CHAPTER 19

# Boyd

Reaching into his tool belt and grabbing a spud wrench, Boyd began tightening the bolts on a newly placed girder. Once the bolts were secure, Boyd replaced the wrench on his belt and carefully moved back across the I-beam; he was secured to the building, standing almost 40 stories in the air. Along with a crew of other ironworkers and welders, Boyd was working to help finish the skeleton of the building, which was mostly welding at this point. Juan and Patrick were already working on welding up the girders, wearing thick welding jackets, gloves, and the big welding helmets. Donning his own gear, Boyd fired up his welder and went to work, hot sparks flying in every direction as he welded the beams together. Welding was precise and painstaking work, but incredibly satisfying at the same time. It was important work too, connecting to the different I-beams and supports.

After about four hours of nonstop welding, Boyd ripped his helmet off, and chugged his Gatorade. He was sweating profusely, the unseasonably hot day in Chicago providing a miserable atmosphere for welding. Leaning against a girder, Boyd checked his phone, smiling to see a text from Kayley letting him know she was on her way to have lunch with him.

"Whatchu smiling about, boss?" Juan asked, taking off his own helmet. He wiped his brow with a rag, taking a few deep breaths of fresh air.

"Oh, you'll see," Boyd grinned. "I'm going down for lunch,"

"Patty and I will finish up where we're at and then meet ya down there," Juan said. He grabbed some fresh copper welding wire from out of a container and headed back over to where Patrick was.

Taking the service elevator down to the ground floor, Boyd put his hard hat back on before leaving the lift, knowing he'd be paying a hefty fine if he was walking around the site without proper Personal Protection Equipment - PPE. On his way to his utility truck, Boyd spotted a few project managers and building engineers talking to some of the other construction workers. The project was ahead of schedule and Boyd guessed the workers were getting praised for being so efficient. His phone started ringing as he stepped out of the fenced in construction site and approached his truck parked on the street.

"Hey!" Boyd answered. "Are you doing ok?"

"I'm fine, I'm fine, my Uber just doesn't know where to drop me off," Kayley explained. "Which side should I go in on?"

"I'm out by my truck," Boyd said. "I'm on the North side, looking at the big parking garage,"

"Ok, perfect," Kayley relayed the information to her Uber driver. "I'll be right there,"

"See you soon,"

Not even a minute later, Kayley jumped out of her Uber and walked over to Boyd's truck, carrying a big brown paper bag of food. She set the food on the hood of the truck and gave him a big hug, kissing him on the lips.

"Hi," she grinned.

"Well, hello there," Boyd returned the smile. He looked down at his dirty hands and sweaty shirt. "Sorry, I'm filthy,"

"Please," Kayley rolled her eyes. "I could care less. How's your day been?"

"Pretty easy so far," Boyd shrugged, fetching another Gatorade from the cooler in his truck. "Would you like water or Gatorade?"

"Water would be fantastic," Kayley said, opening the bags of food. She'd gotten them both salads and sandwiches from a local shop that she'd discovered her first week in the city. Reaching back into the cooler, Boyd grabbed a water bottle for Kayley, twisting the cap off before handing it to her.

"How's work going?" Boyd asked, opening his Gatorade. Kayley paused before answering, her mind still preoccupied by Klint's tirade yesterday.

"It's ok I guess," Kayley muttered. "One of my bosses is a little stressed right now and that just makes my life harder,"

"Yeah, trust me, I understand that," Boyd sympathized. "You wanna vent or anything?"

"No," Kayley said, a little too quickly.

"Alright," Boyd shrugged, digging into his sandwich and salad. Although he technically wasn't restricted to a 30-45 minute lunch, he tried to keep his break short. Since he took over the company, his whole philosophy had been to lead by example. No one, not even the owner of the company, was entitled to longer than a 45 minute lunch, maximum. On a special occasion, maybe that could be stretched to an hour.

"Are you ok?" Boyd asked after Kayley didn't say anything else. She looked down at her shoes and grimaced.

"I don't know how to answer that," Kayley said honestly. Boyd's ears perked up at that comment. He set his food on the hood of his truck and stepped in front of Kayley, grabbing her hands.

"Hey, what's wrong?" Boyd asked, looking her in the eyes.

"I don't know," Kayley muttered, hating having to lie to him. "I'm just having a rough day,"

"I'm sorry," Boyd said softly. "Rough days come and go, I'm sorry you're going through it,"

"What are we, Boyd?" Kayley asked. "I'm sorry, I know that might be a stupid question right now, but I'm not gelling here as well as I thought. I've been giving some thought to moving back to the LA area..."

"Oh," Boyd nodded, lowering his gaze. "That bad of a day, huh?"

"Bad week," Kayley shook her head. Boyd could see that she was keeping something to herself, not telling him the whole truth. It was hypocritical of him to be bothered by that, but it still kind of did.

"Well, look, I mean if you're not happy here, I wouldn't stay here," Boyd said, realizing as he was saying it that it sounded a little harsh. "I would never ask you to stay here on my behalf,"

"So that answers my first question," Kayley muttered. She looked disappointed.

"Kayley, what do you want me to say?" Boyd asked. "If you are not happy here, that's a big problem. I'm not in a position to leave here right now, I'm just not,"

"Well then what am I doing here?" Kayley snapped. "What are we doing?"

Boyd was taken aback by her sudden outburst at him. He felt bad that she was so upset, but they'd only been going out for a month; he couldn't ask her to stay or go with her if she was serious about leaving. If they'd been together for a while, he might've considered it, but being responsible for the business was a big reason for him needing to stay. When Boyd didn't say anything right away, Kayley grabbed her food, and stuffed them back in the brown bag.

"Please don't do this," Boyd muttered. Kayley ignored him and pulled out her phone, opening the Uber app. "Kayley, come on, please don't do this,"

"Forget it, I don't want to bother you," Kayley said.

"You're not bothering me," Boyd reassured her. "I want to talk to you about this, it's just not a good time right now. There's an entire conversation to be had and I have to get back to work in a few minutes. But, I want to talk to you about this. I really do,"

"Ok, ok," Kayley whispered. "I'm sorry, I'm just kind of emotional right now,"

"I understand, you don't have to apologize," Boyd touched her shoulder. "I'm sorry you're going through whatever it is. I'm here if you want to talk about it,"

"And I appreciate it," Kayley finally smiled at him. "I'd like to talk to you about all of this too. I have some more stuff to handle with work tonight, but why don't you come by the hotel I'm at after I'm done,"

"Sounds good," Boyd nodded, returning the smile. He leaned down and kissed her on the lips, holding the back of her neck with his hand.

"Oh boy, boss man making moves!" Juan yelled from the construction site. He and Patrick were walking toward their fleet trucks to take their lunch breaks. Boyd groaned audibly and rolled his eyes as they shifted directions and started walking toward them.

"I'm sorry in advance," Boyd said to Kayley; she laughed and adjusted her hair.

"Now I see why you were in such a hurry to take lunch," Patrick commented. He looked at Kayley. "He's always trying to get out of work, super lazy,"

"Oh yeah?" Kayley asked, looking at Boyd. He rolled his eyes.

"Now, these two are the laziest guys on my crew," Boyd smiled. "Guys, this is Kayley,"

"Patrick," Patrick introduced, wiping his hand on his shirt before shaking hands with Kayley.

"Juan Alarcón,"

"Nice to meet you both," Kayley smiled. The two men gave Boyd a nod of approval.

"You know, you picked a good one," Juan said to Kayley pointing to Boyd. "Just keep an eye on him,"

"Good to know," Kayley smiled, touching Boyd's hand - who was red with embarrassment.

"We'll let you get back to your lunch," Patrick said. "Nice to meet you, Kayley,"

"You too,"

\*\*\*\*

After getting the all clear from Kayley, Boyd took off from his home in Naperville and began the journey back into the city. While it certainly wasn't ideal for him, it was an excuse for Boyd to get to take out his 'gixxer' - the colloquial term for a Suzuki GSX-R motorcycle. At this time of night, the drive into the city would only take him about forty minutes, which could definitely be lessened by the bike's speed. He rarely went under 90 miles per hour when on the highway, making his commute fly by, quite literally.

Parking his bike on the street, Boyd slowly took off his helmet and sent Kayley a quick text, letting her know that he'd arrived. He walked across the street and into the hotel lobby, which was nearly empty at this hour. Making his way to the elevators, Boyd hit the floor corresponding with Kayley's hotel room, and ascended to the correct floor. After finding Kayley's hotel room, Boyd took a deep breath, and rapped on the door three times.

The door swung open a few moments later and Kayley appeared in the doorway. Her hair was pulled back in a messy ponytail and she wore fuzzy socks, leggings, and a black crop top. She smiled seeing Boyd and held the door open for him.

"Hey," he said softly, kissing her on the cheek as he entered the hotel room.

"Hey to you too," Kayley closed and locked the door. Boyd ripped off his boots and set his helmet next to the boots. "Thanks for coming out here, I know it's not exactly convenient for you,"

"Eh, don't worry about it," Boyd shrugged. "Gave me an excuse to bust out the bike,"

"It's nice to see you," Kayley said. "I'm sorry for kind of freaking out today, I've just been having a hard time this week,"

"There's no need to apologize, Kayley," Boyd reassured her. "It's nice to see you too,"

"Well, come in," Kayley offered, leading the way into the small living room of her hotel room. "It's not much, but this is it,"

"This place is nicer than my first two or three apartments," Boyd commented, sitting down on the couch facing the TV. Kayley sat down next to him, criss-crossing her legs. Boyd touched Kayley's leg and looked at her. "I hope you didn't take any offense to anything I said earlier. I just wasn't really sure how to react. I'm not in any position to leave right now, I'm just not, but that's nothing against you,"

"You're not in a position to leave because of work or...?" Kayley asked. Boyd chuckled and shook his head.

"Yeah, you could say that. I don't know if we've ever talked about it explicitly, but I own the company I work for. McTiernan Steel. My grandpa started it, my dad ran it, and now I'm the one running it. That's why I can't leave. I mean, I could for a little while, but not permanently,"

"Well, that's understandable," Kayley let out a small laugh. "I didn't know that,"

"I don't like to advertise it," Boyd shrugged.

"Any particular reason why?"

"I just don't," Boyd said honestly. "I don't want someone to judge me for it, you know? Just left over bullshit from middle school and high school. Grew up pretty wealthy and kids can be demons,"

"Yeah, tell me about it," Kayley rolled her eyes. "Girls are the worst, just the worst,"

"So I've heard," Boyd chuckled. "So, Kayley, what else did you want to talk about? I mean, in terms of us,"

"Yeah," Kayley said softly. "Us,"


Boyd and Kayley locked eyes for a few seconds, staring into each other intensely. Moving his hand slightly up her leg, Boyd inched his body closer to her. The sexual tension between them was palpable, Boyd could feel the physical heat between them. Kayley suddenly reached up and pulled Boyd into her lips, forgetting anything else that she wanted to talk to Boyd about. Boyd's hands shot up to her hair and neck, holding her tightly as he kissed her back. Slowly, he laid Kayley down on the couch, moving down to kiss and bite the sensitive skin on her neck.

"Oh my god," Kayley breathed, running her hands up and down Boyd's muscular back. He sat up and ripped his shirt off, tossing it on the floor. Breathing heavily, Boyd once again planted his lips on Kayley's. They continued making out for a few minutes before Kayley sat up and ripped off her crop top, exposing her bare breasts to Boyd. He exhaled and scooped her up in his arms, carrying her over to the unmade bed.

"You're so beautiful," Boyd whispered in her ear, nibbling on her ear lobe. Kayley squirmed beneath Boyd as he ran his hands all over her body. She hooked her thumbs in the waistband of her leggings and peeled them down ever so slowly, making eye contact with him the entire time.

"Finally, huh?" Kayley commented, looking up at him with a smirk.

"You're wild," Boyd laughed.

"I know," Kayley took it as a compliment. She flipped over onto her stomach and looked back at Boyd, giving him a wink.

****

The morning sunlight bled through the half-pulled drapes, illuminating the hotel room with a bright orange hue. Clothes, couch cushions, pillows, and blankets were scattered around the room, indicating the raucous activities that had taken place the night prior. Even the couch that they'd sat on last night was overturned on its back. It looked like a tornado had torn through the hotel room.

COWBOYS OF THE SKY - 247

Boyd lay in the disheveled bed, his hands resting behind his head as he stared blankly up at the ceiling. A blanket covered his lower half, but he was completely naked. Kayley was still sound asleep, snoring quietly next to him. He had watched her sleep for a while, envious of how peaceful she looked. No matter the situation or scenario, Boyd was consistently unable to find steady sleep. He could sleep fantastic, without trouble for a month, but for the next few months, he'd be plagued with sleepless nights. It made no sense to him, but he equated it to the inconsistent sleep he'd gotten so used to in the military - which felt like a lifetime ago at this point.

That Boyd McTiernan - the soldier, the hero, the recipient of military honors - ceased to exist anymore. Despite all his accreditations and combat missions, that Boyd McTiernan was unbelievably naive to the real world. For all intents and purposes, that Boyd Mc-Tiernan died over in Afghanistan. The worst thing about that was that the current Boyd McTiernan recognized that he was no longer that man.

Stirring in the bed, Kayley slowly moved her hand over and touched Boyd's arm, caressing his skin. Boyd stretched and slid his arm underneath her, pulling her closer to him. Settling in next to him, Kayley rested her head on his shoulder, giving him a quick kiss on the cheek.

"Morning," she muttered, eyes still closed. Boyd smiled and kissed her on the forehead.

"How are you feeling?" Boyd asked. Kayley laughed and buried her head in Boyd's shoulder, blushing.

"Oh, I'm feeling good," she answered, opening her eyes and looking up at Boyd. "Last night was..."

"Awesome," Boyd finished her sentence.

"Yeah," Kayley agreed. "Awesome is one word for it,"

"We never did get to talk," Boyd pointed out.

"I know. We got a little distracted," Kayley sighed. She paused for a moment, sitting up and leaning on her arm. "I'm really ok now. I just had a bad couple of days. I don't plan on leaving anytime soon,"

"You know I like you, Kayley," Boyd said, staring up at the ceiling again. "But there are things about me... things that you don't know about me. If you knew, it might change your mind,"

"What... What do you mean?" Kayley asked.

"I've done things," Boyd grunted. He rolled over in bed and looked at Kayley, touching her cheek with his fingers. "Things that if you didn't know the whole story, you'd judge me for,"

"Honey, I'd never judge you," Kayley whispered. Boyd pulled her against his lips and kissed her; she blushed in response.

"Promise?"

"I promise," Kayley smiled, kissing Boyd again. "Talk to me. I promise you have nothing to worry about,"

"When I inherited the company, I didn't realize how severely in debt it was. I'm not talking a few hundred dollars, more like a few million. It was the kind of money that was unfathomable to me and that was just the stuff on the actual books. My dad owed money to everyone it seemed, some of it to people who don't take kindly to being owed that type of money. They started putting the pressure on me and my company. Threatening to take away everything until they were paid in full what they were owed,"

"Oh my god," Kayley whispered. "What did you do?"

"The only thing I could do," Boyd muttered. Kayley waited a minute for him to elaborate, but he never did. His silence spoke volumes, he could tell that she understood what he was saying. "I'm not a bad guy, Kayley. But I've had to do certain things in order to protect myself. And my family's legacy. I'm all that's left of the

McTiernan's. Someone has to carry on that legacy, that name. I'll be damned if any of it goes to hell to because of me,"

"That's a lot of pressure to put on yourself," Kayley commented. She ran her hand through Boyd's hair, scratching his scalp a little.

"Maybe," Boyd closed his eyes and sighed. "But that's how I feel,"

"I understand," Kayley said. "I'm glad you told me. I'd never judge you for doing what you think is right,"

"I hope not," Boyd wrapped his arms around her and kissed her again, rolling on top of her. "At least, not yet. You want to judge me afterwards, go ahead,"

"Based on last night, I don't think I'll be doing that," Kayley gave him a seductive look. She leaned up and whispered in his ear. "Have your way with me, baby,"

"As you wish," Boyd grinned and pinned Kayley's arms above her head before returning to suck on her neck.

\*\*\*\*

Boyd McTiernan wasn't even totally sure of the name of the bar they were at, just some rundown dive near O'Hare airport. Why Patrick and Juan had chosen it for celebratory drinks was beyond Boyd, but he wasn't one to complain about where his liquor came from. For a dive, it was about as full as it could be, which surprised Boyd. It was a melting pot of different demographics, another interesting feature of the bar.

Polishing off his Miller Lite, Boyd went to the bar to order another one, finding little enjoyment in listening to Craig's latest escapade with a woman half his age. He stood at the end of the bar, waiting for the bartender to come over. It hadn't always been this way between Boyd and Craig. In fact, they were actually pretty close for a while. Not friends, but at least friendly with one another. They were able to tolerate the other, mostly because they had to for the sake of the family. But after Boyd's parents and Craig's wife all passed away, there was no reason for them to continue to pretend that they liked each other. It bothered Boyd immensely that he still had to deal with Craig, but he was still family at the end of the day, and that carried significant weight with Boyd.

"What're you drinking?" the bartender asked, finally making his way back to Boyd.

"Miller Lite. Bottle," Boyd ordered. The bartender nodded and fetched a fresh bottle, snapping the top off.

"Put it on my tab," the man sitting at the bar said to the bartender. Boyd looked over at him and the man merely nodded. The man wore dark colored jeans, work boots, and an orange Hi-Vis shirt. Strangely, he looked familiar to Boyd, but he couldn't quite place it. Based on how he was dressed, Boyd figured he must've seen the man on a site or something like that.

"Thanks," Boyd said.

"Don't mention it," the man answered. He was overly occupied watching the TV, which was running consistent feed from the jewelry store heist, ensuing shootout, and chase. The anchor kept reiterating that the suspects hadn't been caught yet. "Crazy stuff, huh,"

"Yeah," Boyd grunted, grabbing his beer.

"You ever hear about that crew out in Los Angeles?" the man asked, still not really looking at Boyd. "Two separate occasions, two different crews, but they took down a bunch of banks and trucks,"

"Yeah?" Boyd pretended to act interested. He vaguely remembered seeing something about a Beverly Hills bank heist a while back, but that was it.

"Yeah it was kind of a big deal out there," the man continued. "There was a whole big investigation into some connection with a Labor Union out there. Kind of an interesting story. I'd recommend looking into it, you might find it thought provoking,"

"I'll have to read up on it sometime," Boyd dismissed. "Thanks for the beer,"

"You know, Boyd..." the man lowered his voice, finally turning his head so Boyd could see his entire face. He was probably around Boyd's age, maybe a little younger. Boyd stared at him closely, wondering how in the world this random guy knew his name. Had he just overheard Boyd and his crew talking earlier or had they really met before and Boyd just didn't remember? But whatever the case, this guy clearly knew who Boyd was.

"...Chicago isn't the place to find big scores, if you know what I mean," the man said, a smirk spreading across his face. "But, if you're looking to retire, I can definitely provide you with something worthwhile,"

Instantly, Boyd felt his heart start beating a little faster. Not only did this guy know who he was, he knew about the heists. Boyd's hand twitched for the gun tucked in the front of his waistband. The man picked up on that and turned to face him completely. He spoke in a very low voice, ensuring only Boyd would hear him.

"You see Boyd, you and I are the same," he said. "And if you're just like me, then you're probably wondering whether or not you should pull out that gun and kill me. But, since we're the same, ask yourself this - What's stopping me from pulling out my gun? Simple. You and I aren't enemies. In fact, we're the exact opposite. You need a big pay day, right? You've got a guy, a contact who hooks you up with scores? Well, I've got an opportunity for you. You and your children and your grandchildren and your great-grandchildren will never want for a single thing. That kind of a pay day. Sounds too good to be true, doesn't it? Well, I assure you, it's real,"

Boyd was stunned. He paused for a second just to make sure he wasn't having some hyper-real dream. But no, this man was entirely real and being 100% serious. His eyes were dead serious, even if he was still smirking.

"Right now, you're wondering if I'm a cop or something, right?" the man asked.

"That wasn't exactly what I was thinking," Boyd grunted. The man chuckled.

"I've got you spooked, though," he observed. "Rightfully so. I don't know how I'd react if some random guy showed up knowing way too much about me,"

"What do you want?" Boyd asked.

"What any one in our profession wants, Boyd," the man smiled at him.

"And what's that?"

"Listen, you're a talented thief," the man continued. "That much I can see. But your crew... Your crew has one glaring problem. You've got a weak link. I think we both know who I'm talking about,"

Boyd looked over at Craig, who was already drunk and being obnoxious. Everything else aside, Boyd couldn't argue that point. He did have an issue with his crew.

"I've got a crew. A good crew, no weak links. With you, we can take down whatever we so choose," the man explained.

"Why in the world would you want me?" Boyd asked, astounded that he was even humoring this man. "Sounds like you've got it all figured out already,"

"We all have our reasons, don't we, Boyd," the man turned back around. "You have a different skill set. One that I find very, very intriguing," He reached into his pocket and slid a piece of paper over to Boyd. "My number. Give it some thought, then give me a call. Time waits for no one, but I have a feeling you'll make the right decision. Besides, with a woman like Kayley McKenna in your bed, I'd want to give her the best possible life. You and I both know that,"

"What... How do you know about her?" Boyd gasped. Shocked didn't even accurately describe what he was feeling at the moment. He looked Boyd up and down, before standing up, and patting him on the shoulder.

Without another word, the man slapped a few bills on the bartop, covered them with his empty beer bottle, and headed out of the bar. As he walked past Boyd, he adjusted his shirt, revealing the grip of a pistol tucked in the small of his back. Hands shaking a little bit, Boyd picked up the piece of paper and looked at the number, recognizing the first three digits as the area code for Los Angeles, California. By the time Boyd looked back toward the door, the man had already left the bar.

"Who was that you were talking to?" Juan asked when Boyd finally returned to their table.

"Eh, just some guy," Boyd mumbled, feeling the folded up piece of paper in his pocket. "Are you guys ready to go?"

"Yeah I'm good to go," Juan nodded, throwing a few bills on the table.

Making their way out of the bar, Boyd popped a cigarette into his mouth, and lit it. Craig did the same, exhaling loudly as the nicotine flooded his system. Boyd puffed on the cigarette and started walking toward where they'd parked their trucks.

"Are you doing anything tonight, boss?" Patrick asked Boyd as they walked.

"Nah, how about you?"

"So, Boyd!" Craig interrupted, breath reeking of alcohol. "The boys here tell me you've got a new piece of ass,"

"His words, not mine," Patrick put his hands up. Boyd gave Patrick a resigned look and shook his head.

"They did, huh?" Boyd asked, purposely not engaging with his uncle. He focused on the cigarette, trying his best to ignore Craig.

"I heard she's quite the girl," Craig continued, shoving Boyd a little too hard for Boyd's liking. "A real knockout,"

"I just said she was very pretty," Juan chimed in, sensing the growing tension between Boyd and Craig.

"So, what's wrong with her?" Craig asked. "Why's she hanging out with you?"

"You'll have to ask her," Boyd grunted, flicking the ash away from the tip of his cigarette. He kept walking, keeping his gaze straight ahead and not even looking at his uncle.

"Oh I will," Craig guffawed. "So, listen, does that mean things are officially over with Brittany?"

"Craig..." Juan said wearily, knowing Craig was walking on thin ice. Patrick looked at Boyd, trying to gauge if he should intervene or not. Everyone at McTiernan Steel knew that Boyd kept his personal life very, very private. He didn't enjoy talking about that aspect of his life and for the most part, people respected him enough not to ask questions.

"What?" Craig asked obnoxiously. "I'm just wondering! You know what, better yet, before you get too attached to this new slut, why don't you let me take her for a spin?"

Boyd threw his cigarette on the ground and lunged at his uncle, grappling him around the waist. Using every ounce of strength he could muster, Boyd lifted him up off the ground, and smashed him into the ground. Straddling him, Boyd rained down punches, battering Craig's face relentlessly. Jerking his knee upward, Craig caught Boyd in the groin.

"Shit!" Boyd swore in pain, doubling over. Craig brought his fist up and hit Boyd under the jaw, tossing him back on the ground. As Craig was about to pounce on Boyd, Juan grabbed him to prevent the fight from continuing.

"Let go of me!" Craig growled, thrashing wildly.

"Stop it!" Juan yelled at him. "Calm down, stop this shit!"

"Let go of him," Boyd snarled, standing up to his full height and cracking his knuckles.

"Boss, come on," Patrick protested. "Not here,"

"No," Boyd shook his head, glaring at Craig. "Right. Here,"

Reluctantly, Juan let go of Craig. He and Boyd squared up, staring hatefully at each other. Juan and Patrick stood back, letting them have the sidewalk.

"God, I've been waiting forever to kick your puny ass," Craig spat, throwing up his hands.

"Feeling is mutual," Boyd grunted.

Craig moved first, throwing a right cross as hard as he could. Sidestepping the blow, Boyd kicked Craig in the knee, causing it to buckle; he knew Craig had bad knees and went right for the finishing blow. Craig dropped to his knee and Boyd hit him in the face with a devastating kick; his boot smashed off the side of Craig's face. As Craig fell onto his side, Boyd drew the pistol he had on him and racked the slide back, chambering the first round.

"Woah, woah, Boyd!" Patrick yelled, seeing the gun come out.

"Stay out of it," Boyd pointed a sturdy finger at Patrick. He knelt down and pressed the gun to Craig's bloody face.

Craig put his hands up in surrender, wincing in pain. Boyd's heart was beating like crazy. As much as he wanted to pull the trigger, he absolutely could not do it. He was in public and had already let his emotions get the best of him. Drawing a gun in public was a pretty stupid idea and as he took a few deep breaths, Boyd's sense finally came back to him. Slowly, he put the gun away and looked at Patrick.

"Make sure he gets home," Boyd mumbled. Patrick nodded warily.

Turning on his heel Boyd walked back to his truck, jumped in, and sped off. He checked his phone and saw a missed call from Rob. Boyd sighed, knowing that could mean only one of a few things. Their meeting place was set, it rarely ever changed. Reluctantly, Boyd jumped onto the highway and headed West.

\*\*\*\*

There were two wooden bridges that stretched across the Naperville Riverwalk. They looked like something from Colonial America, which suited its location in Historic Naperville. The bridges were a popular location for photoshoots, especially during the fall. Fortunately, it was late enough that the Riverwalk was virtually empty, minus a few couples here and there - walking closely together or sitting on one of the many park benches.

Rob stood at the center of the bridge, hands on the railing, overlooking the Riverwalk; a cigarette was pinched between his lips. Boyd approached him quietly, taking his place beside him, and likewise looking out over the small stream of water. Still without a word, Boyd popped a cigarette into his mouth and lit it, taking a long drag.

"You ok?" Rob finally asked. Boyd nodded solemnly. "Good. That jewelry store pulled in a pretty good haul, huh?"

"Yeah, I've almost cleared my dad's entire debt," Boyd muttered spitefully. Rob nodded his head, understanding the feeling of resentment that Boyd had toward his father. "I'm just so sick of this shit, man. I don't even get to reap the benefits, I have to virtually pay off Craig's loyalty..."

"I told you what you should've done about Craig a long time ago," Rob commented.

"I know, I hired the assholes to kill him!" Boyd snapped. "Not my fault they got whacked,"

"Calm down, ok?" Rob said, always calm. "You wanna talk to me like an adult, go ahead. Save the yelling and screaming for some other peon,"

"Sorry," Boyd took another drag from his smoke. He shook his head, more in disgust with himself than anything else. "I just wish I knew what kind of guy he was before all of this, you know?"

"You know..." Rob said quietly. "You never told me why you wanted to kill him. I mean, I can infer, but you never gave me a real reason. I know you don't like him..."

"That's not reason enough?" Boyd asked. Rob chuckled.

"Sometimes it is," he said with a grin. "But sometimes, there's a deeper reason. I think you and I both know which one this is,"

"Eh, you're not wrong," Boyd shrugged. "It's been a long time coming if you ask me,"

"I don't need to know, I was just wondering," Rob went back to smoking his cigarette.

Boyd mulled over the thought of telling him for a few moments. He'd never told anyone about his deep-rooted hatred for Craig or the reasons behind it. The people at his job could surely see it, but even they only had half of the story.

"The night my mom and my aunt died..." Boyd muttered, tapping another cigarette out of the carton. He lit up the second smoke before continuing. "They went out looking for Craig and my dad. At the time, my parents were having... marital issues. I was still young, never really knew what was really going on with them, but it was bad. Bad enough that my dad was hardly ever home after work. He'd go out with Craig and get shitfaced and roll in after I was already asleep. I'd wake up in the middle of the night and hear him and my ma going at it. They thought they were being quiet, but you know how that goes,"

"Sure," Rob shrugged.

"Anyway, that night Craig and my dad went out. Didn't text anyone, didn't give any indication where they were going, just went out to get fucked up. Happened so many times in the past, I didn't think anything of it in the moment. But for whatever reason, that night, my mom got all worried and panicked. Just had sixth sense or some shit, who knows. She calls my aunt and they go out looking for these two idiots. And that was the last time I ever saw my mother, ever spoke a word to her..."

"Jesus, man," Rob breathed, finishing his cigarette and tossing it into the river. "I'm sorry to hear that, I had no idea,"

"It's ok, I've gotten over it, I guess," Boyd lied. "It was hard to be mad at my dad, I know he wasn't the bad influence in that situation. Craig was always the one encouraging my dad to be a drunk. I don't blame my dad nearly as much as I blame Craig. The guy's never taken on any responsibility, but he's been happy to leech off my family for years,"

"Yeah... I'd probably want to kill him too," Rob admitted.

"I want to. God knows I want to be the one to do it... But I can't. I just can't bring myself to cross that line. I don't know why," Boyd shook his head and tossed his smoke into the river. He took a deep breath and ran his hands through his hair. "So, what was it you wanted to talk about?"

Rob smiled and reached into his back pocket, pulling out a packet of papers. He handed them to Boyd and leaned against the railing of the bridge, letting Boyd scan the packet. The more and more Boyd read, the wider his eyes got. A smile crept across his lips.

"You're serious?" Boyd breathed. Rob nodded.

"Might need an extra guy. Or two. There's no guarantee you walk away from this one. But if you want it, I have an in for you,"

"I want it," Boyd said immediately. "When do we go?"

"A few weeks. After a Sunday night bout with the Packers," Rob said. "I'll need to brief the crew myself this time, there's a lot of moving parts here,"

"Whatever you say. I'll find an extra guy, I think I've got someone in mind,"

"We'll be in touch then," Rob nodded. He turned and walked away, his footsteps echoing across the bridge as he departed.

As soon as Boyd climbed back into his truck, he opened his glovebox and found the number of the guy who he'd met at the bar. It was a risk for sure, to involve someone he barely knew, but the possible reward was worth the conversation. Putting his phone to his ear, Boyd waited for an answer, tapping his steering wheel nervously.

"Hello?" the man answered.
"It's Boyd,"
"I was wondering when I'd hear from you,"
"Listen, let's meet. I got something I want to run by you,"
"When and where?"

# CHAPTER 20

# Kayley

It was true. There was no denying it anymore, no pretending that it wasn't reality. In the last 24 hours, Kayley McKenna had learned a few critical pieces of information about herself and about the man she'd been spending her time with. She was having trouble grasping the reality of the situation, but that didn't change it.

Boyd McTiernan was the man that they had been looking for. Although he didn't explicitly state it to Kayley, Boyd implied enough for Kayely to know. She had no idea how many of the heists he could directly take credit for, but she figured most of them were his. It sickened her. But not for the reasons that one would think.

The right thing to do was to tell Klint that Boyd was their guy that they had been after. That was what she was supposed to do, that was her entire purpose for being there in Chicago. She had done her job to perfection; gotten close enough to Boyd that he confided in her a deep, dark secret. The hard part was over, all she had to do was tell Klint, and she would consider it a job well done.

But as she sat at the warehouse, waiting for the others to arrive, Kayley felt sick to her stomach. Turning the likes of Klint and John loose on Boyd didn't sit well with her. Like her, Boyd was a former soldier and could handle himself. But Kayley didn't want to tell Klint the truth for one massive reason - She was falling for him. She realized when he spent the night in her hotel room that she was falling. Hard. It was totally wrong and against everything she was supposed to believe in. Kayley was still a soldier at heart and on paper, Boyd was the enemy. It didn't really matter if she agreed with that or not, that was just the truth. She had been brought to Chicago to help combat crime and Boyd was a criminal, and a dangerous one at that. The right thing to do was to turn him into Klint.

The garage door started opening, snapping Kayley out of her thoughts. Expecting Klint, Kayley gathered herself and tried to not worry about what was about to happen. Much to her surprise, she saw John walking into the warehouse, clicking his key fob to lock his truck. He waved at her and pushed his sunglasses up on his forehead.

"How're you doing?" he asked, closing the door behind him. Kayley felt her entire body relax slightly to see John.

"I'm ok," she lied. "Are you?"

"Fine, fine," John muttered. "Klint's been pretty quiet. Have you heard from him at all?"

"Can you blame him?" Kayley asked. "But no, I haven't,"

"I guess not," John said with a small smirk.

"You know, you didn't have to stick up for me like that,"

"I know I didn't have to," John put his hands in his pockets. "But he also didn't have to talk to you like that. I can put up with a lot of things, but there are some things that just set me off,"

"John..." Kayley was debating whether or not to confess to John what was troubling her. She felt like she could trust him; the bond between soldiers wasn't easily broken and she felt that unwavering bond between her and him. It was different than the way she felt with Boyd, but the trust was there.

"What's up, Kayley?" John asked. He leaned against the wall, crossing his arms.

Kayley wanted to tell him. She wanted to tell anyone, just to get it off her chest. Maybe he'd understand. Certainly John would be more understanding than Klint would be. Taking a deep breath, Kayley looked at John and spoke in a low voice.

"John, I have to tell you something..." Kayley began.

Suddenly, the garage door began opening and Klint, Kade, and Noah strutted into the warehouse. Kayley hung her head and slapped a smile on her face. It was all she could do to keep her sanity at the moment.

"Hold that thought," John muttered.

"Yeah," Kayley mumbled regrettably.

"Glad to see you all could make it," Klint said, giving John a curt nod. He walked over to Kayley and smiled softly. "Can I talk to you for a few minutes?"

"Uh, yeah, sure," Kayley nodded. Klint gestured for her to follow him and lead her back outside. Once they were alone, Klint turned to face her and sighed.

"I owe you an apology," Klint said. Kayley was taken aback to hear that. She hadn't known what to expect from him, but she didn't expect an apology. "I was wrong to call you out in front of everybody like that. That wasn't fair to you and it certainly wasn't professional. I'm struggling with this case and I took my frustrations out on you. I don't want you to leave and I think you bring a lot of value to the team right now. I hope you're not too mad at me about that,"

"Oh... No, no, of course I'm not mad," Kayley answered. "I understand, I think everyone is feeling stressed,"

"Thank you for understanding," Klint smiled.

Although Kayley wouldn't have put money on it, she felt that there was something Klint wasn't sharing with her. Either something he wanted to say or ask, but either way, he was biting his tongue. There were certainly things on Kayley's mind that she didn't want to share with Klint. She made the decision right there to not tell Klint anything. There was no way Kayley could betray Boyd's trust.

Once back inside, the meeting went about as expected. Klint gave updates on their current objectives, which weren't that different from last weeks. None of their side investigations have proven to be worth anything. As far as Kayley was concerned, Klint didn't know how to handle hitting a wall in the investigation. Part of her felt guilty, knowing she could give him everything he was desperately trying to find. If she did that, however, she'd be putting Boyd in danger, and that was not an option.

Klint dismissed them less than an hour later and left with his brother and Noah, leaving just John and Kayley. Locking up the warehouse, John turned and cocked his head at Kayley.

"You still want to talk?" he asked. "I'm heading into the city if you want a ride,"

"No, it's ok," Kayley responded, having a change of heart. She couldn't risk telling anyone the truth about what she knew. As much as she wanted to trust John, she didn't think that if she told him the truth that it would stay between them. "I'm going out to Naperville for the night,"

"Oh, fancy," John commented. Kayley shrugged. "Well, have a nice night,"

"You too, John," Kayley said with a half-sincere smile.

His truck roaring, John pulled away from the warehouse, leaving a cloud of dust and exhaust in his wake. Walking a few blocks down, Kayley waited for her ride. It took less than two minutes for her to recognize the white utility truck driving towards her; she smiled when Boyd pulled up alongside the curb and leaned over to open the passenger door for her.

"What in the hell are you doing all the way out here?" Boyd asked as Kayley climbed into the cab of the vehicle.

"Location scouting," Kayley said, leaning over the center console to kiss Boyd.

"If you say so," Boyd kissed her back. His tone let on that he didn't fully believe her, but he didn't say so, which Kayley was glad about.

"What's for dinner?" Kayley asked, buckling her seatbelt.

"You?" Boyd answered immediately. Kayley gave him a sideways look.

"Better drive fast then,"

As Boyd pulled away from the curb, Kayley didn't even notice the truck that began to follow them. The truck kept its distance so as not to get spotted, but followed them all the way back to Boyd's home in Naperville. When Boyd and Kayley slipped inside the home, John Shannon slowly drove past the house, discreetly snapping a picture of the front of the house.

****

Boyd and Kayley lay on the couch in Boyd's family room, their clothes strewn about the room. Kayley was still awake, but Boyd was sleeping silently, no doubt worn out from the day. Slowly so she didn't wake or startle him, Kayley got up and went into the kitchen, not bothering to get dressed first. She made herself familiar with the kitchen and looked for anything she could make for dinner. They had planned on going out, but it was getting late and neither of them seemed to be in the mood to leave again. Finding the necessary ingredients for spaghetti and red sauce, Kayley went to work preparing dinner; boiling water and heating up the red sauce. She went back into the family room and threw on her clothes before continuing to work on dinner.

"What're you doing in there?" Boyd called from the couch, about twenty minutes later. His head popped up over the back of the couch; grinning from ear to ear to see Kayley in his kitchen. "You know, I could definitely get used to this,"
"Well, don't," Kayley laughed. "I don't cook,"
"Sure coulda fooled me," Boyd commented. He stood up, groaning in discomfort, and headed toward his bedroom. "I'm gonna take a quick shower. Try not to miss me too badly,"

"No promises,"

While Boyd washed the day off, Kayley finished preparing dinner and setting the table. It had been a very long time since Kayley had put this much effort into preparing a meal. In fact, she knew the last time had been with her ex. She fixed two plates of food, opened a bottle of wine, and sat down at the table. Boyd reappeared from the bedroom a few minutes later, wearing sweatpants and a ripped sleeveless t-shirt.

"Kayley, I can't believe you went to all this trouble," Boyd smiled, kissing her on the cheek before he took his seat. "This looks delicious,"

"I tried, I'm not super confident in my cooking abilities," Kayley said shyly. Boyd took a monstrous bite of spaghetti and nodded in approval.

"Oh yeah, that's delicious," he mumbled through a mouthful of food. He went in for another bite and Kayley felt incredibly happy.

They ate their food, drank the wine, and enjoyed a lengthy conversation about the food they'd eaten during their military careers. Kayley found herself consistently happy with just how easy and comfortable it was to be around Boyd. But no matter how much she enjoyed her time with Boyd, the unfortunate reality of her predicament kept coming back, like an itch that just wouldn't go away no matter what she did to relieve it. The closer she and Boyd got, the harder it would be to admit the truth. How could she tell him the real reason they'd even met in the first place? There was no easy way for her to live a lie, but lying to someone that she was genuinely starting to feel for was a million times worse. The longer it went on, the harder it was getting for her.

"You want to watch a movie?" Boyd asked, setting his fork and knife in his bowl. He grabbed his wine glass and took a sip, offering the bottle to Kayley.

"A movie sounds perfect," Kayley agreed. She grabbed the bottle and poured herself another glass. "More time to work on this,"

"God, you're so perfect," Boyd breathed, like he couldn't believe his fortune. Kayley felt her heart ache, hearing those words. If only he knew.

"I'm not, though," Kayley muttered, avoiding eye contact. Boyd rolled his eyes.

"Don't argue with me on that one, ok?" he laughed. He got up and cleared the table, setting everything in his kitchen sink. "I'll handle those later. Come on, I need a hug,"

Cuddling up on the couch, Boyd turned on a random Netflix movie that he hadn't seen before. With Kayley wrapped around his body like a vine, it didn't take long before he fell asleep, snoring quietly as the movie played on. Kayley smiled and held him closer to her body, enjoying the level of intimacy. It wasn't too long before she fell asleep too, resting her head on his shoulder. In her sleep, she dreamed of the future she wanted. Traveling the world, not as a soldier, but as a civilian. Seeing Rome, London, the Sydney Opera house, all the destinations she'd written down on her bucket list. She envisioned the home in California, the state she loved and felt most comfortable in. The one consistent factor of those dreams was Boyd. He was there, experiencing it with her. Kayley had thought she'd been in love with her ex, but what she felt towards Boyd was something else entirely. She wanted a future with him and would do whatever it took to be able to live out that dream.

****

It was well into the afternoon by the time Kayley got back to TheWit. She and Boyd eventually made it to his bed, sleeping as late as Boyd's job would allow, which was still hours earlier than Kayley was used to getting up. In the military, early mornings were a regular thing. But since becoming a civilian, she'd fallen back into virtually the same sleep schedule she had when she'd been in high school.

Her hotel room was dark, she'd never opened the drapes the day before. Sunlight was trying to get into the room, but most of the living room was shrouded in an eerie haze. Setting her purse and phone on the table by the door, Kayley kicked off her shoes and walked toward the living room to open the shades.

"Hello Kayley,"

Kayley's stomach dropped and she wheeled around to see who was in her hotel room, her self-preservation instincts kicking into overdrive. John Shannon sat on the couch, his leg propped up on his opposite knee, arms spread against the back of the couch.

"Jesus Christ!" Kayley scolded. "What the hell are you doing here?"

"Sit down, Kayley," John said, his voice ice cold. She looked in his eyes and saw an intensity that she'd never seen from him thus far. Kayley just stared at him, narrowing her dark eyes.

"Sit down," John repeated.

"John, stop with the posturing," Kayley snapped, feeling her anger rising. She was incredibly uncomfortable with John's presence; something about the entire situation was so wrong.

"Kayley..." John looked at her and narrowed his eyes. Slowly, he reached into his jacket and pulled out a pistol fitted with a suppressor on it. He didn't aim the weapon at her, but he placed the gun on the couch next to him.

Kayley felt her heart begin to beat a little bit faster and her hands start to sweat. She had two weapons in her apartment, a rifle and a pistol, but they were both tucked away in the bedroom closet; a lot of good those did her now. John's gaze was unwavering, completely stoic and utterly emotionless; it gave Kayley the chills. Reluctantly, Kayley sat down in the chair in front of him, keeping her eye on the gun next to him.

"John..." Kayley spoke quietly.

"No," John shook his head. "You don't get to talk. You get to listen. Klint brought you in because he obviously trusted you and saw something. I wasn't so sure, but you saved my life, which is why we are even having this conversation. I'm gonna give you the benefit of the doubt. But Kayley, I swear, if you give me an answer I don't like, I will not hesitate..."

"Ok," Kayley said, her heart racing now. She was truly terrified because she'd seen what John was capable of; she knew he wouldn't hesitate to kill her.

"He picked you up, far too close to the warehouse for my liking," John said.

"I thought you'd..."

"Left?" John finished Kayley's sentence. "Yeah, I had. But the last few times I've seen you, something's been off. I thought maybe you were having trouble with everything we're doing, but I kept reminding myself, she's a soldier. You were deployed in combat. This is a cakewalk compared to the Middle East,"

"John, you don't understand," Kayley protested.

"What don't I understand? Tell me you're just playing the part. Tell me you're not really doing what I think you're doing,"

Kayley lowered her gaze, falling silent, which was all that John needed to see to know that truth. She wasn't 'just playing the part'. It was more than that, much more. John scoffed and shook his head in utter disgust. She looked at him, feeling the immense weight of his stare.

"Kayley, aside from being the man who nearly killed me, and you I might add, is he the one we're looking for? Was Klint right about him?"

She couldn't lie about it. John would see right through her and she had no doubt in her mind that he'd find out the truth, one way or another. In that moment, fear of the unknown scared her more than admitting the truth to John. Her stomach knotted with guilt at her betrayal of Boyd.

"Yes," Kayley croaked, her eyes filling with tears.

"Christ," John lowered his head and shook it. He was quiet for a while, staring at the carpeted floor. When he looked back up at Kayley, she was crying silently. "Why? Explain it to me,"

"Which part?" Kayley muttered.

"All of it," John said. Kayley sighed and took a deep breath, wiping her eyes with the back of her hand. "I have to understand, otherwise I don't know how much help I can be,"

"Help?" Kayley looked confused.

"Just explain it to me," John repeated. "Your job was just to get close to him to figure out whether or not he was the guy,"

"Exactly," Kayley said. "My job was to get close to him!"

"But not *that* kind of close," John answered curtly. "Come on, you and I both know that's not what the job was,"

"He's not evil, John. He's not even a bad man," Kayley defended. John kept his facial expression as neutral as possible, now letting Kayley take the lead of the conversation. "But I didn't mean for any of this to happen. It just sort of happened. I tried my best to do the job Klint asked me to do, but I started having feelings for him. I genuinely did. And then it became too complicated,"

"When did you find out who he really was?" John asked.

"Only a few days ago," Kayley admitted.

"He told you?"

"He did,"

"Why?"

"I don't know... Maybe he's been feeling as guilty as I have about the entire thing. Leading a double life is hard on a person,"

"Trust me, I understand that," John muttered. "What're you thinking right now?"

"About?"

"Him. What's the plan? How were you going to figure this out?"

"I don't know," Kayley hung her head. "I think I love him, John. I know it sounds crazy, but I fell for him. And I don't know what to do. I don't want to see him go to jail or get killed, but Klint..."

They both were silent for a minute. John looked at her, his eyes softening upon seeing how genuinely upset Kayley was.

"Does he know about you? Your connection to Klint?" John finally asked.

"No, I swear, there's no way he could know,"

"Ok," John said quietly. He reached over the for gun and Kayley jumped to her feet.

"John, wait!" she screamed.

COWBOYS OF THE SKY - 273

"Relax!" John yelled, putting his hand up. He put the gun back into his jacket. "I'm not going to hurt you, my god,"

"Ok," Kayley breathed a sigh of relief.

John pulled the gun back out, releasing the magazine, and showing it to Kayley. The magazine wasn't even loaded with bullets. Giving her a stern look, John snapped the empty magazine back into the gun and tucked the gun away in his jacket.

"I was never going to hurt you, Kayley," John reassured her. "I just needed you to tell me the truth,"

"You're going to tell Klint," Kayley whispered.

"Is that a question?"

"What do you mean?" Kayley looked at John as he stood up and straightened out his jacket. Looking at his boots again, John shook his head and cursed under his breath before cracking a smile.

"Kayley, this whole thing is fucked," he said. "Klint got in way over his head, that much is obvious to me. I'm leaving at the end of the week. I've got some stuff I need to finish on my end. Not going to figure it out here, that's for damn sure. So no, I don't plan on talking to Klint. That being said, my advice to you is the same. Get out of town. If you really love this man and can overlook everything he's done, then take him and go and don't look back. I know what it's like to lose people you love and it's the absolute worst. That kind of hurt doesn't heal, how could it? If it's real, if you think it's real, take a chance. That's what I did and I'll never regret it. But, make a decision and stick to it. Understand that Klint will chase after this guy. Understand that this guy is never going to be able to stop looking over his shoulder as long as he lives. I don't know why he did what he did, but if you respect, understand, and can live with those reasons, then who am I to judge you? Just don't invite me to the wedding, don't think I could participate knowing this dude put a few rounds in me,"

There was an awkward moment of silence before John and Kayley both shared a laugh. He walked over to her and gave her a hug. She hugged him back, relieved to know that she hadn't been wrong about him. John was a good man trapped in the body of something else entirely. There was so much goodness in him, even if he rarely let that side show. And in that sense, he reminded Kayley so much of her own father. He'd been a good man, trapped in the body of a PTSD-stricken veteran; a man who's only escape came on the battlefield. She understood that John was a lot like that. He'd probably never stop fighting, never not answer the call of duty. Like her dad, patriotism was in John Shannon's blood. And at the end of the day, the general population was safer having men like him out there.

"You take care of yourself, Kayley," John whiserped, letting her go and walking out of the room. "I'll see you around, ok?"

"Yeah," Kayley smiled. "See you soon, John,"

# PART 3

# The Devil You Know

*"A man does what he must - in spite of personal consequences, in spite of obstacles and dangers and pressures - and that is the basis for all human morality" - John F. Kennedy; Former President*

# CHAPTER 21

# Klint

Chicago Police Detective Klint Kavanaugh sat on the edge of Mayor Kelly Hart's bed in utter disbelief, watching the local news broadcast. He felt his hands starting to sweat as he watched the TV with complete focus. It was just past six in the morning and the news anchors were talking excitedly to one another about what had occurred the night before.

"...It's hard to explain the scale of what took place here last night," the reporter on the ground was saying to the two anchors back in the studio. "Not a single alarm was tripped, they didn't even show up on the security cameras,"

"Absolutely incredible," one of the anchors commented, really putting on a show for the cameras. "Now as we said earlier, police officials have yet to comment whether or not this heist last night is connected to the several others that have occurred in the last few months. Police all over the midwest have been hunting for a crew of bandits, nicknamed *The Marauders*, but so far all efforts to bring the bandits to justice have proved unsuccessful,"

"What the hell happened?" Klint breathed to himself. He'd missed the first part of the news report. Pulling out his cellphone he dialed a number and put the phone to his ear, standing up and pacing the room while he listened to the dial tone.

"Richard Brown,"

"Rich, it's Klint," Klint said quickly. "I'm watching the news right now, what is going on? What happened? What got robbed? I've been preoccupied, I haven't checked my email or texts yet,"

"Boss, we got a real problem on our hands," Rich said ominously. It sounded like he was walking away from somewhere fairly busy. "Sorry, the Chief and Superintendent are both here right now. They're pissed. You're gonna get read the riot act when you finally come in,"

"Why? What the hell happened?"

"There was a huge heist last night at First American," Rich explained. "It's like they were ghosts. No alarms were tripped, the security cameras were all working, but nothing. These guys didn't leave a single piece of evidence behind for us to go off of. But, they cleared out the entire bank, minus the dye packs and tracers. According to the managers, there was about twenty to twenty-five mil between the vault, cash drawers, and the ATM,"

"They cleared out the ATM?" Klint asked in disbelief.

"Cleaned house, man," Rich exhaled. "Absolutely cleaned house,"

"Shit," Klint shook his head. "Ok, I'll be down there soon. Get a warrant written up for us to search McTiernan Steel Construction. I want the warrant signed by a judge and on my desk by the time I get there,"

"Uh, ok," Rich answered. "I'll get working on that right away,"

"I'll be in as soon as I can,"

Once off the phone with Rich, Klint grabbed his clothes off the love seat in the corner of Kelly's bedroom. Getting dressed as fast as he could, Klint grabbed his shoes and hurried downstairs, pulling the shoes on once he got down to the main floor.

"Kelly!" he called into the house, assuming she was in the kitchen. After getting no response, Klint hurried into the kitchen just to make sure she wasn't there. There was no sign of Kelly anywhere in the house, which wasn't too weird. Usually, though, she never left without leaving at least a note or a text. Klint didn't think much of it as he grabbed his wallet and keys before going out to his Charger; the house had an automatic security system that engaged anytime someone left the house. On his way to his car, he sent Kelly a quick text, wishing her a good day and telling her he'd be back over later tonight. He sent a similar text to his daughter, wishing her a good day as well. Once he was in his car, Klint connected his phone to BlueTooth and started driving toward the police station.

"Call Noah," Klint used the voice command feature in his car. The call didn't even go through before an automated voice spoke to Klint.

"The number you have dialed is out of service,"

"What the fuck?" Klint muttered, picking up his phone to make sure he had the right number for Noah. After triple checking that it was indeed the right number, Klint tried again to call him. Once again, the call wouldn't go through. Klint hung up and found John's number, calling him instead. It went straight to voicemail, only adding to Klint's frustration.

"Where is everybody?" Klint yelled, hitting the top of his steering wheel in annoyance. Something in his gut was telling him that this was wrong. People not answering their phones, another heist... it all just felt wrong. Something was going on, something that he wasn't privy to, and that made him nervous. He couldn't stop thinking as he continued driving, trying to get to the station as quickly as he could.

In his distracted state, Klint didn't notice the minivan that had been following him for the past few blocks. He didn't notice the van speed up and dart into the opposite lane to get right next to him until it was too late. By the time Klint registered that the driver was in the wrong lane, the side door of the van was already sliding open. A man wearing a Jason Vorhees mask aimed an AK-style rifle out of the van at Klint's Charger.

"Holy fu-!" Klint couldn't even finish the curse before the gunman opened fire on his car. Slamming on the brakes, Klint ducked to avoid getting shot. The AK sounded like an explosion every time the gunman pulled the trigger. For the most part, the rounds shredded the engine block of Klint's Charger; a few stray rounds hit the windshield. His window shattered, raining glass shards down all over him. The gunman paused to reload before blasting another thirty rounds into Klint's car, popping the two front tires. Smoke billowed out from the engine block, inhibiting Klint's view of the road. He reached for his gun on his hip, but the second he did, he heard the tires of the van squeal as it peeled off down a one-way street.

Just as quickly as it started, the shooting stopped.

Car alarms were ringing around Klint's car, the gunfire had no doubt set them off. His ears were ringing, his hands were shaking slightly, and he had a few cuts on his face from the glass, but remarkably, he hadn't been shot. The gunman had had him dead to rights; if he wanted Klint dead, Klint would've been dead. That was all he could think about at the moment; he should be dead. Slowly, he climbed out of the shredded Charger, grabbing his cell phone and dialing 9-1-1.

"This is Detectvie Klint Kavanaugh," he said once he got an operator on the line. He was rattled, but still calm enough to tell the operator what he needed. "I was just ambushed by two guys in a black minivan. Shots fired, I say again, shots fired. Need units to respond to my location immediately. Get an APB out on a black Dodge minivan,"

****

Within a half hour, the entire street had been closed and police had swarmed the neighborhood around Mayor Kelly Hart's home. The shooting had drawn the attention of a few civilians and news outlets, as it typically did in Chicago. Against his will, Klint was forced to get checked out by the paramedics, who refused to release him until he cooperated. His foul mood was only worsened when he overheard a pair of patrolmen talking about how the Dodge minivan had been found, burnt to a crisp in an alley a few streets down from where the shooting had occurred. The gunman or gunmen had gotten away. In a city with CCTV cameras to spare, the criminals still always seemed to be one step ahead of the cops. It was a phenomenon that never failed to infuriate Klint.

It hadn't been a random shooting, Klint was sure of that. At least, he was fairly certain it couldn't have been random. The whole thing felt targeted, it felt personal. They hadn't tried to kill him, rather send a message. Well, the message was received, as far as Klint was concerned.

"Are you ok?" Rich asked, propping a foot up on the tailgate of the ambulance Klint was currently sitting in.

"Yeah, I'm fine," Klint muttered, wincing as one of the paramedics stuck a bandage over the cut on his cheek.

"Charger's totalled," Rich muttered, shaking his head. "I'll give you a ride back to the station. Chief will want to talk to you,"

"Yeah... I gotta make sure my daughter is ok first," Klint spoke quietly.

"Do you want me to send a unit to pick her up?" Rich offered. Klint thought it over for a moment before nodding.

"Tell whoever to take her right to the station. She can sit in my office until I get there," Klint said. He stood up, brushing off the protests from the paramedics. "I need a set of wheels, I gotta go find some people. This wasn't a random shooting,"

"Klint, come on," Rich said. "You were just attacked, take it easy, and let me take you back to the station. Whatever you gotta do is still gonna be there this afternoon. Take a breath, man. Trust me, you need it,"

"I need you to trust me on this, ok?" Klint responded. He was typing madly into his phone, texting John, Kayley, Noah, and Kade all at once. They needed to meet immediately, he made sure to make it crystal clear that this was an absolute emergency. "I'll be back later today. I have to go check on something. Take care of Kara, get her some food or something, just don't let her leave the station until I know everything is going to be ok,"

"Klint..." Rich raised his voice, hating how stubborn Klint could be.

"Rich, please!" Klint begged. "Just look after my kid, ok?"

"Ok, ok," Rich nodded. "I'll go get Kara myself,"

"You've got her number, right?"

"I can find her, Klint," Rich grunted, a little annoyed by the implication. Klint nodded respectfully.

"Sergeant!" Klint called to the nearest uniformed officer. "I need your cruiser right now,"

"Sir?" The patrolman looked confused and hesitant at the same time.

"Keys," Klint stuck his hand out. "Now,"

"It's over there," the officer, pointing to one of the CPD Interceptors parked on the street. He dropped his keys into the awaiting palm of Klint Kavanaugh.

"I'll bring it back with a full tank," Klint gave the young cop a wink and jogged over to the car. He hadn't driven an actual squad car in a while.

Flipping on the sirens and flashing lights, Klint sped away from the crime scene, cutting through intersections as he rapidly gained speed. There was one place he needed to make sure hadn't been compromised; his warehouse in Bridgeport. It was the only thing he could think of why the others weren't answering their phones. If someone had figured out what he'd been doing the last few months, that was all the motive a bad guy would need to try and take Klint out. He prayed he was wrong, knowing that if he was right, the others would be in grave danger as well.

****

Shutting off the lights and sirens, Klint came to a screeching halt in front of the warehouse. He leapt out of the car and ran toward the front door, thumbing the key out of his pocket, and feeding the lock as fast as he could. As soon as he entered the warehouse, the smell of gasoline hit him instantly. His nostrils were assaulted with the pungent fumes.

"Oh no," Klint muttered, pulling his shirt over his nose, even though it did little to help the smell. He drew his pistol and cleared the front office, seeing no one and nothing out of place. As he moved closer to the actual warehouse, he could hear low voices. A small sense of relief washed over him. The others had gotten his text and had come, just like he'd asked. Lowering his gun, he pushed open the door and entered the warehouse.

Noah Riordan stood in the middle of the warehouse with two men that Klint had never laid eyes on before. They were all wearing similar clothing; dark jackets, jeans, and black boots. In front of Noah was another man. His back was to Klint, but Klint could tell that it was not his younger brother or John Shannon. Kayley was also nowhere to be seen. Gasoline had been poured over almost every inch of the warehouse, the smell was almost unbearable and it soaked Klint's shoes as he walked toward the group. His internal alarm system was going haywire.

"Noah!" Klint called, approaching the group. "I didn't ask you to bring guests,"

"I know you didn't, Detective Kavanaugh," the man in front of Noah said loudly. "But, given the circumstances, I figured it was past time you and I had a conversation. Noah was kind enough to extend an invitation to me,"

The man turned around and Klint's eyes went wide, the air was sucked out of his lungs in an instant. Boyd McTiernan stood before him, smiling his signature smile at the bewildered police detective. He held a revolver in his right hand.

"Hello Klint," Boyd said.

Klint heard someone come up behind him and whirled around, bringing his gun up. The man in the Jason Vorhees mask walked up behind him, carrying the AK in his right hand. With his left hand, he pulled off the rubber mask. Again, Klint recognized the man.

"I know you too," Klint narrowed his eyes. "Noah's wedding..."
"Pleasure to see you again, Klint," Joe Kado said. He raised the rifle, aiming it at Klint. "Hate to point a gun at you again, but I'm gonna need that gun from you, Detective,"

Boyd raised his gun at Klint too, pulling the hammer back dramatically. He took a few steps toward Klint, keeping the gun level. Joe stepped forward and ripped Klint's gun from his hand, sticking it in his waistband. Klint looked past Boyd to Noah, who crossed his arms and stared back.

"I trusted you," Klint muttered. "Kade trusted you,"
"I know you did and I don't know why," Noah shrugged. "You knew everything about me and you misread everything that was right in front of you. I don't know what to say. I'd apologize, but no one should apologize for being what they are in this world. You are a cop and I am a criminal,"
"No, no," Klint shook his head, refusing to believe that he'd been so wrong about Noah. He hadn't been wrong. On more than one occasion, Noah had provided valuable insight about the case. In fact, it had been Noah who'd pointed Klint in the direction of Boyd. "You were helping us,"
"I was," Noah nodded, stepping forward. "I really did want to, Klint. You're not a bad guy at all, I hope you don't take this

personally. But, in the end, it was all part of the plan. You see, I have no desire to be in debt to a crooked cop like yourself or have a man like John Shannon for an enemy. John's less likely to come after me for something like this, he's got his own problems to deal with. You may have kept the cops off my ass back in L.A., but you don't understand anything about the situation. I may not like it, may not be happy about it, but this is what I have to do,"

"I don't?" Klint snapped. "Noah, you were robbing banks because your boss forced you to! You're not like these guys, you were put in an impossible situation,"

"That's true, Klint. Very true," Noah agreed. He shook his head. "And it turns out I caused more trouble when I put a bullet in Thomas Swaney. The people he was dealing with won't just go away quietly. But you know what fixes almost every single problem on the planet? Money, Klint. Money. And, truth be told, it's hard to walk away from something when you're the best at it,"

"You know, I couldn't have said it better myself," Boyd said, still smiling at Klint. He stepped right up to Klint, leaving only a few feet of space between them. The smile faded slightly and Klint lowered his voice to a low growl. "You know, it was pretty clever getting Kayley to come after me. Pretending to love me and all that shit... That was pretty smart, I have to admit it. I'm almost surprised a cop would play that dirty,"

Klint didn't say anything. He felt like he'd been played. He'd screwed up and he knew it. Looking back, recruiting a bank robber was a pretty horrible idea. But Klint's arrogance had gotten the best of him once again. And now that Boyd knew everything, Kayley was in serious trouble. All because Klint had been too damn cocky for his own good.

"You... You know about Kayley?" Klint asked.

"I told him," Noah said. "Figured the man should know the woman's been playing him,"

"Smart move, Klint," Boyd complimented. "I opened up to her... Not enough to indict myself, but enough for her to know the truth. Which was exactly the goal, huh? Get her to get me to open up to her. For a minute, I actually thought she was serious, "

Klint could see a hint of hurt behind Boyd's eyes, letting him know that Boyd was genuinely disappointed that Kayley had been playing him the entire time. It was small, but it was still a victory in Klint's mind. He'd been able to find a weakness in Boyd, even if it was microscopic.

"So what now?" Klint asked. "You two are going to go rob banks and ride off into the sunset together?"

"Basically," Noah smirked. "I hate to do this to you, Klint, but can't have you interfering with what's to come. I need it just as badly as Boyd does,"

"What're you guys planning?"

"Ha! Wouldn't you love to know," Boyd laughed. "You'll just have to wait and see,"

"You're never going to get away with this, Noah," Klint narrowed his eyes. "I swear, I'll hunt you to the end of the earth if I have to,"

"I welcome the challenge, my friend," Noah answered, flashing a smile.

Noah gave Joe a nod and Joe spun the AK around, smashing the stock off Klint's head with a vicious *crack*. Klint's eyes rolled back into his head and he fell to the ground, losing consciousness as he hit the ground. He exhaled once before his eyes shut completely.

"Boyd, you seriously want to torch it?" Darren asked. Boyd looked around the warehouse one final time. He gave Noah a nod and headed for the door.

"Light it up, Darren," Noah ordered.

Noah Riordan, Joe Kado, Chandler Bannington, and Boyd Mc-Tiernan walked out of the warehouse as Darren produced a Zippo lighter from his pocket.

\*\*\*\*

"Klint! Klint! Come on man, wake the fuck up!" John Shannon screamed. John shook Klint by the shoulders, desperately trying to wake the downed cop. Klint blinked his eyes a few times, slowly coming to. He felt an overwhelming heat around him, his exposed hands felt like they were on fire. It took only a second of being conscious for Klint to realize that the entire warehouse was engulfed in flames, burning violently. The fire had raged through the structure, red hot flames licked at the support pillars holding up the ceiling. Smoke was filling the warehouse, making it hard for Klint to even see John.

Seeing Klint come to a little, John grabbed him by the arm and yanked him to his feet. He threw Klint's arm around his shoulder and began trudging toward the warehouse door. John Shannon had gotten there mere moments after the warehouse had caught on fire; having just missed Noah and Boyd departing.

Coughing profusely, John threw his entire body against the door, smashing it open onto the street. John and Klint collapsed onto the ground as smoke billowed out after them.

Sirens from fire engines wailed as they came to a screeching halt on the scene, organizing immediately to best combat the fire.

"Are you guys ok?" Kade screamed, running over to his brother and John. "Klint, I left as soon as I got your text. I'm so sorry, I don't..."

"Save it," John grunted, getting to his knees. He spat on the ground and blinked his eyes, trying to rid himself of the smoke that covered his body; even his hands were dark from the smoke. "Help him over to the ambulance,"

John and Kade carefully carried Klint over to the ambulance that had just shown up. The paramedics popped the back doors open, allowing John and Kade to lay Klint down on the stretcher. As the paramedics went to work checking him out, Klint reached up and grabbed John's arm.

"Find... Kayley," Klint coughed. His eyes were bloodshot and crazed. "Boyd... He knows,"

"Wait, what?" John asked, ignoring the paramedics trying to move him out of the way.

"Noah... Boyd... Working together," Klint sputtered out. "Warn Kayley,"

# CHAPTER 22

# Boyd

It hurt more than he wanted to admit. But, that was the price of his blatant stupidity. There was no room for relationships, for love, in a world like Boyd's. You couldn't hide an entire part of your life from the person who was supposed to trust you above anyone else. That was a recipe for disaster. Boyd had been foolish to think he could have it all. He was angry with himself for genuinely believing, even for a brief moment, that things could work out with them. No one got it all, everyone had to give up something. And for Boyd, it seemed that time and time again, it was his personal happiness that had to take a backseat. It wasn't particularly fair, but that was the hand he'd been dealt.

To know, however, that Kayley had been lying to him the entire time was a hard pill to swallow. He'd liked her, more than he wanted to admit to himself. He'd let his guard down with her and in turn, put himself in danger of getting caught. The answer was simple - Kayley would have to be dealt with to ensure he was in the clear. Boyd was willing to do a lot of things, but going to prison was not one of them. Before his very first heist, Boyd had made up his mind that if it ever came to it, he'd swallow a bullet before letting anyone drag him away in handcuffs. The only problem with that plan was that Boyd was not certain he could bring himself to remove Kayley from the equation. Killing her... That didn't sit well with him, not even a little bit.

Kayley dug her nails into Boyd's shoulders and moaned in ecstasy; she moved her hips back and forth on top of Boyd, grinding herself over his groin. Her eyes rolled back as the pleasure became too much for her to handle. Boyd looked up at her and had to admire how absolutely gorgeous she was. No doubt, he'd gotten very lucky. He reached up and cupped her bare breasts; Kayley moaned even louder.

"Oh god... I'm so close, baby," she breathed. She leaned down and bit Boyd's neck.

As much as he tried to clear his mind and be in the present moment, Boyd was unable to focus on the task at hand. Normally, Boyd would've been hard pressed to think of anything else while having sex with Kayley. But as Kayley continued grinding her body on top of him, Boyd's brain darted around from the cop to Kayley and then back to the cop. When Noah had first told Boyd the truth, he hadn't wanted to believe him. But, Noah had proof; text messages, phone calls, everything that Boyd needed to see that he had indeed been played by Kayley.

"Are you ok?" Kayley asked, her chest heaving. She leaned down and kissed Boyd on the lips, biting his bottom lip. "You seem distracted,"

"Did I ever tell you how gorgeous you are?" Boyd asked, leaning up slightly in the bed to admire Kayley. She smiled and sat up, placing her hands on his chest.

"As a matter of fact," she purred, putting her hands on her hips. "I think you have,"

Leaping up from the bed, Boyd picked Kayley up and immediately planted kisses all over her neck. Wrapping her arms and legs around Boyd, Kayley giggled in excitement as he flipped her over onto her back.

\*\*\*\*

They lay together, intertwined in each other's bodies with the blankets and sheets in total disarray. Kayley was asleep, breathing quietly on Boyd's shoulder. He was wide awake, staring at the ceiling blankly. How could it all have been a lie? There had been so much about her that Boyd thought was just perfect for him. Their relationship had been easy, fun, the way it should be. He still didn't want to believe it. It was easier to just pretend.

"I'm so sorry, Kayley," Boyd whispered to himself, slowly crawling out of bed. He walked over to his nightstand and opened the top drawer that contained the same revolver he'd held on Klint mere hours ago. Boyd stared at the weapon for a while. Not a single ounce of his being wanted to do what he was about to do, but it had to be done. Going to jail wasn't an option for him.

Swearing under his breath, Boyd grabbed the gun and opened the wheel, double checking that the chambers were loaded. Snapping the wheel back into place, Boyd slowly walked toward Kayley's side of his bed. Using his thumb, Boyd pulled the hammer back.

292 - CARL MICHAELSEN

His hands were shaking horribly as he approached Kayley's sleeping body. He could feel his stomach getting more and more uneasy as he came to a stop right next to her, the gun barely a foot from her head. He raised the gun and ever so gently put the barrel to Kayley's forehead.

Feeling the cold steel against her head, Kayley's eyes shot open. She saw Boyd standing over her. She felt the gun on her head. Her heart began beating rapidly as she locked eyes with Boyd. He looked distraught.

"Tell me it isn't true," Boyd said quietly. Kayley was too stunned to speak. She opened her mouth but couldn't formulate words. Her breaths were shallow and shaky, her eyes began to moisten.

"Boyd..."

"Tell me it isn't true," Boyd repeated himself, pressing the gun a little harder to her head. "Tell me you haven't been lying to me this entire time,"

"Please..." Kayley begged in a voice that was barely a whimper. Tears began escaping from her eyes. "I didn't mean for this to happen..."

"So what... he put you up to this? Told you to fuck me in order to get me to trust you? Is that how it goes?" Boyd raised his voice, only making Kayley more afraid.

"I'm sorry," she whispered. "How...?"

"I had a nice long talk with your friend. Detective Klint Kavanaugh," Boyd explained to her. "Oh yeah, I know everything. Your job was to get close to me so you could then tell Klint and get me killed or thrown in jail,"

"It's not like that, Boyd," Kayley tried to defend herself.

"Bullshit," Boyd snapped. "You lied to me, played me for a fool. You betrayed me..."

"No, I didn't," Kayley cried. "Boyd, I didn't. You have to believe me,"

"Stop lying to me!" Boyd yelled. "I am so sick and tired of the lies! Just tell me the fucking truth!"

"I am telling you the truth!" Kayley screamed back, her military bearing coming back to her.

Before Boyd could react, Kayley threw her legs up, catching Boyd in the head with her knee. She grabbed his wrist, jerking her head to the side to avoid getting shot, and twisted as hard as she could. The gun fell from Boyd's grasp and onto the bed. Flipping to the side, Kayley kicked at Boyd's chest with all her strength, knocking him clean off his feet. He fell on his back, landing hard on the floor. Grabbing the gun off the bed, Kayley leapt up and aimed it at him, standing over him.

Boyd kicked out Kayley's feet from underneath her and jumped up to his feet, catching her by her hair before she hit the ground. Wrapping his strong hand around the revolver, he ripped it from her grasp before throwing her onto the bed, and aiming the weapon at her once again.

"Stop it!" he screamed. "I don't want to fight you!"

"No? You just wanted to put a gun to my head!" Kayley screamed back. It finally registered with her that she was completely naked. She grabbed the sheet from Boyd's bed to cover her body. "You were seriously going to just kill me? Without even getting my side of the story?"

"And what side is that, Kayley?" Boyd yelled. "You've been lying to me this entire time! Making me think you actually cared about me, just so you could find out if I'm really robbing banks in my free time? Well, yeah, I am! I didn't have a fucking choice! I didn't ask for any of this!"

"Then how are you in this situation, Boyd?" Kayley yelled back. "You're a grown man, act like it! Take responsibility for your actions,"

"You don't know what you're talking about," Boyd shook his head.

"You're damn right. And neither do you!" Kayley barked.

Boyd lowered the gun slightly.

"What are you talking about?" Boyd asked. "What else is there to know? Klint told me..."

"Klint doesn't know shit," Kayley shook her head. "Why were you even talking to Klint in the first place?"

"Noah," Boyd admitted. "Noah came to me. He's the one who told me the truth about you working with him and Klint. I wasn't sure I believed him, so I confronted Klint about it..."

"Noah?" Kayley appeared genuinely confused. "Noah came to you? Why?"

"He's a criminal, Kayley. Just like me," Boyd let the gun drop to his side. "He needs a big pay day, just like me. He must've realized it made more sense to work together and I'm glad he did. Found out who I could really trust,"

"Oh yeah?" Kayley asked. "Well, did Noah tell you that I was planning on leaving? Did Noah tell you that I've been lying to Klint about you? Did Noah tell you that I have been trying to protect because... Because I could love you?"

Boyd was silent. He could see it in her eyes, hear it in her voice. She wasn't lying and wasn't trying to save her own skin. Kayley was telling the truth. The gun in his hand suddenly felt like it was scalding hot; he tossed it on the nightstand, disgusted with himself for the entire situation. Turning his back to Kayley, Boyd sat down on the bed, putting his head in his hands.

"I'm so confused," he said, more to himself than to her. "I don't know what to do,"

"Well..." Kayley said softly. She moved across the bed and sat down next to him. "We could start by being honest with each other. You're right, Klint brought me to Chicago to help him. He's been trying to take down a lot of bad people, I guess. My job was just to assist and play a part, so to speak. When you guys robbed that truck and killed the cop... Klint got really obsessed about it. Made it his only priority. That's why I followed you to that bar that first night. He wanted me to get close to you and report back what I could find out,"

"He wanted to know if it was me? How the hell did he connect it back to me so fast?"

"The cables you guys used..." Kayley said. "They were the same cables you used to escape out of the apartment after meeting with those gang guys,"

"How do you know about that?" Boyd asked, looking at her in shock.

"Because Boyd... I was the other shooter who was there that night," Kayley admitted. "You shot one of the other guys on the team, almost killed him,"

"You... You were there?"

"I was," Kayley nodded.

"I'm sorry," Boyd hung his head after a moment of silence. "I'm sorry you were there,"

"You were hiring those guys to..."

"Kill my uncle," Boyd finished her sentence.

296 - CARL MICHAELSEN

"Why?" Kayley asked, the only natural question. Boyd took a deep breath and looked at her.

"Kayley, there's a lot about my past, my family that isn't pretty. But I never, ever, wanted to hurt people. I joined the military because I wanted to serve. I wanted to be a good person, I wanted to give myself to a higher cause. I've never felt more fulfilled than when I was serving our country. But you come home... Come home to the mess that my father left for me to clean and it just changed me. Craig is the reason my mom died. And I'll never forgive him for that. That's why I hired those guys to kill him. I didn't want his blood on my hands, at least not directly. It also wouldn't have surprised anyone if Craig got gunned down by a few gangsters. He's pissed off everyone in this godforsaken city,"

"You've never talked about your mom," Kayley commented.

"It's not something I talk about," Boyd responded.

"Why the robberies then?" Kayley pressed. "And was Craig in on those as well?

"He was," Boyd confirmed. "He's got the skills needed, he's a good asset sometimes. I can separate my personal feelings. As for the robberies, it all goes back to my dad. He took money from guys you don't take money from. All so he could provide for me and my mom. What kind of son would I be if I didn't carry on his legacy? That's why I've been so hell bent on paying back every nickel he owes. I don't want anyone to take the company from me because that's... That's my dad's legacy. That company was everything to him and I am not about to let him down. I can't. I've already failed my parents enough, not anymore,"

"That's too much pressure to put on yourself," Kayley said. "After a while, you have to do things for yourself. You can't keep putting your life on hold for someone who's not even around anymore,"

"Maybe," Boyd muttered. He paused before continuing. "Look, did you... Did you really mean that? That you were lying to Klint to protect me?"

"Yes," Kayley nodded. "I wasn't ever going to give you up to him. I could've loved you, Boyd. At first, it was just the taboo of the whole situation that excited me. But getting to know you... I fell for you. What can I say? I didn't want it to happen, I hated myself for it, but I fell for you,"

"Oh," Boyd muttered.

"For the longest time, I didn't know what to do," Kayley said. "I knew I wanted to be with you, but I also knew what Klint suspected of you. I tried so hard to stop the feelings I had for you, but I just couldn't. In the end, that's what won out. I was never going to give you up to Klint,"

Boyd wasn't sure what to say or how to feel about that. It was nice to hear, but she'd still lied to him. Granted, he had lied to her as well, but it felt different coming from her. He had already made up his mind that he wasn't going to kill her; he never would've been able to really pull the trigger. But they couldn't continue. After the next job, Boyd would have to leave town for good, which meant saying goodbye to the company, to his friends, to the city he'd called home for so long. With the heat from Klint, there was no way Boyd would be able to stay in Chicago. He would have to look over his shoulder for the rest of his life. That was a lifestyle that was better done solo. Kayley couldn't be a part of his life; not now and not ever. She just couldn't. There was nowhere for that relationship to go.

"Please say something," Kayley whispered, touching Boyd's knee. He looked at her sadly and kissed her cheek.

"You know, we could've been something had we met at a different time in our lives," Boyd muttered. He stood up. "I'm sorry, Kayley. I really am. But this... This can't happen anymore,"

"Boyd..." Kayley began to protest.

"No," Boyd shook his head. "Don't make this harder than it has to be. It was never real, it wasn't real. Don't overthink it,"

"Boyd, that's not true. I know it's a lot, but we can still get away from all of this. We can leave tonight, head out West back to California or wherever you want to go,"

"No, Kayley," Boyd shook his head, his demeanor unwavering. She was quiet for a minute and Boyd lowered his voice. "Kayley, I think you need to go now,"

"Please don't do this," Kayley whispered.

"Kayley, I need you to leave now," Boyd repeated himself. He stood up and handed Kayley a ball of her clothes.

Shaking her head, Kayley grabbed her clothes from Boyd, fighting back her emotions. Biting her tongue, Kayley got dressed, gathered her purse, phone, and other items before she walked out of Klint's front door. She slammed the door behind her and waited in the driveway for her Uber. When the car arrived, Kayley looked back at the house sadly before getting in. The whole while Boyd watched from his living room, not returning to his bedroom until she was in the car.

Boyd lay down in bed and was close to falling back to sleep when his phone rang. He reached over onto the nightstand and answered without looking at who was calling.

"Hello?"

"If you hurt Kayley..." a man growled on the other line. "I swear to god I'll bury you,"

"Who the hell is this?" Boyd snapped, sitting up in bed. The man's voice was truly terrifying, unnerving Boyd greatly.

"Shannon. John Shannon," the man said. "You don't know me yet, but you will. You're gonna hate me,"

"Is that so?"

"I'm pretty sure," John continued. "I don't really care for being shot multiple times, but somehow it just seems to keep on happening to me. You'd think one of these times someone would get wise and put me out of my misery... But until then, I'm still here to ruin your day. Also, a word of advice. Next time you want to leave a cop for dead in a burning warehouse... I'd make sure he's actually dead. But, I'm sure Klint will be around to return the favor,"

The call went dead and Boyd stared at his phone for a second before throwing it across the room. He punched his pillow and swore loudly. It took almost five minutes, but once he got himself under control he got out of bed and found his phone. He picked up his phone from the floor and dialed a number, putting the phone to his ear. It rang for a few moments before Rob answered.

"Yeah?"

"We have a problem," Boyd said, swallowing his pride by finally admitting to Rob that the situation was out of control. "Klint's still breathing. He has to be dealt with. Permanently,"

"And he will be," Rob agreed. "The decision to make... before or after this job?"

"What do you think? I'll trust you," Boyd answered.

"After," Rob said without a moment of hesitation.

"Ok," Boyd nodded. "Then after it is,"

"Call the crews. We'll meet tomorrow and discuss everything," Rob insisted. "I'm going back to sleep,"

"See you tomorrow,"

\*\*\*\*

The building was still under construction, not open to anyone outside from the contractors that were authorized to be on site; a gate and fence was set up around the perimeter. Being one of the contractors who had access to the site, Boyd had a key to the gate, allowing him entrance onto the site. It was located in Wrigleyville, close to Wrigley Field where the Chicago Cubs played. The area around the building was largely restaurants, bars, and shops which drew in a sizable crowd most nights. Tonight was no different, the many bars were packed.

They parked their trucks around the bars, choosing a few different garages and lots before walking to the building. On the fifth floor, spot lights were set up for the workers around the massive open floor. The concrete and ironwork was done, but the rest of the building was yet to be finished. Blue tarps, plastic sheets, hundreds of tools and other construction materials were littered over the building. A single large table was in the middle of the sprawling, unfinished room. Blueprints and architectural drawings were all over the table, being held in place by ash trays.

"It's relatively simple," Rob stated, placing his hands on the table. He pointed to three different rooms that were circled on the drawings. "The cashrooms are located here, here, and here. Security is tight and CPD is going to be crawling outside so the key is stealth. Don't blow our cover until we absolutely have to,"

"Make no mistake…" Boyd chimed in. "There is absolutely nothing simple about what we are about to do. Over 60,000 people to deal with, not to mention employees, security personnel, etcetera.

There are a lot of variables to deal with, we need to be prepared for everything,"

Around Boyd and Rob were Boyd's crew - Craig, Juan and Patrick. Also in attendance were Noah Riordan and his crew - Joe, Chandler, and Darren. Craig looked moderately disgusted with Noah and his crew, but mostly his angst was aimed at his nephew, still sour about the beating Boyd had laid on him. Boyd knew it, but pretended to not even notice the looks Craig was constantly shooting at him or the sound effects he was making under his breath as he and Rob continued their briefing.

"We're going to need to hit the cash rooms simultaneously, so we'll be working in teams of two. Three teams on the cash rooms and one team waiting in the North Garage for the getaway," Boyd explained. "We're gonna be carrying rifles and pistols and I want maximum pressure applied to the security guards and cash room employees. These are the nine-to-five types, they're not about to catch a bullet for some cash that doesn't belong to them. CPD outside on the other hand, that's exactly what they want. A cop gets shot on duty, they get to do the news station tour, they're a goddamn hero. We have to do whatever we can to avoid the attention of the cops,"

"What about a distraction?" Noah asked, feeling his input was just as valuable as Boyd or Rob. After all, he was in charge of his crew, they didn't take orders from Boyd or Rob.

"A distraction?" Rob repeated. He folded his arms. "Well what did you have in mind?"

"Something big, something loud, near the stadium. Draw the cops on the perimeter away, give us a few more minutes to work with," Noah said, purposefully being vague.

"Do you have a specific idea or are you just shooting in the dark here?" Rob asked.

"Oh, I've got an idea," Noah nodded. "We ran this same kind of diversion back in the day in L.A. You hit a bank or something like that a few minutes beforehand. Draw all the cops into one location, sneak away when they're completely preoccupied. You'll have at least ten extra minutes to work with, which is a lifetime,"

"Theoretically that could work," Rob agreed. "But our crew is not big enough. We need three teams to hit the cash rooms and not having a getaway team in place is a recipe for disaster,"

"Do we really need two people on the getaway?" Noah asked. "One should be plenty, right?"

"Two is better," Rob held firm. Boyd kept quiet, enjoying hearing how Noah's mind worked. As a fellow thief, it was interesting to hear an alternative point of view. "The extra man can help load the take, speed the entire process up,"

"Oh come on, we don't need an extra man to load the take," Noah protested. "We'll have seven men on site, the two others can hit something nearby; make it loud, make it aggressive, get a lot of attention,"

"You're mistaken, my friend," Rob smirked. "There's eight guys. Total. So, even if seven are in the stadium, that leaves one guy to the diversion,"

"Oh really?" Noah asked sarcastically. He narrowed his eyes on Rob. "Because, I'm looking around here... And I count nine,"

Rob kept his facial expression as neutral as possible, but he clearly didn't like Noah's tone. He took a step toward Noah. Although Boyd was enjoying the macho posturing from both Noah and Rob, he stepped in to defend his friend.

"Rob plans the jobs," Boyd looked at Noah. "That's the extent of his involvement,"

"Ok, so then I'm assuming, because we're the ones taking all the risk, that Rob's cut is significantly less than the rest of ours,"

"Rob's cut is for a fair share of work," Boyd responded evenly. Noah smiled.

"Sure it is,"

"Hey, you want to plan it, be my guest," Rob snapped.

"Easy, both of you," Boyd raised his voice slightly. "You can measure dicks later. We need to figure this out right now. Now, Noah brings up a good point. A diversion is not a bad idea. In fact, it's a great idea. It'll give us more time to work with and that's the truth,"

"I'm not arguing with that," Rob agreed. "But, personnel wise, it doesn't work,"

"Yes it does," Noah countered. He gestured to everyone standing around the table. "There's nine of us here, that's plenty,"

"I already told you, this is all I'm involved in," Rob repeated himself, getting more and more annoyed with Noah.

"Why?" Noah asked. "Look, we all know what kind of a payday we're looking at. It's big. If this is the best way to minimize the risk, why aren't you willing to help out?"

"I'm already doing all the planning and prep," Rob said.

"So do a little more," Noah responded. "Earn that cut of yours. Look, the way I see it, you're not going into the cash rooms or being the getaway. But you can certainly hold up a bank or something with another guy. Hell, a monkey could do that,"

"How many times do I have to repeat myself?" Rob yelled. "God, are you guys from Cali fucking deaf?"

"You know they say living close to the ocean has that effect," Darren commented. "The constant crashing of the waves leaves a hum in the ear. Plus, it's very hard to understand you Chicagoans when you speak. That accent is... truly thought provoking,"

Rob stared blankly at Darren. Noah stifled a laugh. Chandler looked down at his shoes and bit his lip. Joe grinned. The others weren't sure how to react, but Boyd cracked a smile.

"Rob, don't hate me," Boyd spoke up. "But Noah isn't wrong about this,"

"Really?" Rob looked at Boyd, defeated. Boyd shrugged.

"It would help us to have an extra guy," Boyd said. "I think we can all agree on that. If you have another guy who's solid and we can trust, let's hear it. But if not..."

"I know plenty of guys," Rob said quietly. "You need an extra guy, I'll get you an extra guy,"

"Perfect," Boyd nodded, satisfied.

"Just gonna let some stranger in on this?" Noah asked.

"We're letting you assholes in on it," Patrick commented.

"Guys, come on," Boyd looked at Patrick and shook his head. "Can we just be civil?"

"Moving on..." Rob went back to the drawings. "The escape and getaway route should be pretty straight forward. We go right to O'Hare, catch a plane that I've chartered for us, and we're gone. Patrick, I know you'll be coming back because of the kids, but for the rest of us, this might be the last time we set foot in Chicago,"

Boyd had known that it was getting close to having to take an early retirement. He had no real love for the city he'd grown up in, but hearing Rob phrase it like that hit Boyd a little harder than expected. The thought of never coming back, leaving absolutely everything behind, didn't sit well with him. There was a sense of resentment; Boyd hated that he knew that it was the only option.

What they were planning, what they were about to do, would bring a ton of heat. Staying in Chicago was a death sentence. And, contrary to most of his actions, Boyd intended on living a very long life.

"How will we access the cash rooms?" Joe asked, directing the conversation back to the heist itself. "I mean, do we know what kind of security system are we dealing with? Biometrics?"

"Either way, it won't matter," Rob said, picking up a black duffle bag and dropping it on the table. He unzipped the bag and pulled out a small, black cylinder. It didn't look like much, but it was one of the most important pieces of equipment Rob had been able to acquire for the job.

"Anyone know what these are?" he asked. No one spoke up. "These are skeleton keys. Still in the testing phase for the Department of Defense. It'll allow you to bypass any lock or security system. A universal key, so to speak,"

"How the hell did you get your hands on something like that?" Noah asked, impressed.

"Pays to know people, Mr. Riordan," was all that Rob said. "I have three of these, one for each team going into the stadium. Be extremely careful with them. I am *borrowing* these. I need them back in pristine condition,"

"Good to know," Boyd nodded. "Alright, the game is in ten days. That means we have ten days to get the cars, guns, and pick something to hit for the diversion. We'll meet every day until the heist. If anyone thinks of anything, speak up. This is a collaborative effort between all of us, we need everyone's A-game. Understood?"

Boyd was met with a volley of nodding heads. He reached into his pocket and popped a cigarette into his mouth. Craig did the same and started walking toward the service elevator. One by one, the guys started to leave. Darren and Chandler grunted something to Noah as they left. Noah turned to follow them out, along with Joe.

"Noah, hang back a minute," Boyd said. Noah nodded, muttered something to Joe and stayed behind while everyone else - minus Boyd and Rob - left the building.

"What's up?" Noah asked.

"Klint's still alive," Boyd muttered. Noah's eyes went wide and he started fidgeting with his pocket. He did not like hearing that one bit.

"You sure?" Noah asked. Boyd nodded.

"John called me," Boyd explained. "No idea how he got my number, but he's a serious dude,"

"Trust me, John is not to be messed with. He is dangerous and worse, he's totally unhinged," Noah shook his head. "Goddamnit, I knew I should've had Joe just blast him outside the Mayor's home,"

"That would've just brought more attention, which is what we don't need right now," Rob countered. "But, we need to handle him before the job. He's going to be coming for both of you now. I've got a few friends in high places, I read up on John Shannon, and Noah is right, that guy is bad news,"

"So we take them out?" Noah asked.

"I'm not a triggerman," Boyd shook his head. Noah actually laughed.

"Oh, ok," he said, overly sarcastically. "Well, Joe has no problem pulling triggers. I'll have him do it,"

"I think I have a better idea," Rob said, pulling up his phone. "Klint is a relatively simple man to dissect. He's got weaknesses. Now, we can't go anywhere near the Mayor. We'd have a SWAT invasion and be dead within an hour, that's suicide,"

"So, what then?" Boyd asked.

"Klint has a daughter," Rob explained. "She's a freshman at DePaul. We threaten her safety, Klint will fold, without a doubt,"

Boyd and Noah exchanged looks, trying to gauge how the other one felt about a potential kidnapping.

"Are you saying we take her?" Noah asked.

"I'm not saying that explicitly," Rob clarified. He always chose his words extremely carefully. "But, it wouldn't hurt to tail her for a day or two. Get a schedule down, figure out where she's staying, that type of thing. We can make Klint an asset instead of a threat,"

"That's a big risk," Boyd said, taking a drag of his cigarette. "Kidnapping is three to seven years. But kidnapping a cop's kid, that's a death sentence,"

"So we don't kidnap her," Noah said. "We *threaten* to. I have Klint's numbers, let's use it to our advantage. I'll get Joe tailing the girl today, he's good at that sort of thing,"

"Ok," Boyd nodded. "Good plan. I'll handle the cars,"

"Get a van if you can. A Sprinter or something like that," Rob recommended. "It's going to make moving the take a lot easier,"

"I realize that," Boyd gave him a funny look. "This ain't my first rodeo,"

"I'll let you two lock up," Noah said, clapping both Rob and Boyd on the shoulder. "See you tomorrow,"

Once Noah was descending down the service elevator, Rob started packing up his drawings, blueprints, and other plans. Boyd put his cigarette out on the ground and tossed the butt aside.

"This is going to be brutal, you know that right?" Rob said, looking at his friend. "I'd have a back up plan, just in case,"

"I have one, trust me," Boyd reassured his friend. "Might be time for you to retire too,"

"Yeah, sure," Rob smirked. "I'm too damn good at this kind of thing,"

"So why not help us out, Rob?" Boyd asked. "I don't trust some random guy you recommend. I trust you,"

"You really want me on this?"

"It's your job, buddy," Boyd shrugged. "You might as well see it through, right?"

Rob picked up his bags and shook Boyd's hand. He started walking toward the service elevator, stopping just before getting on. Slowly, he turned around and winked at Boyd.

"I'll let you know,"

# CHAPTER 23

# John

As he waited outside the hospital room, John tried again and again to get a hold of Kayley. She hadn't answered any of his previous calls or texts, which worried him immensely. With Noah's betrayal, they were all at risk. Noah knew too much about them personally and the longer time went on without hearing from Kayley, the more concerned John became. He didn't really think Noah or Boyd had killed her, but he couldn't rule out the possibility.

His call to her went straight to voicemail, once again, and John left the same voicemail he'd been leaving for her. Hanging up and stuffing his phone in his back pocket, John marched back inside the hospital room.

Klint was being treated for severe burns to his legs, feet, and back, as well as smoke inhalation. None of it was life threatening, but still gnarly and painful for him to have to deal with. The nurses were constantly making sure the burns weren't getting infected and reapplying dressings to the wounds.

Kade had shown up as soon as Klint arrived at the hospital, having followed the paramedics there. He had zero intention of leaving his brother's side until he was discharged. It was particularly hard for Kade to realize what had happened; he'd grown to be the closest with Noah over the last few months and had genuinely liked the man.

"How's he doing?" John asked Kade, keeping his voice down. Klint was asleep, miraculously. The discomfort from the burns made it hard for him to find sleep without the help of intense painkillers.

"He's fine," Kade mumbled. "I called his daughter, she's on her way here. Haven't been able to get a hold of the Mayor,"

"Ok," John nodded, crossing his arms. "Haven't been able to reach Kayley either,"

"You don't think..."

"I don't know," John shook his head. "When his daughter gets here, come find me. I'll be outside,"

"Why?" Kade asked. John glared at him.

"Because you and I have shit to do," John said, matter of factly. "Klint's gonna be laid up for a minute and we need to find these guys as soon as possible,"

"Where do we even start?" Kade asked.

"First, we talk to the Mayor and find out where Kayley is. Then we can worry about Noah and Boyd," John grunted. He fished his cigarettes and lighter out of his pocket. "I'll be outside,"

It only took about fifteen minutes before Kade jogged out of the hospital towards John's Excursion. John was just about to light up a third cigarette, but decided against it. He climbed inside his truck and turned it on while Kade jumped in the passenger seat. As soon as Kade buckled his seat belt, John handed him a pistol; Kade cocked the weapon and let it rest in his lap.

"Where to first?" Kade asked.

"City Hall," John said as he flew out of the parking lot and onto the road.

\*\*\*\*

John wasn't the least bit concerned with interrupting whatever the Mayor had going on. He'd never cared about being polite or following protocol, specifically when lives were at stake. That trait was just one of many that got him kicked out of the Navy. Of course, John recognized that his passion was often misinterpreted as just another abrasive asshole who thought he knew more than everyone else. But in John's experience, it was often the case that he did know more, and better, than those making decisions. He led Kade through City Hall towards the Mayor's office.

"Can I help you?" the Mayor's young secretary, Molly, asked. She looked at John with a moderate degree of concern.

"I need to speak to the Mayor. Now," he said sternly.

"I'm sorry, but the Mayor isn't available right now," Molly responded professionally. John leaned on the desk in front of Molly and glared at her.

"You seem like a nice girl, so please don't take this personally," John began. "But I truly do not give any kind of a fuck about what the Mayor's schedule looks like. You tell her John Shannon needs to talk to her right now. Is that clear?"

Molly nodded quickly, gulping out of nerves, before she stood up and hurried over to the Mayor's office. She gently knocked on the door twice before entering.

"Hard to believe you're still single," Kade mumbled.
"Not the time," John warned.
"My bad," Kade stifling a chuckle.

Reappearing from the office, Molly waved John and Kade over. They both marched over to the office and John gave Molly a respectful nod. The Mayor was hanging up her phone just as John and Kade entered. She looked exhausted and stressed.

"Gentlemen," Mayor Hart said, forcing a smile onto her face. "What can I..."
"You know Klint's in the hospital?" John said, much louder than was appropriate to be addressing her with.
"Klint's... In the hospital?" the Mayor asked. "Is he ok? What happened?"
"He'll be ok, but he's pretty banged up," Kade answered, giving John a moment. "We have a real problem, Mayor,"
"Noah Riordan, the guy Klint brought in for the team, turned on us," John explained. "He's working with the crew in town here. I'm not sure why, but I'm assuming they're preparing to do a job,"
"Oh my god," Mayor Hart gasped, sitting down in her chair. She shook her head, ran her hands through her hair, and then looked up at Kade and John. "Ok, what do you need from me?"
"Gear, weapons, a couple of fast cars, tactical teams on stand by, a press conference set up within the next hour, and a curfew for the city," John listed off. "We need to find these guys right now and until we do, all of us are in danger. Riordan knows too much about what Klint was into, he could use that all against us. Klint's

daughter is at the hospital, I suggest sending extra units to cover them. You're going to hold a press conference and address all of this. Say your cops are close to an arrest , but do not mention Boyd or Noah by name. The longer they think they're in the clear, the more reckless they'll become. In the meantime, we need 24-hour surveillance on McTiernan Steel Construction and additional units looking for Noah Riordan,"

Mayor Hart wrote all of John's requests on a piece of paper on her desk. She knew better than to argue with John in these types of situations. He was well equipped to handle a crisis like this, she had to trust his instincts.

"Ok, I'll have all of that set up immediately. The cars and equipment you can pick up from the Police Headquarters. I'll make sure everything is ready for you," the Mayor said. She wrote down her personal cell number on a piece of paper and handed it to John. "In case you think of anything else, that's my direct line,"

"Good," John pocketed the piece of paper. "Send those units to the hospital, ok? We're gonna go start working things from our end,"

"John, I don't want to know what you're going to do..." the Mayor said. "But please, the last thing I need is for you to do more damage to this situation,"

"You're gonna have to trust me, ma'am," John responded, stepping right back into his military role. "I've done this before, I know what I'm doing,"

Back in John's truck, they peeled away from City Hall as fast as possible. John weaved his way through the streets, heading West out of the Downtown area.

"Where now?" Kade asked.

"Visit a friend of Klint's," John muttered. "Hoping he can help,"

****

Although John had only been to the house once with Klint, he'd still remembered the general area of where it was. He didn't know the specific address, but figured he'd be able to tell. Sure enough, John recognized the two burly and tattooed men sitting on the front porch of one of the older homes. John had met them a few months prior; he hoped they would remember him as well. Driving past the home, he found a parking spot on the street a few houses down and tucked his pistol into the front of his waistband. Kade did the same.

"Should I be worried?" Kade asked. John shrugged.

"I hope not," he muttered, grabbing two extra magazines for his pistol and stuffing them in his back pocket. "But it pays to be prepared, right?"

"I guess," Kade grabbed two more mags as well.

"Let's do this," John said, opening the door to his truck. "Head on a swivel,"

They crossed the street and hurried over toward the house, slowing down once they got closer. The two men stood up on the porch, watching Kade and John intently. John held up his hand casually and waved at them, getting no such response from either of them. His hand twitched for the gun, his senses telling him that maybe this had been a horrible idea. After all, these men didn't know or trust him. They knew and trusted Klint. Hopefully, the fact that John knew Klint would be enough for these men to help him.

"You in the right place?" the first man asked. John couldn't swear on it, but he was fairly certain that the man's name was Carlos.

"Yeah, I need to talk to Javi," John said, walking closer to the porch. "I'm a friend of Klint's. Klint Kavanaugh…"

"Oh shit," Carlos muttered. "Yeah, yeah, I remember you. You're the guy who took out Miguel Santos,"

"Yeah," John nodded, breathing a sigh of relief. "Sorry to come by unannounced, but it's kind of an emergency. If Javi's around, I really need to talk to him,"

"Yeah he's inside," Carlos cocked his head toward the house. "Tomás, go get Javi,"

"Si," Tomás nodded, walking back into the house. As he turned his back to John and Kade, both men saw the grip of a pistol hanging out of Tomás's shorts.

"Is Klint ok?" Carlos asked, looking at John seriously. John shook his head.

"No, he isn't,"

"*Mierda*," Carlos cursed under his breath, shaking his head. "*No Bueno*,"

"No, no bueno," John agreed.


Tomás and Javi emerged from the doorway; Tomás sat back down next to Carlos to continue his duty of guarding the home. Javi stuck his hand out and shook John's hand.


"Good to see you again, my friend," Javi said with a small smile. He turned to shake Kade's hand. "I'm Javi. Javi Rodriguez,"

"Kade Kavanaugh," Kade introduced. Javi raised an eyebrow. "Kavanaugh? As in Klint Kavanaugh?"

"He's my brother," Kade said. Javi smiled and nodded.

"*Tu hermano* is a good man. So, what brings you here?"

"Well, Klint, actually," John said. Javi looked at John curiously. "Klint's in the hospital right now. He was attacked... Left to die in a warehouse after they lit the building on fire. He's alive, going to make it, but still in bad shape,"

"You're kidding me?" Javi's face got very serious and he crossed his arms across his chest. He exchanged a deadly glare with Carlos and Tomás; the three men spoke without having to use words. "Do you know who it was?"

"Yeah, we do," John nodded. "That's why I'm here. I came here asking for help,"

"With what, specifically?" Javi asked.

"Retaliation," John narrowed his eyes. "I'll be honest, I was on my way out of the city. There's no love lost between Klint and I. But this... one of the guys on our team turned on us. And I haven't heard from one of the others on the team. It's serious. This guy knew a lot about us, our personal lives. They already took a shot at Klint, I'm worried they'll go after his daughter or the rest of us if we get in their way,"

"These guys, are they affiliated or what?"

"Two separate crews, I think," John said. "One is local, one's from California. They're bandits. They hit banks, trucks, stuff like that from what I can tell,"

"Ok, ok," Javi nodded, clearly thinking deeply about the situation. "Klint's daughter... is she safe?"

"Yes. She's at the hospital with him," John explained. "A couple of cops are hopefully getting dispatched to go look after them,"

"Cops are useless," Javi said quietly, shaking his head. "I'll send one of my guys to keep his eye on them. You said you know who did this, *sí*?"

"I do," John nodded.

"Good, you can fill my guys in," Javi said. He pulled out his phone. "I'll make some calls and gather the troops, so to speak. You cool chilling here for a while?"

"I gotta go check on one more person," John said. "She hasn't been answering, I'm starting to get worried,"

"*Claro que sí,*" Javi nodded. "Carlos, Tomás, go with Señor Shannon. Make sure nothing happens to him, he's a friend of Klint,"

"You got it, *jefe,*" Carlos nodded.

"I'll be out by my truck," John said.

Carlos and Tomás ran back inside; Javi led Kade into the home behind them. John jumped in his truck and turned the key, the engine roared to life. He put TheWit Hotel into his GPS. A minute later, a souped up black Chevy Camaro came rumbling down the road, its exhaust screaming. The passenger rolled down his window and Carlos gave John a thumbs up gesture.

"We good to go, homes," Carlos said.

"Follow me," John pulled out from the parking space and sped down the road, the Camaro close behind him.

\*\*\*\*

John slammed on the brakes and brought the Excursion to a screeching halt in front of the hotel. He adjusted his shirttail over his pistol and stepped out of the truck, leaving the vehicle running. Carlos and Tomás followed suit, the Camaro's engine echoing between the tall buildings. The valet attendants hurried over to the vehicles, ready to move them. Thumbing two hundred dollars out of his wallet, John handed the cash to the valet.

"Keep them out front," John growled. "We won't be long,"

"Uh, sir, I don't know if I..." the valet began to protest.

"Keep them out front," John repeated, staring the man down. The young valet nodded, getting the sense that John wouldn't care too much about the hotel rules and procedures for valet parking.

Once inside the hotel, the trio made a bee-line for the elevator, pushing past a family of four to get on first. The father gave them a dirty look, but didn't say anything. John hit the button to Kayley's floor and the doors to the elevator slowly closed. Once they began ascending, John pulled out his gun and released the magazine, checking over the gun one last time. He snapped the magazine back into the weapon and racked the slide, keeping the gun at his side. Carlos and Tomás drew their weapons as well.

"Check your fire, alright?" John said, not overly comfortable with having a duo of cartel enforcers covering him. "Not entirely sure what to expect,"

"We got you, *ese*," Tomás reassured John.

"Great," John grunted under his breath.

As soon as the elevator doors opened, John drew his gun and rushed into the hallway. He took up position in the middle of the hallway while Carlos and Tomás filled the left and the right. Remarkably in sync, the three men moved down the corridor toward Kayley's room. Approaching the door, John put his ear against it. He heard nothing on the other side. There was no way he could know what he'd find inside the hotel room, but he was done being cautious.

John took a step back and kicked the door in as hard as he could. The locking mechanism fell to pieces and the door splintered as it was thrown open violently. Stepping over the shattered door, John moved into the hotel room, leading with his gun.

The first thing he noticed was that the room was unoccupied. The bed was made to perfection, the couch pillows were organized, the towels were folded neatly on the table. It looked like housekeeping had just finished up cleaning the room as well. Not a single piece of luggage, clothing, nothing that belonged to Kayley remained in the room. It was not at all what he was expecting to find, but John was relieved to not find a body. At least if the room had been cleaned and put back together, Kayley had most likely checked out of the hotel under her own free will.

Lowering his gun, John looked around as a sense of dread began to creep through him. The last time he'd talked to her, he'd basically told her to ignore any concerns about dating a bank robber and go for it. That was back when he was planning to leave and he was still irritated at Klint. Not that it made it any better, but John had still been under the impression that Boyd was just a simple bank robber. He'd crossed a line by trying to have Klint killed.

"I'm no detective, but the room looks empty, *ese*," Carlos commented, tucking his gun away.

"No shit, Carlos," John grunted, also tucking his gun back into his waistband. "No one's been here in a while,"

"*Chica* not answering her phone?" Carlos asked. John shook his head a few times.

"We gotta find her," John muttered to himself. He pulled out his phone and tried calling her one last time. Like the last few times, it went straight to voicemail. Wherever Kayley had gone, she clearly did not want to be found.

"Maybe she left, man," Tomás suggested. "No use worrying about something that may or may not have happened,"

"Yeah, I guess you're right,"

Tomás had a point. There was no proof that anything bad had happened to Kayley. Based on their last conversation, Kayley had probably skipped town and headed back to California. But, John couldn't comprehend why she'd be ignoring his calls. In his gut, he felt that something was off. And it bothered him a lot more than he wanted to admit.

"Fuck it, let's go," John shook his head and headed out of the room.

"What about the door?" Carlos asked.

"What about it?" was all that John said, not even looking back toward the busted down door.

# CHAPTER 24

# Kayley

She watched the phone ring and vibrate on the table, not making any move to answer it or send it to voicemail; John's name flashed on the phone screen. In her hands, Kayley held her new phone; which had an entirely new number. iPhones were sometimes a pain to set up, but Kayley had gone through a few too many and was a pro at it by this point. When she'd first moved to Los Angeles, she'd gone through a phase where she refused to put a case on her phones. About four broken phones later, Kayley finally acquiesced and bought a case.

Kayley was waiting on her breakfast order and sipped a coffee as she watched the phone ring. The Starbucks wasn't particularly busy, so she didn't have to wait long for her food. She wasn't quite sure exactly which town she was in, but it was a suburb north of the city. Since moving out of TheWit, Kayley had been temporarily staying at a Holiday Inn as she waited for the day of her flight back to Los Angeles. Being a partner in the talent agency allowed her many privileges, including working remotely from virtually anywhere she chose, which she planned on taking full advantage of.

Coming to Chicago had been one of the worst mistakes of her life and she couldn't wait to get out of town. When Klint had pitched the job to her, she thought she'd really be making a difference, helping out a city that was so very desperately in need of help. The crime and murder in Chicago was disheartening and based on Klint's pitch, Kayley had really believed that they'd be able to make a big impact. Sure, she had known that there might be some undercover work and she was ok with that. She worked hard to keep her body looking the way it did, she certainly wasn't ashamed of how she looked. Women like Kayley held a certain power over men, the kind of power that made it easy to exploit them.

But, Kayley had not been prepared for Boyd McTiernan. As much as she had tried, she couldn't pretend that she didn't develop strong feelings for him. He wasn't a bad man, it wasn't that simple. All of Kayley's life, she'd been witness to the moral gray area of the world. Things were not all good or all bad, nothing was that easy. And Boyd was as complicated as they came, but that was part of his charm, in her mind. She liked how he wasn't one-dimensional, she found his good qualities enamoring and his not so great ones equally interesting. Maybe that said more about her taste in men, but she was old enough to make her own decisions about who she spent her time with. There was no regret on her end about having tried with Boyd. But at the same time, the entire basis of their relationship had been built on a lie, and every time Kayley thought of that, she got sick to her stomach.

After finishing her coffee and sandwich, Kayley threw her garbage away, and headed outside, bringing her coffee with her. She took a sip, breathed in the remarkably fresh suburban air, and started walking back toward her hotel. Her flight was scheduled for tomorrow, an overnight flight from O'Hare to LAX.

Crossing the parking lot to get back to the hotel, Kayley recognized a specific utility truck sitting in the lot, taking up two spaces. She stopped in her tracks as the driver's side door opened. Boyd McTiernan stepped down from the truck, a cigarette pinched between his lips. He had just come from work, still wearing his dirty work boots, jeans, and green hi-vis shirt. Shutting the door, Boyd wiped his hands on his jeans and smiled softly at Kayley. She was pretty surprised to see him, given how their last conversation had ended. Kayley had been resigned to the fact that she'd probably never see him again.

"Hi," Boyd said quietly.

"Wow," Kayley breathed, putting her hands on her hips. "I didn't think I'd be seeing you again,"

"Yeah, me neither," Boyd muttered, looking at his boots.

"You've been following me?" Kayley asked. Boyd shrugged and didn't answer, which was more of an answer in and of itself. "Why?"

"I've just been thinking about you... a lot,"

"Again, why?" Kayley repeated. Boyd looked up at her and stared into her eyes.

"Did you mean what you said to me? Were you serious about all of that?"

"About which part?"

"That you weren't going to turn me over to Klint. That you could've loved me. Was that all just a line or were you serious?" Boyd asked.

Kayley took a step toward Boyd and Boyd took a step toward her. He reached out and touched her hip, pulling her towards him slightly. She looked up at Boyd and leaned up, kissing him tenderly on the lips. Boyd kissed her back, his hands running up her back. Breaking away before things got too heated, Kayley held Boyd at arms distance and looked at him, her heart beating a little faster. Her mind was coming up with a million different questions to ask him, but she was overall relieved just to see him again.

"Yes," Kayley nodded. "I did,"

"Ok," Boyd swallowed and smiled at her. He was still holding her right hand, rubbing her fingers gently.

"I... I was falling in love with you, Boyd," Kayley admitted. "I'm serious. I know it sounds stupid now that you know everything, but I was. I really was,"

"Yeah," Boyd muttered, squeezing her hand. He looked into her eyes again. "I was too,"

"You were?"

"Of course I was," Boyd smiled. "You're an incredible woman. I couldn't stop thinking about you, Kayley. Part of me just wanted to forget all about you and move on, but the more I thought about it... I don't want to move on from you, Kayley. You know everything about me, I have no more secrets, nothing more I'm hiding from you. You are the first person in my life who knows me, the real me. I... I don't want to lose you, Kayley,"

"Boyd... you can't lose me," Kayley whispered. She touched his cheek with her hand. "I promise, you'll never lose me,"

"But you know what I do... you know what kind of person I am," Boyd shook his head.

"And I don't care," Kayley said. "I know the kind of person you are, Boyd, and I'll love you regardless,"

"Are you sure?" Boyd asked again. He had to be sure.

"Yes, Boyd. I'm sure," Kayley reassured him. "I want to be with you, I really don't want to leave without you,"

"When are you leaving?"

"Tomorrow night," Kayley said. "I have a flight booked out of O'Hare back to LAX. I think it leaves around nine or ten,"

Boyd bit his lip and looked at his feet again. He fidgeted with the gloves hanging out of his back pocket. Kayley could tell he was throwing around an idea in his head, working out how to put that idea into words.

"Kayley, can I... Can I come with you?" Boyd asked. Kayley blinked a few times.

"You... You want to come with me?" she looked at him, trying to see if he was being serious.

"I do,"

"What about your company? All of that that you said you couldn't leave behind,"

"Well, after tomorrow, I'm not going to have much of a choice," Boyd admitted. "Arrangements have been made for the company, but I'm gonna need to get out of here,"

"Are you doing another job?" Kayley asked in a quiet voice. Boyd nodded, not offering any details, which Kayley was relieved about. She didn't want to know what he was up to, knowing she'd only worry more.

"Everything is taken care of," Boyd said, equally as quiet. "We just have one last job to do, that's it,"

"That's it?"

"I swear," Boyd assured Kayley. "After tomorrow, I'm done with that life. I'll have enough for me, but I don't want to live out my days alone. I want to travel the world, experience things that I never thought I'd be able to experience. And I want to do all of that with someone I love. Being alone sucks, I don't want to live out my days by myself. So, if you'll have me, I'd love to do all of that with you, Kayley McKenna,"

There was a moment where neither of them spoke. Kayley was doing her best to hide her excitement that Boyd was being completely serious. All she wanted was to leave Chicago and start anew. Doing that with him made that entire situation sound a whole lot better. Boyd looked at her, waiting anxiously for her response. No longer able to keep her poker face, Kayley broke into a big smile, blushing as hard as she ever had in her life. She threw her arms around him and buried her face in his shoulder. Boyd laughed and hugged her back, holding her as close to his body as humanly possible.

"I would love for you to come with me, Boyd," Kayley said, still hugging him tightly. "Don't ever let me go,"

"I won't," Boyd said, patting Kayley's back. "I promise I won't,"

"Good," Kayley took a step back from him. "You promised, so you know that's binding forever, right?"

"Forever, huh?" Boyd asked with a knowing smile. "That sounds like a different kind of promise,"

"Let's get out of this city before we talk about that, how about?" Kayley returned his smile.

"I'm good with that," Boyd put his hands in his pockets. "So what now?"

"Well, I was going to go back to my hotel room, open the cheap bottle of wine I have, and watch a movie until I fall asleep," Kayley listed off her planned activities for the evening. "I'm all packed up, so there's not much more for me to do,"

"I might be able to think of something you could do," Boyd winked at her, smacking her butt with his open hand.

"Yeah, you think you can come up with something for both of us?" Kayley said in her 'sexy' voice. Boyd chuckled and shrugged his shoulders.

"I hope so,"

\*\*\*\*

Kayley awoke with a start caused by a dream that she had no memory of. She rolled onto her back and sighed, looking over to see Boyd sleeping soundly. He looked so calm, so peaceful, which she found odd for some reason. But then again, she'd known many soldiers in her day who could sleep like babies after hours of continual combat. Some people were just wired a little different from the rest, able to handle burdens or stressors better than the average person.

Sliding her hand and arm under Boyd's body, she gently brought him closer to her, snuggling up against him. He didn't so much as stir, a true testament to the man's ability to sleep through almost anything. She stayed still like that for almost a half hour, just listening to him sleep, and thinking about their future. It was reckless and headstrong, but every decision in her life had been that way. So far, things had worked out ok for her, all things considered. What mattered most was that she was happy. Happy and truly excited for the next chapter in her life. With those thoughts at the forefront of her mind, Kayley was eventually able to fall back into a peaceful sleep.

"You seem off," Kayley said that morning, laying in the bed as Boyd laid next to her. "Are you ok?"

"Fine, fine," Boyd muttered, not wanting to get into a serious conversation with her when he knew he had to leave. They were both naked, laying as close to each other as possible. Boyd's arms were wrapped around Kayley, locked at the wrists just under her breasts.

"Come on, Boyd. Are you sure you're ok?"

"Of course," Boyd lied with a genuine smile. He ran his hand through the locks of her curly dark blonde hair. He stared into her eyes, knowing she never looked more beautiful than she did first thing in the morning. He committed every line in her face, every lock of hair to memory.

"I'm excited, Boyd," Kayley whispered in his ear, biting the lobe sensually. "I mean it, I can't wait until it's just you and me,"

"Me too," Boyd grinned, taking her hands in his. He instantly hated himself for the next words that left his mouth. "I'll meet you at the airport tonight. Just have one last thing to take care of,"

# CHAPTER 25

# Boyd

Weapons, equipment, tech, and various other pieces of gear were laid out across four long tables. The men were relatively quiet; calm and collected as they prepared to embark on a dangerously stupid job. And that's what it was, dangerously stupid. But, every single one of them was willing to take the risk for the sake of a better future.

On a separate table lay Chicago Bears football jerseys, hats, jackets, and t-shirts; everything they needed to look like average football fans. The disguises were admittedly crude, but it was often better and easier to just be simple about that type of thing. Plus, Boyd and Rob hadn't gotten any opposition from the rest of the crew.

Boyd was still skeptical of Noah and his crew, rightfully so. He hadn't ever worked with them before. But, they appeared to need the payout as much as he did, which made him trust them a little bit. At least they shared a common goal.

The most surprising thing to Boyd was seeing Rob getting ready with them. Rob didn't appear to be nervous in the slightest. He was his usual self as he went about getting dressed in black jeans, black hoodie, and a pair of black boots; Noah was dressed identically to him. It had taken a little convincing, but Rob had agreed to help with the diversion. Working together, Rob and Noah would create a scene at the Lakeside Bank, which was the closest bank to Soldier Field. The target location itself was not ideal, but Rob and Noah didn't have to actually steal any money, just cause enough of a panic to draw the attention of the cops away from the stadium. Boyd and the others would need all the time they could get, which meant that the diversion had to be both convincing and threatening.

As he mentally and physically prepared for the coming job, Boyd found himself continuously distracted with intrusive thoughts about Kayley. He'd only really ever been in love once in his entire life and even then, there had always been so much drama and tension involved with his relationship with Brittany. While his relationship with Kayley had been extremely, for lack of a better word, unorthodox, Boyd still had a good feeling about her. There were reasons why he maybe shouldn't trust her or be skeptical of her, but their energy, their passion for one another was undeniable. Boyd couldn't deny that he genuinely did see a future with her. Not only a future, but a good one; one where he was happy. His happiness had been something that he'd put on hold a long time ago. For once in his life, Boyd was determined to put himself first. All he wanted was to get to O'Hare and get on that plane with her.

"We are all clear on the plan, right?" Rob said, strapping on a heavy tactical vest. The vest had several pockets for ammo, as well as a built in trauma plate to protect his vital organs.

"You know, we've only gone over it maybe 167 times," Darren answered. "Maybe we should go over it another half dozen, what do you guys think?"

"Is he always an obnoxious prick?" Rob asked Noah.

"Pretty much," Noah smirked. "Don't worry, Rob. We're solid,"

"We're good too," Juan nodded.

"You guys better not screw us on this," Craig said to Noah, an unlit cigarette hanging out of his mouth. Instantly, the room got tense. Chandler and Darren stood up a little straighter, as if they were preparing to get into a fight.

"And you better not risk the lives of my crew..." Noah shot back. He took a few steps toward Craig, puffing his chest out slightly to try and intimidate the man. In response, Craig took a step toward Noah. For a minute, Boyd was wondering if he would have to intervene, but both of them seemed content just trying to intimidate the other.

"You got something to say?" Craig asked. Noah shook his head.

"No. All I'm saying is watch it and be professional. Because I promise you, Craig, you put my guys in danger and I'll blast you myself,"

"Noted," Craig grunted.

Boyd had noticed right away that all of Noah's crew took an immediate dislike to Craig. He wasn't surprised, not in the slightest, but it still made the atmosphere quite tense. The fact that it had taken Noah and his crew about fifteen and a half seconds to realize Craig was a problem and was another reminder to Boyd that he'd made a terrible mistake by involving him in any of this. That was a major liability, one that would have to be taken care of.

"Just for good measure, Rob, why don't you run through it one more time, eh?" Boyd offered. "I'm sure I speak for everyone when I say that one more once over couldn't hurt,"

Rob nodded and set down the half filled rifle magazine that he was working on. He stepped to the middle of the room and looked over the group of guys before he started his last briefing of the job. Taking a deep breath, Rob began to go over the plan one final time.

"You will all be in attendance at the game this afternoon against the Green Bay Packers. Once the game is over, all of the money from the concessions and gift shops will be moved to the three main cash rooms. During that time when the employees are moving the cash, Noah and I will hit the Lakeside Bank. This should draw most of the cops away and give you guys ample time to hit all three cash rooms and make it back to the getaway van. We have our own escape route plotted and planned out, we'll be fine. Once we're away safely, we will communicate that to you all. As for you guys, Boyd was able to secure us a Mercedes Sprinter, it's parked in the garage right now. We swapped out the plates so we should be good.

"Inside the stadium, Boyd and Joe will hit Cash Room #1. Darren and Chandler will hit #2. And Juan and Patrick, you guys have the third one. Craig, you'll be manning the getaway van and helping the guys unload their haul as they come out. The key to your job will be remaining as incognito as possible. The less attention you draw to yourselves the better. The good news is that it's fairly cold so it won't be out of the ordinary for you guys to be wearing layers. We will bypass the security checkpoints via maintenance entrances so our guns and equipment don't get flagged. Once we're inside, enjoy the game. It's gonna feel like a lifetime before the game is over, but try to just be normal, act the part. Feel free to buy some beer or whatever, but don't get hammered, we all need to be on our A-game for this,"

Rob and Boyd exchanged looks, knowing it was the best move for the entire job that Craig would be relinquished to getaway duty. Boyd was surprised that Craig hadn't put up much of a fight when he and Rob had given out the assignments. It was almost as if he knew he was better off in the van.

"Anything you want to add, Boyd?" Rob asked, finishing up his brief.

"Nah, not really," Boyd shook his head. "I think you covered everything,"

"Good," Rob checked his watch. "Alright, let's get a move on and start packing up the cars,"

"Let's go, boys," Noah said to Darren, Chandler, and Joe.

All four of them grabbed handfuls of gear and headed out to the very generic cars that Boyd had secured for the job. Rob followed out after them; he and Noah were driving separately in a Toyota Corolla Boyd had boosted from the Metra station in Naperville.

"Guys, let me get a minute," Boyd said to his crew. Craig, Juan, and Patrick walked over by Boyd. He'd practiced this speech a few times, but he never thought he'd actually be having to give it. He reminded himself one last time to keep it brief and to the point, no use in getting long winded.

"I just wanted to say... It's been a hell of a ride with you guys," Boyd muttered. He was mainly talking to Juan and Patrick. "You know, I'll always wish I had more time with my old man, but getting to take over for him, getting to work with you guys, and getting to become good friends with you guys... Well, it's been one of the greatest honors of my life. You guys, you didn't even blink when I asked for help... Means a lot,"

"You're dad took good care of me for a long time," Juan said quietly. He looked at Boyd and smiled, slapping him on the back. "I owe a lot to him. Least I can do is look after his son,"

"Yeah, man," Patrick agreed. "You're like family to me, always have been,"

"Well, the feeling is mutual," Boyd smiled. "One last thing, I'm not telling the others this. I've got another flight to catch tonight, I won't be leaving with y'all. So, this might be the last chance I get to say goodbye,"

"Where are you going?" Craig asked, suddenly very interested in the conversation.

"Totally irrelevant," Boyd snapped. "The point is, I'm not going to be able to come back to Chicago anytime soon, maybe ever. The company is still gonna be here, though, and someone has to run it. I can't let my dad down that badly, it has to still stay open. Patrick, I know you're staying in the area... if you want it, it's yours,"

"Are... Are you serious?" Patrick gasped. Juan smiled and nodded, understanding how much the gesture meant coming from Boyd.

"Dead serious," Boyd nodded. "You keep the same name and everything stays the same, just keep it open. The paperwork is in my desk at the office, I've signed everything,"

Craig's eyes narrowed on Boyd hatefully, barely able to contain his anger. Boyd expected this reaction, but Craig was on the same boat as Boyd. Neither of them would be safe in Chicago going forward. A guy like Patrick made the most sense, regardless of personal feelings.

"Thank you," Patrick said quietly, sticking out his hand toward Boyd. "It means a lot,"

"Of course," Boyd smiled, shaking Patrick's hand. "Now, come on, we've got a job to do,"

Patrick and Juan grabbed their gear and headed out to the cars. Boyd heaved a duffle bag over his shoulder and was about to follow them when Craig grabbed his arm and whipped him around, his eyes fiery.

"How fucking dare you?" Craig snarled, getting right in Boyd's face. "After everything I've done for you, this is how you fucking repay me?"

"C'mon, Craig," Boyd shook his head. "You and I both know we can never come back to this place. After today, we have to leave everything behind. You know that. Stop acting like a little kid,"

"You've got a lot of nerve," Craig spat. "Ungrateful little shit,"

"Ok, Craig," Boyd nodded, keeping his voice low. He wasn't in the mood to get into it with his uncle, especially right before a job. "Let's just get through the day and then we can hash this out, huh?"

Craig shoved Boyd back and marched out toward the cars. Composing himself, Boyd rolled his head around a few times, and grabbed his burner phone. He punched in the number that Noah had provided and pressed the 'Call' button. Putting the phone to his ear, Boyd grabbed a rifle off the table and headed out toward the cars.

# CHAPTER 26

# Klint

Groaning in discomfort, Klint managed to roll over onto his side, and grab his phone off the nightstand next to his bed. It had been ringing over and over again, annoying the everlasting hell out of Klint. His vision still a little blurry, Klint answered the phone and collapsed back onto his pillow, exhausted from the physical exertion. The burns on his back were stinging, feeling as if they were on fire all over again.

He was definitely getting better, but the constant discomfort from the burns had left him unable to do even the most mundane tasks. The hospital had discharged him under the order of resting and constantly reapplying dressings to the wounds in order to heal faster. In addition, he was on a steady amount of painkillers to help. Much to his relief, Kelly had been staying with him and helping out as much as she could. But unfortunately this morning, she'd had to run into the office for a meeting.

"Hello," Klint grumbled. Part of him wanted to just throw his phone out the window of his apartment.

"Listen to me very carefully, Klint," Boyd McTiernan said. Klint was suddenly wide awake, he sat straight up, ignoring the burning pain on his back.

"Boyd?"

"You are currently laying in bed in your apartment building at the corner of State Street and Ida B. Wells Drive," Boyd stated. "You live on the 12th floor with your daughter, Kara, and small dog, Koda. Kara is a freshman at DePaul and she is currently on campus with some friends doing homework,"

"You son of a bitch!" Klint hissed. "I swear to god if you even look at Kara..."

"You'll do absolutely nothing," Boyd interrupted. "You're gonna listen to every single word I say,"

"And why would I do that?" Klint asked. "I make one phone call and I can send a SWAT invasion to your company,"

"Go right ahead," Boyd laughed. "It's Sunday, no one's there. And you're gonna listen, because as we speak, there is a high-powered rifle pointed at your daughter,"

Klint felt the air get sucked out of his lungs. His entire body tensed up and he felt a wave of nausea course through him.

"Boyd, please," Klint's voice croaked. "My daughter... She's everything to me, she's all I have. Please don't hurt her,"

"Klint, I have no desire to hurt your daughter," Boyd said evenly. "Contrary to popular belief, I'm not a bad man, just a desperate one at the moment. You're going to help me today. You're going to help me for the sake of your daughter. Do it for her, keep her in mind, and everything will go smoothly,"

"What... What do you need?" Klint asked, his heart beating a million miles an hour.

"There's going to be a bank robbery tonight. When the call goes out, you're going to make sure every single cop in the area gets called to that scene. Especially the cops on the Museum Campus around Soldier Field. All of 'em. Is that understood?" Boyd explained.

"Yeah. Yes, I can do that," Klint responded. "Is... Is that it?"

"That's it, my friend," Boyd said cheerfully. "You do that and your daughter will be home tonight in time to dinner without a scratch on her,"

"Ok," Klint hung his head. "I'll make sure that happens,"

"Good man," Boyd ended the call.

Klint threw his phone across the room, enraged. He shot out of bed and went into his bathroom, swallowing two painkillers and washing them down with sink water. The effects of the drugs kicked in a few minutes later. Gathering his phone off the ground, Klint dialed his brother's number.

"Hey, Klint. How're you feeling, bud?" Kade asked. Klint could hear Kade's daughter babbling in the background.

"Grab some gear and come to my place," Klint said. "I'll call John and get him here, too. We're gonna have a busy day ahead of us,"

"What're you talking about?" Kade asked.

"I just got off the phone with Mr. McTiernan," Klint muttered. Kade sighed audibly.

"Alright, yeah," Kade grunted. "I'll be over there soon. Weapons and everything?"

"Everything," Klint nodded. "The door will be unlocked, let yourself in. I gotta make some calls,"

"Ok, I'll be on my way shortly. Gotta explain to Jenna why I'm gonna miss another Sunday with them..."

"I'm sorry, Kade. Blame it on me, I'll talk to Jenna after this is all blown over," Klint felt bad, knowing Kade was trying to make up for lost time with his family.

"Don't be," Kade said. "I'll be over there soon,"

"Thank you," Klint hung up and immediately called John Shannon, praying he'd answer. "Come on, pick up, pick up, pick up,"

"Hey," John finally answered.

"I need your help," Klint blurted out. "Can you get to my place?"

"Uh, yeah, sure," John said, sounding slightly skeptical. "What's going on?"

"I'll fill you in when you get here," Klint said. "Bring equipment, we're gonna need it,"

"Equipment, huh?"

"Yeah, everything you got," Klint implored. "Something is going down. Tonight,"

"Ok," John muttered. "I'm on my way,"

"Let yourself in when you get here," Klint siad.

"Sounds good, see you soon,"

\*\*\*\*

Less than an hour later, Klint Kavanaugh's kitchen table was filled with guns, ammo, and various other pieces of tactical equipment. A few boxes of flashbang grenades and fragmentation grenades rested on the chairs. John, Kade, and Javi stood around the table, waiting for Klint to come out of his room. Having gained the trust of Javi and his men, John had made the executive decision to include Javi, knowing that the man could provide a significant amount of help.

"You have any idea what this is about?" Kade asked John. John shook his head.

"No clue," John said. "He sounded freaked, though,"

"Yeah, same," Kade nodded in agreement. "Hope he's ok,"

"Something's going on if he's that riled up," John commented. There was a murmur of agreement among Javi and Kade.

Klint emerged from his bedroom, limping slightly, but looking remarkably well put together. He had a look of discomfort painted across his face, but he was toughening it out as best he could.

"Thank you guys for coming," Klint breathed, sitting down at the kitchen table in front of the virtual arsenal. "I really appreciate it,"

"What's going on, Klint?" Kade asked, wanting to get right to the point.

"I received a phone call from Boyd McTiernan a little while ago," Klint began explaining. "He asked me for a favor, essentially. And if I don't comply... He's threatening to hurt my daughter,"

"Oh no," Kade shook his head. John lowered his head and looked at Klint, grimly. Even Javi was upset to hear that anyone would threaten Kara.

"What did he want?" John asked. Klint took a deep breath, fighting back tears.

"He told me that there is going to be a bank robbery tonight. When the call goes out, he wants to make sure that I pull all the cops off of the Museum Campus," Klint said.

"That's it?" Kade raised an eyebrow. Klint nodded and shrugged.

"That's it,"

"Well, that doesn't make a whole lot of sense," Kade muttered, struggling to find the connection.

"Where is your daughter?" John asked.

"DePaul," Klint said. "I called to check on her, she's fine, with friends. I didn't want to worry her,"

"I'll send Tomás and Carlos to keep an eye on her," Javi said, pulling out his phone. "Nothing will happen to her on my watch, I promise you Klint,"

"Thank you, Javi," Klint said graciously.

"No need to thank me, *amigo*," Javi excused himself from the room to call his men.

"What about us?" John gestured to himself and Kade. "What do you want us to do?"

"If Boyd's wanting the cops away from Museum Campus, assume it's going down somewhere near there. You and Kade head over there and keep a low fucking profile," Klint said. "I'm gonna communicate the situation to Rich and a few others who I trust. We need to be on high alert. No matter what goes down tonight, Boyd and Noah are either ending up in cuffs or in the morgue,"

"Sounds like a plan to me," John nodded in agreement.

"The boys are heading to DePaul now," Javi said, walking back into the kitchen.

"Great, thanks again," Klint said earnestly. He turned to John and Kade. "Ok, you two gear up and get down there. You still have those credentials I gave you?"

"Yeah," Kade said. John nodded.

"Good. Use them if you need to get in anywhere. I can only imagine what Boyd has planned. We need to let him think we're helping him, ok? Don't make a move too soon, can't risk Kara's safety,"

"We got it," John reassured him. "Trust me, we got this,"

"Ok, ok,"

John and Kade went to work filling a pair of duffle bags with AR-15 rifles, Glock pistols, and tons of spare ammo. Picking up a compact Glock from the table, John slammed a magazine into the breach, cocked the weapon, and tucked it in the small of his back. He handed Kade an identical pistol. Each of them strapped on a tactical vest before grabbing their bags and heading out of the apartment.

"Hey," Klint called. John and Kade turned around. "Good luck,"

"You too, brother," Kade smiled softly.

"We'll talk later tonight," John said, giving Klint a respectful nod. Klint returned the nod and they slipped out of the apartment, slamming the door shut behind them. Klint got up and locked the door before taking his seat at the table.

"How can I help?" Javi asked, leaning on the kitchen table.

"You already have, my friend," Klint smiled. Javi chuckled.

"I'm serious. How can I help?"

Klint cocked his head a few times, debating whether or not he really wanted to ask a known Cartel operative for help. Javi was a friend, though, and Klint did trust the man, regardless of his profession. After all, Javi had already dispatched guys to protect Klint's daughter. Klint could trust Javi to help.

"I could use a ride..." Klint said. Javi grinned.

"That I can do. Where to?"

"City Hall," Klint answered, getting a weird look from Javi. "I need to talk to our esteemed Mayor,"

"As long as I can stay in the car..." Javi said with a wry smile. "I have a feeling I won't be too popular around City Hall,"

"Fair point," Klint chuckled. He stood up and grabbed a pistol off the table. He tossed it over to Javi, who caught it in his right hand. "Let's go, we're wasting daylight,"

# CHAPTER 27

# Noah

Noah Riordan brought the Toyota Corolla to a stop right across the street from the Lakeside Bank. As it was a Sunday, the bank was empty, closed, and the doors were locked. All part of the plan. Rob took a deep breath and eyed the building, taking it all in.

"Have you ever done this before?" Noah asked. Rob smirked and nodded.

"It has definitely been awhile, but yes. I've done this quite a few times," Rob admitted.

"Good," Noah nodded with approval. "Glad you're not as green as you look,"

"Oh, trust me," Rob groaned, cracking his neck. "I'm the farthest thing from green,"

Shutting the car off, Noah put his hands on the steering wheel and lowered his head, muttering to himself for a moment. He'd made a very important life decision in the last few days, one that had changed the trajectory of the rest of his life. Going against Klint, turning on him the way that Noah had, wasn't going to be done after tonight. Noah was nowhere naive enough to believe that he had seen the last of Klint Kavanaugh or John Shannon; those two were borderline psychotic.

Noah fidgeted with his wedding ring, spinning it around on his ring finger a few times. Lexi had no idea what Noah was doing and she never could. When they got married, she'd made Noah promise that he'd give up his criminal life, and he'd tried to keep his word. But, Noah had had no real idea of the extent of Thomas Swaney's criminal dealings. Once some very bad people started coming around asking for money they were owed, Noah didn't see a better alternative. He still had some money from the heists, but that was his retirement fund, something for a rainy day. If he gave up that money, it would be over his dead body. As long as he could make it out alive from this job and keep it a secret from Lexi, he figured everything would be ok. The timing had been perfect, Lexi had flown back to California a few days prior to visit her father. Lexi and Noah had been talking about moving back to California over the last few weeks, just before Noah had made the final decision to partner up with Boyd.

Part of him was certainly still a little skeptical of Boyd, but there were plenty of similarities between them that made Noah feel a little more comfortable. Boyd needed this job to go smoothly, he needed it just as bad as Noah did. Noah had no doubts about his ability to create a convincing distraction, but Boyd and the others certainly had the harder task.

"You plan out all their jobs, right?" Noah asked. Rob shrugged, but nodded in the affirmative.

"Yeah, you could say I have an eye for this sort of thing,"

"Well, let's do this," Noah grumbled. "Good luck, bud,"
"Nah, we don't need luck," Rob answered.

Grabbing his Ghostface mask, Noah pulled the mask over his face and adjusted it so he could see clearly. Fitting an earpiece into his ear, Rob turned the channel to the police scanner, allowing him to hear when the inevitable call went out to the cops. Rob yanked a black ski mask on and took a deep breath, steadying his heart rate. It had been a long time since he actually participated in a heist, that same old nervous-excited feeling was coming back. They both grabbed their weapons and bags of equipment. There was a small crowd of people walking on the sidewalk, Noah and Rob waited until the sidewalk cleared for a moment. Jumping out of the Corolla and keeping their heads down, they hurried over to Lakeside Bank. Knowing they had only a few minutes before some passerby would see them and call the cops on them.

"Go, get that door open," Rob hissed, gripping his rifle and keeping guard while Noah dropped to a knee and reached into his duffle bag. He produced a small shotgun from the bag; he pumped the weapon and yanked the trigger, blowing a hole in the lock. The door swung open and crashed against the wall. Rob and Noah rushed inside the bank and hurried toward the bank teller's desk.

"Come on, let's go, let's go," Noah hissed. He produced a pair of crowbars from the duffle bag and tossed one to Rob. They went to work smashing into the teller drawers and stealing the packs of money, leaving behind any pack with a die pack or a tracer device in it.

Working without a spoken word, Noah and Rob systematically cleared out the drawers before Noah went to work on a safe that was located underneath the desks. Rob knocked over a few computers and generally made a mess of the place, adding to the ruse that a few rank amateurs had decided to try their hand at robbing a bank.

"Hang on," Rob muttered, putting his finger to his ear. "Yeah... call just went out. ETA of response, maybe a minute,"

"Ok," Noah nodded. He kept his voice low. "Remember, we're not trying to hurt anyone, just cause a distraction,"

"I know, I know," Rob said, disengaging the safety switch on his rifle. Noah did the same and moved toward the front door.

"Go get that back door open," Noah said, knowing that was their only logical escape route. They'd sneak out the back, change into their disguises, and move away from the bank before any of the cops could figure out what was happening.

Rob ran back through the employee break room to the emergency exit that opened up the back alley behind the bank. He moved a chair over to the door and propped it open before returning to Noah.

"Thirty seconds," Rob informed.

Noah raised his rifle and aimed down the street, he could hear the sirens getting louder and louder. He looked back at Rob and gave him a subtle nod.

"Alright, tell them we are a go," Noah muttered.

Rob switched channels on his radio.

"Ironside, this is Mastermind," Rob spoke into the radio, using their predetermined callsigns for the job.

"Copy Mastermind, Ironside reads you loud and clear," Boyd responded through the roar of the crowd at Soldier Field.

"We are a go," Rob said. "Repeating, we are a go,"

"Copy," Boyd answered.

"Here they come..." Noah smirked underneath his Ghostface mask. The adrenaline rushed back through his veins instantly bringing him a sense of excitement, like an addict that had gone too long without a fix.

A pair of Chicago Police Department cruisers came to a screeching halt in front of the bank, their tires smoking as they braked hard. A quartet of officers leapt out of their cars, guns drawn.

Noah squeezed the trigger, purposefully aiming at the cruisers and not the cops themselves. He sprayed bullets back and forth, shredding the windshields of both vehicles, and blasting off the entire magazine. Quickly reloading, Noah kept firing, knowing that more gunfire would draw in more attention from the cops. All he had to do was keep them occupied. A few pedestrians and bikers screamed before ducking for cover in a nearby bodega.

"Three more cruisers!" Rob warned, raising his own rifle and taking up a firing position across the lobby from Noah. He fired through the windows, shattering the glass, and driving the cops behind cover. So far, Noah and Rob had yet to receive any return fire; at least none that they were aware of.

The police presence outside the bank was getting larger and larger. Pretty soon, SWAT would be called, and then it would be a full on urban warzone. If Noah and Rob were still in the bank when that happened, they'd be gunned down in a nanosecond. But,

Noah still wanted to buy Joe, Chandler, Darren, and the others just a few extra minutes. Even in the middle of a gunfight, he still knew that he and Rob were taking less of a risk than those guys.

"Reloading!" Rob yelled, ducking behind cover to reload his weapon. Noah stood up and fired off another long burst of gunfire, allowing Rob time to reload.

"Just a few more minutes!" Noah screamed, ducking down. He hit the magazine release on his rifle to check how many rounds he had left. Seeing the mag more than halfway empty, Noah tucked it back in his vest before slapping a fresh one into the gun.

The cops began shooting back, organizing themselves behind a duo of relatively undamaged police cars. Their shots were semi-accurate, causing enough concern that Noah displaced to a different location along the front wall of the bank.

"SWAT has been notified," Rob informed, still listening intently to the scanner. "They are en route, waiting on an ETA,"

"Good," Noah grumbled. He reached into his duffle bag and pulled out two grenades. "When I toss these, you empty that fucking magazine, and run like hell, alright? I'll meet you out back,"

"You got it," Rob nodded, bringing the rifle into his shoulder.

"Ok, three... two... one.... Go!"

Rob leapt out from cover and stood to his full height, shooting wildly at the cops outside of the bank. Once the gun ran dry, Rob ducked and sprinted out through the back of the bank; he grabbed his bag of money and threw it over his shoulder. Yanking the pins out of the grenades, Noah reeled his arm back and launched the first one, immediately followed by the second. He heard one of the cops scream a warning before both explosives detonated, launching one of the cruisers into the air and flipping a second one onto its side.

"Go, go, go!" Noah urged, running after Rob.

There was a noticeable lull in the gunfire. Noah and Rob could hear the cops yelling to each other, trying to see if anyone was hurt, or if anyone had eyes on the shooters. Their uncertainty would buy them a few more minutes, knowing that they wouldn't make a move to enter the bank until SWAT arrived.

They came to a stop, hiding behind a trio or large Waste Management dumpsters and stripped out of their jackets and jeans as fast as possible. In Rob's duffle bag they each had a spare change of clothes - jeans, Hi-Vis T-shirts, and safety vests that had CHICAGO PUBLIC WORKS etched on the back. Additionally, Rob and Noah both put on a hardhat and Noah carried a clipboard, completing their disguise. They stuffed both of their money bags into the oversized duffles, slung the bags over their shoulders, and started running toward their car.

"Did that just go as smoothly as I think it did?" Rob asked Noah. Shaking his head, Noah silently cursed Rob in his mind.

"Don't jinx us, alright?" Noah snapped. "We're not out of it yet,"

"I'm just saying..." Rob muttered under his breath. He switched his radio back to their private channel. "Moving towards the stash car,"

"Copy," Boyd answered. "Ready to commence final operation,"

"Got it, good luck," Rob said.

"Hey, you two!" a cop shouted, pointing at Noah and Rob. "Where'd you two come from?"

"Huh?" Noah asked, squinting his eyes and holding his hand to his ear, indicating to the cop that he hadn't heard. Rob immediately held his breath, his hand twitching for his pistol in his waistband.

"What do we do?" Rob hissed.

"Just stay calm," Noah grunted through gritted teeth as the cop approached them.

"I asked where you two came from," the cop repeated, looking them up and down.

"We were just working down in the sewer, one of the sensors faulted," Noah lied through his teeth. "We were down in the manhole, weren't exactly sure what was going on,"

"Do you guys have any ID on you?" the cop asked.

"I think so..." Noah said, reaching into his back pocket. He looked at Rob. "You got your ID on you or did you leave it in the truck?"

"Think it's in the truck..." Rob said, hoping it was convincing. Rob was impressed with Noah's own ability to deceive so convincingly.

"Ok, you two are gonna have to stay put for now until we get this sorted out. Let me see what's in your bags,"

Noah complied, unzipping his duffle and handing it off to the cop. The cop took the bag and set it down in front of him, watching Noah and Rob carefully before getting down to inspect the bag. Before the cop even had a chance to spread the bag and begin his search, Noah drew his gun and hit the cop over the head, knocking him unconscious with one strike. The cop toppled over onto his side, bleeding from a narrow gash on the side of his forehead.

"No time to hide him," Noah tucked the gun back into his waistband. "Come on, let's go,"

Noah and Rob rounded the corner to a sea of police and SWAT officers, armed to the teeth. The SWAT officers were geared up in heavy riot gear, many SWAT officers held sturdy shields used for crowd control. It looked like they were preparing to enter the bank.

"Jesus," Rob breathed as they walked purposefully away from the bank, trying to act as inconspicuous as possible.
"Just keep moving, just keep moving," Noah whispered to him.

Their stash car was only a block away, but it felt like a mile. With every step Noah took, he was waiting for the cops to scream at them or for the shooting to start up again. He didn't relax, not even for a millisecond. The entire walk to the car Noah held his breath, anticipating the worst. But as they got closer and closer to the car, Noah began to feel like he could breathe again.

Unlocking the door and getting in as fast as humanly possible, Noah turned the car on and sped away; Rob hadn't even closed the door fully by the time Noah was speeding down the street. The adrenaline was fully flowing through him, giving him an exhilarating rush and burst of energy. He pounded the ceiling of the car and yelled as loud as he could.

"Fuck yeah!" Rob echoed Noah's sentiments. "Easy part's over with,"
"Great fucking job, man," Noah slapped Rob on the chest. "Let 'em know we're clear,"
"Ironside, we are clear. I say again, we are clear," Rob said into the radio.

"Copy, Mastermind.  We are a go,"

# CHAPTER 28

# Boyd

Once the call went out from Rob and Noah, Boyd stood up from his seat and headed back into the stadium, Joe was right behind him. They blended into the crowd perfectly, wearing blue jeans, hoodies, and Chicago Bears jerseys pulled on over the hoodies. Boyd was wearing a winter hat, even though it was a little warm for that, to conceal the earpiece he wore.

"Less than a minute left," Joe commented, taking a look at one of the many TV's that were playing the broadcast of the game.

"Ironside to all, let's get it on," Boyd said into the mic hidden below his hoodie. "Get into position,"

"We're on the move," Darren relayed over the radio.

"Same here," Juan echoed.

"Driver?" Boyd asked, waiting to hear anything from Craig. After a beat, Craig's sour voice came over the radio.

"In position," he grumbled.

"Ok, everyone stand by. Get ready to move on my signal," Boyd said. He pulled out his phone and dialed Klint Kavanaugh's number.

"Yes?" Klint answered almost immediately.

"Certainly hope you're holding up your end of the deal," Boyd muttered, stepping away from the crowd of people.

"I am," Klint said, his voice calm. "I've pulled all the cops I could toward that bank robbery..."

"Good," Boyd cracked a smile. "Then I have no reason to harm your daughter. Treat her to a nice meal or something tonight, she deserves it,"

"Fuck you," Klint snapped. "Is that all?"

"Stay by your phone, Klint," Boyd said ominously. "If I run into any complications because of you, I'll be sure to give you a call,"

"Can't wait," Klint said sarcastically.


With a scoff, Boyd hung up his phone and stuffed it in his back pocket. He gave Joe a subtle nod and they started walking. Boyd and Joe moved with the crowds toward the escalators, following the mass exodus of angry, drunk Chicago fans. The Bears had gotten completely walloped by the Packers, which wasn't weird. Boyd had been raised a Bears fan and still followed the team passionately, but had long gotten used to the endless seasons of disappointment. Despite a Wild Card playoff appearance every few seasons, the Bears were stuck in mediocrity.


"Lot of fucking people," Joe muttered to Boyd as they rode the escalator down to the 100 level seats.

"No shit," Boyd shook his head, wondering why in the world Joe felt it necessary to make that comment.

"I'm just saying, lots of potential collateral. Lots of variables,"

"Should've said something during the meetings,"

"I did say something during the meetings," Joe rolled his eyes.

Their temporary alliance was an uneasy one at best, but still quite necessary to get the job done. Alone, neither crew had the manpower to succeed. But by combining their forces, they actually stood half a chance. On paper, they all looked relatively similar, but they couldn't have been more different. Noah and his crew were brash, bold, and adaptable. Boyd had always been a meticulous planner, not liking to improvise or 'wing it'. So far, he had already noticed that Noah's crew had made a name for themselves on winging it. They weren't as fine tuned as Boyd and his crew were, yet, their skills complemented each other nicely.

"Less than twenty seconds left," Joe said, eyeing another TV. He checked his watch. "Right on schedule,"

"Once we get behind the scenes, it's gonna turn into a fucking labyrinth. Sure hope this route is accurate,"

"One way to find out," Joe shrugged.

Their route involved bypassing a door for employees only, a small feat for the skeleton key they possessed. From there, they would have to navigate through the back hallways of the stadium to the cash room that handled the VIP lounge and United Club. After securing their haul, they would have to double back to the general parking garage, all without drawing attention from the plethora of security guards on the scene. These guards weren't actual cops though, not even armed. Boyd wasn't worried about them. As long as the distraction worked and Klint stuck to his word, Boyd was confident in their abilities to pull this off. And if they were able to pull it off, they would be richer beyond their wildest imaginations; not to mention being ingrained in sports history for a long time to come. A robbery at a major NFL stadium was unheard of.

The last twenty seconds of the game dragged on for another ten minutes. When the clock finally read zeroes, Boyd and Joe made their move. Once again blending into the sea of blue and orange, they maneuvered toward the specific door marked AUTHORIZED PERSONNEL ONLY. There was a keypad to the right of the door where employees punched in their specific codes to gain access.

"Alright," Boyd muttered to Joe. "Let's do this,"

Boyd reached into his hoodie and pulled up a neck gaiter over his nose and mouth. He slipped a pair of sunglasses over his eyes to shield his entire face. Wearing a backwards hat, Joe pulled up a similarly themed gaiter over his own face, along with a pair of sunglasses. Reaching into the front pocket of his hoodie, Boyd pulled out the skeleton key and touched the device to the keypad. After a few seconds, the door unlocked and began slowly opening. Putting his body against the door, Boyd pushed as hard as he could, bypassing having to wait for the door to automatically open. He and Joe rushed inside and Joe shut the door behind them, the lock reengaging once it shut.

Having memorized the route to the cash room, Boyd led the way down the hallway. His hand rested on his hip, just above where he had his gun hidden. Time was of the essence now; each team would have to hit their designated cash room in near synchrony. If one team was even a few seconds off, one of the cash rooms could possibly be alerted and call the cops.

Making their way through the inner sanctum of Soldier Field, Boyd turned right and led them down another long hallway. They passed by several offices belonging to different coaches and medical trainers. They passed an employee pushing a garbage can on wheels, but the man didn't even seem to notice them. If he did, he certainly didn't care. Again, it appeared that luck was on their side as well.

"Approaching target," Chandler's hushed voice crackled over the radio. After a few moments, his voice came through again. "In position, ready to go,"

"Same here," Juan reported. "Awaiting go ahead,"

"Copy, hold positions," Boyd muttered. He turned to Joe and cocked his head forward. "Come on, we gotta pick it up,"

Picking up the pace to a light jog, Boyd and Joe completed the last leg of the journey as quickly as they could without drawing attention to themselves. The door to the cash room was unmarked, but according to the blueprints, it was located right in front of them.

"In position," Boyd whispered. He pulled out the skeleton key and moved over toward the lock. Joe drew his pistol and got into position on the other side of the door, ready to swoop in as soon as Boyd granted them access. "Move on my mark..."

"Copy,"

"Copy,"

"Ok..." Boyd put the skeleton key to the lock. He could see the small device going to work at cracking through the lock, but he realized instantaneously that it was taking longer than he'd thought. "Stand by... Stand by..."

"We have to go now, man," Chandler's worried voice said. "We're like sitting ducks out here,"

"There's been a delay, hold on," Boyd snapped, gritting his teeth. He cursed the skeleton key, willing it to work faster. "Come on, you son of a bitch, work!"

"I can try and boot the door open," Joe offered.

"And then what?" Boyd looked at him with incredulity. "You're just gonna make a shit ton of noise and alert who's ever in there,"

"Just an option,"

"Come on, you piece of shit!" Boyd's hands were sweating now as the key still struggled to unlock the door.

They were losing valuable time and he knew it. The longer he kept screwing around with Rob's super secret technology, the more time they were allowing for something to go horribly wrong. Boyd felt his heart beating a lot faster, sweat dripping from his forehead, anxiety rising inside him. It had all gone pretty smoothly up until the most pivotal moment of the job. He didn't have a better idea or a backup plan. There was no way he and Joe could break through a reinforced steel door with brute force. And there was certainly no way to do it quietly. The key had to work, it just had to. There wasn't another option.

The door to the cash room swung open from the inside. An older man, probably in his mid-sixties, stepped into the doorway, mid-yawn. He froze when he saw Boyd and Joe, giving them both a confused look.

Boyd and Joe held their breaths for what felt like an eternity. In reality, it was less than a second. The man saw the gun being openly carried by Joe. He saw the masks, the sunglasses, the hats, and put two and two together. His eyes went wide and he instantly turned to run back into the cash room; throwing the door closed behind him.

Before the door could shut completely, Boyd kicked it open as hard as he could. He and Joe rushed inside, with Joe closing and locking the door behind them. Boyd grabbed the same old man by the collar, just as he was reaching for the phone. Jamming his pistol against the man's temple, Boyd held him in a headlock, and wheeled around to face the other two employees in the cash room - an older African American woman and a younger Hispanic man; they both looked completely stunned. Joe aimed his gun at them both, freezing them in their seats.

"Listen to me very carefully," Boyd began, speaking clearly and concisely so there would be absolutely no confusion about what was expected of them. "We are here for the money, we don't want to hurt any of you, but we will not hesitate if it comes to that. Is that clear?"

Three nods.

"Ok, I'm gonna need you all to put your hands up and stay quiet. This will all be over before you know it. The more you co-operate, the faster this will go. Think of your families, don't do anything stupid. My friend and I do not want to hurt anyone, please do not make us," Boyd sat the older man next to his two coworkers. They all slowly put their hands up, their hands trembling. Joe used their jackets to tie their hands tightly behind their back, preventing them from doing anything to alert security.

"We're in," Boyd said into his mic, alerting the entire crew.
"Copy, so are we," Juan answered.
"Clearing the room now," Chandler reported.
"Two minutes," Boyd let everyone know. Their window was tight, they had to move quickly.

There was a table in the back right corner of the room, every inch of it covered in stacks of green bills. The sight was thrilling for both

Joe and Boyd, who could only imagine just how much money they were about to come into possession of.

Joe tucked his pistol into the back pocket of his jeans and quickly unbuckled his pants. He pulled his jeans down slightly and produced a folded up duffle bag. Unzipping the bag, Joe shook it a couple of times so it would return to form. Grabbing it and slamming it on the table, Joe grabbed the first stack of money he saw and stuffed it in the bag.

"You guys think you're gonna get away with this?" the old man asked as Joe and Boyd went to work clearing off the table. They moved as fast as they could, transferring the money into the bag. "You have to be the dumbest boys out there to try something like this,"

"Shut up!" one of his coworkers hissed.

Boyd and Joe ignored the comments, focusing solely on their job. Every second counted and they couldn't waste any time on insignificant banter from one of their hostages. They cleared the entire table in under thirty seconds, Joe shook the bag a few times to clear some more room in the bag before moving on to a cabinet full of banded bills. Boyd went to work clearing on shelf at a time, dumping armfulls of cash into the bag while Joe held it open for him. As he went back in to grab another stack, he checked his watch. Again, Boyd found himself smiling beneath his disguise. They were ahead of schedule, making good time, and stealing a whole lot of money in the process. He prayed that the others were making as good of progress as he and Joe were. So far, Noah's crew had not disappointed in the slightest; Joe was a total professional and conducted himself with poise that it seriously made Boyd jealous. There didn't appear to be a weak link in Noah's crew, whereas Boyd's had a blatant and obvious one.

"Hurry up," Craig's voice grumbled over the radio. "We're running out of time,"

Boyd felt his blood pressure rise. They were doing just fine, there was absolutely no reason for Craig to worry or pressure anyone right now. He was only doing that to make himself feel more important than he was.

"We're fine, we're fine," Boyd repeated after seeing Joe check his watch.

"Are you sure?"

"I'm positive, keep moving,"

Boyd and Joe went on clearing out every single dollar bill they could find, even snagging a few rolls of quarters from a drawer; they completely emptied out the room with a solid twenty seconds to spare. Joe zipped up the equipment bag and heaved it over his shoulder, groaning as he adjusted to the weight. He pulled the strap across his chest, trying to balance the weight throughout his upper body as best as possible. It was awkward, bulky, and heavy, but Joe could manage it. He had to be carrying close to or over a million dollars in the bag itself. They left behind the three employee's wallets, not even bothering to look through them. Those people had nothing to do with their job, they were simply people who, on that particular day, had gotten into the wrong profession. It wasn't their fault they'd drawn the short straw and had been working when they decided to rob the place, Boyd had absolutely no quarrel with them.

"Thank you so much for participating in today's robbery," Boyd said to the three employees. He tipped his hat slightly at them, relishing in the persona he got to live in when he was doing jobs. "We appreciate your cooperation and hope you have a fantastic rest of your weekend. Go Bears!"

"You're never going to get out of here!" that same old man said, still appalled by Boyd and Joe's brazen heist. "It's absolutely insane! Insane, I tell ya!"

"Don't you worry about it, gramps," Joe muttered, patting the old man on the head dramatically. "Ain't no one going to jail today. Maybe someday, but not today,"

"As I was saying..." Boyd continued. "You all have a wonderful day,"

Without another word, Boyd opened the door to the cash room, and he and Joe slipped out, closing it behind them. He figured it would take the employees anywhere from five to ten minutes to get out of their restraints, which was more than enough time for them to reach Craig and the getaway vehicle.

"Ironside to all, we're moving to the garage. Say again, moving to the car," Boyd alerted the others.

"We are on the way, haul in hand," Juan informed.

"Stand by, just finishing up," Chandler reported, sounding more stressed than he had the last time he'd been heard over the radio. Boyd checked his watch as he and Joe hustled down the hallway back the way they'd come.

"Get out of there now," Boyd said. "You're out of time. Get to the garage,"

"Hang on..." Chandler muttered. Boyd shook his head.

"Get out, now!" Boyd urged, knowing that Chandler was burning time by staying even a second past the allotted two minutes. If he wasn't at the garage at the right time, the entire job could be jeopardized. Boyd turned to Joe. "What the fuck is your boy doing?"

"Relax," Joe grunted, praying that Chandler and Darren knew what they were doing. "They're pros, they've got it all under control,"

"We don't have seconds to spare," Boyd responded, getting more and more annoyed that Joe didn't appear to feel as urgent as he did. Joe was the definition of calm and collected as they approached the door they'd come through a few minutes prior; it would open back up into the stadium.

"Relax," Joe repeated. "It's all under control.

Boyd rolled his eyes, but didn't say anything else. Putting his body weight against the door, Boyd pushed in open, holding it open while Joe slipped past. Once they were back into the stadium, they both pulled down their gaiters slightly to look as normal as possible. They kept the hats and sunglasses on, though, keeping their heads down to avoid their faces getting picked up by the security cameras.

"Ok, we're on the move," Chandler finally said, just as Joe and Boyd were exiting the stadium and entering the parking garage.

"Good, we're closing in on the car," Boyd responded. He turned to Joe, lowering his voice. "Let Noah know,"

"On it," Joe nodded, dialing Noah's number on the burner phones they were all utilizing at the moment. Noah answered right as the phone started ringing.

"Joe?"

"Yeah, we're moving to the car now," Joe relayed. "Haul in hand,"

"Understood, keep me posted," Noah said.

"Will do," Joe hung up and stuffed the burner in his back pocket.

Taking the elevator up a floor, Joe and Boyd kept a solid pace through the garage, avoiding eye contact with many fans who were still in the garage drinking beer, smoking cigarettes, or eating food while chatting amongst themselves. The fact that most of the people in the garage were either intoxicated or just too involved in their own lives to notice Boyd and Joe worked to their advantage.

The dark Mercedes Sprinter was parked in the back corner of the garage. Boyd and Joe exchanged nods of approval to see the van sitting there, just as planned. Picking up their pace to a jog, Boyd activated his radio.

"Craig, we're coming in," he said. "Open the back,"

"Got it," Craig grunted. The two back doors to the van swung open and Craig appeared, jumping out of the van onto the floor. He eyed the bulging bag of money and gave Boyd an evil smile. "That's a lot of money,"

"No shit," Joe huffed, sweat beading from his forehead. He dropped the money down on the ground, groaning in discomfort. He bent over at the waist, stretching his back out. "I'm getting too old to be hauling this shit around,"

"Craig, give me a hand," Boyd said, relieving Joe from having to carry the bag. Craig nodded and bent down toward the bag while Joe turned around and covered them, making sure no one was coming up behind them who shouldn't be. Boyd and Craig each took a strap of the equipment bag and heaved it into the back of the van, throwing it on the floor.

"Heads up, guys," Joe warned. Boyd and Craig wheeled around. Juan and Patrick were hurrying towards the van, each one of them carrying two backpacks that looked as if they could burst at any given moment.

"Pick it up, pick it up," Boyd hissed, willing them to hurry up. Hearing Boyd's urges, Juan and Patrick ran towards the van, leaping into the back and shedding their packs.

"Whew," Juan breathed, smiling from ear to ear. "Well, that was fun,"

"Couldn't have gone better," Patrick said to Boyd. "How'd you guys do?"

"Great," Boyd said quickly. He checked his watch again. "Joe, where the fuck are they?"

"How would I know that?" Joe responded, giving Boyd a disapproving look. He shook his head. "I'm not their babysitter,"

"Chandler, where are you?" Boyd asked into the radio.

"Stand by," Chandler answered calmly.

"Jesus, don't tell me to 'stand by'. Where the hell are you?"

"Boyd, calm down, alright?" Joe said with another dirty look. "What the hell are you so worked up about? We're all going to the same place,"

Boyd fell silent, not wanting to explain to a man like Joe that he was ridiculously anxious at the moment. The last thing on the planet that Boyd wanted was to miss his flight to California with Kayley. He realized being overly concerned with that was definitely a distraction, but he didn't care. All he wanted was that fresh, new start; a chance to leave all of this behind him. He was so close to it he could practically taste it, but even still, it felt lightyears away. Chandler and Darren's delay wasn't doing anything to help either.

"We need to go," Craig said to Boyd. "No way to know if Klint was really able to pull all the cops away from here. Can't take any more chances than we already have,"

"Goddamn, will you two calm down?" Joe turned around, now definitely agitated by both Boyd and Craig. "You guys are unbelievable, just have some faith,"

"We don't know you guys," Boyd spat. "No offense, but I don't have faith in people I don't know,"

"Fair enough," Joe muttered. He clicked on his radio. "Chan, hurry up, alright? The new guys are getting anxious,"

"In... elevator... towards... now..." Chandler's staticky voice broke through the radio. Joe asked him to repeat what he'd said, but got no response.

Boyd was about to voice another complaint with Joe when he saw a white SUV driving slowly towards them. His initial thought was that it was just someone else leaving the game. The SUV came to a stop in the middle of the garage, its engine still idling. The one-ways in the garage were narrow, the SUV was blocking any traffic from getting past it. Although he couldn't see the driver or tell if anyone else was in the car, Boyd got a horribly sick feeling in his stomach.

"Guys..." he muttered, cocking his head toward the SUV. Joe looked at it and visibly let his shoulders sink. He shook his head and groaned before pulling out his burner and calling Noah once again.

"We have a problem," Joe said once Noah answered. Still staring at the car, Joe grabbed his radio. "Chandler, get over here right fucking now,"

"What's wrong?" Chandler asked, hearing the worry in Joe's voice.

"Just get here," Joe said. "We have company,"

"What do we do?" Juan asked.

"Well, nothing yet," Boyd answered, thinking realistically. "Whoever they are, they haven't made any moves at us. Could just be a few drunk guys,"

"You and I both know those ain't drunk guys," Joe muttered, not taking his eyes off the car.

"Klint pulled all the cops away from here, right?" Craig asked, looking directly at Boyd.

Before Boyd could answer that he truly had no idea if Klint had held up his end of the deal, a gunshot exploded through the parking garage, echoing loudly in the depths of the concrete structure. Boyd instinctively ducked, knowing the sound of a sniper rifle all too well from his military days. Patrick's head popped like a water balloon, spraying gore all over the side of the van. His body fell over, blood pumping out of the grotesque wound. Boyd's eyes went wide with realization.

"Sniper!" Boyd screamed. Joe hit the deck immediately and Craig dove back into the van. "Craig, guns!"

"Catch!" Craig yelled, throwing an AR-15 toward Boyd. He grabbed two more rifles and tossed one to Joe and to Juan.

Racking the charging handle, Boyd blankly stared at Patrick's corpse. There was nothing he could do for the man now, but the image transported him back to the streets of Iraq in an instant. He wasn't in Chicago, his hometown, anymore. No, Boyd McTiernan was in a warzone.

# CHAPTER 29

# John

The second John saw the man's head explode through the reticle of his rifle, he yanked back the bolt on his rifle to eject the spent shell. John quickly pushed it back into position, chambering the next round in the magazine. He steadied his aim again and scanned for his next target, hearing the men screaming at each other as they tried to figure out where the shot had come from.

"All units, one bandit down. Four are still standing, two un-accounted for. Move in, I've got you covered," John whispered into the mic on his throat. His radio was connected to the SWAT frequency, allowing him to communicate with an entire squad of Special Weapons And Tactics officers, as well as Klint and Kade Kavanaugh.

All four doors of the white SUV swung open and six Chicago SWAT officers jumped out, their rifles pointed at the Sprinter Van parked in front of them. They moved around to the front of the SUV, making a triangle formation behind the pair of SWAT officers carrying a ballistic shield. The SWAT Lieutenant, Alex, raised a megaphone to his mouth - not that it was needed; he did so more for the effect.

"This is the Chicago Police Department!" he yelled into the megaphone, his voice bouncing off the concrete walls. "We have you surrounded! Put your weapons down and come out with your hands in the air!"

The garage was eerily quiet. The screeching of tires could be heard as a few remaining fans jumped in their cars and scurried out of the parking structure.

"What do you see, John?" Klint asked over the radio.
"Nothing right now. They're behind cover," John muttered. He was positioned on the roof of a sedan in the back of the garage on the ramp, giving him a slight advantage. His police issued M24 sniper rifle was awkwardly propped up on a bipod. It wasn't a comfortable sniping position, but it gave John a good enough line of sight to be deadly.

"Outside the garage is locked down!" Kade's voice yelled over the radio; the wailing of police sirens nearly drowned out his voice. "They're not going anywhere,"
"10-4. John, you get a clear shot, you take it, understood?"
"Affirmative," John acknowledged. He took a deep breath and stretched his trigger finger around the trigger guard. "No shot, at the moment. Say again, no shot,"
"You have ten seconds!" Alex shouted. "Lay down your firearms and come out with your hands up!"

"Calm down, don't push 'em," John said into the radio. "We can't start a gunfight right here. Wait 'em out and I'll pick them off one by one,"

"We're not waiting for shit," Klint snapped, his emotions rising to the surface. "Alex, keep pressing them!"

"Klint, I'm telling you, that's a bad move," John kept his voice as calm as possible. "This is a bad place to exchange shots,"

John knew that Klint's ego was getting the better of him at the moment. He'd disagreed wholeheartedly with going into the garage in the first place. It was a bad location for a gunfight; minimal opportunity for cover, confined space, and the bullets would ricochet like crazy. But, he understood that it was better than getting into a shootout on the street. Still, backing Boyd McTiernan into a corner spelled disaster and John could feel it. Boyd was a Special Forces vet, just like John. If anyone could get out of a situation like this, it was him. John's military sixth sense was going crazy, telling him this was a bad idea. He put himself in Boyd's shoes, wondering how he'd handle the same situation. In John's mind, it made the most sense to try and draw the enemies in and then hit them with a surprise attack, which was what it appeared that Boyd was trying to do. And Klint's over zealous attitude was feeding right into that plan.

"Kade, is your team ready to move in?" Klint asked. John shook his head. Klint was being far too aggressive for this delicate of a situation.

"Copy, we're ready and waiting," Kade answered. Kade was positioned outside the parking garage on the street with an entire squad of SWAT officers ready to move in at any given time. At least two dozen other officers were positioned around the garage entrance, blocking traffic from entering.

"If I give the word, you get your ass in there, alright?"

"You got it,"

"This is your last chance!" Alex yelled again. "Drop your weapons and come out with your hands up or we will open fire on you!"

"Damnit, this is a bad idea," John repeated himself.

Klint's response was drowned out by the sudden barrage of gunfire thrown at John and the SWAT officers. John could feel the repeated concussion of the guns against his chest, shaking the ground with each salvo. In an instant, the parking garage was thrown into utter chaos. The SWAT officers retreated to cover, ducking behind the still open doors of the white SUV. Officers who were manning ballistic shields drew their pistols and started shooting back at the van.

John kept his reticle on the van, slowly scanning back and forth to try and get a clean shot. For the most part, the shooters were staying behind cover, only popping up to spray bullets at the cops before ducking down behind cover once again. Centering his crosshairs on the back of the van, John fired off another round, the supersonic bullet exploding from the barrel of the M24 with a deafening crack. The round cut a hole through the van, but didn't appear to hit any of the shooters. Twisting the bolt, John chambered another round and fired again, hoping a few impossibly loud sniper rounds would disorientate, and or, frighten them into doing something stupid. But despite his best efforts, John's rounds seemed to have little effect.

The cops and the robbers were in a good, old fashioned stand off. They exchanged rounds, but were unable to inflict any significant damage on either side. It had only been maybe two minutes since John had fired the first shot, killing one of the guys on Boyd's crew, but it felt like a lifetime.

More gunfire erupted to John's left and a SWAT officer went down, clutching his leg as blood began pouring out of him. John whirled his head around and saw two men darting across the parking garage; they both carried bulky bags and rifles. The two men sprayed bullets all over the cops as they ran, freeing up their path to the van. Their rounds came dangerously close to John, slicing through the car that he lay on. He felt a round go right past his head and grabbed his rifle with both hands before rolling off the top of the car. Finding cover behind the car, John dropped to a knee and slung the rifle across his back, opting instead to arm himself with his pistol. In a fast-paced environment like this, the sniper rifle wasn't ideal due to its slow rate of fire.

"Is he ok?" John yelled to one of the SWAT officers who was dragging the injured man behind their SUV.

"Upper leg!" the officer yelled back. "Doesn't look good!"

"Klint, we're taking casualties!" John yelled over the radio. "Need to reassess!"

"Kade, get in there!" Klint yelled back. John rolled his eyes and shook his head.

"Negative, we need-" the rest of John's sentence was cut off by another insane bombardment of gunfire.

Moving out from cover, John raised his pistol and blasted off the entire magazine as fast as he could, aiming right at the van. When the gun ran dry, John dumped the empty magazine and snapped a fresh one in, ready to go again.

Alex came running up and knelt beside John, along with a duo of unharmed SWAT officers. They were all a little disoriented from the repeated gunfire; their ears ringing and eyes burning from the smoke and gunpowder in the air. Alex and his SWAT officers unhooked flashbang grenades from their vests.

"We're gonna smoke these guys out and kill them all," Alex said, matter of factly.

"Sounds good to me," John agreed.

"On three..." Alex said, hooking his finger around the pin of the grenade.

Before Alex could finish counting to three, several silver orbs came flying at the SWAT officers and their car. The orbs hit the ground, rolling all over the concrete. John only needed a millisecond to glance at the object to know exactly what it was; his eyes widened with fear. He didn't even have time to shout a warning to his comrades before the fragmentation grenades detonated.

The entire floor of the garage shook as the grenades went off, engulfing two SWAT officers in the first series of explosions. A second later, the white SUV's gas tank caught fire, exploding in a violent eruption, and sending shrapnel from the car in every direction.

John Shannon was knocked off his feet and thrown against the wall of the parking garage, hitting his head on the concrete, and falling into a haze. His vision blurred and his ears ringing, John rolled onto his back, fighting the urge to throw up. He didn't even register Klint's angry voice on the radio, begging anyone for an answer as to what was going on.

# CHAPTER 30

# Boyd

As soon as the grenades went off, Boyd threw his rifle in the back of the van and virtually dragged Juan away from his friend's body; he manhandled him into the van. Joe, along with Chandler and Darren, jumped in as well, moving toward the front of the van to make room. Grabbing Patrick's mangled body, Boyd carefully pulled him into the back of the van, slamming the door closed behind him.

"Go! Go!" Boyd screamed, his voice hoarse from yelling.

Craig threw the van in reverse and slammed on the gas, speeding out of the parking space. The van had taken some damage, but was still driveable, which was a relief. Shifting into gear, Craig spun the wheel and sped toward the exit. As they flew past the shredded SWAT Team, Boyd rolled down the window and tossed two more grenades out of the window, just for good measure.

"What the fuck, man?" Juan screamed from the back, unable to take his eyes off of Patrick's body. "I mean, what the hell was that?"

"I don't know, just calm down," Boyd said, trying to get a grasp on the situation.

"Don't tell me to calm down!" Juan cried. He gestured to Patrick's corpse. "Look at him and then tell me to calm down,"

Boyd didn't want to look at him, not even remotely. He'd seen his fair share of dead bodies when in the military, but this was different. Patrick had been in this situation because of Boyd. It hadn't quite sunk in yet, but Boyd was already dreading the guilt he would have to deal with later in life.

Joe, Chandler, and Darren remained quiet, almost as if they understood what Juan and Boyd were going through at the moment. They exchanged a silent look of understanding sympathy with Boyd, but said no words. They seemed to understand that they were still strangers to the dynamic of Boyd's crew and right now it was better to not say anything that would bring up more negative emotions. Right now, everyone still had to be level headed. The crew was nowhere near out of danger yet. Almost as if on cue, Craig slammed on the brakes, jerking the van and its passengers.

"What the hell?" Boyd snapped.

"Boyd, we have a problem..." Craig said, slowing down to a crawl. He turned around and looked at Boyd with uncertainty.

Boyd looked out the front of the car and could see the blue and red flashing lights around the exit of the parking garage. He hung his head. For the first time, he truly did not know what to do. It wouldn't take more than a minute for the SWAT officers to reorganize themselves and come after them. For all intents and purposes, they were surrounded. Surrounded with no avenue of escape. There was a second exit from the parking facility, but they would have to go up to the floor above and then double back down from the opposite side, which would take time they didn't necessarily have.

Unless...

It wasn't a good idea and Boyd knew it. But he felt resigned to it at this point. He'd had a good run, they all had. Patrick had died because of Boyd and he was not going to let Juan suffer the same fate. He honestly couldn't care less about what happened to Craig, only he knew that if Craig went to jail, he'd sing like a bird. Boyd had waited too long to deal with that problem.

"Juan, go up one floor and go out the second exit," Boyd said calmly. "Craig and I are gonna buy you guys some time,"

"We are?" Craig asked. Boyd glared at him and nodded. Juan also looked like he hated the idea.

"Come on, Boyd," Juan said. "We're not doing this,"

"We don't have time to argue," Boyd said. "You guys get out and get to the airport, ok? Craig and I will meet you there,"

He reached under the bench in the back of the van and grabbed his backpack; he knew exactly what was in there and he'd need every item. Grabbing his rifle and as much ammo as he could fit into the pockets of his jeans, Boyd threw the pack over his shoulders and opened the back door of the van. Craig shook his head, muttering expletives under his breath, but he grabbed his rifle and followed Boyd out of the van. Juan climbed into the driver's seat of the van.

"Hey," Joe said as Boyd was closing the doors behind him and Craig. "Good luck,"

"Thanks," Boyd grunted. "Craig, let's go,"

Juan put the van in reverse and turned around, heading toward the ramp that led up to the next level of parking. Once they were out of sight, Boyd crept toward the blue and red flashing lights. Craig followed, but at a distance, still unaware of Boyd's plan. Boyd had one last grenade left in his arsenal; he pulled the pin out and tossed it aside, moving closer and closer to the exit. Peering around the concrete, Boyd could see the uniformed police officers standing there, hands on their weapons.

"Get ready to run, ok?" Boyd said to Craig.
"This is a stupid plan,"
"Very," Boyd agreed.

Boyd heaved his arm back and threw the grenade as hard as he could. As soon as it left his hands, he and Craig turned around and started running. A few seconds later, the grenade exploded, sending the formation of cops outside the parking garage into utter chaos.

"Follow me!" Boyd yelled, darting toward the stair access in the corner of the garage.

Gunshots cracked over their heads as they ran; the SWAT officers were back in pursuit. Boyd stopped and dropped to a knee, letting Craig run past him. He leveled his rifle and squeezed the trigger, blasting off ten rounds, and dropping one of the officers chasing after them.

"Stairs! Go, go!" Boyd screamed, firing off another burst to keep the cops at bay. He quickly reloaded his rifle and exchanged fire with the cops one last time, injuring another over eager SWAT officer.

Getting to his feet, Boyd ducked down and ran after Craig, bursting into the staircase. "All the way up!"

"Where are we going?" Craig asked, already panting. They kept bounding up the stairs, taking them two or three at a time.

"Trust me!" Boyd yelled back. "I have a plan!"

\*\*\*\*

Boyd had studied the blueprints and layout of the different levels of Soldier Field religiously in his preparation for this job. He'd always been thorough, but with the added risk and potential dangers associated with such a job, he went above and beyond in his planning. Under normal circumstances, all that extra time spent looking at drawings, memorizing access points, wouldn't have changed the outcome. But now, Boyd was relieved he had. He had a plan. It wasn't a good plan, but it would at least do the two things that needed to happen right now. It would create major confusion for the cops, hopefully allowing the guys a chance to escape. Secondly, it would give Boyd his own opportunity to make it out alive.

"Come on, come on, keep up!" Boyd urged, looking back to see Craig falling behind. They were sprinting through a maintenance hallway, dodging electrical boxes, pipes, and the inner workings of the stadium, having lost the cops a few minutes ago when they slipped inside the corridor. Even still, Boyd knew it wasn't going to last, they'd be on them again soon enough.

"Where are we going?" Craig asked. He paused for a moment, putting his hands on his knees and sucking in air, exhausted.

"Trust me, I've got a plan,"

"Care to share it with me?" Craig asked, wiping the sweat from his forehead. "God, I need to get in shape,"

"Just keep up with me, ok?" Boyd said. "I know the way, we're almost there,"

"Almost where?"

Boyd's phone started ringing, stopping him from answering Craig, not that he was going to tell him anyway. Craig would have objected to the plan vehemently if he really knew. Listening for a moment, Boyd didn't hear any sign of the cops around them, and figured they were ok for the time being.

"Take a breather," Boyd said. He picked up his phone and put it to his ear. "Hey,"

"Where are you?" Rob asked. "Noah and I are on the way to O'Hare and I just got off the phone with Juan..."

"I've got it under control," Boyd assured his friend.

"Boyd, what are you thinking?" Rob sounded genuinely worried.

Boyd looked at Craig, still bent over, breathing heavily. He still needed another minute.

"Hey, eyes up," Boyd said to Craig. "I'll be back in a minute, just got to make sure the route ahead is clear,"

"Alright, I'll be fine," Craig grunted. Craig took a seat on the ground, resting his rifle across his lap. "Anyone comes up on us, I'll riddle 'em,"

"Good," Boyd nodded. He jogged down the hallway before putting his phone back to his ear. "Are you still there?"

"I'm here," Rob answered. "Where are you?"

"Inside the stadium," Boyd said, still searching for the correct access hatch. If his memory was correct, the hatch should lead to a ladder.

"What the hell are you still doing there?" Rob asked. "Juan said they made it out the other end and are already on their way out of the city,"

"Good for them," Boyd muttered.

"Craig's with you?"

"Yeah,"

"Boyd..."

"What?"

"For your own sake, please don't do what I think you're going to do," Rob said, lowering his voice. "As you friend, I'm begging you, please don't. I know you think it'll solve everything, but it won't, it just won't. The only person you'll be hurting is yourself,"

"I didn't ask for a lecture,"

"I know you didn't, but I'm giving it to you anyway," Rob snapped back. "You don't have anyone else to answer to, no one to tell you when you're going too far. This... This is too far, Boyd. This is one of those things you can't come back from. Once you do that, it's done,"

"You have no idea what I'm thinking," Boyd lied. Rob knew exactly what he was thinking. Boyd finally found the correct access point in the hallway, relieved that he'd been right. "I have a plan, I just need a few more minutes,"

"Please, man," Rob pleaded with him. "Just get to the airport, ok? I want to see you on that plane,"

"You'll see me, I promise," Boyd lied again. He was getting out of here alive and there was nothing anyone could do to stop him from making his flight with Kayley.

Rob and Boyd both fell silent, neither one of them really wanting to hang up and leave things like that. There had always been a mutual understanding between them. They had the ability to read each other's minds without needing words. Boyd was certain that

Rob was thinking the same thing he was - this was possibly the last time they'd ever get the chance to talk. Ever. It was a heavy thing to even consider. Boyd wasn't scared, but he wasn't naive either. There was no guarantee that he'd make it out of this alive, there never was.

"Just be careful," Rob said quietly. His silence after spoke volumes. He didn't need to say anything more, Boyd knew how he felt, and vice versa.

"You too, buddy," was all that Boyd could muster up.

Rob hung up and Boyd put his phone back in his pocket, pushing the building emotions back into the depths of his soul. Boyd grabbed his rifle and jogged back to Craig.

"Come on," he ordered. "Get up, I found our way out of here,"

"About damn time," Craig groaned, getting to his feet. "You better have a great fucking plan to get us out of here. I've been thinking of how I'm gonna spend my cut of the job,"

"I'm sure," Boyd huffed, hoping that for once in his life, Craig would take the hint and stop talking. But, like millions of times before, he did not. And as they walked back toward the access hatch, Boyd felt himself getting more and more tense.

"A new motorcycle is a must," Craig began, talking loudly. Boyd wasn't worried about them being overheard, not in this type of hidden access corridor, but Craig's blatant disregard for the seriousness of the situation was infuriating. "Probably get myself a place in Mexico. Somewhere close to the beach, but not too far from the city. Still need the nightlife, you know? Have you heard about Mexican coke, man? Shit is legendary, so I've been told,"

"Right here," Boyd said, opening the door to the ladder. He ignored Craig's babble. "You go up first, I'll cover you,"

"Where does this lead?" Craig asked, grabbing a hold of the ladder.

"Just go, alright?" Boyd snapped, annoyed.

"Dick," Craig snorted under his breath. He began climbing up the ladder, his rifle clanging against the rungs with each climb.

Boyd put his foot on the ladder and was about to start climbing up after Craig when he heard a commotion down the corridor. A door got kicked in, violently smashing against the concrete wall. SWAT officers rushed into the maintenance hallway, shouting to each other as they cleared every inch of the hall.

"Move your ass!" Boyd hissed. "I'll buy you some time,"

Crouching down and putting his back against the door frame, Boyd leveled his rifle, and stuck the barrel into the hallway. Even though he couldn't see the approaching cops yet, Boyd squeezed the trigger. The gun spat out rounds as fast as it possibly could. Shell casings clinked off the frame, forming a pile beneath Boyd. He finally let off the trigger when the gun went dry. Working the weapon smoothly, Boyd ejected the spent magazine and slammed a fresh one in before slapping the bolt to chamber the first round.

"Anyone hurt?" a cop yelled. "Everyone ok?"

"Where the hell did that come from?" another yelled.

The advantage of the corridor was in its design. It was extremely narrow, not designed for more than one, maybe two, people walking through it at a time. The confines left the SWAT officers vulnerable to a forward attack, leaving them no place to turn and seek cover. The corridor was a death trap and the cops were just starting to realize that, unwilling to go any further when there was an active shooter in front of them.

While the cops were distracted, Boyd threw his rifle over his shoulder and gripped the ladder. As quickly as was humanly possible, Boyd began ascending, feeling like he was running up the ladder. The higher and higher he climbed, the darker it got. Only a single red light at the top of the shaft illuminated the ladder for him. He didn't hear Craig up above him, which meant that he must've made it out. Boyd kept on climbing, his arms and legs beginning to burn slightly. The red light got closer and closer. Once he was right below it, Boyd reached up and grasped blindly for a handle, lever, or something to open the hatch. His hands met a steel handle and he pushed with all his strength.

He was instantly attacked with a rush of frigid Chicago air and wind. The wind was strong, sucking his breath away as he pulled himself out of the hatch and closed it behind him. It was so windy and cold that it stung Boyd's face and hands. Craig was on one knee, a few feet from the hatch, cursing wildly at Boyd, who could barely hear him.

Boyd and Craig were now on top of Soldier Field, near the massive scoreboard, and above all of the executive suits. It was the highest point of the stadium that Boyd could get them to, just over 150 feet in the air. The city skyline was illuminated, but still slightly shrouded by the looming rain clouds. If it wasn't such a dire situation, Boyd would've taken a moment to admire that view. How many guys got to witness a view of Chicago like that?

"This was your brilliant fucking plan?" Craig shouted over the wind, police sirens, and city traffic. "Are you fucking insane?"

"Shut the hell up and get over to the ledge!" Boyd shouted back, pointing his finger toward the edge of the building.

"Are you nuts?" Craig shouted, his eyes wild. "What the fuck are we going to do?"

"Just trust me! I know what I'm doing!"

"No, fuck you!" Craig was enraged. "I can't fucking believe I trusted you to get me out of this! This is the stupidest thing I've ever seen"

"Stop bitching!" Boyd yelled. "Start moving,"

"Fuck you!" Craig repeated, shaking his head in vile disgust.

Boyd balled his fists, fighting the internal battle within himself. He had to remain calm and focus on getting to Kayley. That was the only priority. He'd put up with his uncle's scorn for years, a few more minutes wasn't going to change anything in their relationship.

"Come on, Craig!" Boyd started moving toward the edge of the building. "We don't have time for this,"

Boyd inched closer and closer to the edge, still not standing up to his full height yet. The powerful wind made him nervous, knowing how dangerous the shifts in wind could be for what he was planning to do. He shrugged out of his backpack and unzipped it carefully. Before he could unzip it fully, Craig snatched the pack away from him, trying to see what was inside.

"What the hell are you doing?" Boyd screamed, launching himself at Craig. They wrestled over the bag, Boyd delivered a solid punch to Craig's face, connecting with his eye. Craig stumbled back and fell to the ground.

"Craig, we are wasting time!" Boyd shouted, getting more and more angry by the second. "What the hell is wrong with you?"

"You always were such a prick," Craig shook his head. "After everything I've done for you..."

"Everything *you've* done for me?" Boyd cocked his head. "All you've ever done is make my life fucking miserable! Every bad thing that's ever happened to me I can trace right back to you!"

"Oh my god, get over it!" Craig shot back.

"Get over it?" Boyd screamed, his eyes full of rage.

"God, I knew your dad was soft on you, but I never imagined he would have raised such a little bitch,"

Boyd shuddered with anger. Craig sneered, satisfied with getting such a visceral reaction out of Boyd. But he wasn't done yet.

"You know what?" Craig continued. "With the rest of my cut, I'll buy that agency your girl works for,"

Boyd gritted his teeth and balled his fists, his nails digging into the skin on the palm of his hands. Craig's smile got unsettlingly devious, seeing Boyd's physical reaction to his comments. He stood up.

"I'll make sure she gets behind a camera every single day, just to spite you. And if she wants to keep her job, she'll have to suck my dick whenever the fuck I say so,"

Boyd stared at him blankly for a moment, a wave of calm crashing over him. He suddenly didn't feel so cold, so exposed. Closing his eyes, Boyd took a deep breath. Opening his eyes and staring at Craig, Boyd leaned down and picked up the bag, tossing it at Craig's feet. Craig looked at Boyd quizzically, but bent down and picked up the bag. He looked inside the bag and rifled through it, narrowing his eyes as he realized.

"I knew it!" Craig shook his head, throwing the bag on the ground. He raised his rifle, having every intention of killing his nephew where he stood.

Before Craig could do anything, Boyd closed the distance between them. He grabbed the barrel of the rifle, keeping it pointed away from him. With his free hand, Boyd grabbed his revolver and jammed it right under Craig's chin. Boyd pulled the hammer back with a click. Craig trembled and stared at Boyd with huge, bug eyes, terrified.

"Too fucking slow, old man," Boyd growled.

The revolver was a Ruger GP100, chambered in a .357 Magnum. It was spotless, recently cleaned. He had inherited the gun from him after his dad had passed. Boyd had brought the gun along for one simple reason - it had belonged to his father. There was a sense of justice in that, poetic even. When Boyd had made up his mind to kill Craig, he knew exactly which of his guns he was going to use. If anyone deserved justice for a lifetime of Craig's antics, it was James Boyd McTiernan I. It would never bring his dad back, but Boyd would sleep a little better, a little more peacefully, knowing that justice had finally been served. Craig had finally gotten what had been coming to him.

Craig slammed his eyes shut. Boyd squeezed the trigger, blowing Craig's head apart with a single round. Blood and gore exploded out the top of Craig's head as his body fell backward, landing with a wet thud on the concrete. He stood there for a moment, staring at the body, watching the blood pool out from underneath him. Slowly, he lowered the revolver and tucked it into his waistband. After catching his breath, He looked around for the back pack. Boyd's heart sank when the bag caught a gust of wind and started blowing across the ground. Thankfully, it got snagged on an exposed pipe and stopped blowing away.

Quickly grabbing the bag and opening it, Boyd pulled out a single parachute rig. He pulled the harness through his legs and over his shoulders, securing and tightening everything. The parachute was already out of the container. Because he was jumping from only 150 feet, he'd have to throw his chute as soon as he jumped. BASE jumping from such a low altitude was a major risk, but the lowest recorded successful BASE jump was just above 90 feet. Boyd had an extra 60 or so feet to work with, which made him feel a little bit more comfortable.

Leaving his rifle and backpack behind, Boyd walked over to the edge, chute in hand. Timing was everything and Boyd would have to wait until the wind was not as strong. Sure, it could pick back up at a second's notice and throw off his entire jump, but at least he'd have a chance to get a solid start.

The tips of his boots were hanging off the edge as he stared at the ground, 150 feet below him. Heights didn't bother him at all, those feelings of nervousness or anxiousness had vanished years before. He was more nervous about the wind than the actual jump, even though to date he'd never attempted a BASE jump from this low an altitude. The lowest he'd ever gone was just under 200 feet and even that had felt like he was pushing his luck. Boyd took one final deep breath and bent his knees, preparing to jump.

"Twitch and I will drop you where you stand," a voice said from behind Boyd.

# CHAPTER 31

# John

"Step away from the ledge, drop the chute,"

Not moving his feet, Boyd angled his head around to see none other than John Shannon standing behind him, aiming a pistol at him. John's brown hair blew in the wind as he took another step toward Boyd. Turning back forward, Boyd chuckled.

"You know, you and I have met before," Boyd said, loudly. "You remember?"

"No, I don't," John answered.

"Afghanistan, a long time ago," Boyd said, still having his back to John. "I remember it so vividly. I was Army SF at the time. We all heard stories about you. John Shannon. You and Gray Saxon were legends, we all talked about you guys,"

Boyd turned around and looked at John, kind of sadly.

"I was sorry to hear about Gray. I'm sure that was hard for you," Boyd offered.

"It was," John grunted.

"Gray was a good guy, I knew a lot of guys spoke very highly of him. That story about him going after that pilot... he was a hero,"

"They're not *stories*," John responded. "That was just who he was,"

"Look, former soldier to former soldier, I don't expect you to understand why I'm doing what I'm doing. But I'm asking... Just let me go. I'm so close,"

"Not an option," John said, his pistol still aimed right at Boyd, not wavering in the slightest. Boyd finally turned around and looked at John, face to face.

"I wish I had time to tell you everything, to make you understand,"

"I don't need to understand," John shook his head. "I just need this entire thing to be behind me,"

"I don't want to fight you, John," Boyd said warily. He softened his expression a little bit, trying to find some common ground with John. "She's waiting for me at the airport, man. I'm just trying to get to her, that's all I'm trying to do. I promised her I'd be there and I intend to keep that promise,"

"Kayley?" John asked. Boyd nodded.

"Yeah,"

"You're serious, huh," John muttered.

"More serious that I've ever been about anything," Boyd answered him honestly. "She's an incredible woman, one that doesn't come around ever for a guy like me. She's my chance to leave all this shit behind..."

John thought of Anna and felt pain all over again. She had been that to him, an amazing woman who he'd never deserved in a million lifetimes. Yet, she'd loved him. During those years, there wasn't anything that would've kept John apart from her. He would've moved mountains to be with his woman. He understood how Boyd felt, which made it harder for him to want to stop the man. There were just so many similarities between him and Boyd. John looked at Boyd and saw bits and pieces of himself. When he really thought about it, John would give and do anything to have Anna or Riley back. Although he had loved Riley Hanna in a very different way than he'd loved his wife, he would still give anything to have just one of them back in his life. How could he stop a man from trying to be with the person he loved? Life wasn't fair, John had learned that the hard way. It wasn't fair that a veteran like Boyd had had to resort to robbing banks, for whatever his reasons may be. As much as his actions contradicted his sentiments, John didn't want to be a judge, jury, and executioner. If Boyd was going to get caught, the real cops should do it, not John Shannon.

"Go," John muttered, lowering his pistol. Boyd cocked his head, clearly surprised to see John's change of heart. Putting his pistol into the holster on his hip, John took a step back from Boyd. "I'm serious, go. The real cops will be here any minute,"

"Thank you," Boyd said, genuinely. He turned back around to face the sky in front of him.

"Hey," John said. Boyd turned his head back toward the former Navy SEAL. "Take care of her, ok? Just be there for her. You're lucky to have her,"

"I know, John," Boyd nodded at him. "I'll take care of her, I promise I will,"

John gave him a nod, mutual respect between two former soldiers. Separate branches, different lives entirely, but bound by respect through the fact that they were brothers in arms at the end of the day.

Standing up straight, Boyd bent at the knees, and prepared to launch himself into the air. He let the cold air sting his fingers and hands. Closing his eyes, Boyd took six steps back away from the ledge.

Opening his eyes, Boyd sprinted toward the ledge, throwing himself into the air as he threw the chute behind him. Spreading his arms and legs, Boyd waited a nanosecond before the chute deployed and caught air. Grabbing the toggles, a smile crept across Boyd's face as he angled away from the stadium, catching a merciful gust of wind.

The explosion of a sniper rifle echoed across the lakefront, freezing John Shannon in his tracks.

He instantly dropped to his knees and swung his rifle around, snapping open the reticle to start scanning. The first thing he tried to locate was Boyd McTiernan's chute, but he couldn't find him anywhere.

"Target down," Klint's icy calm voice crackled through John's earpiece. It actually sent a chill down John's spine as Klint repeated himself, hatred oozing from every single word. "I repeat, target down,"

# CHAPTER 32

# Kayley

Horrified and heartbroken, Kayley stared at the TV, which was tuned to CNN. She couldn't hear what was being said by the anchors, but they kept showing the clip of a man jumping from the edge of Soldier Field, followed by a still image of the man slumped over in his parachute rig, very obviously dead.

Even though the still image was too distant, too blurry to get a clear look, Kayley knew that that had been Boyd. She knew, in that moment, that Boyd wasn't going to be meeting her at the airport. They weren't going to be starting their lives over again in California. Everything that she had been looking forward to was gone in a matter of seconds.

Tears were falling freely from her eyes, she didn't care who saw her, or if anyone recognized her. Her phone sat on her leg. Kayley would go back and forth from staring at the TV to staring at her phone, praying that Boyd would call or send a text to let her know that he was alright.

But that was never going to happen. Boyd McTiernan was dead.

Kayley waited until the final boarding call for her flight, her makeup a streaky mess on her face. She didn't care. She felt numb, incredibly numb. Her heart was broken in a way that she couldn't even begin to process.

Lip quivering, hands shaking, Kayley managed to walk over to the airline employee and scan her boarding pass off her phone. The gate attendant gave her a concerned look, but didn't offer any words of comfort. He had probably seen many people in bad shape about to get on flights, it was probably easier to just ignore them.

"Have a good flight," he said with an insincere smile.

Keeping her face hidden beneath an Adidas ball cap, Kayley found her seat. She put her back pack up above in the luggage compartment before taking her seat on the window. The seat next to her was empty and it would remain empty for the duration of the flight. She had to try very hard to avoid looking at it, knowing it would break her.

When the flight reached its cruising altitude, Kayley got up and went to the lavatory. Behind the security and privacy of the locked door, Kayley sobbed silently until she ran out of breath.

# CHAPTER 33

# Klint

The following weeks were hard for Klint. His 'team' had all disappeared, minus Kade. Noah was gone without a trace. Kayley had refused every call or text that Klint sent her, but he knew she was back in California. And John Shannon had left without a word. The last time Klint Kavanaugh had seen John Shannon had been through the reticle of his sniper rifle, just before he fired the bullet that killed Boyd McTiernan.

Klint was subjected to countless interviews, interrogations, and questioning by Internal Affairs. They seemed hell-bent on finding out exactly what he'd been up to the last few months, regardless of the Mayor's attempts to shut down the investigation into her right hand man. But, the detectives over at I.A. didn't seem to care about what the Mayor's thoughts on the matter were. As a result, Klint was resigned to desk duty until the investigation was closed.

Klint and the Mayor continued to see each other, although it was admittedly more complicated than both of them had originally realized. They hadn't yet put a label on their relationship, but neither one of them needed it. Both of them were happy with how things were and that was all that mattered.

As had become the routine, Klint got off work, left the Precinct, and drove home in his car. He was working no cases, no leads, and had nothing to focus on off hours aside from being a father to Kara and Koda. Even though he felt incredibly dissatisfied with his professional life, being able to have more time for his family was important.

He was sitting in traffic when his phone rang, buzzing loudly in the cupholder of his Charger. Klint used the button on his steering wheel to answer the call via Bluetooth.

"Detective Kavanaugh," Klint answered.

Silence.

"Hello, this is Detective Kavanaugh," Klint repeated. "How may I help you?"

Again, silence.

"Hello?" Klint asked one final time, his thumb hovering on the button to hang up.

He was about to press it when he finally got a response.

"Should've aimed for the heart,"

Klint's eyes went wide and he froze in his place, unable to drive forward even after the lane opened up in front of him. That voice sent chills down his spine.

"Boyd?"

"Watch your back, Klint,"

And the call went dead.

# CHAPTER 34

# Kayley

**Four Months Later...**

The early morning sun was just starting to rise over the horizon, covering the beach and ocean in a beautiful orange haze. Her Air-Pods blasting a J. Cole song, Kayley jogged along the path that ran adjacent to the beach. It had become a ritual at this point, getting in a quick morning jog before going to work at the talent agency. She'd already been promoted to Talent Manager and was working with a number of well-respected models for companies like Playboy and Vogue. Work was picking up, with more and more men and women wanting to get into the industry.

As impossible as it had seemed, Kayley had slowly gotten over what had happened in Chicago. She'd deleted and blocked Klint Kavanaugh's number, having absolutely zero desire to talk to him ever again. The week after she got settled back into Los Angeles, Kayley found herself a good therapist and went bi-weekly, diving head first into the long road of making herself whole again. So far, Kayley had been very happy with the progress she and her therapist had made, but still recognized that she had a long way to go. She'd yet to get into the entire complex relationship with Boyd. And the truth was, she wanted to date, wanted to be in love again, but she just wasn't ready. Yet.

Coming to a stop, Kayley drank from her water bottle, and started walking down the pier on the beach. It was still relatively early in the morning and there weren't many people out and about. The morning sunrise was always super calming for her and just started her day off on the right foot.

Leaning against the railing, Kayley hugged her arms and sighed, taking in the beautiful view. She was lucky to call California home and definitely appreciated it more and more every day.

"Hell of a view, huh," a male voice said from behind her.

"Yeah," Kayley said softly, not turning around to see who the voice belonged to for fear of ruining her zen.

"You don't have views like this in Chicago, I'll tell you that right now,"

Kayley's heart skipped a beat. She whipped around, her own hair smacking her in the face.

He wore tan Timberland boots, ripped jeans, and a camo hoodie with the hood pulled up over his Chicago White Sox baseball hat. His hands were in his pockets and he was smiling from ear to ear.

Kayley put her hands over her mouth, truly believing that she might be seeing a ghost.

"Hey, Kayley," Boyd McTiernan said, now grinning at her.

"Boyd!" Kayley squealed, running over and jumping into his arms.

They embraced and sealed their lips to each other, kissing passionately. Kayley instantly started crying, overjoyed to see him alive and well. For almost a full minute, they didn't break their kiss or embrace, just relishing the opportunity to be together again.

Holding Boyd's face in her hands, Kayley looked into his eyes, unable to stop smiling.

"I thought you were dead..." she whispered. Boyd smiled and kissed her forehead.

"I made you a promise," Boyd shrugged.

"Tell me... Tell me everything," Kayley said, leading Boyd to one of the benches on the pier. "I want to hear it all. God, I've missed you so much,"

"I missed you too,"

Boyd touched her chin and pulled her in for another kiss.

# CHAPTER 35

# Noah

Noah Riordan got home just before six in the morning, the sun was barely making an appearance. Los Angeles, for all of its problems and faults, had a beautiful sunrise. He opened the front door as quietly as he could, closed it, and locked it just as quietly. Taking off his boots, Noah set them neatly by the other pairs of shoes before walking upstairs to his bedroom. The door was cracked open just a little bit and he peered inside, smiling at what he saw.

His wife, Lexi, lay in bed, still sound asleep. Ivy, his loyal golden retriever, was next to her, facing the door; her paws were crossed and her head was nuzzled next to them. She popped her head up as Noah pushed the door open further, wagging her tail enthusiastically.

"Shh, don't wake up mom," Noah whispered, kneeling down in front of Ivy and scratching her head. She crawled forward, licking his face, delighted to have her boy back. Smiling softly, Noah continued petting his dog until she was satisfied. After Ivy got comfortable again, Noah pulled off his shirt and climbed into bed alongside

Lexi, gently easing himself next to her so as not to wake her. As soon as his head hit the pillow, Noah was asleep.

Their escape from Chicago had been rather uneventful, minus the loss of Boyd and Patrick. In all honesty, Noah had been expecting to lose a few of them, and he was relieved that it wasn't one of his guys. He had been able to pull off something no other thief on the planet had done and that made him extremely proud. However, his pride was slightly tainted by the fact that he could never, under any circumstance, tell Lexi why he really went to Chicago. As far as Lexi knew, Noah had construction business there. He'd take that secret to the grave with him.

When Noah awoke hours later, Lexi was resting her head on his chest as she pet Ivy's back. He smiled and gently touched her cheek. Lexi looked up at him and grinned. She moved up and kissed him.

"When did you get back?" she asked, sleepily
"This morning," Noah said. "I didn't want to wake you,"
"You did," Lexi said. "But it's ok. It's nice to see you, I missed you,"
"I missed you too, Lex," Noah ran his fingers through her light blonde hair. "I'm off for a few days now, why don't we do something? I got a pretty good bonus from this job,"
"Yeah? That sounds fantastic,"
"I'm gonna take Ivy out and make some coffee," Noah kissed Lexi one more time before getting out of bed and sliding into his slippers beside the bed. He turned to Ivy and bent his knees a little bit. "Ivy, wanna go outside,"

Ivy barked exactly one time and then jumped off the bed. Noah followed her out of the bedroom, downstairs, and through the house to the back door. He unlocked the door and let Ivy run outside to do her business; he stepped out onto the patio, taking in a deep breath of the fresh morning air.

"That's a pretty dog," a man's voice said from off to Noah's right. He whipped his head around and cocked his head for a moment.

Boyd McTiernan stood in his backyard, hands in the pockets of his ripped jeans. He looked a lot more alive than Noah had thought he would. Noah chuckled and shook his head.

"I figured you weren't dead," Noah said.

"Yeah?"

"Yeah. Guys like you and me don't seem to know how to die,"

"Fair enough,"

"Why are you here?" Noah asked.

"You guys seem to have a good thing going on here," Boyd took a step toward Noah. "I was gonna ask if you'd consider letting us in on your next job..."

"What makes you think there's a next job?"

"C'mon, Noah," Boyd rolled his eyes. "There's always a next job. We always have a next job, something in the works. And besides, you still owe me my cut of the Soldier Field job,"

"Rob has your cut," Noah muttered.

"I figured, he's very thorough,"

"As far as another job... I don't know if that's a good idea. Crossing Klint the way I did isn't gonna come without consequences. Doing another job right now-"

"I'm not saying right now. But think about it Noah. To the rest of the world, I'm dead. Being dead has its advantages,"

"I suppose," Noah said. Ivy sauntered back into the house, brushing past Noah's leg.

"You're gonna seriously sit there and tell me you don't have something else in the works right now?"

"No," Noah shook his head.  "I'm not saying that,"

"So, tell me," Boyd pressed.  Noah stared at him and then looked back inside his house.

"You drink coffee?"

# Epilogue

Chicago Executive Airport, formerly known as Palwaukee Municipal Airport, was located outside of Chicago in Wheeling, Illinois. It was an extremely small airport, compared to O'Hare and Midway, only logging about 77,000 flights a year. But, for executive travel, it was much easier to navigate than either of the other options.

John Shannon stood on the tarmac next to his truck, a pair of large duffle bags and a gun case at his feet. He watched the Gulfstream G500 jet taxi down the runway from behind his sunglasses. Taking one final puff of the cigarette, John flicked it on the ground, and stomped on the butt. The jet came to a stop in front of John and his truck. It only took a couple of minutes before the door opened and the stairs folded down to the tarmac.

An older man in a crisp black suit stepped out of the jet, a sincere smile on his face as he made eye contact with John Shannon. Heaving his bags over his shoulder, John picked up the gun case, and headed toward the jet. The older man stepped off the stairs and two men hurried down after him; each of them was wearing a suit, bullet proof vest, and carried an M4 carbine. Around their massive thighs, each man had a pistol holstered and several spare magazines in a bandolier.

"John Shannon," the man said, sticking out his hand. "I cannot tell you how happy I was to get your call,"

"I was glad the offer still stood, sir," John responded, shaking the man's hand.

"Please, call me Jasper," the man said. "No need for any formality between us,"

Jasper Crane had a truly commanding presence that John had to admire. That hadn't been given to Jasper, no, that had been earned by many, many years of critical work for the United States government. All of that hard work had paid off and Jasper now had his dream job - the Director of the Central Intelligence Agency.

"Come on, my men will handle your bags. I've got a couple guys on board who are going to be excited to see you," Jasper said. Despite Jasper's offer, John brought his bags up the stairs by himself. The two armed guards followed him and Jasper back into the cabin, raised the stairs, and locked the door behind them.

Already sitting in the cabin were two of John's former teammates from the SEALs; Smoke and Clancy. Clancy was asleep on the luxurious couch, his face buried in a throw pillow. Smoke, however, set his phone down and stood up, a bright smile on his face.

"I didn't believe it when Crane told me," Smoke said. "It's good to see you, my man,"

"Good to see you, bro," John returned the smile. He stowed his bags with others and took a seat across from where Jasper was sitting. "I was glad to hear you and Clancy were on the team,"

"Smoke and Clancy were a great addition to our unit," Jasper said, giving Smoke a respectful nod. He had a glass of whiskey on the table in front of him. "Can I get you a drink, John? The fridge is stocked,"

"I'm ok, thanks,"

"Well, the pilots have to do a few things before we take off again," Jasper said, folding his hands. "I wanted to know if you had any questions or anything,"

"No, not really," John answered. "I'm just ready to get back in it. I'm good to go,"

"I'm glad to hear it. We've got a real good shot at finally getting Yusuf,"

"We're really going after him?"

"We are,"

"Good,"

"I know this was never a motivator for you, but since you're technically going to be a private contractor, there is a significant amount of money in it for you as well. We can discuss all of the specifics when we get back to Langley,"

"Alright,"

"Is there anything else you need or want?" Jasper asked with a smile. "You can negotiate, you know,"

"I'd like to have someone else on the team," John said. "If she wants to,"

"Who?"

"Her name is Kayley McKenna, Army vet,"

"Done,"

"Also, I want my salary split. Half of it goes to Cassidy Minor and her family,"

"Done and done," Jasper said with a smile. He stuck his hand out to seal the deal. John shook Jasper's hand.

"Welcome aboard, buddy," Smoke reached over and slapped John on the shoulder.

# ABOUT THE AUTHOR

Carl Michaelsen is a graduate of North Central College in Naperville where he studied Small Business Management. It was during college when he wrote his first book. His love for writing stems from early elementary school where creative free writes were the best part of his days. Since publishing his first book, *Phantom,* Carl has gone on to write many more books and plans to keep writing. In addition to writing, Carl works as a Project Engineer. He also enjoys reading, going to the movies, collecting comic books, and spending time with his three dogs.

## Contact

Instagram - @cmmichaelsauthor

Website - https://carlmichaelsenauthor.com/

E-Mail - @cmichaelseniv@gmail.com

Printed in the USA
CPSIA information can be obtained
at www.ICGtesting.com
LVHW012317111223
766263LV00045B/1156